From a Distance

From a Distance

VERNON BARGAINER

iUniverse, Inc.
Bloomington

FROM A DISTANCE

iUniverse books may be ordered through booksellers or by contacting:

iUniverse
1663 Liberty Drive
Bloomington, IN 47403
www.iuniverse.com
1-800-Authors (1-800-288-4677)

ISBN: 978-1-4759-8161-2 (sc)
ISBN: 978-1-4759-8162-9 (hc)
ISBN: 978-1-4759-8163-6 (e)

Library of Congress Control Number: 2013904676

Printed in the United States of America

iUniverse rev. date: 3/15/2013

ALSO BY VERNON BARGAINER

I Remember Running

It Is Morning

At the Feet of Angels

1

A RACKETY OLD PICKUP finally misfired its way out of town while a distraught young woman strained at the wheel and prayed to the gods for mercy. Nineteen-year-old Sarah Lock was running. After a while, she looked in the rearview mirror, sobbing, and nodded as she saw her hometown, Dallas, receding in the distance. Maybe a little speed on the open highway would thwart the backfiring of her stolen truck. She peeled away like a shot tiger. *Must be the cheap gas*, she thought.

Sarah glanced toward the grassy roadside outside the passenger window and flinched at the sight of the little wad of money she'd pitched into the seat just minutes earlier—five one-hundred-dollar bills she had dug out of a jar in the pantry, her last tangible effort before bounding away. Now she was thinking, *What am I going to face trying to buy a hamburger with a hundred-dollar bill?* At once, she sobered, knowing that in the days ahead, she would face many other such pesky and much more compelling questions.

But this is it, thought Sarah. *The dream is gone; it's over.* No one would understand why she ran, no one in her life. But it had to be done; it had to be settled at once, nipped in the bud. With good luck, she should be in Oklahoma City by noon. She stomped the accelerator, fixed her eyes on the road ahead, and drove on, brokenhearted but resolute in what she was doing. At once, the trusty old vessel backfired again. *One more for the road.*

Now that she was settled on course, Sarah tried to relax. Gently, she caressed the left side of her jaw with two fingers, and the tears came again. Before she could dwell on that matter, she was startled by sirens screaming in the rear. The red-and-blue lights of the police car were closing fast—much to her delight. "Come on down," she taunted, as if they could hear her. She raved on, "Nothing would serve my cause any better than to be identified as going north out of Dallas, heading for Oklahoma City in this forsaken old 1999 Chevy pickup." At this point, there would be no reason to suspect it was a stolen vehicle, so it was unlikely they were after *her*.

Sarah sped to seventy-five miles an hour and started driving nonchalantly with one hand. Now she was rocking her head from side to side as if in rhythm to music in the car. At once, the blaring police chaser was at her back bumper. She laid on a seductive smile and glanced toward the car as it whizzed by and proceeded on ahead. "Curses!"

All the excitement seemed to be over. Traffic was monotonously light, and the highway had become boring. Even old Grumpy managed only an occasional backfire. Too bad, for she would have preferred to be distracted, fully occupied with mundane thoughts. Instead, she was taken back to thoughts of her shattered dream. Once more, she tested her aching jaw and jerked back when she felt the deep pain of a bruised bone. At once, she tapped her lips, as if calling for *their* help, and started shaking her head.

Sarah's whole life had been a wrangle, trying to overcome a demoralizing stigma placed on her during her early childhood. Years later, providence allowed her a life-changing event, which brought great promise—but it was not to be. The battle was not over after all. Within this crisis, it wasn't physical pain that hurt so much; rather, it was the emotional devastation, the destruction of her dream, the denial of freedom from the humiliating disgrace thrust on her as a child.

⌒*w*⌒

Oklahoma City was positively inviting. There were no visible little battles going on, either in the traffic or on the sidewalks. The only thing that possibly might have enhanced this picture would have been a sign, reading "Welcome Fugitives." *Forget it,* thought Sarah. *This isn't a stolen truck after all. It's mine.* She slapped the steering wheel and snorted loudly. *So, by golly, I'm not a fugitive; I'm just a missing person. No law against that, right?* Otherwise, life certainly seemed to be at ease in this warm Southern city—just what a desperate, heartbroken woman needed.

Having frequently visited her late aunt who had lived near the city, Sarah generally knew her way around. Now, she drove straight through town and into the parking lot of a four-story apartment building. She just sat for a while, resting her head on her clenched hands near the top of the steering wheel. After a while, she leaned back, took several deep breaths, and stared for a few moments vaguely into the sky. Then she glanced toward her lap, shaking her head at the dull mid-length black skirt pulled tight around a green satin blouse with sparkly magnolia blossoms and a huge, double-ruffle neckline. This outfit was familiar to all who knew her, and since it would now be missing from her wardrobe, it surely would be held as the primary ID element in tracing her.

Okay, it's time!

Sarah crammed the little wad of money into her gaudy over-the-shoulder, black leather bag; snatched the keys from the ignition; and bumped open the door with a determined shoulder. As she twisted her way out of the old relic, she made a quick survey of her surroundings. There was no one in the parking lot; a couple of people were just entering the building. She slammed the door, locked it, and strolled toward the apartment, trying to appear calm and confident. Once inside the building, she glanced at the desk which, mercifully, was very busy at the moment. She hurried to the elevator, rode it alone to the fourth floor, found the stairwell, entered it, and walked half a flight down. The plan was in motion.

In the stairwell, she lifted a pair of sleek black slacks from her bag, as well as a tan, short-sleeved silk blouse and a pair of black high heels. No one would notice that these items were missing from her wardrobe, for they had been on loan to a very close friend who had returned them a couple of weeks ago when she moved to Arizona. Sarah had stored this outfit in a dry-cleaner's bag and then replaced it with another set of clothes when she ran. Now, quickly, she donned the new ensemble. When it was fully in place, she twisted around a bit, somewhat prissily, as if modeling in a fashion show. Then she stuffed her runaway clothes into the bag, whirled it over her shoulder, tightened her lips, folded her arms, dipped her head, and whispered, "There!"

Back on the street, Sarah walked away from town for a block and then circled back, walked two blocks, and caught a bus to downtown. She rested inside a busy shoe store until it was almost her turn. In a few moments, she eased out of her seat and headed for the door, mumbling, "I'm sorry, y'all; I forgot something. See you later." She dawdled out of the store and proceeded toward the Greyhound bus station. It had been a long day, and she was sleepy and hungry. No matter, she had to press ahead.

Soon, she was hit with a sense of needing to hurry. It was 1:15 p.m., and the bus was scheduled to depart at 2:30. However, the station was just minutes away. *So now is the hour,* thought Sarah, *for that strategic though dreaded phone call to Mommy Dear.* Dreaded, because, as supportive as her mother had always been, there was still one critical issue in their relationship, one that had haunted her for ten years.

Leaning against a storefront with her huge bag slouched on the pavement behind her ankles, Sarah lifted her cell phone and nervously dialed her mother's number in Dallas.

"Hello."

"Mom?"

"Hey."

"Mom, no problem; I just called to let you know I'm fine, but I'm somewhere else."

"Than where?"

"Than there."

"Explain!"

"I'm in Oklahoma City, headed north. I just didn't want you to worry when you would find out I'm missing."

"Is Mack with you?"

"Ah ... no."

"Does he know?"

"Later, Mom."

"Sarah, what's going on?"

"It's okay, Mom; it's okay. Trust me. I'll fill you in later."

"Your dad's not gonna like this."

"Tell him to just take it easy, and please don't worry. Everything's going to be all right. So I'll call you again."

"Wait, wait, wait, wait! What's—"

"Check you later; bye."

Sarah closed the call, turned off the phone, and heaved her unwieldy bag back up to a weary shoulder. "Ouch!"

As she hurried away, she was hailed by an old man, seemingly in a desperate hurry, yet straining to make his way along the sidewalk. As he approached, he smiled bashfully and dipped his head briefly as if apologizing for the interruption. "Pardon me, ma'am," he creaked. "Can you tell me how to get to Dewey Avenue?"

Seizing a chance to escape her anguish for a moment, Sarah smiled mischievously and chortled, "Ah, I recommend walking; it's so close, you know."

Quickly catching her jest, the old man joked, "How ... close ... is it?"

Sarah giggled, tapped his shoulder warmly, and said, "Okay, here's what you do. Turn around and go back the way you were coming, just to the far edge of the courthouse. That's Hudson. Turn left onto Hudson, and walk one or two blocks to West Main. Turn to … ah … your right, then walk about a block, and, bingo, you're there!" She threw out her hands excitedly and piped, "Deal?"

"Deal," said the old man. He paused for a moment, looking serious. "And, my dear, I must say, it was worth getting lost to find you. Your warm sense of humor and not being in too big a rush to help somebody has made my day. I'll never forget this moment. God bless you!"

As he turned and lumbered away, Sarah brushed a lone tear from her right eye and sighed. "You, too, sir. I'll not forget you either. I wish you goodness and goodwill every day of your life."

It was still a little bit early when she arrived at the station, so she grabbed a package of peanut butter crackers from a vending machine and sat down to wait for the preemptive right moment to buy her ticket. Clearly, this strategy was a gamble. The bus could well be fully booked already—one more thing to worry about. So she just sat bedazzled, fidgeting with her crackers and trusting the grace of God. *I don't know why I'm so nervous; I'm perfectly incognito, whatever that means. Guess I'm just instinctively nervous.* "Oh … oh!" *Chewing hurts.*

Precisely at two o'clock, Sarah walked toward the ticket counter, trying to look snappy and proud. *Not a worry in the world.*

"Good afternoon, miss. May I help you?"

"Yes, thank you. One-way to Dallas, please."

2

SARAH LINGERED IN THE bus lane, smiling at passengers hurrying to board, politely stepping aside and waving them ahead. It was her premise that this would cast her as an unconcerned traveler who had no fear of being recognized. Surely her behavior was the opposite of what one would expect of a girl on the lam.

Now the commotion was beginning to settle, so Sarah stepped smartly to the bus, holding her chin up, climbed the steps resolutely, and handed her ticket to a harried-looking driver. At the top of the aisle, she paused. All the front seats were taken except for one beside a woman who looked as though she might not have had a bath in a few days. Sarah started down the aisle, meeting the easy smiles of seemingly relaxed passengers as she strolled on. Near the back, a middle-aged man flaunting a certified extrovert smile, nodded toward the empty seat beside him as if to say, "This one's for you."

"Be my guest … please," he said.

"Thank you … Believe I will. How kind of you to save me a seat."

"Well, I always try to look out for pretty ladies."

Uh-oh. This could get ugly. Sarah smiled.

"I'm Leon Garner," he said, bowing and exaggerating his grin.

"I'm Michelle Wheeler; it's very nice to meet you, Leon. Again, thanks for sharing your quarters with me."

"Quarters? Yeah, I guess you're right; each row is sort of

a ... what would you say—a billet?" He slapped his stomach, laughing vigorously, apparently thinking he'd gotten off the better quip. Then he cleared his throat and mused, "Surely there's more behind that modest countenance of yours than I thought."

"Hmm." *This bird obviously wants to flirt. If only he'd just shut up. How am I gonna handle this for five hours?*

"So anyway," continued Leon, "I hope I meet with your approval as a seatmate. I've already been criticized for this gear I'm in today."

Sarah shook her head lightly and glanced up into the face of her partner. "Someone around here?" she asked.

"No, no," he said, "my wife ... when she let me out at the station. See, she brought me down here; so, like, why not? She didn't have a damn else thing to do. Maybe she was on edge because she had to get off her rump and drive the car four miles."

As Leon rattled on, Sarah pretended to listen intently while slyly scanning him for her own assessment. He was a bit overweight and slightly balding, but not to the point of detracting from his somewhat handsome face. But, ugh, his attire was totally out of character for this man of obvious self-confidence. He was wearing a long-sleeved blue dress shirt with button-down collar and no tie. This might get by for most occasions, but he had paired this slightly fashionable top with denim pants.

Finally, Leon slowed to catch his breath. Then he leaned back hard against his seat, raised his chin, thumbed his collar up to it, and smirked. "What do *you* think?"

"I think your wife was right."

"Hmm. So you don't think this outfit looks good on me?"

"Sure, I think it looks good," she droned, halfheartedly. "I just think a button-down looks better with a tie."

"Well, you girls. I like it this way just fine—by golly."

"And that's all that matters," said Sarah politely.

"Woohoo! What a surge of support."

Sarah smiled. Then she looked away from him, taking in the small horde of passengers. Generally, it was a well-groomed, vibrant crowd, apparently happy with their decision to take a bus. Some were already sleeping, or their posture made it appear they were. *Maybe this is a good technique for dealing with an incessant talker when you want to signal disinterest without being overtly rude.* She winced when Leon started up again. "Where're you headed?"

"Dallas. Aren't we all?"

"Oh, that's right; this *is* an express, isn't it?"

Sarah smiled but said nothing.

"Is that home?" blurted Leon.

"Is what home?"

"Dallas."

She didn't answer for a while, hoping he'd forget the question. However, he continued to stare right at her, lifting his eyebrows from time to time, remaining unusually patient for an extrovert. So she swallowed, dropped her head, and murmured, "Sort of." She gazed into her lap, hoping to signal that she didn't want to talk about it. Apparently, he got the message, because he didn't press the issue. *Maybe he's not a bad guy after all,* thought Sarah. *In any event, he's proved to be sensitive on that one. Score one for Leon.*

At once, the driver's voice blared over the loudspeakers. "Welcome aboard, everyone. Thank you for choosing Greyhound. Everything's looking good for our flight—heh, heh. Sit back, relax, and enjoy the trip. We should be in Dallas by about seven forty-five. Hang in there, as they say—heh, heh."

Just as the bus jerked and started to ease forward, some of the passengers began calling out to the driver. Some were waving their arms and pointing toward the right rear of the bus where a young boy was running, desperately trying to catch the driver's eye. He was yelling and waving his ticket in the air. He was actually gaining on the bus until it started to pick up a little speed. Still, he raced on.

Suddenly, the presumably unwashed woman up front bounded out of her seat and shot up to the driver, screaming, "That young man is going to get hurt! He has a ticket. Look!"

The driver grumbled something unintelligible, but he did stop the bus and open the door.

The young kid scrambled aboard, struggling for breath as he stretched toward the driver holding his ticket at arm's length.

The driver snatched the ticket and admonished, "Find a seat, *quickly*."

Thoroughly exhausted, the boy hesitated at the head of the aisle, panting and swallowing hard, clearly out of shape. He looked to be about fifteen years old. His garb was a sharp contrast to that of Sarah's seatmate. He was wearing baggy pants, an Old Navy T-shirt, and a bib cap turned backward. At least his outfit was consistent throughout, unlike old Leon's. Suddenly, the boy swung himself into the seat next to the woman who, unknown to him, had interceded on his behalf.

As the young lad settled in, the passengers applauded. At that, he rose somewhat out of his seat, turned half around, and nodded to the crowd. Then, he waved a limp finger in the air, humbly accepting their kindness.

As they rolled out of the station, an obviously irritated Leon tapped Sarah's shoulder and smirked. "What's with the kid, I wonder?"

"He's late."

Leon chuckled. "I dare say, Sarah, you're certainly a woman of few words."

"Most comments only need a few."

"Touché! And I must say, my dear, for a girl who doesn't have much to say, you're really sharp."

"Thank you."

Leon began shifting around in his seat, visibly ill at ease with this scanty conversation, obviously wanting to really open up and interact with his seatmate. Finally, he sucked in a deep breath and blew it at the window. Then he sat up straight and started in again. "So anyway, I'm going there on business." He chuckled and added, "Sorry, but I can't tell you what the business is."

"That's okay; I don't want to know," said Sarah, smiling impishly.

"Well, the thing is, there are certain self-protecting mechanisms—fences, I call them—that people wrap themselves in, and that tendency—I guess it's just human nature or instinct—is really prominent in the corporate world." Leon was on fire now, one word breeding another in rapid succession with little inflection.

Every now and then, Sarah would cut her eyes up to him as he rattled on, but nothing seemed to have any influence on his constant stream of chatter.

Leon marched on. "I maintain it's nonsense, overreaction. Why all the insecurity? What are we afraid of? I think studies would probably show corporations actually flourish on what they make visible rather than what they hide. You know what I mean? I think it's all pretense. What do you think?"

"I try not to think about it."

"Ouch. Sorry."

"No, no; no problem. I just don't trouble my brain with puzzles about the nature of the corporate world. I see your point, though." As she talked, Sarah was smiling full tilt.

Leon pursed his lips, visibly deep in thought. "So what do you think here? Am I talking too much? I think I'm boring you."

"I'm so sorry, Leon. I know I haven't been very responsive, and I apologize. I'm just tired; it's been a wearying, somewhat trying day for me—physically and emotionally. You deserve better for a seatmate. Your warm, kind effort to help us both relax has gone unheeded because of my preoccupation. Please forgive me."

"Not at all …"

"Thanks."

"Yeah, on the contrary, I find you to be a very supportive, excellent listener, and when you do respond, it's always relevant and to the point; you don't throw in all that superfluous stuff like most of us do."

"It's kind of you to say that."

"No problem. Anyway, maybe the springtime sights along the roadway will be inspiring and relaxing—more than talking; that's for sure."

"Doesn't really matter," yawned Sarah. "I'll probably sleep the whole way."

"Me too," muttered Leon.

"Does that mean we'll be sleeping together?"

At that, Leon doubled over laughing, his stomach rolling and shoulders bobbing like two bouncing balls. Finally, his spasms abated enough that he was able to giggle out a word or two. "Hey, that's cute. See what I mean about you? Your reticence is actually kind of charming. So you don't sing much, but when you do, you're on key all the way."

"That's an interesting comment. I'm not sure I get the metaphor, but anyway, so much for that." Without giving him a chance to comment further, Sarah dropped her head and slumped slightly, using the technique the bus crowd had taught her earlier.

Night, Leon.

Sarah's eyes flicked open. At the moment, she couldn't grasp where she was, whether in a dream or somewhere on earth. Her first impulse was to think that she had overslept and missed an appointment or was late for some event she was supposed to attend. Gradually, the real world started to fill in around her, and she realized she was on a bus. Then it all popped into focus. As she began to shift around in her seat and, with much labor, straighten up, she noticed that her loquacious seatmate was just rousing also. She watched, amused, as he stretched his eyes, plainly going through the same exercise she had just experienced.

In a while, Leon smacked his lips, looked squarely at her, and murmured, "Is this a new world or what?"

"It's whatever you want it to be. I'm just glad to be *in* a world."

Now the traffic was really getting rancorous, even though, at least technically, it was well beyond the evening rush hour.

Soon, the weary voice of a tired bus driver announced the obvious. "Welcome to Dallas, everyone; we should be at the Greyhound station in about ten to twelve minutes. I sincerely hope you enjoyed the cruise, and it's been a joy to serve you as your driver. Now, listen up! Something unusual has come up, and you will not be able to disembark immediately. I'll have to hold the door closed until certain unexpected activity has been completed by the local police. They say it'll only take about ten to fifteen minutes. So please bear with us. I'm in the same boat with you, heh, heh."

True to the driver's promise, the bus pulled into the station in just a short while. Also, true to his word, two policemen approached the bus as soon as it stopped.

Sarah froze and began to summon all the grit she could manage to keep from showing her sudden shock.

"Damn!" said Leon.

"I agree; very annoying." She knew better than to try to smile or gesture in any other way, for she would begin shaking all over at the least physical effort. She just swallowed, turned her head away from Leon, and prayed. She was so lightheaded it was hard to hold it up, and the sticky feeling in her scalp was bearing in on her. *Just can't afford to tremble,* she pleaded in her prayer.

In a moment, a little buzz ran through the crowd, causing Sarah to glance forward. Two policemen were climbing aboard. One of them remained at the front while the other started down the aisle, looking left and right at each passenger. He stopped abruptly at Sarah's seat but mercifully did not look directly at her. She was ready to react if he should. She just held a steady expression, her mouth crimped in one corner, and let her head drift around nonchalantly. She didn't look directly at her seatmate but could tell that he was just sitting still with his arms folded across his stomach. Uncharacteristically, he said nothing.

Sarah so wanted to look up at the police officer to gauge his expression but decided eye contact might not be the best strategy. However, when he suddenly started to turn, she glanced up directly at his face and saw only an unrevealing frown just as he headed back toward the front. Sarah and Leon looked at each other and shrugged.

Now the two police officers stood at the head of the aisle, conversing. At once, they confronted the young kid who had caught the bus literally on the run. The boy became very animated and loud. Apparently, the officers were asking him to stand up, but he refused. Finally, one of them took the kid's arm and literally dragged him out of his seat. Then, the other officer got involved, and they all struggled for a while, until finally, the kid succumbed and relaxed somewhat as the officers cuffed his hands and walked him off of the bus.

Shortly afterward, the driver announced that passengers could disembark. Leon and Sarah kept up a little idle chatter as they strode up the aisle and out of the bus. After a few steps toward the waiting room, they stopped spontaneously and stood in place for a moment, just looking at each other.

"Someone meeting you?" asked Leon.

"Yes. How about you?"

"I'm picking up a rental car."

They both shifted in place for a bit, and then Leon touched

Sarah's shoulder and smiled. "Gotta get serious for a moment," he said. "First of all, you've been a jewel; I learned a lot from you. Thank you for listening to me."

Sarah smiled up at him and said, "Thank you for talking. I learned a lot from you, too." She paused, making eye contact, and then added, "We need both, don't we? Talking and listening?" Leon nodded. There apparently being nothing more to say, they turned from each other and walked in opposite directions.

Now Sarah wandered back to the spot where she had last seen the young kid as they marched him away. One of the passengers had remarked that they had seen an officer remove something from inside his shirt, apparently a stolen watch or some money or something. Sadness filled Sarah's heart. In her mind's eye, she could see them taking him away. *Poor, misdirected kid*, she thought, *starting out all wrong—so much potential going to waste. Dear God, please see what you can do. Please!"*

After a few minutes, she drew a heavy breath and set out to look for a payphone. Using her cell phone would be too risky.

"Hello?"

"Okay, Mom, I'm on I-35 heading toward Kansas City."

"Why are you doing this?"

"First, answer this: Who all is there with you at the house?"

"Just me and Dad. What difference does it make?"

"Because I have some secrets and I need you, Mom; I need you maybe more than I've ever needed you in my life." As she finished, she could hear her mom crying. "Mom, I'm so sorry; I'm sorry to cause you and Dad trouble like this." With that, she began crying herself, and for a few moments, the two of them cried together—a dumbfounded Denise (Morgan) Lock and her frightened daughter, Sarah Grace Lock. Finally, Sarah stiffened and exclaimed, "Okay, we have to brace up, Mom; we have to face what is, and I will tell you all about that over the next couple of days."

"All right, Sarah, please go on."

"Mom, what I said at the beginning of this phone call was a lie. I'm actually back in Dallas." Now, she could hear her dad grumbling in the background.

"That's absolutely incredible, but at this point, nothing surprises me. When did you eat last?"

"I just had some crackers and a hot dog since I left. I think more than that, I am so tired and weary and shaken; I need sleep. But, Mom, I have to hide out for a while, and I need your help on that."

"That's it; 'Hide me, Mom; thank you very much'? Come on, Sarah, give me something to go on, here. This is your mother you're talking to. Sure, you know I'll do all I can, but don't be coy with me. Give me some answers."

"Okay, Mom—okay, okay. I'm sorry; I'm just so desperate. I'm on the run because of something my short-term husband did. I fully intend to explain everything, but right now, I'm just rattled and so very tired. So yes, please help me hide. And I can't do it there because Mack will surely be knocking at your door any hour. I'm frightened, Mom; please, help me on this!"

"Okay, sweetheart. I'm sorry for exploding, but don't you see? It's just that I care. Hold on just a minute and let me talk to your dad."

Momentarily, Ed Lock came on the phone and asked brusquely, "Sarah, my dear, why all the mystery? Why can't you tell us right now? In fact, why didn't you tell us right away—with that first … err, mysterious … phone call from Oklahoma City?"

"Daddy, if y'all will just please bear with me until I can rest and pull myself together. The fact is that I had to run away from my husband this very day—just a few hours ago. So this is as *right away* as it gets. Like I said, I'm so sorry." She began to sniffle, and she could tell by the timbre of her dad's voice that he was fighting tears also.

"You're right, sweetie; it really doesn't matter how this came about. The fact is we all need each other. Surely, you know Mom and I are here for you. So why do you need to hide?"

With that, Sarah broke down and cried openly, railing at her own guilt and at the heartache she knew she had brought on her beloved parents. Unable to control herself, she was making enough commotion that some travelers had started toward her with concerned looks, obviously ready to offer help. *Like what could you possibly do?* she thought. Before they got any closer, she waved a hand in the air, signaling everything was okay and smiled brokenly.

"Sorry, Dad, I'm not avoiding your question. I just sort of gave in to it all for a moment. I'm just so weary, so weary that I don't even feel hungry. But, to answer your question, the reason I need to hide is that I absconded with Mack's truck this morning, and he'll have the police looking for me when he finds out I'm not coming back with it tonight."

Again, Sarah waited patiently while her mom and dad conferred. Then her mom came on and said, sympathetically, "Okay, darling, give us a moment to contact your aunt Gina out in Mabank. Do you want to call us in about fifteen minutes, or do you want me to call your cell phone?"

"I'll call you in fifteen … and, Mom, thanks." She hung up and took several deep breaths. For a while, she reflected back over their conversation of the last few minutes. It struck her as odd that in all that time and in all of their grumbling, nobody, including her, ever said, "I love you." *I guess it goes without saying,* she conceded. After the designated time period, she dialed home.

"Okay, Sarah, here's what we're going to do, so—"

"Mom, could you hold up just a sec?"

"Sure, darling."

"First of all, I'm sorry for the consternation I've caused you and Dad. Please believe me. Next, I just want to say I love you."

"Oh, my goodness, I haven't said that, have I? I guess the

shock of it all just took away our senses … but, darling, we love you, so very much; please forgive us."

"It's okay, Mom; I didn't say it either."

"Hold on; here's your dad."

"Oh, Sarah! Sweet Sarah, can you ever forgive us? We're just so scared."

"We'll just all forgive each other."

"It's me again," said Denise. "Here's the plan: Your aunt Gina wants you to come live with them for as long as you want. As you know, you've been a favorite of hers ever since she babysat you when you were a toddler. So Dad is coming to the station; he's leaving in a couple of minutes. He will pick you up and drive you to Mabank. He plans to stop somewhere for you to eat, so please go along with that. Okay?"

"Okay, Mom. Ask Dad to bring some underwear, a couple of dresses, and a gown, and don't go near Mack Turbo's house."

"Right, but what shall I say if Mack comes a-callin'?"

3

IF YOU CAN SLEEP through the aroma of hot sausage gravy, fried eggs, and buttermilk biscuits, you have achieved the ultimate in sleeping. So thought Sarah early the next morning as she squirmed her way out of bed, yawning and stretching, even before her feet reached the floor. She smiled when she heard dishes rattling in the kitchen, three rooms away. Now she sat on the side of the bed, pondering her situation, wondering what this day would bring, and trying to reckon whether she had time for a shower before breakfast. *I'll hurry.*

After a quick shower, she dressed and sat down to catch her breath. Suddenly, she heard a loud crash. When no other sounds followed, she smiled and started shaking her head. Surely, her mom's younger sister, her klutzy aunt Gina Evans, must have dropped a skillet or mixing bowl or something. This was her trademark. Everyone accepted that she would drop something every day—maybe several things—and no one made a big deal of it. This was just Gina. It never seemed to bother her unless the object struck her foot or careened off her knee or something like that. Then she would groan, very matter-of-factly, "Damn the devil!" When questioned about this proclivity, she would just laugh and say, "I was born without a grip."

Everything must have turned out all right because as Sarah entered the dining room, she came upon her aunt Gina and uncle Kyle kissing and teasing each other like two mischievous kids. In fact, they were known for kissing loudly and for chuckling as they pulled apart. These two devoted people were admired widely for their total acceptance of each other; they made love and marriage work. They also had generous room for others in their lives. They had always treated Sarah like a queen.

"Okay, you two, this is not the huggin' hour," belted Sarah as she bounced cheerfully into the room.

"Hey. Hi, little punkin!" shouted Gina. "Well, you know, Kyle still needs the practice. He hasn't gotten it right in ten years. Bear with him; poor baby, he still tries."

"It's worth the effort," chuckled Kyle. "Anyway, dear Sarah, welcome home. I guess you heard your aunt bouncing a skillet lid off the floor this morning; she's getting really good at it."

"Let's hear it for Aunt Gina," cheered Sarah, laughing exuberantly. At once, she ran into the arms of her dear uncle and held on, drawing energy not only from the hug but from the heartwarming welcome she had just received from these two genuine, beloved people. As they drew apart, Sarah looked from one to the other and remarked, "Thank you all for having me—I love you so much."

"We love you too, sweetheart, and you're welcome here for as long as you want." Suddenly, she frowned and began kneading her hands. "But, ah … well, surely you can understand that we're near panic with worry and curiosity as to what's happened to you. Denise didn't take the time to tell us very much. Have mercy, Sarah; give us something to go on, here. How can we support you? Please, Sarah, *say* something!"

"Okay. I just need a hideaway for a little while. Something dreadful happened on my wedding day, and, ah, I guess you can say I ran away from home."

"But *what*? What happened? Why do you have to run?"

"I'll tell it all just a little later, but for now, just know that it has to do with something my new husband did. The thing is, I want to go through the telling of it just once because it's so stressful to recount. I want us all to get together, y'all and Mom and Dad. Then, I'll spill it all."

"Okay ... I guess," said Aunt Gina, lifting her hands as if conceding defeat. "For now, let's have some breakfast."

"Yeah," interjected Uncle Kyle, "since it's Saturday and nobody has to go to work today, we delayed breakfast to let you sleep as long as you could."

"Thanks. You've always been so considerate. Thanks for indulging me for just a while. I *will* let you know everything."

Breakfast was relaxing and reassuring. It was a buzz. It was communion. The three reunited kin talked freely and cheerfully of old times, and all seemed to radiate the joy and peace of those bygone days. During that roughly ten-year period when the two families lived in the same neighborhood in Dallas, Sarah's aunt and uncle took care of her during the daytime, five days a week.

At once, Uncle Kyle burst into laughter. He turned toward Sarah and drawled, "Remember the time when you were in the third grade and came home from school one day and said to your mom and dad, 'Does anybody know where I can get a job?'"

"Sure. I still don't know what was so baffling about that. I think it's a very reasonable question, even for a third-grader. But Daddy couldn't quit laughing. Mom, of course—well, you know Mom—she doesn't laugh at anything for more than three seconds. Anyway, she cleared up fast and said, 'Where in the world did you get that silliness?' I just said, 'From my teacher.'"

"I remember," broke in Aunt Gina as she slapped the table, knocking over a bottle of syrup, "your mom, in her inimitable way, just said, 'Explain!'"

"Yeah, and I told her that the teacher talked about jobless people and said times were hard for them and that they hurt a lot."

With the merriment soon winding down, the three revelers simultaneously grew serious, as though grieving the loss of those wonderful old times. They just sat for a while, smiling and nodding reassurance to each other—soaking in their love, wishing they could go back in time.

Even so, Sarah was actually a bit irritated with all the frivolity at a time like this. She wanted to cry, and they were trying to keep her laughing. She had given it a halfhearted effort at a time when all she wanted to do was be quiet and think. She excused them, however, because she knew this was their unique way of being supportive. They were trying to provide a comedic relief scene for her, and she really didn't want to play her part.

Momentarily, Sarah's mood changed, and she shook her head at her own reverie, thinking, *We can go back there; we just did.* She continued to sit quietly, reflecting on their past lives, thinking back to her own feelings in those days. She recalled that, at that early time in her life, she sensed that her aunt and uncle loved her more than her own mom and dad did. At once, she remembered dismissing that impulse after she grew up, realizing that the love of one was not greater than the love of the other. Now she was thinking, *You can't weigh the love of one against another. Each person loves through their own personality.*

Now, chairs began scraping away from the table. "The party's over," chimed Uncle Kyle.

"So it is," said Sarah, rubbing her hands together. "This may well be the most strategic breakfast in my entire life, coming as it does at the time of grave need for me. And I think, Aunt Gina, Uncle Kyle, it will likely turn out to be the most memorable of my life. This is really a pivotal moment, and, my dear aunt and uncle, you are at the center of it. Thank you so much."

"Our pleasure," declared her loved ones.

Uncle Kyle went out to tinker in his workshop as Sarah and her aunt withdrew to the living room to relax and entertain whatever would come up. At this point, Sarah decided it was high time she opened up and did some explaining. Much to her pleasure, nobody had really pressured her to talk explicitly about her strange, somewhat precipitous situation. In a while, she took the initiative to open the bag. "Aunt Gina, I know you must be simmering with curiosity about what's going on with me. I know *I* would be."

"Of course, dear; you're right. We can't help but wonder what's up, but you deserve the freedom to decide when to talk about it. That's why we're leaving it up to you."

"How very kind; you two are all class."

"Thanks. As a matter of fact, your mom called earlier this morning asking when she might come out and talk. She wants one of us to call her back as soon as we can."

"Could we just please put it off until tomorrow, maybe tomorrow afternoon? That would give me a little more time to settle down, and everybody will have time to go to church and get back. You know, I want to be coherent and make sense when we get into this thing. I know it's inexplicable and confounding to you all, but I won't make you wait much longer. Can we?" pleaded Sarah, looking up through the top of her eyes.

"You bet. I'll call Denise. Be back in a jiff."

When she returned, Gina was smiling and punching the air with a thumbs-up. "They'll be here for lunch tomorrow, after church, about twelve thirty."

After breakfast dishes Sunday morning, Uncle Kyle settled in to watch church on TV, while Sarah and Aunt Gina sat side by side on a couch, each thumbing through a women's magazine. Now and then, they glanced at each other, smiled awkwardly, and turned back to their books, trying to appear engrossed. Clearly, everybody was nervous and jittery. It seemed as if the air was loaded with nerve endings. In a while, Gina closed her book and said, "Think I'll go get lunch started."

"I'll help," said Sarah as she scooted to the edge of the couch.

"No, no!" exclaimed her aunt. "That's okay. Nothing much to do; I got it covered."

As Gina started out of the room, she glanced back at Sarah, who was still sitting on the edge of the sofa, looking dejected. Gina hesitated and said, "Something you wanted to say, sweetheart?"

"It's just that being busy might help me."

"Oh my, yes of course! What was I thinking? Come on with me."

Time seemed to pass rapidly for the two ladies preparing lunch for five. Later at the front door, the reunion of these five ensnared kinfolks was warm, excited, and as jubilant as they could possibly make it seem under the circumstances. Still, Sarah felt the nervous atmosphere remained in command. She sensed they all had tried to make dining lighthearted and cheerful, but it wasn't working for anybody. Mercifully, it was quickly done—dining, that is.

While the men set out to watch a baseball game, the ladies retreated to the front porch, apparently believing it the most neutral place for serious talk. For a while, they just looked out across the countryside and occasionally at each other. In a while, Sarah, staring at the door, exclaimed, "Aren't the men going to join us?"

"It's all your call," said her mother. "I thought maybe you didn't want a big show. Your dad said last night that he figured you intended this to be a mommy thing, so he wouldn't push himself into the … err … situation."

"But it's family," pleaded Sarah. She had already decided to go public, so to speak, in order to avoid being heckled in a one-on-one situation with her mom, who predictably would have a piece of advice or a sarcastic question on every point she made, interjecting "explain" after every other revelation. Also, doing it with everybody present meant that she would have to tell her horror story only once. Much to her surprise, her mother seemed perfectly at ease with this approach.

"Why, sure; I agree. I just didn't want to make assumptions about your wishes. Really, sweetheart, I'm glad you clarified it. Let's get the two unsung sports heroes out here."

The men came tripping onto the porch the minute they were called. Without further ado, they took up chairs and leaned in to listen. After a short period devoted to fidgeting and heavy breathing for each of them, Sarah set out on her painful journey.

"Okay, y'all," she began diffidently, "are you ready for my confession?" She tried to laugh, but it was not to be, so she pushed on. "First, I just—well, you've been so patient—and I ..." She paused for a moment hoping to stifle the overwhelming temptation to cry. She stiffened her body and stretched as tall as she could. "I think what I want to say is, I owe you big-time. I'm not sure I deserve your love and devotion, but I'll accept it. I guess all I can do is say, from the bottom of my heart, thank you, thank you, thank you—I love you so."

An instant rumble of approval rose from the little assembly as each of them voiced full support and love.

"Okay, bear with me as I wade out into this thing. I know that the main thing you want to know is why I ran. I'll get to that shortly. The fact is that early last Thursday night—my wedding night—my one and only dream was shattered. This was a dream I had totally invested myself in. I literally clung to it as a matter of life itself; all my hopes were in it, and, oh, I was so sure of it. I was positive, and it was everything."

Everyone continued to listen, clearly giving their undivided attention—no questions, no suggestions, no interruptions of any kind.

Sarah pressed on. "Okay, get ready, everyone; this is it. On that night, my husband of just a few hours tried to break my jaw and almost did. Listen, he didn't just slap me; it wasn't just a little hit. It was a jolting slam of his clinched fist into the side of my face. Y'all, Mack Turbo—yes, young, innocent, impeccable, devoted Mack Turbo—punched out his new wife."

Instant pandemonium broke out in the little assembly. Everybody was waving his or her arms and talking at once. Her dad shot out of his chair, fisted the air, and screamed, "Mack Turbo is gonna know what that felt like."

"Wait, Daddy! Please, wait. Please, everybody, hold up for a bit. There's more you ought to know before anybody makes a move in this thing." As she began caressing her jaw, she continued, "My jaw is still sore, and it's very uncomfortable trying to chew or even talk. But, okay, I can deal with that; I'm aware that it's already healing. But this is the thing: it isn't the pain that made me run; it was the dream."

After her dad returned to his seat and the others settled down, Sarah continued, "See, it had always been my dream, ever since—probably since I was about nine years old—ah, it was my dream to have a sweetheart someday. I just dreamed of having someone to please and love and laugh with and play with and work together with and someone to just love me and watch over me and who I could do all the same things for. Before anybody says anything, I'm well aware this is not conventional thinking for a child, but, Mother, as you so pointedly let me know one day, I was different. That's when you saddled me with that awful label." She stopped and continued to stare accusingly at her mother.

At this, her mom shifted nervously in her seat for a moment and then, pointing a finger into the air, exclaimed, "I *did not* label you; it was your teachers who hung that word on you. Don't try to burden me with that one!"

"Take it easy, Mom," said her dad.

"Okay, I didn't mean to turn this into an argument," said Sarah. "The important fact is that I had a dream, and Mack Turbo blew it to hell."

Dad opened his mouth to speak, but Sarah held her hand up to stop him and then went on. "So again, it wasn't the pain of the physical blow; it was the loss of a life-fulfilling hope. Maybe that's not a reason to run, but consider this: that purportedly meek, innocent young kid suddenly exploded. The real Mack Turbo surfaced. He popped. If he'll pop once, he'll pop again, over and over. My immediate response was to run away from him, to nip it in the bud. Being different as I am, I don't believe in second chances. He got all the chances due him and blew them all in that one fell blow."

Now, her family members were nodding their approval. "I agree with that," said Aunt Gina. "When you use up all your chances in one heinous mistake, it's over. You get more chances only if there's some reason to believe the first instance was a fluke. In this case, it sounds to me like there's something wrong with Mack, an illness or some problem that he was able to hide during all your courting days. And, sad as that is, it's over with that jerk; he earns no sympathy from anybody. He's his own damn problem."

"Absolutely," said Sarah. "I'm sorry Mack has a problem, truly sorry. I had no idea ..." With this, she broke down, held her hands to her face, and cried into them for just a few moments. "But, no matter what, it's over. Believe me; I don't hate him, and I don't want anything bad to happen to him, but I can never trust him again, even if there are excuses for his behavior. That's why I ran. To me, his was an act of ending our marriage."

Uncle Kyle, looking around at the rest of them, apparently seeking their attention, said, "Sarah dear, you're okay. Understand, darling, you're okay." As Sarah nodded, he continued, "I think you saw in Mack Turbo the fulfilling of your dream because you so yearned to *have* the dream. Lucky old Mr. Turbo just happened to be in the right place at the right time—for him, that is. Your decision to limit his chances to one was absolutely the right one. Still, sick as he might be, I'd like to show him what a hard right to the mouth feels like."

"I'm with you," said Ed Lock.

"Stop it, you guys. I've already taken care of that."

"What did you do? Pee in his house shoes?" chortled Aunt Gina, obviously attempting to lighten the situation.

"That would be too mild," said Sarah, frowning at her aunt's continued attempt at humor.

"Yeah, but okay," began Mom Lock, "what did you mean when you said you'd already taken care of the guy?"

"Okay, here's the big surprise, and I can tell you that you won't be nearly as surprised as I was. The fact is that when he struck me, I instinctively hit him back, socking him in the mouth. I couldn't get much force into it because, pinned to the bed as I was, I couldn't draw back and ram it into him like he did me. See, since he was on top, he was able to draw his fist all the way back behind his shoulder and rocket the thing brutally into my face. Anyway, I hit him."

"Way to go!" shouted Uncle Kyle.

"Yeah, right on," agreed her dad.

"Maybe so," said Sarah, "but you should have seen the look on his face when I did it. He was visibly stunned. He didn't move a muscle, not even a twitch. He just stared at me in total disbelief. Finally, he just rolled over to his side of the bed and— well, I guess—fell asleep."

"Weirdest thing I ever heard," said her mom.

"I know," said Sarah. "See, Mack was already mad at me because I had made him wait till our wedding night for sex. He would always say to me, 'This is the twenty-first century; people don't do that waiting thing anymore.' I would just say, 'What people?' He'd grin and say nothing more."

"So what do you plan to do?" asked her mom.

"First, I will hide for a while, not for always, but long enough for everybody, including Mack, to come to grips with this whole thing. I would like to hide here with Aunt Gina and Uncle Kyle for maybe four to six weeks, if they'll have me. After that, honestly, I don't know what I'll do. Obviously I'll have to find a job. Other than that, I just don't know what kind of future I'm supposed to have. I know one thing for sure; I'll never want a man in my life again."

"You don't *have* to know what you'll do right now," said

Gina. "Otherwise, have no doubts that this is your home, period."

"Thanks. Your love and the love of Mom and Dad are worth a shattered dream. I'm sorry to put everybody through this. Please tell me, y'all: Do you understand why I ran and why I feel I have to hide for a while?"

Everybody nodded agreement, then Dad, scratching at his chin, said, "So now, Mom and I need to think through what we'll say when Mack comes a-calling."

"Right, and be assured, he'll be at your door, probably several times. I don't know what all he will do, because now he's unpredictable to me, but you can bet he'll do something. I don't want to ask y'all to lie, but if you could just figure out a way to have him believe that the last thing you heard was from a phone call when I said I was in Oklahoma City, heading north. What do you think?"

"We'll take care of it," said her mom.

Dad nodded and asked, "What do you plan to do tomorrow?"

"I want to help Aunt Gina with anything I can. And then, I have a lot of thinking to do, like what I'm going to do with Mack, how I can get our marriage annulled, what to do if they charge me with theft of the money and truck, and mostly, how I can restructure my life."

"Hey, girl, just keep your head up! Remember, life goes on," said Uncle Kyle.

"Well, you know, until last Thursday night, my life seemed so secure, resting all cozy in a dream."

"Maybe you can start a new dream after a bit."

"I don't see that happening."

"Don't say that," chimed in Aunt Gina. "Never stop dreaming. For that matter, you might even find a new sweetheart."

"Sure, out here in this prairie. Besides, remember, I said I would never have another man."

4

SARAH STOOD ALONE IN the front yard, just a little ways from the porch steps, and tried to embrace the day. She stroked her hands gently, not looking anywhere in particular, just standing still, waiting for inspiration. In a while, she started to stroll on out, pausing now and then to look at the sky. Again, she stood in place for a few moments. She bowed her head and prayed, and then she drifted on out into the sweeping prairie grasslands.

As she stood just inside her vast, awe-inspiring meadow, she tried to think philosophically. *A new day is always welcome,* she thought, *no matter what's going on in life. It's a chance to refresh and get a new grip, free from the clutter of yesterday. A new day is an invitation to search for new pathways, raise a new voice, sing a new song. Maybe it's a chance to rekindle hope. I just gotta do something; life is too miserable this way.*

Her healing smile was instinctive, triggered by her reverie and the peaceful meadow, which just lay across the land, calmly yielding to the day, whatever it might bring: hot winds; thunderstorms; gentle rain; light breezes; a warm, healing sun—whatever life delivered.

Sarah gazed out across this wonder of God's world and held her smile. Inspiration had arrived.

The prairie was about two city blocks wide and seemingly endless in length as it swept toward the horizon. The thick grass was at least a foot tall, its rich golden color fading to light blond in the distance. The sky was clear. The air was tinged with a light haze, casting a soft veil over this pastoral countryside, giving it a sense of mystic charm. The sun was just rising over the treetops as soft shadows crept out over the tall grass.

Sarah stood immobile and closed her eyes to let the full sense of this serene setting envelop her. Now, she could feel herself swaying lazily as she gave way to this consuming spell. She breathed deeply and began to absorb the fresh aroma that filled the air—the seedy, crisp smell of meadow grass touched with the delicate fragrance of sparsely scattered wildflowers. All around her, it was still and quiet—perfectly quiet except for the intermittent warble of a distant songbird and once, the faint crack of a fallen twig as it landed in a bed of dry leaves at the edge of the surrounding woods.

"I wish I were a bird," said Sarah to the wind. "Then, I could honor this spectacular prairie land the way *they* do when they drift peacefully above it. Maybe I could twirl slowly, like a ballerina." So it was. She curled her arms above her head and spun in place for a while; then she began moving back toward the house, still twirling.

As she neared the house, her twirl winding down, something caught her eye. Looking toward the east, she spotted a little white wood-framed house sitting atop the gently sloping land, which was still a part of the meadow. It looked to be about two football fields away. There, a short distance from the small house stood a figure; as best she could tell, it was a man. Soon, she looked away and moseyed on into the house of her gracious aunt and uncle.

As she entered, she could hear her aunt talking on the phone in the den. Sarah decided not to disturb her at the moment and so slipped into the guest bedroom (now *her* room) to rest for a few minutes. It was a rather small room, highly decorated with trinkets, paintings, and brightly colored accent rugs scattered randomly over the dull, dingy-looking carpet. Besides the ceiling light—and fan—there were three lamps in the room, none of which was located at a place where one would likely need light to read. Most of the resident figurines had been patched with Scotch tape where they had lost a leg or arm or some other body part. However, the two rag dolls lounging on a bench at the foot of the bed were in good shape, apparently immune to breakage—from being dropped, that is.

"Hi, Sarah," chimed Aunt Gina as she breezed into the room. "Your mother's on the phone; you can take it in here. I'll leave you two alone. Come on in when you finish," she said, waving an arm back over her shoulder as she left the room.

"Hi, Mom; what's up?"

"Just touching base mostly. Your dad is anxious to talk to you about your jaw."

"What about it?"

"Oh, you know, you shouldn't let it go unattended, and I agree with him on that. Anyway, I'll let him cover that with you. So what about if we drop by tomorrow after dinner and visit for just a short while?"

"Sure, if it's convenient with Aunt Gina."

"It is indeed; I've already talked to her about it. Meanwhile, how are you doing?"

"Okay."

"Any new developments in your hideout plans?"

"Let's talk about that tomorrow. Have you heard anything from Mack?"

"No, I haven't. How should I play it if he calls or shows up unexpectedly?"

"Like we said before, you don't know where I am."

"Got it."

After mom and daughter ended their call, Sarah went to the den to be with her aunt. They visited genially, talking mostly about the beauty of the day and hardly any about the phone call.

"Aunt Gina," asked Sarah, grinning with curiosity, "do you know the people in that house at the top of the rise?"

"It's just one person, an older man. He's probably about

sixty-five, kind of large. He lives there alone. We haven't had a lot of contact with him outside church. We all go to the Harbor Baptist Church in Payne Springs near Mabank."

"Is that house on the road to Mabank?"

"Not exactly; it's on this little tributary country lane that passes by that house and comes within about fifty yards of where we are now. It sort of circles off the highway and comes back onto it just about right at the Meadowlark Café. Planning a surprise visit to the house up the meadow, are you, dear?"

"No, no. I was just curious because I saw a man standing in the yard looking this way ... I'm pretty sure it was a man. Anyway, he seemed to be frozen in his tracks, gazing down the meadow. It just roused my curiosity; that's all. You know how I am."

"Yeah, I do indeed; you've always insisted on knowing everything in your environment and its purpose," chided Gina.

"Hmm, guess you're right. Somehow, this guy didn't strike me as being an older person or really large, but after all, I couldn't actually see his face. He may be a visitor there. Anyway, it matters to nothing."

As planned, the two families met again Tuesday afternoon. After the usual few minutes of harmless banter, throats started to clear. Mom Lock was the first to jump in with something serious.

"Ed, you want to do the jaw thing first?"

"Well, sure," he said, twisting around to face Sarah more directly. "Sweetheart, we need to have your jaw examined and the sooner the better. How about tomorrow morning? I can get us in with Dr. Debosky the same day I call, and ..."

"Whoa, whoa, wait a minute! What's all the rush? For that matter, I don't see any need for it. I can tell it's healing day by day ... It's healing. Okay, Daddy? It's healing. Please."

"No matter; it could be broken and you not know it. Then one day, it might flare up and cause some real trouble. The whole point is, Sarah, it could be serious, and we need to check it out."

"I don't think so. I'd rather not bother with remote possibilities like that, not now. Anyway, what if somebody sees me and recognizes me out on the town like that?"

"Very unlikely. The point is we have to play the odds here; we have to take that chance. Okay, listen, Sarah, there are other reasons for checking into it. We need to document it right now. You know what I'm saying? We need to establish just exactly what your condition is and the extent of your injury as of the date Mack pumped his fist into your face. That's all I'm saying."

"Where will that get us?"

"Well, duh!"

"Come on, Daddy; I can't stand that *duh* thing that people do, apparently believing themselves so superior. Just because we're not thinking along the same lines doesn't mean I'm an ignoramus."

"Okay, I'm sorry, but surely, you're not just going to let this thing go. Surely you're going to be filing for annulment of your marriage or whatever it takes to end it. Otherwise, why did you run away? That run ended your marriage but not legally. You're going to need evidence to end it legally. Do you understand that, Sarah? Evidence?"

"I ran because I didn't want to be hit again and because I needed time to think."

"Hoo, boy."

"Hold on, both of you," said her mom. "Let's all just take some time to think. Try to understand what Sarah's going through."

As that comment unfolded, Aunt Gina was vigorously nodding and mouthing "*Yes!*"

"Crap," scoffed Ed Lock as he looked away from the group.

Sarah, weary of it all, just shook her head as her patrons began to drone tediously about little irrelevant issues related to domestic living, reaching agreement on every point, essentially because none of it mattered. As the buzz wound down, her mom announced, "Well, as I say, let's all think. For now, Ed and I need to run along so you all can settle down and get ready to hit the hay."

The last one through the front door was Dad Lock, who turned half around and said, "Let me know, Sarah."

While Uncle Kyle headed for the shower, Gina and Sarah sat quietly commiserating in the den. At one point, Gina said, "Sarah, my dear, this is a lot for anybody to bear. It's a mountain. Honestly, I don't know what I'd do. Whatever you decide, Kyle and I want you to know that we love you. You've always been our little girl."

Teary-eyed and sniffling, Sarah murmured, "I know you love me; you two may very well be the most loyal people in my life. I love you too, and I treasure *your* love. I will try not to disappoint you. I thought this was going to be simple, but Dad has put some things in my head that I am just now beginning to fathom."

"Uh-huh, and keep in mind, he loves you unconditionally or he wouldn't be working on you so hard. He's trying, sweetheart; he's trying. He's doing what he has to do even if it comes across a bit gruff. You're his daughter."

"I'm glad you said those things, Aunt Gina."

They sat quietly for a little while, each politely allowing the other time to think, neither driven to fill time with talk.

"Aunt Gina, I'm beginning to waver a little bit as to my position on the medical exam issue. My mind is beginning to clear on one point, a very crucial one. Now, I'm thinking that I ran—and that I'm here—because my life with Mack Turbo is never to be. That is giving me another dimension of the run."

"Uh-huh. I'm glad you're thinking. Keep it up, dear one."

"Well, I don't want Mack to die or suffer or anything like that, but I positively don't want him in my life ever again. Aunt Gina, as far as I'm concerned, Mack Turbo is out of here."

"Sounds reasonable."

"So, that means, some legal things are going to be necessary, and I might as well start gathering some—as Daddy says—*evidence*."

"Probably so."

"Aunt Gina, I get the impression that you agree with his advice on this—as Mom puts it—*jaw* thing."

"Honestly, I do, but you are bright and need to be given time to think it out for yourself."

"Wow! Did I hear *bright*? What a breakthrough!" whooped Sarah, clapping her hands.

Gina smiled.

"I think I'll call Dad tonight. Maybe he can work out a doctor's appointment for real soon, hopefully for tomorrow."

Her mom answered the phone after the first ring, and Sarah blurted out at once, "Mom, let's do the doctor thing!"

"Oh, Sarah, I'm so glad to hear that. Let me get your dad."

"Hey, young lady, what's up?"

"Dad, I've totally changed my mind. Will you get the doctor's appointment set up for me?"

"Indeed. I'll start working on it first thing in the morning. Oh, Sarah, I'm so glad to hear you say that. Darling, I wouldn't be pushing on this if I didn't think it vital. I don't want you to go through any discomfort in all this, but some things just demand a little sacrifice. I'll be there with you. I'm so relieved."

"Thanks, Dad. I owe you big-time."

"Not at all."

"There's something else I think we need to be working on, and that's the legal stuff. Don't you have a lawyer friend you might be able to sound out on these things?"

"I do indeed, and as a matter of fact, he owes me one, so I

should be able to get some free consultation, particularly on the prospect that you might become a client of his."

"Right. I hope it comes out that I can get the marriage annulled, because I would like to lead the rest of my life as though Mack Turbo was never a part of it. Actually, I think *he's* the one who needs to see a doctor."

"No question about it, but personally, I don't give a damn about his problem."

"Uh-huh."

"So okay. I'll call Dr. Debosky at eight in the morning. We'll get it done."

"Ah, Dad, actually ... well, do you think you can work out something with an out-of-town doctor. If I come into Dallas, someone might see me, recognize me, and blow my cover, so to speak." She smirked, giggling awkwardly.

"Come on, Sarah! Oh, never mind, I'll try to find one in Mabank or somewhere a ways out of Dallas. Sure, I'll work on that. Forgive my blunt reaction. I'll try. It's just that I already know that Dr. Debosky would work us in early. But that's okay; that's okay. I'll give it my best shot."

Dr. Michael Burrell, nodding at an X-ray he was holding at eye level, spoke confidently with Sarah and her dad in his Mabank office early Wednesday afternoon. "Don't let this shock you, but I see a little displacement of the jawbone. Before you shoot me, let me say it is a very tiny fracture. Technically, it's not a fracture; your jawbone has been shifted ever so slightly back toward your ear, and it's that end of the bone that is probably giving you some pain. Am I right?"

"You're right," said Sarah. "It mostly hurts when I open my mouth real wide. Most of the time, it's just a little uncomfortable. But sometimes, I forget and open wide, and that's when it kills me."

"Understand," said the doctor. "With that in mind, I don't really see putting you on heavy pain medication. I think if you feel you need some help at times, an aspirin should do it. Also, I don't have any other therapy to recommend right now—just, you know, avoid real tough foods until it heals a lot more."

"I was gonna say, 'Keep your mouth shut,'" joked Dad Lock.

"Very funny," said Sarah.

Dr. Burrell declined to join the banter. Still looking serious, he said to Ed Lock, "And yes, on the question of documentation, I will provide you with everything you need. I won't be able to fix the time of the injury precisely, but I'll have a professional estimate based on scientific criteria."

"Thank you so much, Doctor—for everything. Especially thanks for working us in on short notice."

"Not at all. Glad we could. Also, if you do get into legal proceedings, call me as a witness." At that, he chuckled for the first time during their visit and added, "Neither defense lawyers nor prosecutors like to cross-examine medical professionals."

As they crossed the waiting room and made their way to the elevator, Sarah's head darted this way and that; she was sorely afraid she might see an acquaintance. In the parking lot, she was still distracted, flinching at every little sound and sudden movement. In the car, she took a deep, *loud* breath and whooshed it through loose lips. "So there!" she said.

During the ride back to Sarah's hideaway home, her dad briefed her on his conversation with his lawyer buddy. "So he sees no problem in achieving dissolution of your marriage, but he's uncertain at this point as to which proceeding offers the best outcome for the long run. He would like to do an annulment, and he says that would have no effect on the stolen property issue, if it comes up."

"Wouldn't that be community property?"

"He doesn't think so. Sure, he'd like to be able to argue that the truck and money were community property, but he says the laws of the State of Texas define community property. Anyway, he's not at all optimistic on that question. Also, on the point of annulment, he indicates that if you weren't in fact married, there would be no grounds for a community property argument. Oh, here's one that will please you. He said your abandoning the marriage by running away was a great choice on your part. His words were, 'smart girl.'"

"So maybe I'm not so different—*Mom*."

"Well, okay, whatever. Anyway, the lawyer also cautioned that the sooner the better. He points out that there are precise time limits. Concerning your allegation—he calls it an allegation—ah, your allegation that Turbo slammed you in the jaw, he says that has to be substantiated somehow, even if by circumstantial evidence. On that matter, he said it'll likely be your swear against Mack Turbo's swear. So sharpen your memory on the details of that horrendous attack."

"Actually, I'd like to forget it, but I see the point. In fact, I'm going to write it down, you know, sort of journalize it."

"Great idea."

Soon, they were at Sarah's hideaway home. Kyle and Gina were at work, so Sarah proceeded into the house with the key they had provided and started looking for something to do to help out. Uncertain of where she could begin, she decided to hold her question on that matter until she could talk to her aunt. She was vehemently opposed to freeloading on them. That decided, she found a notepad and began a journal of her life since the preceding Thursday.

After breakfast the next morning, Sarah became aware that she was smiling. Thereupon, she nodded to herself and headed for her enchanted meadow. As she pushed through the tall grass, all of nature seemed to be singing, "Good morning, Miss Sarah." With that little fantasy, she began to dance as before, twirling gracefully (she hoped) in gratitude for the meadow's warm welcome.

Once again, Sarah spotted someone standing a ways into the meadow near the white frame house at the top of the rise. *Hope it's not a spy for Mack Turbo.*

5

A YOUNG MAN STOOD at the top of a deep meadow, gazing hypnotically toward a lone woman dancing in the tall grass some two hundred yards away. He was convinced that the dancer was a woman by the way *her* skirt flared, rising and falling, as she twirled like a ballerina.

Kevin Eric Lane was up at the crack of dawn to catch a breath of early morning air. Now, he wondered whether perhaps he was still dreaming. Strangely, the distant woman seemed to be a captive of her own dance, enraptured somehow, as though riding it out for its own will. He was spellbound, studying her every move. There was something dreamlike about this scene. Soon, the young lady pirouetted and hopped her way to the little blue house waiting at the edge of the woods.

Kevin Lane was not used to very much reverie in his life, so this experience was arresting for him. Now, he stood still, staring at the spot where the woman had frolicked gracefully in the enchanting meadow. After a while, he turned away and began to amble toward *his* house, head bowed, arms dangling loosely beside his legs. Still entranced, he stumbled up the two porch steps and fell gently to floor. At once, he pushed up in stride, barely aware that he had fallen. As he proceeded to the door, he continued to look back at the steps that had attacked him, trying to understand how he had managed to fall while looking down.

The instant Kevin shoved in the front door, he was greeted

by the raspy bass voice of a newfound friend. His landlord and housemate, Grover Geesling, croaked, "Find any good air out there, Kevin?"

"Pardon?"

"Air. How was the prairie air this morning?"

"Great. Yeah, it was refreshing ... relaxing. You know?"

"Glad to hear it. I take it you didn't have breakfast; I don't see any evidence of making cereal or cooking eggs."

"You're right; how about cold cereal this trip?"

"Let's do it."

As they dawdled over soggy cornflakes, the two newly acquainted bachelors began to visit a little, attempting to learn something about each other. But Kevin was getting restless with this mundane chatter because he yenned to bring up another subject. This was his second day in the splendid old country home of Grover Geesling. The rent was cheap, and the location was absolutely perfect as a point of operation for his assignment as an amateur photographer for an upstart magazine called *Lands Alive*. Abruptly, Kevin blurted, "Oh, by the way, Gro, what do you know about the people living in that blue house down the pasture?"

"Yeah. It's a middle-age couple living there. They bought that old blue house when they got married about ten ... twelve years ago—fine, fine people. We don't visit, really at all, but I have talked with them some at church. Were they out this morning?"

"I only saw one person outside, playing around in the meadow, but I'm pretty sure it was someone in their teens or possibly twenties. Of course, it's pretty hard to tell from that distance. Still, I just got the sense that it was a young girl. Do they have children?"

"No. Must have been a visitor."

"Hmm. Okay, another thing that struck my curiosity; why is that house blue? It's the only blue house I've seen in all my roaming around in these parts."

Grover chuckled at the novelty of that situation and then drawled playfully in his low, manly voice, "For distinction, my boy. You'll notice it's not *very* blue."

"True. No problem; I was just curious why this house was different."

"That's the whole point, Kevin—to be different. See, there's not a lot you can do with a two- or three-bedroom floor plan. You know, not a lot of latitude for variety there. So what does *that* mean? It means you have to rely on some other variation of styling if you want your house to be distinctive. So, Kevin, my boy, it's the cut of the roof and the windows that give a house its distinction."

"Honestly, I've never paid attention to that, but now that you mention it, I can picture that whole situation. In fact, it's making me recall, right now, some really beautiful roofs I've seen. In fact, some are just spectacular."

"Right, and what the builders do with windows, if done right, can accentuate the roof lines and add to the overall uniqueness of the house—or they can do nothing ... just blah. You know, you can make them tall, slim, and masterful looking, or you can make them fat and dominating—I don't like fat windows—or they can just blend in with the house and create a calm portal for looking outside at the wondrous world we're privileged to live in."

As Kevin listened to his landlord, he was impressed with the old man's optimistic outlook, his evident acumen, and his accepting countenance. He was easy, well adjusted, and clearly very bright. When he seemed finished with his very provocative clarifications, Kevin nodded vigorously.

"That's amazing, Gro. Most of us just accept all those things without really understanding what's going on. I'm with you; I like a pretty roof, you know, with steep gables and exciting lines. Yeah, and I have never thought about windows making much of a noticeable difference in the styling of a house."

"Yeah, windows matter."

"Hmm, I'm just thinking of the blue house down there. I remember the windows, now that we're on that subject. I could only see those on the very front side of the house that peeps out from the edge of the woods. Anyway, I recall that they were peaceful-looking windows, not show-offy, having more of a calming effect—as you say, portals to the outside world."

"I dare say, Kevin, I believe something has really captured your attention about our neighbors down the prairie way."

"It has indeed. I'm fascinated. It's probably that there's a young mystery woman in that picture. Reckon?"

Grover winked, and that was all.

Kevin was up early again the next morning, hoping he would catch the carefree dancer in the meadow once more. She wasn't there; neither was she there the next day. *She must have been an overnight visitor*, he thought.

Undaunted, he attempted it again the next day. Something seemed to be drawing him to the same spot every day. However, this time, he moseyed around in the yard for a while, trying to stay optimistic and patient. After about a half hour, there was still no sign of the young woman. "Something gnawing inside me tells me to stay out here all day if I have to," he mumbled to himself. At once, he realized this notion was utterly foolish, that there was no sane reason for him to be outside waiting for an inexplicable image to appear in the distance. "What is this? I have no connection with anything or anybody out here in this country neighborhood."

Almost an hour had gone by, yet Kevin waited. Soon, he wrinkled his brow, chastised himself for talking to himself, and started moseying back to his house. Before he reached the front steps, he instinctively glanced outward again. No luck. He sighed and started on again, but this phantom thing, whatever it was, still held its grip. As he glanced out for the last time, he gasped and stopped cold in his tracks. He had just seen an arm poke out into the air from the edge of the woods at the blue house. At once, he hurried back into the meadow and took up watch there as he had the day before.

The young lady sauntered slowly on out, hesitating frequently, with no apparent intention to dance. She seemed engrossed, as if coveting the wonder of nature, hoping it would bring inspiration. It was as though she was trying to work out a problem or was trying to heal herself from some major disappointment. Notwithstanding all that seemed to be going on with her, there was grace in her every movement.

After a while, she seemed to give in and twirled one time in place. Again, she paused, just looking down at the grass. Even though it was impossible to discern her facial expression from the distance, Kevin felt he knew what it was: pensive, sad, hopeful. All at once, she pirouetted around in a broad circle, and when she finished, she seemed a new person. Kevin felt himself cheering for her. *Go, little ballerina! Go, girl; you're gonna be all right.* Then he wondered curiously to himself, *How can you pirouette in the grass?*

He watched for a long time, to the point that he was worried he needed to be about the business of the day. He had to drive into town to pick up some photo accessories, lenses, filters, an external flash, and some software. He would be placing all his photos on the Internet in a password-protected file set up by *Lands Alive*, his magazine. At this point, he knew he really needed to get on it; after all, he had a job to do.

Still, Kevin could not shake the sensation of wanting to stay outside with his mystery girl for as long as she did. *What's she doing to me?* he wondered. *I can't make out anything about her, really, yet I stand here staring across this meadow as if, somehow, I want to be with her, like she needs me or something. I don't get me.* In a while, he left the meadow and his little curio dancer to be alone with her rapture until—as Kevin assured himself—they met again.

After a quick frozen dinner for lunch, Kevin headed out. He had decided that the trip into town would be doubly useful if he followed a scenic route, giving him a chance to explore the countryside for photo opportunities. His magazine assignment was to get aerial and still photographs of the complete range of scenery throughout the East Texas landscape.

As he cruised away from the little white house, he was again deep in thought. The encounter with the young, distant dancer was puzzling, primarily because he had not been seeking a girlfriend and really had no particular interest in finding one. His romantic affairs since graduating high school seven years earlier had all been short-lived, essentially because he was not interested in marriage and children. There was no good reason why the little prairie ballerina should now absorb him. After all, he knew nothing about her. As that thought slipped his mind, he slapped the steering wheel and exclaimed, "I do so know her; I don't know details about her, but I *know* her—whatever the heck that means."

Kevin selected a route that cut straight through the fields and woods, a county highway that would hook up with the interstate from Houston to Dallas. The handsome, serene prairie fields came first, lavish in the afternoon sun, just calmly doing their job. Most served as feed farms, typically oats, hay, or barley, while others were given to grazing for what few cattle were left in East Texas. All seemed at ease with this world—no visible turf wars raging in these parts.

Momentarily, he came upon a little herd of cattle, all grazing in the same direction, a short distance from the barbed-wire fence that secured them. The fences were low enough that a really agile cow probably could have stepped over them, especially where the wires sagged. *But why would they want to?* thought Kevin. *They have everything they need in this girded pasture.* Surely, cattle would wander through a fence that was down simply because they could. Kevin smiled as he tried to put himself in the place of a cow. As cows looked at the issue of evading their fenced land, they probably thought something like, *When the fence is up, why bother? When it's down, why not?* In any event, one thing about a cow he had always found repulsive was their ever-loving habit of chewing their cud. He had accepted it for a while until he found out ... what a cud was.

Kevin cruised on, marveling at God's creation. Just ahead was a long, winding curve that would wrap him into the woods. Now, he felt that he was once again roaming the timbers he grew up in. It was fascinating, inspiring, and cooling. And it was peaceful. Soon, he emerged again into the meadowlands, leaving only about two miles until he would meet the main highway to Dallas. Suddenly, he was overtaken by a speeding car that whizzed around him, honking, and raced away. At once, Kevin noticed a little animal dart across the road just in front of the racing car.

The peace of the lands was shattered. It was as though the world had been suddenly swallowed up. Kevin slammed on his breaks and watched in horror while the car spun in circles, skidded sideways, and finally sailed across the highway where it slammed into a light pole. There was an instant explosion under the hood. Kevin could see vaguely the head of the driver bobbing and weaving, but no one emerged from the burning car. Flames were rapidly approaching the man. On a gamble, Kevin pulled a little closer to shorten the distance he would have to run, jumped out, and raced toward the flaming car.

When he looked into the car, the driver appeared to be pinned, unable to lift himself out of the seat. Now fire flickered on the right side of his head. The door was jammed, and the window was stuck. The fire was creeping toward the man's left side. This was no time to ask questions. Kevin yelled at the man, "Turn your head; look the other way." The driver appeared confused and did nothing. "Turn your head, damn it!" Slowly, the victim turned toward the passenger window, all the while slapping at the flicker of fire that had just jumped into the long hair on his right side.

Kevin treaded back a few steps and, with a running start, literally rammed himself into the window, breaking it at the bottom, leaving shards sticking up in the bottom edge. He reached in and grabbed the man's shoulders, but he didn't budge; he wouldn't help at all. So Kevin clamped his hands around the man's neck and began to pull on him, inadvertently choking him at the same time. This gave the man a change of heart, and he started to push with his legs. Working together, the men finally wrestled the victim's body through the broken window. They fell to the ground, too exhausted to move.

"We have to get out of here," exhorted Kevin, almost too weak to talk. "Roll off of me. I know it'll hurt, but none of that shit matters, Jack; just get off!" As the man labored on over, Kevin ripped off his shirt, slinging buttons, and smothered it over the man's head. It worked, but, poor guy, his hair was singed and his right arm was scarred with burns and bleeding from fresh cuts. Now, he reached to take the man's arms and began pulling. "Come on; give me a hand here, dude," he warned. Finally, the victim started pulling up to his rescuer. Kevin slung his head at the stench of burned flesh and scorched thick hair. "Phew!" He turned his back on the reluctant stranger and ordered, "Now, put your arms up my back; ride my back! Damn, where is the traffic when you need it?" Finally, the rebel did as told, and the two dragged their way down the shoulder of the road to a safe distance just as the car exploded. At once, a car stopped behind them.

Back home that night, though weary from the day's events, Kevin decided to write what he jokingly referred to as his "semiannual letter" to his mom in Philadelphia. He wanted to let her know that he was settled at his new location and cheer her with the word that he was doing fine. He was an only child.

His mom and dad were divorced and living in different corners of the country. His dad hadn't spoken to him in years, while he and his mom talked by phone about every six months and exchanged letters not much oftener. They considered themselves endeared to each other but were not conspicuously close.

Kevin and Grover tarried briefly at breakfast the next morning. They sat quietly, neither tempted to talk further about Kevin's drama of the day before. Finally, Grover relieved the moment by opening up a new subject.

"Kevin, my boy, have you quit flirting with the blue-house meadow girl, the prairie dancer, as you call her?"

"No way; I saw her briefly yesterday morning. That's when I really should have been heading for Dallas. See what a grip she has on me?"

"Hmm."

"Come on, Gro," snickered Kevin. "You can't just drone *hmm*. We owe this girl more than that."

"By all means. Forgive my seeming indifference. I just didn't want to seem too inquisitive."

At that moment, Kevin was rubbing his shoulders. The cuts on his arms were just minor and should hold up just fine under the Band-Aids. But his shoulders were painfully sore from all the pulling and tugging while fighting to get a modicum of help from the crash victim. *That was one strange dude,* he thought. *That bird was justifiably suffering mental hysteria, but at times, it seemed as if he didn't really care.* Finally, it occurred to Kevin that he hadn't responded to Grover's last comment.

"Oh, sorry, Gro; I was just thinking back to yesterday's caper."

"No problem; I figure you're entitled to some rest, and talkin' is really not rest."

"Yeah. By the way, speaking of girls, let's talk about that

mystery lady for a moment if you don't mind. I think … well, I have some questions I'd like to test against your wisdom and insight."

"Me? Wisdom?"

"Sure, Gro—especially you."

"Okay, shoot!"

"Quite simply, do you think one person can feel another from a distance?"

"Feel? I think not."

"Well, like, I mean, when I'm watching her, I sort of sense the essence of her—vibes—you know what I mean?"

"I know vibes, but really, now, how far do they travel?"

"Depends on the sender, I guess. See, when she's dancing out there, sometimes, she sort of sweeps the sky, holding her arms up and away from her head as if praising God for the meadow and asking Him to bless it. Then she'll twirl like a ballerina, curling her arms above her head. After a few of those pirouettes, she'll pause and extend her hands out to the meadow as if expressing gratitude and at the same time, asking for a complete rescue; from what, I can't imagine."

"Well, Kevin, that's kind of a novel sensation, and I've never really felt another personality like that without being right there with them. But who's to say? I do believe there's such a thing as extrasensory perception. You may be the one."

"That's the word I've been looking for." Kevin chuckled and added, "That's it. I feel closure now. See, now I have a label for it."

"Well, you know, they say all you need to explain anything is a word."

"Yeah. I do think this is an extraordinary situation. It's as if I can sense what her life is like, what's churning in her heart—and mind, I guess. And it happens to the point that I feel like I care, you know, like I don't want this young loner to have burdens."

"Well, maybe that kind of rapport is remotely possible. Almost anything can happen with human beings. On the other hand, Kevin, it could be just a fantasy, like a dream, one where you *want* to know her that well. Still, how could you want her, since you've never even seen her or said one word to her?"

"It was no fantasy. It was real."

"Understand. Tell me, Kevin, is she pretty?"

"Darn right, she's pretty. From a distance, I can make her anything. But I don't have to this time; I can tell by her grace and poise that she's pretty."

With that, the two shoved away from the table and started fumbling with the dirty dishes. When Grover headed off to work on a broken door latch, declining Kevin's offer to help, the young boarder proceeded to the outside.

At the door, Kevin turned and said, "I'm going to the top of the meadow to build an air castle."

6

DENISE LOCK CAME ALONE to Sarah's hideaway home Friday afternoon. Dad Lock was working, and, as he had indicated, Mom was the only one who had any eyewitness news to report. She, her sister Gina, and Sarah decided to gather on the front porch to speak of the matters at hand. En route, Gina dropped an open sack of cookies and then kicked the sack as she leaned down to pick it up. The three women dropped to their knees and started scooping cookies. *Sometimes, life goes awry*, mused Sarah.

Three fully recovered conferees finally made it to the shady front porch and began speaking and sipping lemonade.

"You mean you actually invited Mack Turbo into your home?" asked Sarah of her mom.

"Of course; might'n it arouse suspicion if I hadn't?"

"Yeah, you're right. How did he act?"

"Mostly, he just had this strange look that I can't really read, kind of stern and like he doesn't really believe people. As I talked, he just looked into me as if he doubted what I was telling. I sense he knows something is being hidden from him. He shifted a lot in his chair, and I could see by his countenance that he was really being tempted to, well … *blow up*, I guess is the word. But, surprisingly, he restrained himself. And, I have to say, he was polite when he asked me to have you call him, and he left smiling."

"Really! Did you lead him to believe we're regularly in touch?"

"Of course not. He's just making that assumption. Wouldn't you? After all, I'm your mother."

"I'm sorry, Mother. I shouldn't be so edgy. I just stay nervous about this all the time. Anyway, what was his main purpose in coming to the house?"

"He didn't explain."

"What were his first words?"

"Well, after we greeted each other and I invited him to have a seat in the living room, the first thing he said was, 'Any news?'"

"And you said …?"

"I just shook my head. Then he said, not rudely but abruptly, 'We have the truck;' just like that: 'we have the truck.' No lead-in or anything."

Said Aunt Gina, "Sounds like he was struggling to remain civil, like he would really rather just explode."

"No question about it," said her mother. "Otherwise, he said he needed to talk to you, Sarah; in fact, he pleaded with me to locate you and have you call him or let him know where he could find you and meet with you. He kept emphasizing that it was very important for the two of you to be in touch. He said to impress on you that it was especially important for *you*, personally."

"What is there to meet about? We no longer have a relationship; there's nothing to talk over."

"How so?"

"It's over!"

Mom Lock and Aunt Gina just nodded and kept nodding until Sarah finally broke the ice.

"Okay, y'all, I know I can't stay in hiding forever; that would be no life. So I guess we might as well get all this jazz over with."

"Jazz?" Gina chuckled.

"Okay, *misery.* Anyway, I want Dad to get things underway for an annulment of the marriage. In reality, it no longer exists, anyway. I know I can't stay in hiding forever, but I'm a long ways from being ready to come all the way."

"Explain," said her mom.

"Mommm!" Suddenly, Sarah slapped her head and pleaded, "Oh, I'm sorry; please forgive me. The thing is, I know I'll have to surface to pursue the divorce—I mean annulment—but I want to stay low long term. Mack still doesn't have to know where I'm … ah, *holed up,* so to speak."

"We understand, and we'll honor your wishes. Right, Gina?"

"You bet. Tell, me, Sarah, does this mean you're ready, or let me say *willing,* to talk to Mr. Mack, or meet with him?"

"Let's kill two birds with one stone. Mom, will you talk to Dad and see if you all are willing to have him come to the house one more time, and all four of us can face off together?"

"Be assured, Dad would never allow such a meeting unless he was there."

"Okay, let's see what we can do? I'll just simply come over under the cloak of night, and Mack boy doesn't have to know where I came from. Tell Dad not to make it too soon; give me another week or so."

They continued to chat about the general hazards of life and other trivial matters until her mom started scurrying around getting ready to leave. She excused herself for just a moment as she struck out for her car in the driveway. "I have something for you, Sarah." She was back in a flash, totally breathless.

"Hey, Mom," jeered Sarah, grinning broadly. "Me thinks you're not in shape. Did you scrap your exercise program?"

"I never started it, you little rascal. You would notice that, wouldn't you? But whatever; here's your violin. Thought it might be a welcome companion to you when you visit *your* meadow."

Sarah reached excitedly for the violin, brought it to her chest, hugged it a few moments, and then eased it into a chair and stepped forth to embrace her mom. "I love you."

"I'm the blessed one in that deal. No matter how treacherous things may get for us around here, I will always love you, my child. Our love for you makes us do sometimes the harsh things we have to do."

"Same here," stressed Gina.

"Now, I must run," said her mom as she headed for the door waving her arm behind her.

After their dinner Friday afternoon, Sarah begged her uncle Kyle and aunt Gina to name some things she could do around the house to help out. Reluctantly, they agreed she could vacuum and help with dishes, but both swore they would allow no more than that. In a while, the three of them sprawled in recliners in the small den and spoke in subdued tones. While Sarah listened, Gina briefed her husband on the news reported by Mom Lock during her afternoon visit. Sarah didn't interrupt as her aunt talked.

"Does that pretty much cover it?" asked Gina, looking at Sarah.

"It covers it exactly," said Sarah modestly as she stared into her lap. The others waited patiently as she continued looking down, twisting her fingers. She felt they knew full well that she needed time with herself more than anything. In a while, she coughed and murmured, "Would it be all right with y'all if I retire early? For some reason, I feel tired. I haven't really done enough to *get* tired, but I just feel lazy—mentally, I guess."

Gina and Kyle agreed instantly. Sarah curtsied and started away. As she reached the door, her uncle Kyle said, "Sarah, my dear, lift your head! Let this Mack stuff go for a while. Don't go to bed thinking about it. Everything's in motion to solve it all, so there's nothing to do at the moment. Just think about the boundless, steadfast love that's still in your life and always will be."

"I will. Thanks."

Sarah was up Saturday morning before anyone else. She had fallen asleep Friday night, vowing to do as her uncle had advised: lift her head, lay her troubles on the meadow, and let its incredible healing take over. But the cold, hard morning was now in charge as she sat on the side of her bed, yawning and shaking her head. She reached up to push back her hair and frowned at the sight of her trembling hands. Why was she trembling? At once, she felt the tension in her shoulders. *There's no reason for all this. I just have to get to the meadow.*

As she pushed away from the bed and started to stand up, she was shaking all over, like someone in a deep chill. She couldn't remember ever feeling such overwhelming anxiety in her life. A lingering shower would surely ease the morning's pressure. But she couldn't; the rattling water pipes would wake her family. Now, she was laboring to stand fully erect and at once collapsed back onto the bed. At this point, she just wanted to give in, go back to sleep, and sleep the whole mess out of her life. If she was really lucky, maybe she wouldn't wake up. She continued to lie across the bed, clenching her fists, trying to squeeze out the tension. Then her mother's words of the last afternoon came floating back into her mind, and she started to whisper to the ceiling.

"Why does Mack need to see me? There's absolutely no way he can fix anything. So he's bound to have some self-serving strategy in mind. What kind of games are we going to get into? Why was I so blinded to his dark side during all those too-sweet courting days? I really didn't know him; I tried not to. I've really only known him since the night he smashed my jaw."

Now Sarah was rocking from side to side, still flat on her

back, crosswise on her bed, as she continued to murmur, "Forgive me, dear Lord; I've screwed up so much. I've messed up my own life by overreacting to an innocuous statement that I was retarded and then trying to quash that by courting and marrying a man who turned out to be a screwball. Actually, I've messed up his life too by leading him on. We were actually using each other—me, to surmount a cruel stigma levied on me as a child, and Mack, by sacrificing everything to get me in bed."

In a while, Sarah was just played out and started to settle a little physically. With that, she turned her thoughts to gentler matters. As she began to work her way out of bed, she heard commotion in the house. With that, she proceeded to the shower and a while later stood fully dressed before a mirror. Her hands still trembled somewhat as she attempted to put on makeup. She hoped her face would be free of any stray traces of lipstick when she showed up for breakfast. Finally, it was done. "Whatever!" she grumbled as she turned away and hurried to the dining room.

The morning had been a tough one, so much so that Sarah felt breakfast was simply a procedure she had to get through. Fortunately, her aunt and uncle did not try to make her talk, and all three of them broke genially in different directions afterward.

Sarah strolled—feebly but hopefully—toward the front door, deep in thought. *Meadows know what you're going through,* she chided herself. *Oh my, but what if they should ever run out of magic? I have to find out.* At the porch, she gently laid her violin in the swing and sat down beside it. She would swing lightly for a while and try to strike a new mood before venturing out. Every few minutes, she caught herself dozing. Each time, she would quickly shake off the drowsy feeling. But she drifted again, and the next conscious sensation she had was the experience of waking up. Her eyes just lifted, and there was the world. *Welcome aboard, Sarah.*

She began to swing again, staring out across the beautiful

prairie, fascinated by the dancing of cloud shadows across it. These dark, dreamy shades were full of surprises. They would begin and end unexpectedly, each one sweeping briefly across a certain little piece of the field as intermittent clouds passed in front of the sun. Smiling to herself, she picked up her violin and began to play, "You'll Never Walk Alone."

After a while, Sarah laid down her violin and moseyed out to her little dance square in the meadow. For a few moments, she just picked at her fingers, abruptly questioning whether this was going to work. Suddenly, she smiled a joyful, stretching smile, for even as she pondered her fate, the infallible ambiance of her steady, faithful old meadow rose to embrace her. She turned, smiling, raised her arms, and extended them toward the vast field, as though casting her blessings upon it.

Now, Sarah was twirling and hopping around cheerfully in her little square of short grass cut into the thick field. Originally, this was intended as a small picnic area. In one turn, she spied the mystery man at the top of the rise and lifted her arms toward the sky as though beckoning to him, which she was not. Nevertheless, this was a part of her dance; if it fit in with anything, so be it. Still, she wondered why this person was consistently in the meadow at the same time she was. Recent developments had made her dismiss the idea that this was a spy for Mack Turbo. But who was it, and why did he appear every time she ventured out?

7

KEVIN LANE STROLLED INTO the meadow, knowing he'd have to wait but fully willing to do so. As he reached his usual surveillance spot at the top, he glanced instinctively down the wide prairie lane. At that very instant, he saw his meadow ballerina, and his heart jumped. *Why?* he wondered. *I'm here just out of intellectual curiosity; there's no reason why it should touch me emotionally. You'd think she was a long-lost sweetheart or something.*

The timing was incredible as they both reached their fairyland at virtually the same moment. At first, the young lady seemed reluctant to engage her outing. She just sort of stared at the ground, essentially motionless, although she did lift her head from time to time. All of a sudden, she turned half around, raised her arms, and extended them out toward the vast field, as though she were blessing it.

As the young woman continued to twirl and frolic, she seemed to become more cheerful and friskier. Kevin watched, his heart pounding, strangely wishing he could see her at close range, maybe stand close enough to feel the essence of her, hear her voice, see her smile, touch her. Suddenly, she finished a pirouette facing his direction and immediately raised her arms high above her head as if hailing a friend.

Kevin started to raise his hand to wave to her but aborted before he could get it high enough in the air. He was afraid the girl's gesture was not for him, that perhaps it was just a part of her dance. It was his conviction that when building air castles, you try to avoid initiatives that might lead to disappointment. Even so, he decided to quit toying with this whole game, his meadow fantasy, and make an unprecedented move. So he began walking farther into the meadow. He tromped on until he'd gone about seventy-five yards. From that point, he was able to discern a few more details about the young maiden and her surroundings. Sadly, his endeavor was too late, for the object of his interest suddenly danced her way out of the meadow and into the blue house.

Kevin hurried inside and immediately began preparing to leave for his day's survey of landscape photo opportunities. Just as he turned toward the front door, Grover sauntered in.

"So how did you two make out today?"

"Ah, well, we simulated waving at each other."

"Tell me, how do you simulate waving?"

"In my case, it means I didn't raise my hand above my waist."

"And?"

"And what?"

"What about the little meadow nymph?"

"She held her arms up in my direction, but I don't think it was for me."

"Kevin, my boy," began Grover, grinning mischievously, "I think this mystery chick has some kind of hold on you."

"Perhaps. But, Gro, I can't help but sense that she comes out there for therapy, that she's trying to dance away some distress in her life. There's a sadness in her endless twirling. I think I would just like to find out that she's okay; then I'd leave her alone."

"Come, now, Kevin; she's a *girl*, right?"

"I don't feel that she's just any girl."

With that settled, Kevin hurried to his car and took off. It would be a full day. He needed to plan for his photo anthology to cover East Texas all the way to the Arkansas and Louisiana borders. It worried him that at this point, he hadn't taken a single shot and all of his reconnoitering had been in the afternoon light, which cast a different glow from that of the morning. Perhaps he would have to curtail his morning girl-watching. "Yeah, right."

Back home that evening, Kevin and Grover played dominoes until both were yawning.

Kevin got up somewhat early Monday morning, choked down breakfast while Grover was still snoozing, and then bounded outside. This time, he proceeded a little ways into the meadow right in the beginning. He was thinking, *This field itself would be a worthy study for my photo essay.* He snickered at that notion, which made him think, *Amazing! I can now mix business with … with what?* At that moment, he could hear music, way off in the distance. He cupped his ears with his palms and listened intently. "Yes," he said to his meadow, "you're serenading this morning." Then it stopped, and in less than a minute, the sun rose in his soul. She was there!

He continued to slog through the tall grass toward his target. The twirling little maiden appeared not to notice. As he drew ever closer, he was able to see clearly that she danced within a square of short grass, mowed like a lawn.

On he marched. On she danced—still appearing not to notice him. At once, Kevin stopped within about fifteen yards of her. There, he stood perfectly still and watched.

Now, the ballerina seemed to be caught up in an endless pirouette. Finally, she stopped dead still, with her back to him. She remained in that position with no evident inclination to turn toward her intruder. Then, after a seeming eternity, she started to circle in Kevin's direction, very slowly.

Finally, they faced each other squarely, but neither seemed able to say a word. Then, Kevin raised his hand as if to signal a greeting and so did she. Just as they started to wiggle their hands in a somewhat formal but genial way, someone in the blue house called out, "Sarah, I need you!"

The young girl jumped, waved determinedly, and dashed toward the house.

A downcast Kevin began walking back up the meadow, mumbling to himself, "Sarah ... Sarah. Her name is Sarah." He plodded on, still deep in thought, and then spoke out again, "Sarah, you're beautiful."

Grover was standing just inside the door, grinning fiendishly, as Kevin trudged on in. "Well," he chortled, "I see you managed to find your way back to the house, young hunter; catch anything?"

Kevin forced a weak grin. "Almost, but she got away just when I had her in my sights."

"Uh-oh, I'm sorry for jesting, Kevin; I see you're a bit down. Forgive me."

"Hey, no problem. It's just that I was so close, when she suddenly loped off toward the blue house."

"My boy, look at it this way: you're making progress. What's your impression of the young lassie?"

"I only managed to get within about fifteen yards of her, but that's all I needed. She's all that I dreamed she would be."

"That's it?"

"Her name is Sarah, and she's pretty. Someday, I will hold her hand."

At that, the two bantering men raised their eyebrows at each other and said no more.

Kevin thought their near meeting must have been a harbinger to future extended encounters, for they were both in the meadow early the next morning. Kevin was high-stepping through the tall grass with new energy. When he was about midway to Sarah's dancing patch, he hesitated. The music of her violin filled the cool morning air. He lingered a while, just listening. It told him so much more about his dream girl. It was the touch of her soul, her heart—indeed, her *life*. In some sense, her soulful music seemed to be crying out. In another sense, it reflected full acceptance of whatever life presented her.

In a while, Sarah began to turn, ever so slowly, still playing pensively. Kevin moved on in to stand at the edge of her prairie oasis. He waited. Nothing else was as important as this scene. Somehow, he knew positively that this youthful artist was worth waiting for. At length, she stopped everything. At this point, she just stood gracefully in place, with her violin and bow pointing toward the ground, her back turned to Kevin.

After a while, Sarah turned to face Kevin and smiled, obviously striving to make her expression appear both resolute and friendly. She said nothing.

Kevin just stared into her face, letting her innocence, her grace, her pretty face fill him. She was somewhat slender but not skinny, right on the edge of being tall, and she was, as Kevin thought, *perfectly contoured and proportioned throughout, head to toe, with just the right emphasis on her impressive chest.* She had the look of an innocent child and at the same time, the dreamy expression of a young high school girl. Her face was sort of oval, her blue eyes clear and bright, her features soft and shapely. Her rich brown hair just cushioned her face without distracting from its natural loveliness. To Kevin, she was perfect. While he admired her visually, he simply could not help but also feel passion for her. Suddenly, he realized it was time to say something.

"Do you take requests?" he asked.

"For what?"

"Ah, for songs," blurted Kevin quickly.

"Really now. What songs?"

"Err ..." He hesitated for a few moments, trying to reckon with this unexpected and difficult first exchange. "'Ave Maria,'" he said finally.

Sarah raised her violin, smiling now more confidently, and played an absolutely haunting rendition of—you guessed it—"*Ave Maria.*" When she finished, she curtsied and Kevin applauded.

"That was beautiful. By the way, I'm Kevin Lane, a short-term renter from the man of the house at the top of the rise."

"Nice to meet you, Kevin Lane. I'm Sarah Lock, and I live right there," she said, pointing with her bow.

They nodded to each other awkwardly and began shifting in place, both frantically searching for something else to say. In a while, Kevin cleared his throat and said, "I'm sure you know that I've been watching you from a distance."

She nodded curiously and with a teasing smile, asked, "Why?"

"I was, ah, just fascinated."

"Actually, I did wonder about you. And, by the way, I'm sorry I teased you about, you know, taking requests. That's just me. Forgive me."

"Oh, not necessary; that just helps me know you better. Forgive me for spying on you."

"Okay, but tell me why you *were* spying, so I'll know whether to be frightened or honored."

"I just wanted to *know* about you, because I had this feeling, sort of—"

Bam-crash! Thus came, in that instant, a loud sound from the blue house.

"Uh-oh!" screeched Sarah. "Gotta run. I think my aunt has dropped the icebox or something."

Sarah was not out Sunday morning; neither was Kevin after 10:15 a.m. He had checked on her just before he headed for his church, the First United Methodist Church in Mabank.

Back home after worship services, Kevin persuaded old man Grover Geesling to allow him the privilege of preparing lunch. And so he did: tuna fish sandwiches and watermelon. *Go, Kevin!* After lunch, each spent a leisurely day, independently seeking his own thing, two essentially private bachelors with little interest in social interaction.

Kevin got an early start on his business project the next day. Sarah was missing again. As he drove along East Texas deep-country roads, he pondered what that might mean. Might this be her diplomatic way of saying, "Get lost, Jack!" He quickly shook that notion, for he didn't even want to entertain the painful hint that he might not be welcome in her world. Somehow, inexplicably, Sarah Lock had become the focus of Kevin Lane's life.

Now, Kevin was in a thickly wooded area. It was cool and dark inside this wonderland, all of which made it conducive to deep, unfettered thinking. He didn't have to pay attention to details because he had already decided there were no redeeming photo shots in these tight timbers.

As he cruised along, he tried to figure out what his obsession with Sarah was all about. It had started so theoretically, just basic human curiosity. "Like hell," he said aloud, pounding the steering wheel. "It has never been curiosity. It has always been fascination. It has always been a longing to be near her." From the very beginning, it had been as though he cared about this young woman, whom he'd never met, whom he'd only embraced from a distance. How could that mean anything? Still, he yearned to know that she was going to be okay. Now that he had interacted with her, face-to-face, he was more certain than ever that she was troubled and the meadow was her clinic.

When he returned to his rental house, he was uplifted, for he was convinced he was now ready to start shooting haystacks, rice fields, and wild turkeys—and so to bed. *Good night, noble scout.*

Bingo! Heeere's Sarah.

It's not possible to run fast through a field of thick, tall grass, but Kevin did his best. Before he could get halfway, Sarah moseyed out of her paradise and into the blue house.

"Damn!"

He was late getting away on this disappointing day. Possibly to change his luck, he decided to drive down the country lane, which would take him near Sarah's house, and then on out to the main highway. There was not the slightest sign of any activity or even life at the house, so he proceeded on, slowly, halfheartedly.

All at once, he rounded a gradual curve and spotted his dream girl just ahead. She was walking gracefully, with perfect posture, her arms swinging rhythmically. *I can't believe it. Where could she possibly be going?*

While he crept on, still a little ways behind her, Sarah never looked back or lost a step. Kevin thought, *Knowing her in the small way I do, I'm sure she knows who's behind her. Sarah Lock is one sharp lady.*

Ultimately, he pulled alongside of her. At that moment, he lowered the passenger window and called out, "Where you headed?"

"Meadowlark Café," she answered, interrupting her walk.

"Hop in, and I'll give you a lift."

"Why would you deny me this walk?"

Kevin hesitated. This extraordinary young lady had a solid record of always being one up on him—and he loved it. Presently, he said, "To make it easy for you."

"This *is* easy," she shot back, smiling. "It doesn't get any easier than this."

"Oh?"

"Yes. The air is stale in cars. Out here, it's all new air, all fresh and cleansing."

"You got somethin' there."

"So come walk with me. Come breathe with me."

At that, Kevin hopped the shoulder of the road, away from Sarah, bounced through the weeds, and pulled underneath the canopy of an ages-old red oak tree. He locked up, slapped the roof of the car, and sprinted over to meet Sarah, who was waiting patiently. As he approached her, it was his sense that she had been smiling throughout the course of his impromptu preparations.

"Hi," said Sarah sweetly.

"Hi, Sarah; will you have lunch with me?"

"Only if we'll go Dutch."

"Unh-uh; I'm the escort here. You know, I asked *you*."

"That sounds kind of final, but that's not going to happen. We'll get separate checks and each pay our own."

"No."

"But we don't even know each other."

"Dear Sarah, I know more about you than you could ever imagine. Don't forget, I've watched you on your soul-searching journey through the meadow for several days."

"What do you mean *soul-searching*, and why did you call me *dear*?"

"I called you *dear* because I feel kindly toward you, and it is my feeling that the meadow is catharsis for you. Please forgive me if I'm out of bounds here, Sarah. I only mean to care."

"So you have pity for me?"

"I don't exactly have pity for you, mostly because I feel you can handle whatever you have to; I can tell you're a well-adjusted, bright, capable person. So it's not pity, I tell you. I care about you for other reasons."

"Again, I say, how *can* you? You don't know me."

"Someday, I will. For now, I think I feel I know you because I've *yearned* to know you. If you continue to let me come around you, I'll reveal some things that I think are possible even when observing someone from a distance. Right now, I'll say it depends on the one being observed, the vibes arising out of their heart, their life."

"I guess I'm supposed to ask you about this some future day," she said, propping her chin on one thumb, staring blankly into his eyes.

"Only if you want to."

"Now, what about those *other* reasons that you say make you care about me."

"Could we save that for another day also? Actually, I'm not even sure I can explain it all to myself."

"Whatever you want, *dear* Kevin."

They walked on down the middle of the narrow country road, talking less and less. Now and then, they chuckled as their shoulders brushed together when one or the other bounced over a bump or struck a shallow hole. It took quite a while for them to reach the Meadowlark Café, which sat alongside the main highway.

Inside, they dawdled over their menus for several minutes. Sarah seemed to have drifted. She just sort of looked away from her menu vaguely out the back windows in the direction from which they had just come. Kevin didn't push. If she needed time for reflection, she was entitled to it. In a moment, as he thought back to their conversation along the road, he felt some remorse. Now, it occurred to him that he had not been as understanding as he should have been, and he felt sorry about that.

Kevin began breathing deeply. Sarah still seemed to be in a contemplative mood. Momentarily, she took a deep breath and looked sympathetically at Kevin. They both spoke at the same time:

"Sarah, I'm sorry—"

"Kevin, I'm so sorry—"

Their confessions mingled because they came out simultaneously. This caused them both to laugh out loud. Then Sarah held a finger in the air to claim the floor, and Kevin waited, smiling and caring all the more for this little jewel, as he thought of her.

"I guess I was a little argumentative, and I'm sorry, Kevin; you don't deserve that. Will you please forgive me?"

"My dear Sarah—oops, I mean, Sarah—I can't visualize there will ever be a time in your life when you'll need to ask for forgiveness. I'm the one who was inconsiderate."

The sudden appearance of a server saved them from further anguish on this issue. "May I take your order?"

"Sure," said Kevin. "Do you want to go first, Sarah?"

"No, you go."

"I'd like the chili burger, with shredded cheddar and many, many onions."

"And to drink?"

"Ah, a root beer."

"And you, ma'am?"

"Me too."

"Exactly?"

"Sure, including many, many onions."

After the server breezed away, they looked at each other and winked. Kevin said, "I guess with all these onions, we've effectively ruled out any heavy kissing tonight—I mean, you know, like, with *anyone*."

"Good save, Kevin."

"Well, you know, I don't want to come across as some kind of flirt."

Sarah shook her head, grinning. In a moment, she motioned toward his bare arms. "Looks like you've been in a fight with a wildcat."

"I was at an accident. I mean, I wasn't *part* of the accident, but I was there when it happened. I was driving behind a car that lost control and exploded. I just pulled the driver out of the flaming car."

"Brave man."

"Not really; I just did what you do if you're at an accident."

After a leisurely meal and some guarded conversation, they walked back toward their homes, again shoulder to shoulder. Finally, they reached Kevin's car.

"Taxi," sang out Kevin. "If not, I'll walk you home and come back for the car."

"No, no; I'm ready to ride now, but thanks for offering to walk me."

As they pulled away, Kevin exclaimed, "Oh, by the way, is everybody okay at your house? I was just curious about that loud crash-bang noise that roared out of your house the other day."

"Everything's okay, thanks. My aunt dropped a hair dryer, and when she tried to catch it, she bounced it off a wall. Nobody hurt."

At the blue house, Kevin parked, turned off the engine, and tripped around to open the door for Sarah. "Thanks," she said and ambled toward her house without another word. At the door, she turned and waved, and Kevin returned the courtesy. This was no time to press anything.

At his own house, Kevin and the ever-jolly Grover watched television, or rather they *looked* at it. Not a lot of concentration involved.

In a while, and somewhat suddenly, Grover leaned toward Kevin and said, "Oh, by the way, did you see the article in the paper about the young scout who wrecked his car in front of you a few days ago."

"No, Gro, I didn't see that. But I haven't been reading the paper very thoroughly at all. What does it say?"

"Not very much, just mentioned that he lost control when an animal hopped across the road in front of him. He's been released from the hospital with third-degree burns down one arm and one side of his face. But, apparently, he's okay."

"Praise God for that. Did it give his name?"

"Ah, it was Grady somethin', like Grady Singles or whatever. Anyway, mostly, it just talked about him being a scout, searching the woods and fields for animal eggs and other zoological specimens."

That night, Kevin fell asleep, wondering what Sarah was thinking about. Every time he thought about some event of their day, he smiled. *Night, Sarah. I, ah ...*

8

PREPARATIONS TO HELP SARAH meet with her newly appointed lawyer took front burner at the Evans household Friday morning. Kyle and Gina had the logistics worked out well ahead of time. Sarah would ride with her uncle Kyle to his job in Crandall, near Dallas. Her dad would take a break from his job and pick her up from that point, drive her to downtown Dallas, and introduce her to Mr. Buford Crump, Attorney-at-Law. Her dad would leave it in their hands and go back to work. Her mom would skip her lunch break and pick her up when their consultation was finished.

Uncle Kyle was unusually quiet during the drive to Crandall. *Thank you, Uncle Kyle.* Sarah welcomed a little respite with time to let her mind wander to little innocuous subjects, thus saving her the anxiety of dwelling on the feature story of the day. Now she was thinking back to yesterday and her impromptu luncheon date with Kevin Lane.

How's he going to feel when I'm not out there this morning? It seems we've actually become close, like friends, in just about a week. Can that happen? In a way, I've sort of given him a hard time, but not to hurt him, and he takes it so well. He keeps coming back, smiling timidly. He seems to enjoy that of me. I can't let any of this go on. It's not fair to him. I just have to find a way to brush him off. It's the only humane thing to do. The only problem is, I ...

They cruised on in virtual silence for only a few more

minutes. Suddenly, Kyle shook the calm with his unnecessarily loud announcement that they had arrived at their destination. "We're here!"

"Hooray! The rendezvous point. Oh, and there's Dad, waiting in his car over there near the entrance to your building."

"Right, my little buddy, our very cunning covert plan is unfolding splendidly. Way to go, us!"

Her dad was considerably more talkative during their ride into downtown Dallas. Most of his conversation was aimed at briefing Sarah on what to expect in her meeting with *her* attorney. He continued to emphasize that Buford Crump was now *her* attorney, not his. "Do your best, sweetie. You know I have to say that, and I didn't want to do it in front of *your* attorney."

They were in the waiting room for only ten minutes when they were called into the attorney's office and invited to sit down.

Momentarily, a slightly overweight, middle-aged, neatly dressed man hurried into the room and stepped forth to meet his company. He had the air of a man who was fully focused, confident, and unwilling to concede control to anyone. Still, his smile seemed genuine. He just simply looked like he knew what he was doing.

Said Ed Lock, "Buford, I'd like to have you meet my daughter, Sarah Lock—Sarah, this is Mr. Buford Crump."

"A pleasure and an honor," said Mr. Crump.

"And it's my pleasure also, Mr. Crump; thanks for seeing us—I mean, me." With that, Ed Lock left the room.

"Ms. Lock, before we get into anything technical, are you okay? Are you comfortable with this situation—that is, talking to an attorney about very weighty matters?"

"Yes, I'm perfectly at ease with that."

After some brief conversation, helping them get acquainted, Mr. Crump pulled his chair up to his desk, opened a file and a notebook, uncapped a ballpoint pen, looked up at his client, and declared, "Okay, we're on our way. Please forgive me for having to ask so many questions, but there is no other way I can prepare myself for giving you top professional representation."

"I understand, and I'm okay with that."

"First of all, I understand from your dad that your preference is to pursue annulment rather than a divorce."

"That's right."

"Am I correct in understanding it's your position that annulment might give you some advantage because of community property laws?"

"That's part of it. Also, it'll help me keep my name."

"Okay, we'll proceed accordingly. First of all, tell me what happened on the night of April 12, 2012."

Sarah related the whole gruesome story, point for point, leaving out only the graphic details of their sexual exercise. Otherwise, she did give explicit details of the brutality involved at the end.

"Had he ever hit you before?"

"Never."

"Do you have any reason to believe he was under the influence of drugs or alcohol?"

"Not really. I was with him most of the day, and a good portion of it was given to the wedding and reception and to other social stuff."

"Did you, at any time, notice any unusual behavior on his part?"

"I don't know what you mean."

"Anything that might have seemed out of character for him."

"I can't say that I did. I mean, he was all smiles and giggles the whole day."

"Can you tell me the things that were done and said by both of you before you retired for the evening?"

Buford Crump was beginning to look impatient even though Sarah was rattling off short answers to his terse questions. He just sat straight up as he questioned her, never leaning forward as most interviewers eventually did, trying to be convincing. He seemed hurried, as though he really didn't have time for this process, leading Sarah to sense maybe her case was not all that important to him.

Finally, she decided it was high time that she answer his last question. "Well, okay, before we retired for the evening, we just talked about the wedding and how it went."

"Did either of you mention anything about your future?"

"No."

"Did the two of you say, '*I love you*'?"

"Gee. Actually, I don't remember that phrase coming out again at that time."

"Tell me, what was the last remark you remember hearing him say before you, ah, retired for the evening?"

"I distinctly remember him saying, rather raucously, 'And now for the main event.' He had always been peeved because I made him wait until we married before having sex."

"I see. After the two of you exchanged punches, what happened?"

"He passed out, and I lay in bed literally plotting my course. His lily-white image was destroyed, and I knew—I mean, I was positively convinced—that someday, he would do that again. He just lost it; he could no longer hold back his true character."

"So I understand you drove a truck to Oklahoma City and caught a bus back to Dallas."

"Right. That was a decoy move—to get him looking for me in the wrong place."

"Where did the truck come from?"

"It was his."

"Okay, on that point, I'm obliged to tell you, Ms. Lock, that makes the truck separate property."

"Since we had just got married, wasn't it community property at that point in time?"

"Not in Texas."

"Well, I also took five one-hundred-dollar bills that he brought to the marriage; I guess that's separate property also."

"Right you are. Where are the truck and cash now?"

"I left the truck at an apartment building in Oklahoma City. I don't know where it is now. And the cash is in my purse."

"See, this also raises the question of stolen property. Keep your fingers crossed on that one. Mr. Turbo may well elect to press charges on that issue, but we won't speculate on that. I just want you to be ready for that matter if it comes up."

"Oh my! This could get difficult."

"Indeed. Ms. Lock, I really believe we need to file for divorce in this matter; I don't think annulment will help you, and I would be at a loss as to how to present a case for annulment, considering the facts and the law. I take it neither of you was a minor at the time of the marriage."

"Correct."

"So is there really any reason why divorce won't serve your interest as well as annulment?"

"It's mostly an emotional thing with me; I had just hoped that we could have it turn out that I was never married to that ... ah, that man. Also, in a divorce, I wouldn't have my name back. But I guess I have to face reality."

"Okay, we'll sue for divorce. What we have is cruelty, and I can prove that one. Keep in mind, it's very likely going to be your swear against his swear. If so, our job is to convince the court that you're believable and he's not. My job will be to impeach him as a witness before the court, assuming, of course, that he testifies in his own behalf. In any event, we shouldn't have any difficulty in proving abuse that so frightened you that you took the truck to escape further danger to your life." He chuckled (a rarity for this guy) and added, "Sort of like self-defense. That will also help us on the question of stolen assets if that issue surfaces at some point."

"Okay. Meanwhile, who am I?"

"You'll be presented as Mrs. Sarah Grace Turbo."

"See, that's what I was trying to avoid."

Her attorney threw out his hands and squinted as if conceding that point but offered no relief on the question.

"Okay," droned Sarah. "Let's get it done."

Attorney and client deliberated for another half hour and ultimately agreed that every relevant matter had been covered.

As they stood to exchange courtesies before parting, Sarah said, "Oh, by the way, I am due to meet with Mack Turbo in a few days, as soon as my dad can get it arranged."

"Why?"

"Perhaps we can agree on getting a divorce."

"Well, do what you want, but I really don't advise it. You know, he'll have plenty of opportunity to seek settlement after he's served. But, like I say, do what you want."

"I understand."

"Shall I proceed with the action at once?"

"Ah, give me a couple of days. I'll call you right after our meeting with—what shall I say—the defendant?"

"I'll wait for your call."

Denise Lock picked her daughter up soon after her meeting with the lawyer and headed for Mabank. She seemed preoccupied because, as she put it, a knotty little problem had just come up at work. So it was another quiet ride, leaving Sarah more time to contemplate her total situation. Her mind soon wandered to thoughts of Kevin.

Sarah simply could not understand how anybody could be acquainted with someone for only one week and then give a hoot about what happened to her. So why was she thinking about Kevin and wondering how he would feel when she wasn't there? He would probably argue that they had actually known each other longer, although part of it was from a distance.

As she continued to think about Kevin, she asked herself, *Why am I thinking about him anyway? He's not really chasing me. But he does seem to care about my life. Apparently, that's why he watched me from a distance every day. But that only means he cared about a human being, not necessarily me. At that point, he didn't even know what I look like. Are we to believe there really are such forces as personal vibes?*

Now, Sarah began to rethink her premise that you couldn't care for somebody you didn't know. Indeed, it seemed to her that Kevin actually had a caring attitude toward her as they interacted on those two or three occasions. His reactions to her had seemed to be directly related to *her* personality, which by all outward appearances, he had seemed to enjoy thoroughly. He hadn't appeared solicitous like Mack Turbo had been. Kevin had been more indulging, and he had even said *no* to her one time.

Soon, they pulled into the Evanses' driveway and the contemplation ceased. Sarah was so tired and emotionally weary from her stressful day that she opted to turn in early. It was her hope that fatigue would keep her from lying awake, tossing and turning, while she relived the day. It didn't work. She lay awake, thinking of Kevin and wondering why. How could she give any thought to a romantic relationship ever again, considering the way the last one was ending? Still her mind continued to picture Kevin, his bashful smile and timid way of interacting with her. She was stretching herself in two different directions. She wanted more of Kevin, and she wanted to run from him. Sleep had no chance in this frustrating situation.

Sarah rushed out to the meadow early Saturday morning. Kevin was not out yet. In a while, she saw him just begin to emerge at the top of the meadow. The sight of him made her shiver. At once, she got cold feet and dashed back into her house.

In the late afternoon, her dad called and advised that the meeting with Mack Turbo at their house was set for Monday. He suggested she spend Sunday night with them. The plan was for him to take a circuitous route to the Evans residence and return with her after dark. Sarah agreed, and the deal was sealed.

After dinner, Sarah sat quietly by a window. Still so much to think about: confronting her adversary face-to-face, leaving

Kevin to worry about what had happened to her, putting her mom and dad through so much grief, and many other things. What all was she going to feel when she looked Mack in the eye? What could she say to him? Should she try to see Kevin? If so, what could she possibly tell him that she was willing for him to know? She soon became confused and went to bed.

Sarah did not go to the meadow Sunday. As planned, her dad picked her up after dark that night and took her home with him. It was near bedtime, so they talked very little.

"How did it go with your attorney?"

"Very well. I'm confident that he'll do a professional job for me. Funny thing though, he didn't think our meeting with Mack was such a good idea."

"Of course not. He's a lawyer, right? So if you and Mack meet and agree to an uncontested divorce, he gets a smaller piece of the action."

And so the four brave warriors gathered as planned. It was really a puny little pack of subtle adversaries, all standing in a circle, arms dangling awkwardly by their legs, staring inanely at each other, without the least notion of what to say. *Take it, somebody! Let the games begin*, Sarah thought.

Sarah just stared at the discredited man of her dreams. No word, no thought, no sense of any kind could capture in the tiniest degree the impact of her feelings at this moment in her life. She felt that she was beginning to buckle under the weight of having to stand face-to-face with this man who had once meant everything to her. In a while, she just bowed her head and spoke softly, "Excuse me; I'll be right back."

Sarah went straight to her old bedroom, dropped to her knees, leaned far out over the bed, buried her face in her hands, and cried. And she cried. Nobody bothered her for a while. Eventually, her mother came in and attempted to console her.

"My little punkin, I'm not even going to ask you to explain. Wow, that's a breakthrough, huh? I just came in to tell you to take all the time you want. I don't know the details of what all you're suffering right now, but I can imagine some of what you're going through. The others have taken seats and are pretty well keeping their mouths shut.

"Oh, Mom," began Sarah, still bawling and trying to talk through her trembling voice, "I just stood there, looking at that man and trying to fathom him and our tragic situation." Sobbing and jerking, she continued, "I couldn't even figure out what I was feeling: for him, for me, for life, for anything. As expected, it brought back that horrible nightmare, but that's over and I can deal with that. It also brought back the shattered dream—the dream that I had staked my life on. How am I to deal with that? Oh, Mom, please!"

"It will come to you in time, sweetheart. Please, my precious child, take your time and try to regain your faith. God is with you—with every tear. At some point, if you'd like for me to pray with you, just say so. Meanwhile, you're worth waiting for."

"Mom, I think now is the time. Can we pray?"

"Indeed, we will." Mom Lock knelt beside her daughter and prayed, "O Holy Lord, we come rushing to You with our arms wide open, knowing You'll strengthen us for all that we need, that You will help us seek the things You want us to do and that You will show us how to restore our trust in You. Bless all of us, now, as we begin a difficult journey with each other."

In a while, Sarah rose, dried her tears, and took her mother's hand. A few steps later, they rejoined the others. Dad Lock stood up at once, but Mack remained seated. Momentarily, he stood up also, and then the little huddle was back in place, much in the same pattern as before. Now, Sarah and Mack looked straight at each other, both unflinching.

Mack Turbo glanced around the circle. Then, looking straight at Sarah, he said, "I want to know why you punched me in the mouth."

Sarah just stared straight into his eyes, undaunted, her countenance firm. She let this ride to the point that Mack started shifting around and working his mouth. He pointed a finger directly to her nose at close range and barked, "Why did you break my tooth?"

Sarah's hand flew up to block his finger, and she said unapologetically, "If you can ask that, then you're either phony or crazy."

Mack narrowed his eyes and stared hatefully at her as he spoke, "Just what are you trying to pull?"

"Mack Turbo, I wish you no harm, but you hurt me, hurt me deeply, broke my jaw, shattered my dream, and you have the unmitigated gall to ask me what *I'm* trying to pull?"

"Sarah Grace, that ain't gonna work, young lady. Get yourself ready, because I'm forced to sue you for physical abuse—manslaughter, if you will." With that outburst, he opened his eyes wide and looked down his nose at her.

Sarah bristled and retorted, "Perhaps we can ride to the courthouse together and save on gas. After all, I have no choice but to file charges against you for malicious physical attack and endangerment of life. How about aggravated assault?"

"Yeah, yeah, yeah." He squinted at her and pursed his lips. "And what about the stolen truck and the money? Huh, what about that?"

"We'll ask the court. Keep in mind that under vicious attack, I had no choice but to avail myself of any means necessary to save my life."

Mack chuckled sarcastically and mouthed, "Well, this is gonna be some real fun, ain't it?"

"Mack, I'll be able to deal with the problems you handed me, but you … you, Mack, you have much worse problems. In fact, you need to see a doctor as soon as you can. Save yourself, Mack; it'll only get worse with what you've got."

"You insinuatin' I'm mentally ill?"

"No, I am not. You know me well enough to know that I

don't do insinuating. I'm telling you straight outright, you have a problem. When you have a problem, you see a doctor. You dig?"

Mack stared at her a long, uneasy time. "You're really cute, Sarah."

"I have nothing to gain by being cute. And when it's all said and done, Mack Turbo, I wish you well."

Mack turned and started out. At the front door, he looked back at them and said, "To begin with, I'll send you my bill."

Sarah said, "Mack, I need my clothes."

"Buy some more; you got the money," chortled Mack as he bounded through the door.

The little family furrowed their brows and breathed a deep sigh of relief that it was over. "You all were sure quiet," mused Sarah.

Dad Lock said, "We had no role except to be on hand in case the fireworks started. They didn't, although it did get a bit contentious at times. Otherwise, sweetie, you clearly didn't need us interfering. You handled it well."

Sarah nodded. "Well, y'all, you know, as I looked at him and listened to his voice, I suddenly wondered what in the world I ever saw in him."

"Don't blame yourself for anything," said her dad. "He was just a master role player. Now, changing the subject, it's one thirty; shouldn't we be calling your attorney?"

"What's the hurry?"

"Well, you heard what Mack said about filing charges. I would think your attorney would want to beat him to the plate."

"Oh! Yes, Dad; in fact, I promised Mr. Crump I'd call him right after the meeting, which he really didn't want us to have."

Sarah called her attorney, and he confirmed that he needed to be first on the docket.

"I'm pretty sure we're going to catch this bird lying," said

Attorney Buford Crump, "and if he'll lie on one matter, it's reasonable to believe he'll lie on others. What we have to do is destroy his credibility. So for now, be thinking about all the points of fact you can remember, how he lived, the things he did, strange incidents you can remember, how often he saw a doctor, if at all, and what for. Much of what you can remember may have seemed trivial or meaningless at the time, but now it might very well have weight in our trial. Don't try to judge the relevance of these things; just get them down. You see what I'm driving at?"

"Yes, I do, and I'll get it done. Thank you, sir."

9

BACK IN MABANK ON a sunny Tuesday morning, Sarah and Kevin met in the meadow. She was playing her violin when he moseyed up, smiling broadly.

"Hi, stranger," said Kevin cheerfully.

"Hi, yourself."

"I have a confession."

"Okay, lay it on me."

"I missed you the last two or three days."

"Yeah, I was visiting in town."

Kevin nodded, and then, looking quizzically at her violin, he asked, "Is it hard to learn to play a violin?"

"It all depends on your learning capacity."

Kevin folded his arms across his midsection, bowed over them, and laughed aloud.

While he laughed, Sarah felt tears forming in her eyes. He had always taken her little barbs with such good humor, never seeming the least bit offended. On the contrary, he even seemed to enjoy them. It was almost as if he actually admired that about her; it was her personality and hers alone, and he loved her for it. *Don't say love; that's ridiculous.* At this point, she felt she couldn't hold up any longer without crying in front of him.

Just as Kevin was recovering from his laugh attack and lifting his head to look at her, she turned around and started back toward her house. "Excuse me," she said, barely above a whisper.

"Sure."

Sarah plodded on into her house.

Inside, she sat in the den trying to compose herself. Her aunt and uncle were at work. Facing Kevin was harder than dealing with Mack. It would be easier if she could just walk up to Kevin and say, "Don't come here again; I can't see you anymore." But she cared for him, and she could tell that he cared for her. Neither had tried to push anything because each of them expected the other would believe it was way too early for any strong feelings in their relationship. *Looks like I'm doing a pretty good job of messing up two lives—three, including mine.* Soon, she stood resolutely and tramped back outside.

When she returned, Kevin was standing a little ways into the meadow, hands clasped behind his back, looking up into the sky. *Wonder what he's thinking.* Obviously, he was so deep in thought that he hadn't heard her come back out of the house. She really hated to interrupt his musing, but things had to move along. When she cleared her throat, he turned toward her and smiled. Somehow, she always felt comfortable when he looked at her, and this time was no exception.

Kevin had the countenance of a man who understood human nature and accepted people on their own terms. His face was full and nice looking, and when he smiled, the light in him came shining through. He was a little taller than Sarah and had the physique of a track star, even though his demeanor refuted that possibility. His bearing was more that of a poet than an athlete, and he was a dreamer. He was all man, he was genuine, and he always looked neat.

"To answer your earlier question," she began, "it's really not very hard to learn violin. Mainly, it takes practice and dedication. That's all, my Kevin," she said, trying to sound nonchalant.

"I can't begin to tell you how relieved I am. However, there's just one problem for me."

"Oh?"

"Well, it would be my guess that playing any musical instrument requires some measure of talent, and there's where yours truly drops out of the class."

"Hmm."

"Hmm? That's it: hmm?"

"Well, you know, hmm's its own thing."

"Hmm."

Sarah laughed and then sobered quickly as Kevin's expression turned serious. He seemed to be searching for some way to change the subject, so she waited.

"Know what, Sarah? I'm tired of being Mr. Glum Guy. Let's play something else."

"My, Kevin, how you do run on. Whatever in the world are you talking about?"

"Well, pardon the English, but we ain't havin' no fun. Could we, like, just do something silly out here? We seem so solemn most of the time."

"Okay, this ought to be good; I'll play the violin, and you dance."

"Yeah, right."

"Okay, we'll both dance."

And so it came to pass. Sarah played and hopped in rhythm while Kevin bounced and twisted around in the grass, so awkwardly at times that Sarah laughed until it echoed from the woods. It was the first genuine thrill she could remember having in quite a while.   Now Sarah pirouetted while Kevin clogged like an Irish jig dancer. Suddenly, he got tangled in his feet and fell on his butt. He immediately pushed himself back up, straining and giggling, while his partner cheered him on. The whole exercise was outright silly, which meant it hit the target. When they began to wind down, puffing and reeling, they somewhat gravitated to each other. As they came together, laughing heartily, they just instinctively embraced. It seemed to derive naturally out of their dwindling dance. In a moment, they pulled back, looking shocked.

They headed for the porch and fell into the swing to puff it out and get their breath back.

"I'm more out of shape than I thought," panted Sarah.

"Me too. Maybe we need to do some hiking, say, along the edge of the woods," suggested Kevin.

"Sounds good, but you know … another day." The instant those words left her mouth, she thought, *You're really brushing him off, aren't you, Sarah girl?*

"So," began Kevin, still a little short of breath, "I won't be out tomorrow. Gotta catch some shots just before and after dawn. I need to get some coverage in the early morning glow, and the conditions are predicted to be perfect for that tomorrow."

"Why not get your pictures right here in *this* meadow, in our meadow?" *Oops, I shouldn't have said* our *meadow.*

"Oh, I'm definitely going to, at some point, but these places for tomorrow were already staked out in my assignment."

"I see. Well, good luck, then."

"Thanks." With that, Kevin drew a deep breath, pushed out of the swing, and started away. When he was a few steps out, he turned and waved.

Sarah waved back and went inside. When she thought the timing was right, she set about to cook dinner to have ready near the time her aunt and uncle would be home from work. She had decided to fix a chicken-spaghetti casserole and serve it with a simple salad of cucumbers, red onions, and vinegar. Surely, this would not offer much variety, but with a large casserole, she didn't think a lot of side dishes would be necessary.

After the highly applauded dinner that evening, Sarah and her aunt Gina retired to easy chairs in the den.

"You know, Aunt Gina, I've met a young man out here in the meadow … I say *young*; he's, like, four or five years older than me."

"I *thought* you had met somebody; nothing wrong with that."

"Yeah, I know I shouldn't be messing around, but …"

"Hey, consider yourself single and free. For all intents and purposes, you are. You do what you damn well please."

Sarah laughed and slapped her knees. "Thanks for that resounding endorsement. Anyway, we only met about a week ago, but we've been watching each other for a couple of weeks."

"Watching?"

"Yeah; well, you know, from a distance."

"That's healthy."

"I'm not sure it is, but as hard as I try, I just haven't found the courage to brush him off—politely, of course."

"Then don't."

"You're serious about this, aren't you, Aunt Gina?"

"I am indeed. I don't know if this fellow in the meadow is the right thing for you, but I do know you can't let this calamity with Mack Turbo rob you of the right to a free and happy life. And right now, my dear one, it sorely threatens to do just that. What I'm seeing in you now is giving up on all dreams, giving up on having any kind of life, and I see you with a lot of needless and very harmful guilt feelings."

Somehow, the word *feelings* caught Sarah off guard. Her feelings of late had been so relentless and puzzling that she seemed unable to deal with them without crying. That, in itself, was confounding, because crying had been a rarity in her life up to that point. She'd had a few disappointments, but she seldom cried about them. Now, she could hardly keep from it, and the most unexpected word or event could bring on the tears. So when her aunt spoke of guilt *feelings*, the tears welled up. Finally, she braced up and tried to make some sense.

"Aunt Gina, you're right. I cry a lot these days. Most of the time, I can't even tell what I'm crying about. I mean, I really don't know which one of these guys I'm crying over. Mack's a human being, too, and he just went wrong. Do we get one or two mistakes in life? The one thing I'm positive of is that he gets no more chances with me. Still, he has to try to live, and in that regard, I wish him well."

"As I see it, Sarah, Mr. Mack is at our mercy right now, and like you, I don't wish him any harm, but he deserves no mercy in the issue at hand."

"Right, and there are just too many unknowns with Mack. Of course, I don't know much about Kevin either. But his unknowns are basic, and until I know more, I consider them nonthreatening. The things I don't know about Mack could kill me. The things I don't know about Kevin could bolster our relationship—or end it ...whatever. At least I'd be free to live without fear."

"Pray about it, sweetheart! We're all praying that God will give you trust and wisdom and help you know what to do. Trust, my dear, trust!"

With that, the women fell silent, and Sarah began to contemplate the question of prayer. Surely, she hadn't prayed enough; she hadn't laid her burdens on the Lord, partly because she thought it trivial to ask God's help for what she'd gotten herself into. Now, she was beginning to see the question in an entirely new light. In a while, they both began to yawn. They smiled and said, "Good night."

The next day, Sarah couldn't seem to make herself busy enough. As hard as she tried, thoughts of Mack and Kevin kept creeping back into her mind. The Mack impulses were easy to deal with, for even though she had compassion for his difficulty, he was history, and she could just simply wish him better days.

It was entirely different with Kevin. She just couldn't seem to shake her growing interest in him. Even so, that matter was entirely within her control. In fact, even under present adverse conditions, she had to admit that ultimately her fate was in her own hands.

Bolstered by that resolution, Sarah knelt at her bed and prayed as her aunt had suggested. The one word that hung in her mind from her aunt's counsel was *trust*. "O Lord, please instill within me the will to restore trust in my life. Lead me to where You want me to go and help me to find the things I need to know. In Your own name, I pray."

She got up from her knees and went right out to find Kevin. Of course, he wasn't out there, but she could make him be there; she could picture him from a distance, see him in his car, will him to be thinking about her, see him smile ... *So much for that.*

The next morning, Sarah went to the meadow early to watch for Kevin. Sure enough, he was out early too. Funny thing, he seemed to be laboring to make his way through the grassy field. Still, on he trudged. In a while, she spotted the problem; he was carrying something. In fact, it appeared to require two hands to loft it along. When, finally, he was near at hand, she saw that he was carrying a vase of flowers, holding them chest high.

Kevin marched right up toward Sarah, grinning like a stand-up comic, and handed the vase of flowers to her, reaching his arms way out and up, with great ceremony, as if exalting a queen.

Sarah took the bouquet of red roses, fought back her tears, and awarded him her very best smile. "I dare say, my Kevin, are you courting me?"

"I'm honoring you. I ask nothing. These roses represent you, and the regard I have for you."

"I love red roses. I like *all* flowers, but I think roses are God's best work."

"I agree. Other flowers are best for other occasions, but roses, especially red roses—"

"I understand," blurted Sarah, quickly interrupting. "Indeed, I'd like my aunt to meet the man who brought us roses. Are you okay with that?"

"Absolutely. Want me to carry them?"

"If you like. Come with me."

Just inside the door, Sarah yelled to her aunt that they had company—she hoped—giving her time to prepare for a visitor. Sarah pointed to a table, and Kevin set the roses on it just as

Aunt Gina tripped in and whooped, "Hi, gang. Ooh, what beautiful roses!"

Sarah stepped forth and performed introductions while Kevin and Gina smiled and spoke cordially with each other. Then, in her effervescent way, Gina reached out and dutifully hugged her guest. The three visited for a little while, following protocol for first visits, which entailed laughing at most things said, including and especially those that were not particularly funny.

As Sarah and Kevin were leaving, Kevin stumbled and kicked over a small plastic trash basket.

"Hey, that's *my* job," Gina said and laughed as he stooped to rescue the little container.

"What, recovering fallen trash containers?"

"No, knocking them over."

They both laughed, and Gina patted his shoulder. Sarah stepped forth and took his hand. "Let me guide you so you don't fall down the steps," she said, winking at Gina.

When Kevin and Sarah were safely grounded, they both suddenly became aware that they were still holding hands and even squeezing them gently. Eventually, they relaxed their hands and set them free, more or less instinctively. For a climax, they just looked at each other submissively, knowing there was nothing to say.

"Sarah, you want to take that little hike down the woodline now?"

Sarah shook her head, staring at the ground. She glanced toward the swing.

"Are you going to dance today—play your violin?"

She kept shaking her head at every question. Finally, she said, "Kevin, can we talk?"

"We sure can; wanna do it in the swing?"

"Assuming you mean *talk*?"

"Hoo, boy! I better not perpetuate this one; it could go anywhere. So I'll just say *yes, talk*."

The laughter that followed this halfhearted banter rang a

bit hollow. So they both plopped into the swing. Sarah twisted around toward Kevin, and he toward her, their knees touching. At this point, Sarah was a little short of breath. *Why does this have to be so difficult?*

"Are we ready to talk now?" asked Kevin.

Sarah nodded and began, "I think we both have to acknowledge that we don't really know very much about each other." She hesitated there, just looking at him expectantly, waiting patiently for a response.

Finally, he frowned and started to speak. "I'm afraid of where this is going."

"Okay, here's the thing; I can tell that you're just a little bit fond of me, and honestly, I think a lot of you. But if you knew all about me, you wouldn't, ah, have much interest in me." At this point, the fight to hold back her newfound nemesis lump in her throat was crushing.

Kevin could tell that she was struggling and that she needed him to make some kind of response. "Sarah, my precious jewel, I *do so* know you. I *feel* you, and that's knowledge. My feelings for you go beyond fondness."

"Okay, get ready. Kevin, my sweet friend, here's the news: I'm retarded!"

Kevin turned further around so he could look her in the eyes, and with a thin little-boy grin, he said, "Let's don't tell anybody."

"Is that supposed to be funny?"

"Most definitely not!" Kevin was very nearly shouting.

"Then what are you saying?"

"I am vehemently opposed to spreading rumors and lies, and the suggestion that you're retarded is an outright lie."

"Say what you will, but I'll have you know that's the label my mother and teachers slapped on me when I was nine years old. Well, Mom denies it; she says she was just going by what the teachers reported to her. I still place some blame on her, though, because she never tried to get it retracted, even though I made good grades for the rest of my scholastic life."

"Well, whatever its source, it's all bullshit."

In spite of the gravity of the matter in their laps at this moment, Sarah felt just a tiny bit amused, because her friend was really animated. She had never seen such a dead-serious expression on his face. He was ready to go to battle. They were silent for a few moments, giving each other a little recovery time; all the while, Kevin looked very stern. Again, Sarah felt the hint of a smile tugging at the corners of her mouth. She decided to suppress it with a few spoken words.

"Kevin, are you saying I've been falsely labeled?"

"No doubt about it. It's unfair, and that's the main thing that bothers me about it. It's a lie, I tell you. Sure, we've only been acquainted for a couple of weeks, but I've studied you closely, because I found myself falling for you, and I'm telling you, Sarah, among many wonders, I see the brilliance in you."

"Maybe that means you're prejudiced in my favor."

"Well, of course I am, but that doesn't override my senses, my perception, my judgment!"

"So if I'm not retarded, what am I?"

Before he opened his mouth, Kevin beamed that admiring smile she'd seen on him several times in their brief relationship. Then he said calmly, "You're unconventional."

"I think I like that better."

"Believe me; it's beautiful. And, my dear Sarah, you're unconventional because you are the opposite of retarded. Sure, you're different; you make comments in conversations that people in our culture are not prepared for, so they're caught by surprise. Personally, if I had to use a label, I'd say you are borderline genius. You can see things others of us can't. You can think for yourself; you can figure out meanings of things usually regarded as too subtle to understand. Am I prejudiced in your favor? Damn right I am, because I want to be around someone like you. I have to stop now before I say something you don't want to hear."

"I guess I should tell you that my teachers diagnosed me based on the IQ test."

"IQ tests have a place, but they fail to consider personality. They don't weigh the element of motivation and some other behavioral factors, and they are certainly not conclusive; they only give us an indication of what we might want to watch for."

"Speaking of IQ tests …" Sarah chuckled as a preface to her next words. "I remember it well, my experience with the IQ test, that is. I became fascinated with its questions, so much so that, in my rascally way, I began to look for ways to trick it."

"Sounds a bit unconventional to me."

"So you say. Anyway, back to the test. When I was taking it, I was trying to second-guess how it could measure anything. So I just picked answers that I felt made the question look ambiguous. Honestly, I had done that on some of my tests in class. I guess it all caught up with me. Believe me; I got the message, and I realized how very wrong I was not to follow the conventional way of taking tests. And, Kevin, right here before you and God, I admit that I was wrong, that I thought I was smart and I acted like a smart aleck. But it was too late, I guess. So I got the label."

"Sometimes, I guess it doesn't pay to be too smart."

"Right. So I started making really good grades in my classes, but nobody changed the label. One day, I scored perfectly on a test, and the teachers came after me, saying I had to have cheated. They tortured me mentally, trying to get me to reveal my *accomplice*. But all that jazz stopped when I said, 'Give me the test again, or give me one just like it, and stand beside me while I take it.' They backed off, and nobody raised the issue again … I didn't hear the R-word anymore."

"But nobody retracted the label, right?"

"Exactly. Kevin, I was so distraught. I tried to find ways to keep the labeling from controlling my life. I sought out dreams to help me cope. I thought about it all the time and still do a lot. Can you imagine the questions it made me ask of myself in the beginning?"

"Sweetheart, I feel I need to say something right here, to have you know my silence is support, not disinterest. I'm sitting here listening, wanting to find ways to express to you how sorry I am that you're going through this. Please know that my silence is simply to hear you out so I can understand your feelings and how this all has affected you. When I'm not responding, I'm listening and caring."

"You know, Kevin, you're pretty special. I think that's one reason I'm laying it all on you."

"Thanks. Now, yes, please tell me all the questions that taunted you about living under that egregious label."

"Can I have a job? Can I get married? Can I have children? Can I even fall in love? Can I read and understand the newspaper? What's with me, anyway?"

"Devastating."

"Yeah, we need to go somewhere and get the label changed. Who's the authority on this? Is there a checklist of attributes I'm supposed to manifest under the label? I need to know so I can make sure I'm on course as a bona fide retarded person, you know, to make sure I conform to the stereotype."

"That's a damning satire on our systems, isn't it? You know, Sarah, I think we are but puppets of our words."

"I think you're right. Our words sound out, and we move. So often, we react to the word instead of the thing it stands for."

"My Sarah—"

"Kevin, hold it right there. I told you all this so you would reassess whether you want to get serious with someone wearing my label. So think twice before you refer to me as *my* Sarah."

"My dear Sarah, I love you."

10

THREE LITTLE WORDS. HOW powerful—how dear to life, how vulnerable to abuse. They can change life, save life. They can seal an everlasting bond, mend a broken heart. They can sustain a happy relationship or be used to end one. They can cause tears, and they can bring joy. They can sound regret or yield promise.

In the case of Sarah (Lock) Turbo, they brought confusion. Now, she sat in the porch swing, mulling over the incident that had occurred in that very same spot twenty-four hours earlier. *Why did Kevin say, "I love you?" I could tell he hadn't started out to say that. Was he sincere, or was he just desperately trying to save me from my misery? Does it matter? Yes, it matters, darn it, because I'm a married woman. And even though I'll be single again soon, I'm not about to tantalize myself with another romance. So I lost my bet. I was counting on Kevin losing interest in me when he learned that I was retarded. Instead, he raced to my defense.*

After an hour of swaying in the swing, gazing into the unrevealing sky, she resolved to change her strategy. It was time for Kevin to know the whole truth, namely that she was married. That surely would get the job done. If not, the last step in her scheme was to simply brush him off and ask him to get out of her life. Telling him that she didn't care for him would be the hardest part. But she loved him too much to string him along and allow him an impossible dream. It was the only right thing to do for the two of them. *Stand by, Kevin; I hate this.*

Just as Sarah pushed out of the swing, Aunt Gina came to the door and called out, "Sarah, your dad's on the phone."

"Hi, Dad." There was a little tremor in her voice, and her dad picked it up.

"Sarah, what's wrong, baby?"

"Oh, I think it's the stress of it all, Dad. I have little anxiety spells from time to time. No problem; they go away quickly. I'm okay, Dad. Really, I'm okay."

"My precious daughter, I'm so sorry. Hopefully, it'll all resolve sooner than we think. But, you know, stress catches up with all of us at one time or another, mostly depending on what value we place on any given event in our lives. The big thing is that we don't bow to guilt feelings. They never get you anything."

"Right on, Dad! I know I've got work to do with myself."

"Don't we all?" said her dad. "Meanwhile, I just wanted to let you know of some recent developments. Mack was here yesterday—left your clothes and a note."

"Oh, how nice."

"Well, yeah, maybe."

"You sound a bit doubtful."

"I'm skeptical of anything about that boy at this point."

"That reminds me, Dad; have you heard from Mr. Crump as to the divorce matter? If not, I'd like to call him for a progress report. I'm gettin' antsy already. Maybe he can give me some assurance that'll help my anxiety."

"By all means, and no, I haven't heard from him. Why don't you come spend a day or two with us and call him from here? Or would you rather *I* call him for you?"

"I want to call him, and more importantly, I want to be with you and Mom."

"Okay, I'll pick you up at noon, and you can call him today. He'll be closed tomorrow."

"Deal."

Conversation between father and daughter was low-key during their drive to Dallas. Indeed, there were even a few brief periods of complete—but comfortable—silence. Each of them recognized the delicate situation for what it was and chose not to force any issues. This car ride was not the place for it. *Besides*, thought Sarah, *Mom should be present when we get really serious.* Finally, after one particularly long period of silence, Dad opened up a somewhat perplexing question, one which all of them had been pondering but were hesitant to bring up.

"You know, Sarah, we all thought we knew Mack Turbo, and we were proud of him—I mean *really* proud of him."

"Yes," murmured Sarah.

Dad let his little girl rest for a few moments and then continued, "What's more—I think you could feel this at the time—the marriage between you two had the enthusiastic support of Mom and me. We all liked him. And now, I just don't really understand him."

Sarah didn't answer. She glanced at her dad and then stared down the open road ahead, as if in a trance. In a while, she said, weakly, "Daddy, what's *wrong* with Mack?"

"Well, sweetheart, like I say, I don't really understand him, but I think he's lost."

"That's pitiful."

"Agree, and I don't know if it's a mental thing or an ego thing or a thing *nobody* understands."

"Is it our job to find him?"

"Most definitely not."

Sarah remained with her dad at his job until his workday was over. During that time, she called Buford Crump and left a message. When he called back in a half hour, she told him she was interested in the status of the divorce proceedings in case there was anything she should be preparing for.

"Glad you're keeping up with it," said Mr. Crump genially. "No, there's nothing you can or should do at this particular point. I have filed a petition for dissolution of marriage, and ordinarily at this point, they would be serving notice to Mr. Turbo. I haven't checked on it, but I assume that's being done. Sometimes, it takes a little while to serve a participant, primarily because they're not always where they're expected to be. If I haven't heard something from the court by the middle of next week, I'll check on it. You raise a good question."

"If he decides not to contest the divorce, will we still have to go to court?"

"We'll likely have to *appear* before a judge, but there wouldn't be any, for lack of a better word, *trial*."

"I like that. Meanwhile, as to serving Mack Turbo, they shouldn't have any problem nailing him. We know he's rambling around in the area because, for one thing, he came to our meeting last Monday and for another, he came to the house Wednesday and left some stuff."

"I agree; they should contact him any day now."

Soon after she ended her phone call, Sarah and her dad headed for home. When they arrived, her mom was at the front door, smiling, her arms wide open, ready to welcome her daughter. They visited for a few minutes, inexplicably still standing in the doorway. Perhaps that was protocol for these situations, Sarah thought. In any event, her mom suggested that they all rest awhile and hold up their discussion of recent developments until after dinner, which, she beamed, was ready to serve with but a little warming.

Dinner was great, right? After all, this was home.

Now, the conferees gathered in the family den, and her dad, leaning way forward in his chair, opened the meeting.

"Sweetheart, day before yesterday, while Mom and I were at work, Mack paid us a little visit. Based on what he did, we're sure he deliberately picked a time when nobody would be here."

"Wonder why that was necessary?" grumbled Sarah.

"You're about to find out. Anyway, he left this note in the mailbox." Dad reached far out, grunting, and handed Sarah a sealed envelope. Sarah glanced at it, and before she could begin to open it, her dad warned, "Not yet, sweetie, how about waiting until I give you the rest of the story."

"Okay, Dad," she conceded, dropping the envelope in her lap and looking keenly at him.

"This next one is the real kicker. It may help answer some of the questions we raised with each other during our ride into Dallas this afternoon. All your clothes were on the front porch. Not bad so far, eh? Right, but get this: they were spread all over the floor. I mean every inch of the porch was covered, side to side and front to back. It was like a wall-to-wall rug made up of your clothes. Each piece was spread to its full length and width. Your underwear was scattered helter-skelter over all these garments, and shoes were thrown all around on top of this. That's it. That's the news."

"That little pipsqueak," snapped Sarah. "Glad it didn't rain. Anyway, I know what his strategy is. He wants to get me irritated, upset me to the point where I'll make some tactical mistake. Well, Mr. T., I will not be duped that way. I shall calmly write you a letter, gratefully acknowledging your efforts."

"Wanna hear a good one?" asked her mom. Without waiting for an answer, she nodded toward her husband and said, "Ed took several pictures of the porch scene before we touched a thing. He says you never know when we might be able to use them. You know your dad's a stickler for documentation."

Sarah swung down her elbow with a clinched fist and shouted, "Yes! Way to go, Dad!"

"Thanks. Okay, you may want to open the envelope now; we're very curious, as you can imagine."

Sarah stared at the envelope and then looked at the ceiling for a few moments. The one-line address was handwritten with dark, bold letters: "*TO MRS. SARAH TURBO.*"

She eased open the envelope; twisted the single, half-page note around; and began to read. At once, she could feel her brow wrinkling and soon became aware that this reaction was causing concern on the part of her parents. She could hear their heavy breathing and feel the heaving in her own chest as she read. When she finished, she slammed the envelope and note down in her lap and glanced at the ceiling again. Her parents let her handle these early moments in her own time and way.

"Oh, no—please, God!" Now, she pounded her knees and continued to cry, "No, no, noooo!"

Her mom and dad waited.

In a few moments, Sarah pulled herself straight, held her head up, and proclaimed, "He's gonna lose this one too." Thereupon she decided to read it through one more time before handing it to her parents:

Bill of Charges Owed to Mack Turbo
Debtor: Sarah Grace (Lock) Turbo

Retrieval of truck	*300.00*
Repair of truck damages	*720.00*
Stolen cash	*500.00*
Lost work time	*1,280.00*
Dental charges	*910.00*
Trauma counseling	*3,117.00*
Gasoline for doctor visits	*16.00*
TOTAL	*6,843.00*

All charges due upon receipt.

"My, how clever!" She smirked as she passed the note to her mom.

Mom Lock read the note, working her lips, jerking back from time to time, and shaking her head. She handed it to Dad Lock, who studied it and, like Sarah, just dropped it in his lap when he finished.

"You're right, Sarah; that's just really cute."

"How can this relate to the divorce proceedings?" asked Sarah.

"It doesn't relate at all," proposed her dad. "Our too-clever

Mr. Turbo is planning something much bigger than divorce, but have we got news for him!"

After breakfast Saturday morning, mom and daughter commiserated in the comfort of the den.

"Here's something, Mom, that you might find interesting. It's no big deal, but it's just a point of information. I've met a man."

"Aha! Where have you been to meet a man?"

"In the meadow."

"Ooh, tell me more."

"Really, Mom; it's nothing. This boy from up the meadow comes out most days for the same reason I do—to feel the peace of nature and get some fresh air. One day, he saw me dancing playfully in the meadow in front of Aunt Gina's house, and he was fascinated."

"So how did the two of you meet?"

"Well, he just … I guess he was so enthralled that he wanted a closer view. You know, girls dancing in a pasture is not a common occurrence."

"You two have a thing going?"

"I guess if it was left up to him, we would have. But no, we do not."

"Just friends, right?"

"Yeah."

"Yeah? That's it, yeah?"

"Come on, Mom! I'm a married woman. It can't be more."

"My little punkin, I'm your *mother* and I *know* you; I can tell you'd like for it to be more."

Sarah shrugged.

"Come on, Sarah, doesn't this sound like you're being swept off your feet again. Think this through."

"That's exactly what I'm doing right now as we talk."

"No, you're not. It sounds very final as you discuss your … err … *friendship* with this unknown peeping Tom."

"Whatever! I just wanted you to know that a man had entered my space. That's all—nothing serious going on."

"Sarah, dear, I'm not sayin' this is not the guy for you, but get real; you'll be single pretty soon, and maybe you ought to get used to that for a while before you let your mind dwell on the prospect of a new *man*."

"Don't worry; after my divorce, I'll be too broken to ever care for a man again. I'd always be suspicious and reluctant. I'm afraid I can never feel love, so, I'll not be romancing this young man. He's about four years older than I am." She chuckled. Now, she was smiling as she thought of this guy she was about to let go. "And he's … he likes my little aggressive humor. He never gets offended; he just laughs, and, Mom, sometimes, it looks like he wants to come hug me when I pull one of my little verbal pranks."

The daughter was on a roll, and her mother picked it up. How could she not? She was Mom. When Sarah paused for breath, her mom chided, "Well, he should be easy to brush off, then."

"Very funny, Mom."

It was her mom's turn for a wordless shrug.

Ed Lock took his daughter back to her so-called hideaway home Saturday afternoon. On the way out of town, she dropped a letter in a roadside mailbox. It was distinguished by its simplicity and brevity:

> *Dear Mr. Turbo,*
> *Thanks so much for the clothes. You really didn't get them matched up too well, but at least they're all here. As to your bill of charges, my attorney has them under advisement. Thanks again. Sarah.*

Saturday afternoon in Mabank, Kevin Lane knocked at the door of the blue house where he had met Sarah's aunt Gina Evans. When a man appeared at the door, he introduced himself and explained that he lived at the top of the meadow and that he and Sarah had become acquaintances, so to speak.

"Come on in, my friend," said the man. "I'm Sarah's uncle, Kyle Evans. Yes, Gina mentioned your visit. It's good to meet you, and I admire your taste in flowers. We think that was a nice gesture on your part."

"Thanks. I just felt that red roses are her."

"Right you are. Sarah has sort of been our little girl since she was six. She is quite remarkable. Bet you're looking for her right now."

"Yessir; I mainly just want to find out if she's okay, you know, sort of like a worried neighbor."

"Sure," said Kyle with a twinkle in his eye. "She's actually with her mom and dad this weekend."

At that moment, Gina pranced in and hooted, "Mr. Lane— Kevin Lane, right?"

"Yes, thanks, Mrs. Evans."

"Gina," she insisted. "I see you've met the man of the house."

Kevin was getting restless because all he wanted to do was find out about Sarah. He didn't really have any interest in generating a social affair. Suddenly, he realized that was an ugly attitude. After all, here were two people whose house he had invaded, perfect strangers to him, and they were being gracious and accommodating.

"We *have* met. And, y'all, thank you for inviting me into your home. That's kind of you." *Much better, Kevin.* "As I mentioned to Kyle, I miss my little meadow friend and just wanted to make sure she's okay."

"Oh, sure, Sarah's fine," Gina assured him. "Want to have a seat and visit for a while?"

"Well, for a few minutes, I guess. I don't want to interrupt your day. The thing is, Sarah and I have come to be ... well, I would say very good friends. We have one very major common interest: the meadow. Plus, she just makes my day, every time we have brief contact. She is pretty, brilliant, and fascinating—"

"Whoa, sounds like more than, ahem, close friendship."

"Well, I think it's still clearly platonic—for her anyway."

"Kevin," began Gina, turning very serious, "there are some things about Sarah that may make her seem disinterested in many ways. That's because she's going through some troubling times in her life right now. Out of respect for her, we can't talk about any of it, but I just wanted you to know that she's burdened a bit at the moment. It'll all work out someday. It'll probably be better if you didn't mention this disclosure to her. Meanwhile, thanks for being her friend. We love her as our very own."

"I'm so sorry. But, y'all, I knew something was wrong. We may be just friends, but I care about that."

"On that point," said Kyle, "please don't get disappointed if she seems unable to deal with caring at the moment."

Gina cleared her throat loudly and said, "That's probably enough, Kyle."

"Right, that's all I'll say. Keep your head, Kevin!"

At this, the three sat quietly for a few moments, just nodding their heads in full agreement, each likely looking for a polite way to close their conversation on a difficult subject. Kevin rose to transact his departure and said what he hoped were all the right social things. Then, he set off while his hosts stood at the door, again offering their encouragement. When he was outside alone, he glanced back at the house and said aloud, "Thanks, God, for good people."

As he trudged up the meadow, dejected and worried, Kevin thought back to his pleasant, yet disturbing, visit. He recalled glancing at the vase of red roses as he was leaving and noticing that they were holding up well. *Hope that's a sign,* he thought.

11

NEITHER SARAH NOR KEVIN came to the meadow at any time on Sunday. They both went to their churches. Then, they each spent a solemn afternoon at home, grateful for what they had in their lives, yet longing for something they were afraid they could never have. Their meeting the previous Thursday had ended on a note so provocative as to jostle their senses and—more severely—break their hearts. And if they were to be fully honest with themselves, they would have to admit they were a little ticked off at each other—Kevin, because Sarah seemed rigidly unreceptive to his demand that she had been mislabeled, and Sarah, because Kevin persisted on that point. Still, they were heartbroken, for there was an invisible force, gnawing at the edges, still trying to push them toward each other.

Sarah was the first out Monday morning. When she didn't see Kevin in his spot at the top of the meadow, she retreated to the porch swing. She continued to dwell nervously on the impending revelation with which she was about to shock him. *He's a dream I didn't go looking for,* she thought. *Bless him, he just came calling. I hate to prolong this, but there's one thing I just must give him. Heaven only knows why, but he seems to have his heart set on hiking down the edge of the woods. There's no way I can deny him that. But, Kevin, my love, that's it.*

In a short while, Sarah cried her way back into the meadow, and there he was, waiting. His arm shot into the air the instant he saw her, and he was on his way. He was really sailing through the tall grass. Soon, he was near her, holding his arms out, obviously intending to step right into an embrace. When he was within a couple of steps of her, she backed away. He dropped his arms, looking so very disappointed. But he had never tried to push her, and he let it go at that.

"Hi, Kevin," she said, sweetly.

"Hey, what's up?"

"Oh, just sittin' rouna-house," she chortled.

"Well, that's good duty, if you can get it."

"Right. So, Kevin, are you still wanting to go hiking through the woods?"

That sounds so formal, thought Kevin, *like's she's making a big concession. I guess this is what happens sometimes when you tell someone you love them. And I love her for what she's doing right now.* Suddenly, he realized he hadn't answered. "Oh, yes, indeed, I just want to be a little boy again for an hour and play in the woods."

"Good, well, just in case you did," she said, trying to giggle excitedly, "I wore cotton slacks and a long-sleeved shirt today. Shall we forge ahead?"

As they tramped along just inside the meadow, still in the shadow of the tall trees, they instinctively looked up from time to time. Kevin said, "Why do we keep looking up toward the heavens? Is it just a reflex born of nature's inspiration?"

"I think we're praying subconsciously; we're saying, 'Thank you, God; how can we bring this rapture into our own souls?'"

Both nodded, and they pushed on.

As they treaded quietly along their way, Sarah was at once aware of a somewhat carefree feeling; she had a sense of being at ease, as though she was actually having a pleasant time. She looked up again and then all around. It was a grand day. It was clear, cool, and restful, the kind of day you could see all the way through. It seemed so tranquil out across the fields and grasslands. The day was everything it could be, a sweet song, a peaceful melody—even for those who were not at peace with themselves.

After a while, the hikers, each still scanning the fields and the sky periodically, looked at each other pleasantly and nodded. At that moment, a gentle morning breeze rose to touch their faces and force the easily yielding meadow grass to quiver in little waves. This seemed to have the effect of bringing them physically closer together as they hiked along. How could the day be so grand with so much at stake? Was it taunting them?

They walked on, really close together now; as they listed occasionally over uneven terrain, their arms would brush against each other for a second. Although unsolicited, at least by Sarah, those moments were as engaging as the incomparable field they walked in. There was something about an honest, unintentional touch of two people that confirmed or denied any feeling of attraction between them. In a few moments, Kevin fell a step behind, simply because he couldn't quit gawking.

All of a sudden, Sarah lost her balance as her foot found a shallow, invisible hole in the meadow bed, and she started to fall. Kevin instantly reached forward for her, vigorously pulling her steady with one hand on her shoulder and one hand in front of her. They continued to hold this position to ensure everybody was fully balanced and to wait for their panting to abate. After an awkward period of time, Sarah cleared her throat and started to speak, though a little weakly.

"Err ... Kevin, I don't know if you've noticed it or not, but your hand is on my breast."

Kevin's hand instantly flew off her shoulder.

"Wrong hand, Kevin."

"Oh, sorry," he said, grinning like a little kid caught with his finger in the pie filling.

Sarah was struggling to keep from laughing, but so far, had managed to hold it at bay. She suppressed as hard as she could, but in the end, she could hold out no longer and settled for a little snicker into a cupped hand. Then she glanced at Kevin who was making like he hadn't noticed her predicament. *How nice of him,* she thought.

"Know what, Sarah? Let's move over a little closer to the woods and start looking for a promising place to enter."

"Gotcha!" whooped Sarah as she turned toward the woods. "My uncle Kyle told me one time that if you walk far enough down this field, you'll come to a narrow trail that leads through the woods all the way over to a creek."

"Okay, let's go for that. In fact, there *is* a creek north of here that runs near the highway at one point and then cuts in and goes for miles, and I believe finally empties into the Trinity River. You know, I bet that's Whistle Creek the little trail goes to."

After about twenty minutes, they came upon the prize. Sure enough, there was this little trail leading into the woods. The hikers could only see about fifteen yards down the trail before it disappeared in a long curve. They stood at the head of the trail, contemplating their course, looking at each other for confirmation.

"This is bound to be it all right!" exclaimed Sarah.

Kevin nodded. "You mean this little trail will take me all the way over to Whistle Creek?"

"Well, not if you don't want to go," chided Sarah.

Kevin chuckled and looked admiringly at his very bright, very adorable sweet friend. After he recovered from his daydream, he said confidently, "Let's go at least a little ways down the trail. It looks enchanting."

"Onward!" ordered Sarah.

They moseyed along, stooping to peer through underbrush, gazing up to the tops of the tallest of trees, bending young saplings, twisting vines, raking leaves with their feet, and kicking at stumps. They were clearly trying to catch the full measure of the woods. It was growing dark inside the thicket when they came upon an old fungus-covered log. It sat just inside a small cove, apparently created by the fallen tree they were headed for and perhaps a few others. In any event, the results made a nice little room inside the enchanted woods.

"Why don't we sit a spell?" suggested Sarah.

"Capital idea," piped Kevin.

After they sat down, Sarah looked askance at Kevin and said, "Why are you frowning?"

"Well, I just don't understand it. Where do these stumps and logs come from? I mean, what accounts for their presence inside these dense woods? You think people came in here and cut trees to get firewood or something?"

"Well, I don't know what for—they came in here, that is— but this is clearly people work. I've never seen a Spanish oak wield an ax."

Kevin smiled and, again, just shook his head at the marvel of his young companion. "I agree; people did it."

Suddenly, Sarah was distracted by something in the cove. She was leaning way out, looking at a cottonwood tree, well sheltered by the towering oaks.

"I hope you don't fall off the log," mused Kevin.

"Well, there's something irregular about that tree over there," she explained, pointing past Kevin's nose.

"I don't see anything."

"You're too close. Here, let's take a look," she said as she shoved off the log.

At the tree, there was—mostly toward the back side of it—a

small man-made trapdoor hinged to a limb right above a hole in the tree trunk. The hole was made partly by a big bump apparently left by the healing of a wound.

"I'll be darn," said Kevin, lifting the little door and fishing around inside the hole with his other hand. "It's like a mailbox."

"Fascinating," said Sarah, unable to break her fixation on their discovery.

"It was definitely intended for something."

Sarah chuckled, poked a finger in the air to make a point, and sang out, "I know what. *Think*, Kevin!"

Kevin tilted his head and pooched his lips but was unable to come up with anything.

"It's a secret post office for two forbidden lovers. Do you see, now?"

"They used it to exchange l-l-love notes," stammered Kevin.

"Exactly. Like, they were too young to be romancing—or something—so they had to do it on the sly." Suddenly, Sarah sank into sadness while Kevin continued to poke around in the tree-trunk mailbox. Then she slipped into a fantasy of what it might have been like. She saw two innocent young lovers battling the stigma of being too young for romantic passion, yet feeling that unspeakable quiver of love so deeply inside and knowing it was real and right. It had to be so disheartening, indeed scary, to know they were seen as violating some public definition of heartfelt love. Sarah quickly shook herself out of her dream. That little harmless fantasy had at once been both thrilling and demoralizing. She looked away, sighed, and moved back to the log.

"So much for that little bit of intrigue," said Kevin as he moseyed back to his place on the log.

Sarah nodded, and the two sat quietly for a while. The unexpected little snippet of merriment was over. They had needed that, for they both sensed they were on borrowed time.

Time passed while they rested, perfectly content to hold their journey indefinitely. During this time, Sarah was becoming increasingly restless. Finally, she decided it was time.

"Kevin, I have something to tell you, and this is as good a place for it as anywhere. Are you okay with that? It won't take very long, but it's another serious matter in my life that you have a right to know about. I'm sorry I waited so long, but I didn't know we would be growing serious about each other. I don't want to ruin your hike in the woods, so if you're not okay with this now, I can wait until we're back at the ranch, so to speak."

"Fire away," said Kevin. "I'm a big boy, but I dare say, you *do* have me worried, so let's get it done."

"Okay, it's actually very short and simple."

Kevin nodded, staring intently at her.

"Kevin, I'm married."

He twitched but said nothing. He just kept looking at the ground. Finally, he looked at Sarah and tried to smile but just couldn't get it going. "That's certainly daunting news all right," he murmured.

"I'm so sorry. I've done you wrong. I should have told you in the beginning."

"That's ... that's just ... I can't speak to that."

"Understand," said Sarah.

After a deep, deep sigh, Kevin droned, "Well, I guess I'm committing adultery, sitting here talking to you and feeling love for you. You know, I can quit the talking, but the other ..."

Now, Sarah's head was buried in her hands. She had just let it all go. Weeping turned to crying aloud, and her hands did little to muffle it. She was shaking and straining to come out of it. Her man didn't interfere. *Oh, how I wish he'd never come along.* That thought plunged her yet deeper into her anguish. *I didn't mean that, Kevin.*

After a while, Kevin rested a hand on her shoulder. Gathering all the strength she could possibly summon, Sarah lifted her head, sniffled for a few moments, forced a weak smile, and then looked into his eyes. "I guess I messed it up pretty good."

"Actually, I think I'm probably the culprit in this affair."

Sarah shook her head; Kevin said nothing more.

After several minutes, she said, "Kevin, I know you're angry, and you have every right to be."

"No, I'm not angry." He shook his head to emphasize that statement. "I'm not angry." Then, smiling, he added, "I'm glad I had all those sweet moments getting to know you."

"Honestly, so am I, Kevin, and I never thought I'd say that."

"So is your husband in the military somewhere?"

"No."

"I guess, probably, we need to be heading on back."

"Yes, Kevin."

Sarah knew the trip back was destined to be lonely. She was already feeling it as they mounted the meadow. She was also aware that it was a lonely hike back for Kevin. Now, she questioned whether her decision to give Kevin his longed-for hike was really the right thing to do. Unfortunately, she had failed to consider possible negative consequences. It was in her *heart* to do it for him, but she failed to tune in to her *mind* also. *Maybe I am retarded.* It just seemed she couldn't do anything right. Somehow, trying to reckon with reason and feelings at the same time was altogether too confusing—with a broken marriage on the one hand and forbidden love on the other. *What a mess.*

After what seemed like an endless walk, they were back at Sarah's hideout home. It was time for parting. Instinctively, they turned and faced each other. They seemed so much alike in their reaction to Sarah's confession, as in so many other things. Even that perception itself was one they shared on this sad occasion. Now, still facing each other, they dropped their eyes and just stared at the ground for a few moments. Finally, they smiled perfunctorily and shifted in place for a bit. Then, Kevin quit smiling.

"I would attempt to embrace you," he said, "but I know that would not be the right thing to do. So I'll just say, God bless you, my dear Sarah."

"God bless you, too," said Sarah, and they parted.

That night, Sarah confided in her aunt Gina as to what had transpired that day between her and Kevin.

"Now, I'm at odds as to whether to tell him I have a pending divorce action. What do you think, Aunt Gina?"

"Sarah, I can't believe you asked that."

From the intonation of that snap reply and the instant change in her countenance, it was entirely clear that Gina was disturbed and dead serious.

"I didn't tell him, because I don't want to string him along. The whole point of telling him I'm married was to liberate him from an impossible dream."

"Sarah! Listen to me! *Tell* your man. He's proved he can handle it. Don't let Mack Turbo rob you of a real dream."

"I just don't want to give Kevin false hope, because when this is all over with Mack, I'll not likely ever trust romance again. Can't you see that, Aunt Gina? Put yourself in my place."

"Phooey! Sure, talking about a divorce will likely renew Kevin's hope, but who knows? It may not be *false* hope, as you assume. Don't try to predict yourself while you're stressed out. Give God a chance to work on this! Where's your trust?"

"I see your point."

"So *tell* Kevin you're getting a divorce!"

"It may be too late."

12

KEVIN AND SARAH DID not return to the meadow for the rest of the week. Why would they? It was over! Kevin did not have the motivation to make the three rather long trips he had scheduled for distant East Texas points. He plodded along at home, working at the computer, refining digital pictures and filing them on the Internet with his employer. Even with those simple tasks, he was having a hard time keeping his heart in his work. *I gotta quit whipping myself,* he thought as he shoved back from his desk for a break.

In desperation, he decided to distract himself by interacting with his landlord. *Woohoo.* It didn't work; Old Man Geesling, speaking candidly, essentially scolded him for getting involved with the—as he judged—clearly irresponsible young girl. He was very negative about the whole thing. It seemed to Kevin that Grover G. was attempting to be almighty counselor in the matter.

"Gro," began Kevin, hesitantly, "I hear you, okay? I agree that I probably shouldn't have gotten involved with the young prairie nymph, as you call her, but I did. So you see, that's where I am, and I have to take it from there."

"Take what?"

"My life."

Grover just looked at him wordlessly.

Kevin let it go for a while and then moaned, "Okay, I guess I'm just feeling sorry for myself. Thanks for listening."

"Anytime."

At this point, Kevin was wishing the day would hasten along; he was sorely ready for it to end, so he could try for a good night's rest. Usually, that helped. Meanwhile, perhaps it would help to get out of the house, drive around locally for a while, and meditate.

Cruising along country roads, he began to question himself. His mind and his feelings were tugging at each other, giving way to a prickly internal battle. *Who's in charge here?* he pondered. *Should I follow my brain or my heart? Either could well lead me astray. The rational, indeed proper, thing to do is forget the girl. Yeah, right. Still, I have to respect her and the others involved in her life. So for the sake of Christian values and social propriety, I herewith resolve to drop Sarah Lock from my mind. I will think of her no more.*

Kevin's resolution worked for about three miles. Suddenly, he slapped the steering wheel and spoke aloud, "What the hell! I don't *want* to forget about her. Dear God, please forgive me if thinking about her is adultery. I will not try to go around her or bother her in any way. It's just that she's someone I could truly love if she was free. My mind will keep me from carrying out my heart's desire." He drove on, and in a while, the thought struck him: *That doesn't mean my heart's wrong.* With that, he went home.

For the rest of the week, it was a matter of methodically transacting each day and night, carrying out the rudiments of living. In his emotional state, the best he could hope for was to choose tasks that involved simple procedural steps. Therefore, he concentrated on eating, sleeping, some mundane work at the computer, and a little dismal bantering with Grover Geesling. One light spot was the receipt of an e-mail from his employer, saying, "Kevin, your work is looking great. Good quality. Keep it up." Although somewhat terse, the message was uplifting and offered some incentive to carry on.

Two hundred yards away, resting reflectively in her hideaway house, Sarah Lock was having similar experiences. The difference was that, in her case, she had so much more weighing on her. Even so, she could not shake Kevin from her thoughts. She now knew that the only humane thing to do was to let him know about her pending divorce. But to tell him meant she would have to break their tacitly agreed-upon silence. She would have to see him again, which might be a problem. In any event, she simply had to let him know. *But how and when?*

The whole question was taken out of her hands when she received a phone call from her attorney Wednesday afternoon. He indicated he had some new developments to bring to her attention and asked if she could meet with him in his office the next day. She agreed readily and called her dad at work.

When she arrived at the office of Buford Crump the next day, she was struggling to keep from trembling. She could not remember being so nervous in all her life. So much was at stake. In a short while, she was called in by her smiling, cordial attorney.

"Mrs. Turbo—"

"Could you just call me Sarah? I'm sorry, sir, but as you know, I'm trying to shake that name out of my life forever."

"Oh, of course, and thank you for pointing that out. So, Sarah, they have successfully served Mack Turbo, and his attorney has already contacted me and let me know that they will oppose the divorce action. Not a surprise, really, but I question the rationale for that position. Anyway, that's up to them."

"That means we'll be going to court; we'll have a trial?" queried Sarah nervously.

"You're exactly right, but worry not; we will be prepared. I can't imagine what kind of defense he can offer, since he's filed a bill of monetary charges with you and accused you of cruelty.

Why would one want to continue a marriage so fraught with nuisance? If he wants to remain married, why is he seeking compensatory damages from his wife? I can see him doing that after a divorce but not before. That doesn't make sense, but that's not our problem. As irrational as it may seem, we still have to be prepared for every scenario."

For the first time, Sarah breathed a sigh of relief and felt her jitters beginning to fade. It was so comforting to hear her advocate declare they would be prepared for any- and everything. She smiled. "I can't tell you how good those words sound to me. And, Mr. Crump, I will do everything I can to help you prepare."

Now, Buford Crump was smiling at his determined client. "Sarah, you are a very bright person. You just spoke the reason for this meeting. Yes, I have an assignment for you, and I know you will carry it through. We will get it done. Now, let's speculate a little on what tactic Mr. Turbo and his attorney might use. See, our job is to anticipate. That's the whole game at this point."

"I'm in," said Sarah, shuffling around in her chair, clearly more at ease.

"Good. Now, here's the thing. As you are obviously already aware, this is going to be a tactical exercise, a game of strategy. So here's what I want you to do. Delve into your memory. Think of all the things you can that describe Mack Turbo's courtship with you, that is, things that stand out from that period covering the full term of your relationship with him. Pay particular attention to what you can remember of his habits, tendencies, attitude, and so forth during that period. Try to recall instances in which his reaction may tell us about the way he thinks. We're going to use all this to anticipate lines of defense he may pursue in court and then get you ready for it."

"I'll begin at once. In fact, I will write it all down, sort of journalize it in reverse. My mind is already thinking about it, so I'll already be in gear by the time I get home and I can start writing at once. I'll hurry."

"Fabulous. We don't have a court date yet; this is something I can't predict very well. They could give you an early date or a later date; it all depends on what's on the docket right now. Anyway, we'll be ready."

"Do you think you'll need it before, say, this coming Monday?"

"No, I'm pretty confident we won't have a date by then."

"Why don't I work toward faxing it to you by close of business Monday?"

"That would be splendid, but do take more time if you need it to be entirely thorough."

"Mr. Crump, I sure do like the way you operate."

"You know something, Sarah? I thoroughly like dealing with *you*. It makes it so easy for me. I marvel at how you are perfectly tuned in all the time. It's *you* that's going to make this easy."

Back home Thursday evening, Sarah hurriedly gathered her pen and notebook and sat on the side of her bed with her feet propped on the side rail. First, she just had to spend some time thinking, not a welcome task considering her present disposition toward the subject of her writing, one pitiable Mack Turbo. In a while, she lifted her head and touched the pen to her chin, trying to think of where to start. As she brought it down to begin, she stopped it in midair.

Sarah's mind had flashed back to the quandary she had been in just before her attorney called the day before. She frowned as she recalled reaching a decision to tell Kevin about her divorce situation. The last thing she had pondered was the question of how to get in touch with him. Ideally, she needed to get that issue off her mind as soon as possible so that she could give her undivided attention to the journal. The problem was that during her and Kevin's present period of detachment, neither of them was going into the meadow. At once, she resolved that she would go into the meadow several times a day, just in case he might wander outside at some point, maybe just for a little fresh air.

For now, she would think about her experiences with Mack

Turbo and begin to make notes. She would organize them later and work in some continuity so that the whole thing would make sense. After dinner that evening, she made a cursory swing into the meadow. No Kevin. She was not surprised, considering the manner in which they had parted on their last outing when she gave him the worrisome news of her marriage. Still, she knew Kevin was infatuated with the meadow for its own sake, so it was reasonable to expect that he would continue to visit. On the other hand, the whole experience might have soured him on the meadow or anything connected with their relationship.

During breakfast Friday morning, Sarah discussed her whole situation with her aunt and uncle. They would be her best sounding boards; she knew they would be both candid and loving in offering their counsel. She felt so very blessed to have them in her life. They, along with her staunchly devoted mom and dad, would give her all the support anyone could ever hope for. Though it was her aunt Gina who had urged her to tell Kevin about her pending divorce, at the present meeting, it was Uncle Kyle who took the initiative.

"Why don't I mosey up there to Kevin's quarters on the pretense of visiting with Grover and at some point, casually mention to Kevin that you have some information for him?"

"Thanks, Uncle Kyle, but I'd rather not stage it with that much formality. I'd rather have Kevin and I meet accidentally."

"Why does it matter?" asked Aunt Gina.

"See, I don't want Kevin to think it's all that important, that it's any big deal. I just want it to be a casual point of information."

"So it's on to the meadow several times a day," grumbled Kyle. "I still think my way is the best. I could stop by the Geesling house on my way to work this morning and get it started; know what I mean?"

"For that matter, Kyle," said Gina, "you could just give him the so-called routine point of information yourself, and Sarah wouldn't have to even see Kevin at all."

"Okay." Sarah sighed. "You all have convinced me, and I thank you for your help and caring. But let's compromise; Uncle Kyle, you could alert the Geesling man—not this morning, but maybe Monday—that I have a routine bit of information for his boarder, who could drop by here briefly—I say *briefly*—one day, and I'll relay."

With that, the matter appeared to be decided, and their discussion ended with smiles—followed by raised eyebrows.

Immediately after the breakfast meeting, Sarah went back to her journal, but she was having trouble concentrating. She just couldn't seem to get into it. Finally, she slammed her book down and stomped out to the meadow. For a change, she decided to try to relax, so she played a couple of pieces on her violin and attempted halfheartedly to dance a little.

Suddenly, coming out of a twirl, she saw Kevin at the top of the meadow. He was perfectly still, looking straight in her direction. In a while, he raised his arm high in the air. Although she had pledged not to make a deal out of the situation, she just didn't have the heart—indeed the will—to ignore his gesture. Although the matter seemed to have been already worked out with Uncle Kyle's initiative, she couldn't just watch this young man wave for her and let it go. She lifted her hand just a little above her shoulder. Now, Kevin was walking toward her. She stood in place, breathing heavily, holding her violin and bow down beside her knee. After a while, they were face-to-face. Neither said anything for a while, each bearing a serious countenance. Finally, Kevin spoke.

"I just wanted to check to make sure you're okay."

"I'm okay. How about you?"

"Fine."

"Oh, by the way, Kevin, since we happened up together like this, there's one little point I neglected to mention in our last … err, the last time we talked."

"Okay." He smiled and added, "It's never too late, they say."

"Right. Anyway, no big deal, but just to be, you know, ah, just to be complete, I failed to mention that I have filed for a divorce." As Kevin began to smile, she quickly added, "Now before you say anything, this doesn't change a thing."

Still smiling, Kevin said, "Okay, but I wish you luck in getting the divorce. Really, I wish me luck, too. My dear Sarah, please forgive me for smiling; it was just so automatic. I'm not smiling at your adversity, because I don't want you to suffer anything *ever*."

"Like I say," said Sarah, trying hard to sound matter-of-fact, "I didn't mean to mislead you by omitting that little fragment of information. I didn't think it material at the time. Then later, I decided I needed to be complete and honest with you. So I guess it doesn't really matter all that much, because after the divorce, I'm not going to be able to have any kind of relationship considering all I will have been through—all this mess. Maybe I never will."

"Guess that takes back my premature smile."

"I'm sorry, Kevin."

"That's okay; I'm not giving up, even if I have to start all over again—from the top of the meadow, mind you."

Neither said any more for a few minutes. Finally, Kevin broke the silence. "How will I know when you're free?"

Sarah just shrugged. She had no strength to talk, for tears were already filling her eyes. She turned and walked away, and so did Kevin.

Inside her home, Sarah marched straight to her bedroom and closed the door. Her family would understand. She picked up her journal and sent it sailing across the room until it hit a wall and fell to the floor. She vowed she wouldn't work on it any more that day. She now was aware that she could easily finish it over the weekend, and her uncle could fax it to her attorney from his office Monday morning. E-mail was out of the question because she didn't want it even touching the Internet. For now, all she wanted to do was go to bed, and so she did.

When Kevin was near his house, after the tense rendezvous with Sarah, he hesitated and stood for a while at the top of the meadow, looking far out over its vast province. It looked so crisp and innocent, so relaxed. Remarkably, the surrounding woods, as tough and invincible as they seemed to be, looked peaceful and free. It was as if they took pride in keeping guard over the grasslands. They looked so resolute, standing there against all foes. Kevin just lingered quietly for a while and reveled in the rapture of nature. *How does nature do it?*

He was careful not to look at Sarah's distant spot in the prairie. At this moment, he was entranced. He couldn't separate himself from this reverie. He so longed for his fairy tale to come back. Suddenly, he gained new grit and stomped the ground. He positively would start over. He would not let his little angel go. He would do whatever he had to. Someway, he would have to find out when the divorce was final. Maybe he could send Grover down to check with the Evanses on some pretense of covering a church matter. Grover could find out when Sarah was going to be away. Then Kevin would visit them on that day and make some sort of deal to find out about her divorce. Maybe it wouldn't break their loyalty.

13

KEVIN HAD ALWAYS THOUGHT that the magic of night had a way of filtering out the risky, impulsive ambitions of the day, leaving for the cold, hard morning the thankless task of restoring reason and focus.

In Kevin's case, the cold, hard morning hit him like a brick—one brick. All the bold plans he had ardently dreamed up the day before now looked totally foolish. He ditched his plans to visit Gina and Kyle Evans to learn of Sarah's situation, and he even scuttled his notion of keeping track of her in any way. If Sarah had wanted him to know of her changing status, she would have told him how to find out. In fact, he decided, he would merely forget his sweet young maiden. *I will simply drop her. This is plan B.*

To make plan B work, he would have to stay brutally busy. So he set about to make his three somewhat distant trips to East Texas points, to Marshall near the Louisiana border, to Lufkin, and northeast to Texarkana. The trips went well. The scenery was breathtaking; the river lands lent a novelty he hadn't encountered in his earlier ventures, and, all in all, he felt very pleased with himself. He was confident he had a collection of award-winning photographs. If not, it was strictly his fault, for the lands were incomparably beautiful and inspiring. It had been a soundly productive, highly rewarding week. Then why wasn't he clicking his heels? Why did he feel such melancholy?

He started out the next day, lonely and weary of heart. He

caught himself moping around like a forlorn old hound dog. He was sure Grover had noticed, but the man had said nothing. Plan B was the pits. It wasn't easy to let Sarah out of his life physically, but dropping her from his heart and mind was impossible, he soon discovered. He didn't really want to. If he couldn't have her in his arms, he could at least hold her in his soul. He'd rather grieve than lose her from his memory altogether. This way, she would still be in his life. *Guess I'm just feeling sorry for myself. Poor baby.*

One evening, Kevin and Grover were resting on the back porch, which looked directly into the woods. In their division of labor, Grover did all the cooking and Kevin did the dishes and other housework and maintained the grounds. They had finished their chores late that day, so it was dark by the time they opted to rest. As a rule, these two men, while perfectly comfortable with each other, didn't converse much. So they just sat quietly and watched the fireflies pierce the night and listened to the crickets, whose songs, though monotonous, were consistently upbeat and sometimes very loud.

All of a sudden, out of the blue, Grover leaned toward Kevin and, in his deep, grating voice, blurted, "Kevin, my boy, I notice you haven't been going to the meadow lately. Is your fair young maiden on vacation?"

"No. Actually, we broke up."

"Wow! That's a surprise. What happened? Did you find yourselves incompatible?"

"No; not that, but our relationship just reached the point where it was impractical to continue."

"That's vague enough. What you're really saying is, 'I don't want to talk about it.' And, Kevin, I respect that and I apologize for bringing up the subject."

"Oh, that's quite all right. I just have more to do than play in the meadow. As to Sarah, I've pretty much dropped her out of my mind."

"Sure you have," teased Grover.

Monday morning following her and Kevin's de facto breakup,
Sarah took one last look at the summary section of her journal
before handing it off to her uncle to fax. She shook her head all
the way through the reading of it:

*In summary, Mack Turbo was good to me all through
our six-month courtship. He did everything I asked him
to do. He opposed me in only one thing. But he was
mostly careful not to offend me. He was totally agreeable
on just about everything. All of this led me to predict
he would be a gentle, caring husband. He did nothing
that made me think he could be violent. There was just
this one thing: he wanted sex. Now, I realize that's all
he ever wanted of me. In fact, he did get angry with me
for making him wait until we were married. As he put
it himself one time, he was "obsessed with my body."
He thought that I was mentally challenged and said I
needed him to take care of me. Sometimes, he did come
down rather hard on that, saying something like, "You're
gonna need my help."*

With the journal project complete, Sarah was left to think
of Kevin, not that she had forgotten him for a minute. She had
simply summoned all her will to concentrate on the journal and
get it done. That had to be the overriding priority in her life at
that hour. Now, head bowed, she thought of her dream, of how
Kevin came along, out of the blue—fully qualified to be her new
vision of life. Oh, how she did ache to see him, to tease him
and marvel at his instant smile, to have him hold her! They had
rarely ever embraced, but now, she could feel herself in his arms
and instinctively hugged her shoulders.

Sarah was aware that Aunt Gina was nearby while she
was deep in thought, and she was grateful that her aunt didn't

question her or otherwise interrupt her thoughts. She was also aware that the woman adored her, knew what she was going through, and would try to comfort her. In a moment, Sarah raised her head, looked directly at her, and smiled. With that, Gina smiled back and strolled over to be with her.

"My dear Sarah, please tell me what I can do."

Sarah just shook her head and smiled weakly.

Gina tried again. "I hate to see you toughing it out all by yourself like this."

"Thank you, Aunt Gina."

"Well, you've got more on you than you should ever have to bear."

Sarah sighed, looked up at her aunt, and said, feebly, "I guess I brought it all on myself."

"No, you did not! It just so happens that *trouble* is always out there rambling around trying to find someone to dump on."

"I got a load of it, I guess." She managed a halfhearted snicker.

"Yeah." Gina tightened her lips and added, "If you ever want to talk about any of it, Kyle and I are here for you."

"I know."

They were both silent for a few moments. In a while, Sarah said, "Believe it or not, at this particular moment, I'm more preoccupied with Kevin than Mack Turbo, maybe 'cause in just a little while, Mack will be history."

"Good riddance."

"Right, but unfortunately, he will still control my life."

"Hmm. Tell me about Kevin."

"Aunt Gina, I have to tell you that I have feelings for him, and I have tried not to. I have feelings for him more than I've been willing to acknowledge, even to myself."

"How did you meet anyway?"

At that, Sarah's countenance brightened, and for a change, she started to speak with some enthusiasm. "See," she began, sitting up straight, "the first time we met, we didn't even come up close to each other. We stood a ways apart in the meadow, just looking—I guess, timidly—at each other. After a while, Kevin raised his hand, like about as high as his shoulder as a sort of *hello* sign. In a moment, I lifted my hand also. He didn't rush to me, but he seemed so enthralled."

Now, Sarah was really getting into her tale, smiling and gesturing and twisting around in her chair. Gina picked up on this drastic change in demeanor and exclaimed, "Sarah, my darling, how wonderful! This total change in your mood as you talk of your adventures with Kevin *tells* me something."

"Oh my," said Sarah, quickly covering her mouth.

"Hey, don't dismiss it; this is a positive element in your life right now."

Sarah nodded. Now, feeling a little dreamy, she proceeded with her story. "So anyway, that was the first time we met, and it was interrupted when you called me in for something; I don't remember what."

"Sorry."

"Hey, no problem. That was probably the best ending for that first meeting. Now, we met again the same way, sort of tentatively at first, but the second time, we actually said, '*Hi.*' What a breakthrough, huh? Okay, so we met other times after that and actually began to talk. One day, he walked me to the Meadowlark and we had burgers together. Everything was always low-key, calm, unhurried. Still, I could tell we were drawing close."

"Really now, that all sounds a lot more romantic than meeting in a bar or a checkout line or even at church or a concert."

"Actually, it *was* romantic in the sense of … well, it was like a fairy tale."

"I think—"

Sarah interrupted before she could get any further. "I can see adoration in Kevin's eyes when we talk or just glance at each other. Honestly, Aunt Gina, there are times when it looks as if

Kevin wants to bound over to me and hug me, but he doesn't. He never pushes."

"I think he's a gentleman," said Gina, finally wedging in a word.

"I feel that he is. Tell me, Aunt Gina, what was your first impression the day you met him when he brought the roses?"

"I thought he was a nice-looking, clean-cut young man with good bearing. And really, even from that brief meeting, I had the sense that he was genuine, that he was a man of good character. I didn't sense any pretense in him like Kyle and I saw in Mack."

The mention of Mack changed the entire atmosphere of the moment, leading Sarah to lament, "I guess the ordeal with Mack will forever be my albatross. And that's mainly why I can't get serious with Kevin."

"Oh, Sarah, I'm sorry I mentioned Mack's name. How thoughtless of me!"

"No, no, no. That's okay. He's already on my mind in some spot pretty much all the time. Don't feel bad about bringing it up."

"Maybe, if you could get really busy, you wouldn't think about it all so much. Want me to find a project for you? Seriously."

"You know, Aunt Gina, if you wouldn't mind, I'd like to spend a few days with my mom and dad."

"Splendid. Tell you what; I'll drive you over there myself after dinner tomorrow afternoon. I'd like to visit with my sister a couple of hours, too."

"I'll pack!" Sarah giggled, clapping her hands.

"Meanwhile, Sarah, don't try to intellectualize this thing too much. This is probably one of those times when the heart is right."

The next morning, Sarah did indeed get up to pack for her trip home to Dallas. After she finished, the day seemed to drag and grind on unmercifully. Finally, it was time for dinner, and after dinner, it was on to Dallas for the two excited women of extraordinary rapport. They babbled all the way. They had risen above the heartaches and turned their minds to things they could laugh about. Somehow, someway, the dogged demands of character would always come through and eventually prevail.

Welcome home, Sarah! While the two Morgan women, Denise and Gina, visited, Sarah and her dad escaped to the front porch to spend some truly lighthearted, loving time together. Her dad was very astute during their visit. He didn't come near the subject of his daughter's present misfortune, and Sarah didn't volunteer anything.

Dad and daughter—nothing worked like dad and daughter. They spent those precious moments together, reminiscing, reliving the good times, and not even remembering the tough times. They remained upbeat, mainly because they knew they had to. Though they stayed above the scandal, they felt it all the while, and they knew it was there, gnawing at the edge, demanding attention. But they refused to toss it a bone. So they rallied on, snubbing life's occasional madness. They did this because, as her dad would say, *"That's what you do."*

After Gina left, mom and daughter clung to each other. Now, it was time to face the ever-present nemesis. Somehow, it was nonthreatening in this setting. Mom and daughter—nothing worked like mom and daughter. They got the Mack business out of the way in short order and turned to the subject of Kevin.

"Actually, Mom, we really don't know a thing about each other. All we have is what we've observed in our casual meadow contacts."

"That's okay, sweetheart; you can learn a lot from surface facts."

"Yeah, we *feel* a lot about each other. I guess all we have is what we feel."

"Just one caution: go slow—be careful."

"That's two."

"Not really."

They laughed together. Momentarily, Sarah began to yawn,

and soon thereafter, the household shut down and all went to bed.

About midmorning on Wednesday, Attorney Buford Crump called and—referring to it as good news—advised that the hearing of Sarah's petition for divorce had been set for Friday, May 25, at 9:30 a.m. He also indicated he would like to meet with Sarah a couple of days before. Sarah agreed and hung up, trembling.

She slumped into the nearest chair, dropped her head into her hands, and continued shaking. Her mom and dad were at work, so she had the house all to herself, which was just as well. This was one of those times when it worked best if one was left alone to tough it out with her own resources. Sometimes, over-consoling, as well intentioned as it was, had the effect of perpetuating the emotional crisis. Though she had prayed hard for this day to come, the reality of it was frightening. She was going to court. She would come face-to-face with her adversary. She would swear to the truth, and she would tell it. Right then, the truth was that the whole ordeal was unnerving. She prayed and went to bed for a healing nap, saying lastly, "Thank you, dear God."

Kevin Lane's ears must have been burning, for some mysterious force had hurled him back to plan A. Essentially, this plan said: *Find the girl. Don't let her get away. Know when she's free. Don't let her out of your mind.* "So be it," said Kevin to the meadow he had just wandered into early one morning. "Just like old times."

Although his dream girl wasn't there in her distant spot, he could plainly see her. So clear was her image in his mind that he wished upon her—asking for a new day, just for her. The first time he ever watched her twirling so gracefully in the meadow, he could sense her anguish, her trouble. Now, he could actually see it. He could see it in her face and in her dance, and he could feel it and shudder at its brutal indifference. How could anything pick on so innocent, so precious a being as this little jewel?

Now, Kevin began to wade through the tall grass over the width of the meadow to a vantage point near the woods on the other side. When he looked in the direction of the blue house, he saw her again, very distinctly. Sadness filled him; he so wanted to do something about her troubles, whatever they were, and his heart ached because there was nothing he *could* do. Then, right there in the midst of his quandary, staring hopelessly into the meadow, there came to him an impulse. There *was* one thing he could do.

"Dear Holy Lord, please hear the cry of Your child, Sarah Grace. She is dear to the world, and she is my friend. We love her—and so, we pray. Reach for her hand, Lord; hold her. Give her divine courage and the will and strength for whatever she is to do. Watch over her when she sleeps; walk with her when she's on the go, and stand with her when she's challenged. We humbly lift her up to Thee. Praise Thee, O Lord. Amen."

From his prayer, Kevin lifted his head just as a gentle breeze swept through, pushing the tall grass into rolling waves across the meadow. Surely, this must be God, acknowledging his prayer. He smiled and headed back to his house, where he was met by a serious-looking Grover Geesling, who clearly knew of his suffering and was offering his support and caring.

Days passed uneventfully. Then on the following Sunday, Grover mentioned to Kevin, rather casually, that he didn't see Sarah in church with the Evans couple.

Kevin's head popped up instantly. "Really, Gro? Is that all you know about it? Did they mention her or anything?"

"They just said she was visiting with her mom and dad in Dallas for a few days."

"Uh-huh."

"Does that make a difference, Kevin, my boy?"

"It does, indeed. It means I can take the first step in carrying out what I call my *plan A*, which begs that I try to see her again."

"Do you know yet what that first step will be?"

"Yes. I will pay a visit to the Evans house tomorrow evening."

Sure enough, on Monday evening, Kevin knocked at their door. He was invited in by a smiling Kyle Evans.

"Come on in, Kevin. Good to see you again; hope all's well. Gina's told me a lot more about the situation facing you and our Sarah, and I empathize with both of you."

"Thank you, Kyle; that's very kind of you."

At that moment, Gina came rushing in, holding her arms wide, and hugged their guest. "Welcome, Kevin. Come and have a seat."

Kevin marveled at how he and Gina both made it all the way to chairs without stumbling. "Hope I'm not interrupting anything," he said.

"Not at all," said Gina. "Tell me if I'm right, but I'm thinking you are just a little bit lonely."

"Indeed, I am. But that's not the main issue for me right now. I'm worried about Sarah. Mind you, she doesn't owe me the time of day, but ..." His voice was beginning to crack, so he cleared his throat and struggled on. "I just ... well, can you at least tell me if she's okay?"

"She's okay," chimed Kyle and Gina at the same time.

They laughed at that, and Gina continued, "She went to visit with her mom and dad for just a few days, but today, she received some news that will probably cause her to stay there at least through this week. And, Kevin, I know you miss her, and I know that both of you are grieving the situation between the two of you. I'm sorry. Maybe time and future developments will see you together again."

"I'm sure counting on it. Most of all, I want to see the day when she's happy. She deserves to be happy, darn it!"

"Okay, Kevin, you sit right there; I have something from

Sarah's room that I want to show you. I'll be right back." Gina was gone for less than a minute. She returned, walking very slowly and carefully, carrying something with both hands, as though it were some delicate object. As she stepped up to Kevin, she handed him a crystal bowl.

Kevin bowed his head and gazed into a bowl of dried roses. He was entranced. The petals still had color; if anything, their hue was richer than when they were in full bloom. They were actually a soft purple now. Each flower had been cut from the very top of its stem. And, amazingly, they had drawn back into their childhood, into small buds, perhaps a little plumper than when they were originally preparing to bloom. Kevin couldn't speak. All he could do was stare, through tears, into the pretty stoic rosebuds and feel Sarah's heart.

"You see her there in that bowl, don't you?" asked Gina.

Kevin could only nod.

"Well, Kyle and I want to see you two together again for whatever might work out. At least, you need that time together."

"Thanks. Knowing that helps me a lot. Please know that I'm not here meddling in her affairs. I care too much about her to do that. So I don't want to know anything that's private to her, but I was just wondering if there are any points y'all feel free to make that will help me be sensitive to her needs."

"Certainly," said Kyle, "there *are* some things that I think we can mention that won't break her confidence but may at least ease your mind. You see, she has been suffering under a very heavy and unexpected load since the middle of April. That has pretty well absorbed her every moment."

"Right," added Gina, "and you already know she's filed for divorce; she told you that herself." Gina paused and just stared at her clasped hands. Kevin didn't intercede. In a while, she continued, "The main thing is, Kevin, she's frightened—very."

Kevin almost broke at that disclosure, but he braced up and said as strongly as he could, "She needs us. Oh, how she needs us, and I praise God that she has you all. Please, I just want to help her; is there anything you can think of that I might could do?"

"Kevin," said Kyle, "you're already doing it. Otherwise, all any of us can do is just pray and be patient. I think, right now, that's the best support we can give her." Gina was nodding as he talked.

"I understand," said Kevin. "Just one more thing, would it compromise your loyalty to her if you got word to me when her divorce is final?"

"I think we can do that," said Gina. Kyle nodded agreement.

"Okay, okay," said Kyle. "Here, now, surely we can tell you this much more. She is presently married to a man named Mack Turbo. We can't tell you about what she thinks of him or their relationship, but we can give you *our* opinions, which we formed on our own cognizance."

"Yes," said Gina. "See, we saw this old boy quite a bit during their courtship. In our opinion, he's for the birds."

"That's putting it mildly," grumbled Kyle. "I can tell you this: I didn't trust that guy from the beginning. He's phony. We watched him make a big show of doing everything Sarah wanted, bowing to her every wish. He clearly had an ulterior motive, but Sarah so wanted a dream that she didn't pick up on it. All Mack wanted was to get her in bed, which she refused until such time as they might get married. Well, they did get married, and something happened on their wedding night that we can't discuss because it's private."

"Maybe someday, she'll want you to know about that, and perhaps she'll tell you," said Gina.

"I understand perfectly," agreed Kevin, "and I don't want you to reveal anything not in her best interest."

"There's one very significant fact that we *can* reveal," began Kyle, "because it will actually be a matter of public record. Just today, we learned that a court date has been set for this coming Friday."

Gina quickly raised a hand and insisted, "Now, we don't know what she'll be like when it's over. We don't know what she'll want to do or where she'll want to live. It's my guess that she'll probably hibernate for a good week and get in a bit of crying. That's okay; maybe it'll help get it out of her system."

All Kevin could do was just shake his head interminably. There was no way he could speak. Finally, he pulled himself together and stammered, "Thanks for everything, and, Kyle, Gina, you two are the real thing; thank you for having me in and confiding to me some things that will help me serve her."

"God bless you, Kevin," said Kyle as Gina leaned out to pat his shoulder. "Now, at the right time, we will tell you this one more thing, because this too will be a matter of public record. I will personally get word to you when the decision is final on her divorce. Of course, seeing you is going to be entirely up to her. You understand that, do you?"

"Oh, absolutely."

"Frankly, we both hope that you will indeed see her again," said Gina.

"Meanwhile," chimed Kyle, "the next time *we* see her, we'll be in court."

14

HOW DOES ONE GET ready for court? That was the all-consuming question pressing Sarah Turbo at this moment in time. On the same Monday that Kevin visited the Evans, she was trying to gather her wits to the point she could prepare herself for the upcoming ordeal.

What'll I wear? The more she thought about that, the less sure of herself she was. She stared for a while at the ceiling and then through the window in her bedroom. Nothing became clear. Perhaps she would have better luck with other questions. *Will I have to look directly at Mack? What will the lawyers ask that I can predict? I know they'll make a big fuss over the truck. What can I say? Shall I just say I was scared numb? What the heck! Why am I troubling myself with this stuff? That's what I have a lawyer for.*

She picked up the phone, dialed Buford Crump, and made an appointment for early Wednesday morning. Her dad would drop her off on his way to work. How she would get back home was a question to be reckoned with later. Her dad would come up with something. She suddenly felt very humbled by the loving support she had all around her, from all of her family. If only they could keep her from being scared. She chuckled at what she knew was impossible for anyone. *When you're scared, you're scared.*

Wednesday morning at the Crump camp brought an unexpected measure of relief from her fears. After all, she was getting professional help. Business at her attorney's office was clearly in motion, yet everything seemed calm and orderly. Before she had time to find a way to get frightened again, she was called in and invited to sit at the conference table across from her attorney.

Buford Crump began in his usual polite, reassuring way. "I find this setting works best," he said. "It seems less formal and maybe more conducive to a free exchange of thoughts and ideas. I have a little standard briefing about court conduct that I want to pass along to you; otherwise, we're here to help each other. So please feel free to ask questions and offer suggestions and even challenges if you have misgivings about anything. This is going to be *your* day in court, and my job is to be part of your strength and help you do your best."

"I can't think of anything that could be more reassuring for me than that," said Sarah, smiling confidently. "As a matter of fact, I have already been wrestling with some questions about what's going to happen in the courtroom, but I have to confess that I didn't come up with many answers. Mr. Crump, I sure am glad I have you, and I want to thank you for the serious attention you've given my case from the very beginning."

"It's my pleasure, Sarah. Now, first of all, thanks for the journal; it is outstanding. It will also probably help that you conditioned yourself somewhat by going through that memory exercise. Okay, as I believe I mentioned to you once before, to a large extent, this hearing is going to be a game of strategy. I'm sorry; that's just the way it is. That's made necessary in large part because of the rules of civil procedure that regulate these courtroom processes. Now, while court action is necessarily procedural, it is also solemn—very solemn. Among other things, that means you'll be under oath. In that context, our rules don't cover conduct of witnesses, especially those who are parties to the action. So we'll do it here. How's that?"

"Super."

"Sarah, we will be making our case before one judge. So our first order is to avoid any conduct that might irritate that judge.

In that spirit, I can tell you that I will try to keep it as short as possible. You won't hear me making a lot of tactical objections unless I think they really make a material difference or help protect you from abusive inquiry. Usually, by the time you object to a question, the damage has already been done. So I'll be pretty conservative in this matter. You know, a lot of judges consider divorce actions less important than other cases on their docket, particularly where there are no custody or division-of-property issues.

"Moreover, I will keep my direct examination of you very short, and it will contain no surprises. Likewise, if Mr. Turbo takes the stand, I will hold my cross-examination to the minimum necessary to respond materially. After all, this is a hearing, not a criminal trial. Also, if we counselors are permitted to make opening and closing statements, I will keep mine short. There's a point at which judges quit listening to these arguments anyway. What do you think?"

"I think I'm feeling very relieved about the whole thing. I might as well confess to you right now that I've been terribly frightened."

"Everybody is, Sarah. Believe me; that's normal. Since we're on that subject, how about a few pointers on how you should present yourself?"

"I'm ready, sir."

"Okay, here's where I get pretty blunt, but please keep in mind, it's for your own good. First of all, what to wear."

"Hoooray! I got out of bed this morning worrying about that one."

"Then here's what I want you to do: Dress neatly; look sharp. Look like you respect the dignity of the court. Dress a little bit up, but not overly. Know what I mean? Don't dress like you're going to the opera, but at the same time, don't dress like you're going to a hockey match. And do your hair. Make sure it's neatly coiffured." At that, the attorney started laughing outright and teased. "Don't put glitter in your hair and that sort of thing."

"Oh, that's disappointing, sir. Are you sure? I was planning to wear a huge red bow in the top of my hair and be eating popcorn out of a grimy little sack while I'm on the witness stand. Maybe I could ask His Honor, the judge, if he has anything to drink back there."

When Buford Crump recovered from his laughing binge, he pushed a thumbs-up toward Sarah and said, "You've got it. My, how you do catch on!"

"Seriously, Mr. Crump, I promise to do my best not to destroy the solemnity of the court."

"Moving right along," said the attorney as he glanced at his watch. "As to your demeanor, not just when you're witnessing but also as you just sit there in the courtroom. Look serious but not sullen. Look confident but not cocky. Don't get cute. Just answer the questions, and, Sarah, let me come down hard on this point: don't answer more than the question. If a question can be answered by yes or no, then say that. Don't try to embellish it or justify it or otherwise explain it. No answer is as clear and powerful as a simple *yes* or *no*, especially under oath. If more is needed, the interrogator will ask you."

Client and attorney continued for another fifteen minutes. Most of that time was given to Buford Crump disclosing to Sarah the actual questions he would be asking her before the judge. Lastly, he advised, "We will be in Judge Lawson Tillman's court."

"Thanks for everything," said Sarah as she turned to leave.

"You're quite welcome," said the attorney. "See you in court."

Then came the day! The court seemed to be at order, although nothing was happening, except for some whispered dialogue at the bench between the judge and the bailiff. The court reporter sat at the front side of the room with a direct view of the witness stand. She was casually studying her fingernails but clearly ready to go at an instant's notice.

Sarah and her attorney sat at one end of the front row; Mack Turbo and his attorney were at the other end. Mack was wearing a tie, a big breakthrough for him. The attorneys wore suits. Sarah had dressed herself rather conservatively, wearing a long, tailored black silk dress with no ornamentation and a short string of white pearls. Her hair was combed from a center part straight down to her ears and tucked under toward her neck. She had the sense that she looked quite matronly, but apparently for this occasion, matronly won out over flashy. She sat straight up in her chair, with her feet close together, and her hands resting lightly in her lap. She was wearing what she called a pre-smile and thinking, *Okay, bring it on!*

Of boundless comfort to Sarah was the presence in the courtroom of her ever-loyal support group, which included her mom and dad, Aunt and Uncle Evans, plus an aunt and uncle and two male cousins who had flown in from San Diego. They were from the Lock side of the family. Otherwise, there was a sparse scattering of spectators and one haggard-looking woman whom Sarah recognized as Mack Turbo's mother. At this point in time, he had no father.

Suddenly, the bailiff stepped away from the bench and crisply announced the case. "Now comes the case of Sarah Grace Turbo versus Mack Lindsey Turbo." Sarah flinched when she heard herself referred to as Turbo. *Oops, can't flinch.*

Holding his gavel toward the court, without pounding it, Judge Lawson invited opposing counsels to make opening statements. Buford Crump was on his feet in an instant and began to speak.

"Thank you, Your Honor; I'll be brief. Simply stated, we will show, through testimony and documentary evidence, that because of cruelty, the marriage in question ended the day it began. Mrs. Turbo's own testimony will be the conclusive element showing, as it will, that she was subjected to physical abuse to the point she had to run for her life. We are also prepared to corroborate her sworn statements through the testimony of other witnesses if needed."

As Mr. Crump returned to his seat beside Sarah, Mack Turbo's attorney, Peter Masterson, stood up and began to speak. "Thank you, Your Honor, for the privilege to open. We will show that Sarah Grace Turbo is so challenged psychologically that she is incapable of making decisions about her life and marriage and is in need of the care only a devoted husband can provide. We will also present evidence demonstrating that the abuser on the night in question was actually Mrs. Turbo, not Mr. Turbo. Nevertheless, my client is willing to dismiss her abusive behavior in deference to her mental condition. Further, the evidence will demonstrate that Mrs. Turbo was so beset emotionally on the night in question, that she was led to flee the scene with a stolen truck and other assets of Mr. Turbo. In short, the evidence we will present will establish that this marriage should continue for the sake and well-being of Sarah Grace Turbo—essentially for her own good. Thank you, Your Honor, for hearing this case." Masterson returned to his seat.

It was disturbingly quiet in the courtroom as the judge turned to Sarah's attorney and said, "Proceed."

"Thank you. I call the plaintiff, Mrs. Sarah Grace Turbo."

Sarah was sworn in and took her seat in the witness chair.

"Mrs. Turbo, when were you and Mack Lindsey Turbo married?"

"We exchanged vows at about one thirty in the afternoon on April 12, 2012. We were pronounced husband and wife immediately thereafter."

"Had you courted each other for a period before that?"

"Yes."

"To the best of your reckoning, how long was your courtship?"

"Just about six months."

"How would you describe your courtship?"

"It was wonderful; it was unblemished."

"How would you describe Mack Turbo's treatment of you during that period?"

"He was always good to me, respectful in every way. He tried to do all that I asked and just did everything to please me. We only disagreed on one thing."

"And that one thing was what?"

"Sex; I insisted on waiting until we were married to have sex, and he disagreed."

"Did he press the matter physically?"

"No, but he kept bringing it up verbally."

"I see." Now, the attorney turned away from Sarah and started nodding. Sarah sensed that he was trying to demonstrate that he was about to come up with a really big one. Finally, he wheeled around and pointed a finger in the air as if to say, "*This is it.*"

"Now, Mrs. Turbo, tell me, during your courtship, did Mack Turbo ever threaten you or abuse you physically?"

"No."

"Mrs. Turbo, what events stand out in your mind as occurring at your wedding?"

Oh how I wish everybody would quit calling me Turbo. "We had a reception following the wedding vows. Just about everybody stayed—my family and several friends of Mack and me. We had cake and other refreshments. It was festive and a lot of fun—a lot of laughing and joking and frolicking around. It lasted for about three hours, and then people started to drift away. Mack and I, his mother, and my mom and dad had an early dinner together, and then Mack and I went home to watch TV and go to bed early."

"Did you eat anything at the reception?"

"Oh yes, indeed; I ate some of everything. I ate a lot."

"Are you aware that people there saw you eating?"

"Of course. We were talking and eating at the same time."

"So to the best of your knowledge, are there witnesses who would be able to confirm they saw you eating?"

"Objection!" declared Mack's attorney. "Leading the witness."

"Overruled," began the judge. "Plaintiff's counsel didn't state."

This is almost fun, thought Sarah as her attorney, masking any sense of victory in that round, simply returned methodically to his questions. "Mrs. Turbo, what specifically happened that leads you to ask for a divorce?"

"On our wedding night, after we went to bed, we had sex, and on its conclusion, Mack who was still over me, drew his fist back behind his ear and rammed it into my left jaw. I jumped and hit him back."

"Why did you hit back?"

"It wasn't something I thought to do; it was just reflexive."

"What happened next?"

"He finally rolled off to his side of the bed and I presume went to sleep. He went to work early the next morning."

"What did *you* do?"

"After Mack left for work, I took the truck and drove to Oklahoma City where I left it in the parking lot of an apartment building. Then I caught a bus back to Dallas."

"Whose truck?"

"It was Mack's."

"Why did you do that?"

"I was scared to death."

"Why did you immediately come back to Dallas?"

"To hide."

"What about this frightened you to the point that you ran and took to hiding?"

"Mack had an unblemished record with me, so when he tried to break my jaw—"

"Objection," chimed Mr. Masterson.

"Sustained," said the judge. "Witness will refrain from assigning motive to the accused."

"Well, okay, when Mack hit me, I was shocked because he had never done anything like that. So I knew at once that he had lost control of himself. My instant thought was that if he would do this once, he would do it throughout our marriage."

"Mrs. Turbo, do you have any other testimony you wish to offer in your behalf for the record?"

"No."

"Okay, if it please the court, I have two documents which I will enter into evidence. I will hand originals to the bailiff for the court and provide opposing counsel with machine copies. The first document is a medical statement provided by Dr. Michael Burrell, who examined Sarah shortly after the wedding. I will just point out that, based on an X-ray and examination of Mrs. Turbo's jaw, he found a slight displacement in the jawbone. He acknowledges that he can't fix the time of the injury precisely but offers evidence at least fixing the range of days in which the injury could have occurred."

During this exercise by her attorney, Sarah glanced a couple of times at her soon-to-be former husband. He never looked her way. He just sat rigid, his jaw firmly set, staring straight ahead. At these and other times during the proceedings, she could not help but feel some empathy for Mack Turbo, actually a little remorse for his situation. Indeed, it was not her purpose in this matter to hurt him but rather simply to ensure her own freedom—and safety. At this point, she felt a trace of moisture in her eyes; she hated to see anyone in trouble, and she truly hoped that Mack would find help for his problems and be reborn into a healthy and prosperous life.

When Sarah's attorney finished distributing the second proffered document, Mack's attorney objected on the basis of relevancy.

"Your Honor," said Buford Crump, "it goes directly to the

question of defendant's regard for his wife, whether he recognizes her as his true spouse."

Up to now, Sarah had been able to stay calm by just finding fascination in the games. But this question blew it. She felt the tension hit her shoulders and instinctively pressed her elbows against her sides. This question went directly to her own fitness to serve as an acceptable spouse. The attorneys seemed so matter-of-fact about it all—and that was as it should be, she conceded—but she just couldn't strip the emotion out of it. At this early point, she was sorely aware that, though she could feign calmness during the heat of the battle, someday, she would have to look back on this experience, and the shock of it could be devastating. *I was wrong; this is no fun,* she thought, just as the judge raised his seemingly irritated voice.

"Objection overruled. Proceed, Mr. Crump."

"Mrs. Turbo, do you recognize this document?"

"Yes." Her attorney was doing his practiced good job, which helped Sarah's confidence somewhat. From their previous interactions, she had felt him to be a bit conceited. Now, however, watching him in action, she felt he was just serious about his role. Clearly, he did not waste time on side issues and distractions. *He may seem arrogant, but he just gets it done,* she thought.

"What is this document you have in your hands?" he asked. "It's like an invoice ... ah, it's a statement of charges that Mack says I owe him."

"For what?"

"Like, well, he has on here, charges for retrieving the truck, for some cash that I took out of a jar in the house, for some dental work, lost time from work, medical counseling, and so forth."

"When did you receive this bill of charges?"

"A few days after I left."

"Thank you. Your Honor, I have no further questions of this witness."

Thereupon, Judge Tillman turned to Mack Turbo's counsel and invited cross-examination.

"Yes, thank you," said Peter Masterson, politely, as he approached the witness. Somehow, the expression on his face belied the swagger in his hips as he marched toward Sarah. For one thing, he glanced back at his client a couple of times and once looked down at himself as if checking his zipper. When he got to Sarah, he just looked at her for a few moments, nodding his head before saying anything. Finally, he pulled himself tall and started to speak.

"So I understand you stole a truck, drove it to Oklahoma City, and caught a bus back to Dallas. Is that correct?"

"No."

"But you testified earlier that you did exactly that."

"I didn't say I *stole* the truck. I just took what was there."

"Why?"

"As I testified, I was frightened and instinctively ran from the source of my fear, so I could buy some time to think."

"No. I mean, why did you come back to Dallas?"

"I figured it would be the last place Mack would look for me after he got word I had gone to Oklahoma City. I wanted him to be looking for me there while I hid out here."

"So in effect, you returned to the scene of the crime."

"Objection!"

"Sustained. Witness will not answer," ruled the judge. "Counsel, this is a divorce hearing. Criminal charges have not been entered."

Now, Sarah was beginning to lose her composure, inwardly at least. She started kneading her hands, which heretofore had reposed calmly in her lap. At once, she willed them to relax again. Then she smiled confidently at her interrogator.

"Mrs. Turbo, are you mentally challenged?"

"Yes."

"That's all? Just *yes*?"

"That's all you asked."

"Okay, let me ask you this; has it ever been reported to you by any authority that you have a mental impairment of any kind or degree?"

"Yes."

"Explain."

Sounds like my mother. "Sir, when I was in the fourth grade, my teacher said to my parents that I had been shown to be mentally retarded by the IQ tests we all had taken." This question hurt more than any other that had been asked. It literally hurled her back in time to that dreadful day when her mother reported her teacher's comment that she was retarded. The comparison with this present situation was dreadfully unsettling. Now, she recalled how she had approached the IQ test as a joke, believing it to be stupid and irrelevant. Accordingly, she had deliberately fabricated answers to the questions she thought the most ridiculous. Today, she was trying to entertain herself by indulging in what she saw as the gamesmanship at play in this so-called solemn setting.

"I see," continued Mack's attorney, "and after a disappointing wedding night, you chose to run away."

"Objection!"

"Sustained," said the judge shaking his head.

Sarah could not suppress an all-out grin. Now she felt in control of her situation again. With that, she sighed as subtly as possible and relaxed her hands and shoulders.

"Your Honor, I'm finished with this witness," said Masterson.

Sarah's attorney came forward to face her again. Having received Judge Tillman's permission to redirect, he asked of Sarah, "Did you graduate from high school?"

"Yes."

"Do you know what your grade point average was?"

"Yes; it was three point six."

"What does that equate to?"

"It's kind of a low B-plus."

"Have you ever been given or been referred for medical or psychological counseling, to your knowledge?"

"No."

"Your Honor, this concludes our case. I reserve the right to call other witnesses if it becomes necessary."

At that, Judge Tillman turned to Mack's attorney and said, "Mr. Masterson, you may proceed with your defense."

From this point, Sarah just watched with indifference as Attorney Masterson called Mack Turbo as his only witness and proceeded to slog through a torturous hour-long session with his client. It all centered on their claim that she was incapable of knowing what she was doing during the night in question and therefore was incapable of accurately reporting on it or reacting to it sanely.

Sarah felt by now she had been indoctrinated to the point that she had actually acquired some sophistication in courtroom business. Accordingly, she had personally concluded that most of her adversary's questions involved leading the witness and were otherwise irrelevant. However, as her own attorney had promised, he did not object to anything. By that, she knew he was playing his best card by choosing not to prolong the hearing. When offered the opportunity to cross-examine, it seemed like he used only about three minutes to cover two points.

"Mr. Turbo, you've testified that you didn't actually hit your wife, that rather, you just gave her a friendly tap on the cheek. Was your fist clinched when you tapped her?"

"Well, it might have been, but it's like when you hit a guy on the shoulder with your fist as a friendly gesture. I certainly wasn't trying to hurt."

"All right, do you recall the bill of charges we entered into evidence earlier in this hearing?"

"Yeah."

"Did you recognize that as a document you delivered to your wife's parents?"

"Yeah."

"Okay, so how is that going to work?"

"She just pays me."

"From what source?"

"Wherever she can get the money; that's her problem."

"After she pays you, will she have access to that money as something you own jointly?"

"Huh?"

"That's okay; no further questions."

Judge Tillman invited the parties to make closing statements, and Sarah's attorney went first. "The record will show that Mack Lindsey Turbo subjected his wife, Sarah Grace Turbo, to cruelty by way of damaging physical abuse on their wedding night. It also demonstrates that Mr. Turbo does not regard Sarah as his wife, or that he has any plan for taking care of her as he claims. Finally, we submit that the court must find Sarah Grace Turbo fully capable of taking care of herself. Among other indications, her demeanor during this hearing shows her to be mentally healthy, capable, and alert and that she is able to understand and interpret questions and facts and to articulate responses showing her to be fully in touch with reality. We pray the court grant her the requested divorce and restore her freedom to live in peace."

Peter Masterson used his closing argument to revisit all the muddle he'd plowed through with his client during his testimony. Again, he apparently was trying to convince his client that he was doing the best job possible for him simply by performance volume.

When it was done, Judge Tillman declared that he was prepared to issue an immediate decision without retiring to his chambers to analyze the evidence. Thereupon, he declared as follows:

"The court finds that the petitioner, Sarah Grace Turbo, was in fact subjected to unprovoked physical abuse at the hands of Mack Lindsey Turbo, and this abuse was of such order as to dissolve the marriage. Further, the court is persuaded that the petitioner is fully competent to take care of herself and make reasonable decisions about her life. Therefore, the divorce is granted. Further, I find that the dissolution of the contested marriage, occurring as it did within twenty-four hours of initiation, is tantamount to annulment. Therefore, I will sign an order, at the petitioner's request, restoring her name to Sarah Grace Lock."

When she was leaving the courtroom, Sarah walked over to her former husband and said humbly, "Mack, I wish you well."

As she walked away, she saw him mouth, "I'll get you for this."

15

SARAH RODE HOME WITH her dad after court. The others had gone on ahead while they waited for Judge Tillman's order restoring Sarah's name. When they stepped in the front door of the Lock home, the gathered devotees all stood and applauded. Dad Lock proceeded into the crowd to join them in their standing ovation.

Finally, Sarah raised her hands acknowledging their greeting and urging them to settle down.

She continued to stand near the front door as her supporters quieted down and took their seats. She looked mischievously at them for a few moments. Then, she cocked her hip to one side, tilted her head coyly, poked a finger in her dimple, and—grinning like a seductive little imp—said, "Anybody know where I can get a job?"

There followed a round of raucous laughter, over which the voice of Ed Lock could be heard musing, "Guess that takes us back a few years."

At once, Uncle Kyle Evans blurted, "You do that on the streets of Mabank, and the police will pick you up in two minutes."

Sarah curtsied and said, "Seriously, at this point, I will have to come out of hiding and, err, go to work."

For the next hour, the liberated family just simply lived it up in a way that only healthy, happy families can do. In a while, Sarah excused herself, saying she was going to the kitchen to get some juice. As she closed the refrigerator door, her mother sauntered in, wearing a modest, almost pleading smile.

"Sarah," she said, "could we talk privately for a moment? I have something I want to say to you and something I want to ask of you."

"Sure, Mom. Want to sit at the bar?"

"No, we can stand; this won't take long. The thing is, my Sarah, I have wronged you, and although I don't deserve it, I want to ask your forgiveness."

"Oh, Mom, why, of course. I forgive you no matter what you think you've done." She reached out for her mom, and they embraced for a moment.

"I did it all right; back in 2001, your teachers gave that IQ test to all of you, and your main teacher reported to me that it showed you were retarded. As you will recall—only too well, I'm sure—I passed this along to you and told you not to worry about it. Okay, what I failed to do was challenge the teacher's contention, and there is where I really failed you." Now, both mom and daughter were sniffling and swiping tears. "So ten years later, I'm asking for your forgiveness. Will you please forgive me?"

"Mom, yes, I forgive you." They embraced again.

"You don't have to, darling. I mean, I'm your mother, but I didn't act like it. I'm so sorry; I feel guilty, and I deserve to."

"No, Mom, not anymore. You asked for forgiveness, and I gladly do forgive you. That has liberated both of us."

They nodded to each other and fell quiet as Sarah began to relive those heartbreaking days following her mother's news that she'd been determined marginal. It was an obsession that had lived in her mind and heart for ten years. Although she had come to accept it academically, she never got over it emotionally, partly because of her own senseless regard for the IQ test. Now she recalled vividly her cavalier attitude toward the test, thinking it was so foolish and she was so smart, she could just make a joke out of it, play with it, and expose it for the nonsense she thought it was.

In a while, her mother embraced her again and then turned away, obviously deep in grief, and leaned over the counter, resting her head in both hands. Sarah came to her and began rubbing her back gently. In that poignant moment, it occurred to her that it was her mother's sense of guilt that consumed her so intensely. It also dawned on her that it was this feeling of guilt that had made her mother appear distant in the past few weeks during Sarah's sudden struggle with life. It seemed that her mother was reluctant to get deeply involved with her problems. In a few moments, they straightened up and smiled instinctively, possibly to show they were still good friends. *Oh, but I don't need a friend; I need a mother. Maybe she's back.*

As they started out of the kitchen, they heard clamoring and excited chatter coming from the living room. Then family members laden with vessels and baskets started filing pell-mell across the den and out the back door. When they caught up with the crowd, they learned that Kyle and Gina had brought picnic lunches for everybody. Ed Lock was in on the secret and already had the tables and benches set up in the backyard.

The surprise party was fun and rewarding. It was a rare get-together for this particular configuration of the families, so the unending social hubbub rattled on. At one point, Sarah wearied of the whole thing, exciting as it was, so she escaped to the front of the house and found a lounge chair on the porch. To some extent, the excitement, which should have been uplifting, was actually making her sad. In a while, her dad drifted out and asked if he could sit with her.

"Sure, Dad. I'm sorry I sneaked out of the convention, but it's been a tiring day for me, and I just wanted to rest a little."

"Actually, me too," said her dad.

"Well, you know, it was becoming too predictable, what with people interrupting each other and finishing each other's sentences and laughing at things that weren't funny. It's okay.

Believe me; I accept this as protocol for social interaction, but it just takes energy, and mine is about played out at this hour."

"I'm with you all the way, sweetheart." Sensing full agreement, they smiled and fell silent for a few minutes. Then, her dad scooted to the front of his lounge and twisted around so he could look directly at his daughter as he talked.

"My precious Sarah, what are you gonna do now? Tell me what we can do to help you."

"I wish I knew—really. Maybe I'll just lie in bed and cry for a week. I'm serious. All of a sudden, I don't have any grasp of the future or of my place in it."

"But you will, my dear. You will. And you'll do it your own way and in your own time. Be assured, neither I nor anybody else has any right to tell you what you ought to do. There is no *one* way to deal with the horror you've been through. Your personality, that wonderful mind and kind heart of yours, will guide you. I have absolutely no doubts."

"Thanks, Dad. Believe me, that helps: just knowing that you have that kind of confidence in me." She yawned unexpectedly, giggled about it, and murmured, "I feel like I could just go crawl under a bush somewhere, like a sick cat, and cuddle up there on the bare dirt—you know, and sweat it out. Maybe the dirt of life can heal me." She tried to laugh, but it came out as a muffled sob.

"Oh, my dear, deserving daughter, I know you have the patience and the courage to see it all through. One day, you'll be free. Believe me; you'll be free. I just pray that all of us in your life will have the presence of mind to be patient with you. There is absolutely no reason to be in a hurry for tomorrow. We don't even need to know what it might bring, assuming it comes, and we're not even sure of that. There is one lasting thing we *can* be sure of, and that's the love of God and our love for each other."

"I'm with you on that. Again, I realize I need to quit

freeloading, get off my butt, and go to work. I've built up quite a debt."

"Someday perhaps, but not now. None of us wants you to go to work just yet. Take it easy for a week or two. Let this thing die. Then, by all means, it'll help you to be busy. For now, don't worry about the debt thing."

"Whatever you say," she grumbled.

"Before we go any further with anything, I want to tell you, sweetheart, that you were absolutely brilliant in court—I mean *brilliant*. You were also the epitome of grace and poise. I'd sure hate to try to win a case against you. I just want you to know that I'm exceedingly proud of you."

"Thank you, Dad. I guess ... just looking back at the whole fiasco, I think I probably wrecked Mack's life by letting him into mine—because I so wanted a dream. See what happened? Instead of bringing out the best in him, I inspired the worst."

"If it's there, it needs to come out, and as painful as it was, it's best that it came out early like it did. Actually, you probably did old Mack boy a favor by drawing out that demon in him—screwball. You know, if there's a demon in us, the sooner out, the better. So now, maybe Mr. Mack can get some help."

"You just may have something there, Dad. Hmm, yes, I believe you do."

Her dad yawned and drawled, "So I guess that's all, huh?"

"Right, Dad. See you when we wake up."

"Uh ... *dirt of life?*"

Sarah shrugged and raised her eyebrows, and that was all they had on that strange subject.

Indeed, the two did drop off into light slumber. They awoke simultaneously at the slamming of the front screen door as the two Lock cousins scampered out to join them. The jolly banter that followed was welcome and perhaps refreshing but, to Sarah's chagrin, sadly boring. Fortunately, it ended when Aunt and Uncle Lock started hustling around to leave. Soon, they and the cousins were gone.

After they left, Sarah stood quietly, leaning against a porch column, staring after the disappearing car. She was shaking her head and roundly chastising herself for being so moody: *I'm sorry, y'all. Please forgive me. Right now, nothing seems to please me. I'm so sorry. You came all this way to support me. You're angels. For now, I must get myself well. Then, I'll write to you.*

Then came her mom, bearing the countenance of a woman clearly on a mission. "Where would you like to live for now, Sarah dear? You're in demand, you know. Dad and I want you and so do Gina and Kyle. Still, we all want it to be your call."

"Ideally, I wish I could be with all of you, but that's not possible." She sighed deeply and continued, "Mom, to start with, I'd like to stay here with you and Dad for four or five days. I can just read and sleep during the daytime when y'all are at work. Then we could enjoy the evenings together. I'll try to cook something."

"Beautiful, we'd like that."

"Thanks. After a few days, I'd like to go back to live with Aunt and Uncle Evans, not to hide out, but to be out there in the peaceful country. That way, I can help them some and also enjoy the serenity of the woods and meadowlands."

"Believe me; that'll please them big-time."

Now, mother and daughter stood quietly, neither tempted to talk for a while. They glanced at each other and smiled from time to time but said nothing. In a few moments, Sarah looked directly at her mom, frowned, and shook her head, obviously preoccupied with solemn thoughts. When she continued to stare vaguely past her mom, the woman said, calmly, one word: "Kevin?"

Sarah nodded.

Kevin had decided it was time to get serious with plan A. To begin with, he would write a note for delivery to Sarah when she returned. This was predicated on his full conviction that she would win her case and would return as a free woman to live with her aunt and uncle. It took less than a minute to write what he wanted to say to his dear friend.

His next step was to task old Grover-buddy to snoop at church for whatever he might learn of Sarah's unfolding status. As it developed, that strategy worked far better than he had expected. On Sunday, as soon as they returned from their respective church services, Grover handed Kevin a sealed envelope given him by Sarah's Uncle Kyle.

Still standing, Kevin ripped open the envelope and read the short note:

Hey, Kevin, hope all's well. Here's the info you wanted on our niece. As of last Friday noon, Sarah is a free woman and her maiden name (Lock) has been restored. There is nothing linking her to her former, short-term husband. Also, we expect her back here about midweek. She's staying with her mom and dad for a few days first. Kevin, she's tired and very distressed. She's been through quite a bit. Thanks for caring. Kyle.

Kevin was so touched by the last part of Kyle's note that he went immediately to the meadow to pray. "Dear Lord, I'm here for Sarah Grace. You already know her needs and are waiting for us to pray for her. So, Holy Lord, here I am, praying for my dear friend. Please reach to her with your love, grace, and mercy."

Kevin's next planned move was a visit with Gina and Kyle Evans. On Monday evening, he waited until he felt they would be finished with their dinner. When he knocked at their door, he was soundly welcomed by both.

"Thanks for the note, Kyle. It really lifted my spirits, and I want you all to know that I will not press Sarah for anything. I know that, even though she won her case, she is thoroughly beaten and demoralized. I just hope someday, this innocent little angel will see me again. Not that she's obliged to—I just want to please her."

"Kevin, we're convinced that you do, that your love for her is true," said Gina. "And I must say, I think your perception concerning her feelings—actually her condition—is very sensitive."

"Thanks for having confidence in me. Please, I love her so much I don't know what to do. When she returns, would you just hand her this envelope? I have a note in it for her that she's welcome to respond to or not respond to as she sees fit and which she may share with you at her discretion. It's really just a little invitation."

"Consider it done," said Kyle. "We expect her back here this coming Wednesday. Kevin, if you think you have pride in her now, you should have seen her in court. She was all class; she was simply dazzling."

Tears hit Kevin instantly, and though his voice cracked when he spoke, it was strong and determined. "I can just see that picture; that's Sarah. I so want her to be happy, to reach a point where all this torture in her life is history. She deserves to live, to be free." He apologized, for he was now torn to the point that he needed to stop for a few moments.

"Take your time, Kevin," said Gina. "We feel the same way as you. She's been in our lives since she was a baby, and our love for her is still growing."

"I thank God that she has you two. Knowing you helps me understand where that class character of hers comes from— along with her mom and dad, of course."

"That's quite a compliment," said Kyle. "Thanks."

"Well, thanks for having me in. I don't want to take up any more of your time. Please be honest with me if you think I'm pushing too much. I'm afraid I may be a burden on Sarah. If that's ever it, I'll back off in a heartbeat."

"No, you're not a burden, Kevin. She needs to be forced to

face things," said Gina. "Really, for her own health of mind and spirit, she needs to face the reality that, in spite of what's happened in her life, she can live again and she can have a loving relationship. As I'm sure you know, right now, she doesn't think she ever can. You, Kevin, can be the facilitator in that, whether she comes to love you or not."

As Kevin was leaving, he turned back to face his newfound friends, chuckled, and chimed, "Right now, I would pay good money to have her thump me with one of those clever little gibes that only she can wield."

Gina and Kyle laughed. Then Kyle's expression turned serious, and he said, "All of us, of course, typify Sarah by her humor and good-natured teasing. We say variously that it's cute or it's refreshing, or sharp, ingenious … you know, all that, and it's true. But, Kevin, my friend, whatever *we* say it is, for Sarah, it is her way of coping. We all have to draw on something in our personalities that helps us cope with life's trials. And that ingenious trait you obviously admire in Sarah is *her* way, and I believe it works for her."

"Wow! I never thought of that."

Kevin went to the meadow on Wednesday morning. She was not there, and although disappointed, he was not surprised. To comfort himself, he rationalized that it was much too soon to expect a response from Sarah.

Sarah's reunion with her country home life was the most comforting event in all the days since the divorce hearing. She could actually feel her face relaxing somewhat when she laughed and the tension drain a little from her shoulders when her dear aunt and uncle resumed their regular loving roles.

She waited until bedtime that evening to open Kevin's envelope. Sitting on the side of her bed, in her pajamas, she

bowed before the short, handwritten note and whispered it to
herself:

Dear, dear Sarah,
If you ever change your mind, come to the meadow. I will
look for you every day, hoping for your return. I don't
mind waiting. I will come as long as the mornings keep
coming. Just hope you're well. Love, Kevin

Sarah pressed the note over her knee and stared across the
room. She tried to reckon with her feelings for Kevin. *Am I
letting this thing get out of hand with him? Why can't I just
blow him off and set us both free?* She continued to ponder her
feelings for this solicitous man who had come into her life so
innocently and yet cunningly. Too bad he hadn't come on the
scene earlier. She gasped at that thought because it sounded so
conceited and self-serving. Suddenly, she was aware that her
hand covering the note was pressing unmercifully into her knee.
Ouch!

The next morning, still undecided about Kevin's message,
Sarah elected to stay in the house until late in the afternoon.
Finally, she decided to go out back to the wooded side of the
house. She wandered around the grounds for a while, glancing
into the treetops, as if seeking solace or inspiration from them.
That seemed to have limited effect, so after a while, she decided
to sit down in their shade and see if that worked any better.

She sat stiff-legged in a swing hung from the limb of a tree in
the backyard. She stretched her legs straight out, as stiff as she
could, trying to squeeze out the tension. In a while, she heard
an awkward fluttering overhead. She glanced up and saw a little
bird with a broken wing settle on a twig at the tip of a tree limb
across the yard. She relaxed her legs and began to speak with a
gentle voice.

"Hi, little friend, I'm sorry about your wing. How can you
fly with it broken like that?" She thought for a moment and then

said softly, "Oh, I know; it's because you *want* to fly. For you, little spirit, flying is living. Flying is what you do. So maybe that tells me what my problem is. Maybe I don't *want* to love. Oh, but I do want to love … but I'm afraid. What do you think, my little stoic friend?"

In a while, the young bird flew away without a chirp and Sarah left the swing.

16

Turn, turn, my little prairie ballerina. I will come to you. Way across the meadow, I can see the heartache in your dance, hear the cry of your soul. Yet, I find hope in your lifted arms. From a distance, I can see in you all that I know you to be. I am there, my love.

Kevin stood at the top of the meadow, much as he'd done some six weeks earlier when he first spotted the young lassie, dancing in the distance. She was back. He was ecstatic, yet tension still nagged him. *What if she doesn't stay long enough for me to get there? What if she's just there to tell me to butt out?*

Suddenly, he sprang away and began hustling down the meadow, staying close to the tree line where the grass was short and easy to tread. As he drew near Sarah, he slowed down and started to stroll on in.

Sarah had stopped twirling. She just waited, facing him, still and quiet, thinking about him, knowing he loved her and trying to quell her love for him. Now, he was only a few feet away. Then he stopped short, a courtesy that she found typical of him and that she so admired.

Kevin looked neat, as always. It was the warm, late days of May, and he was wearing a short-sleeved, wine-colored cotton shirt and dark-blue Dockers. In fact, he never ventured far from this crisp, conservative, starched look. He was no baggy-pants, patched-jeans, funny-T-shirt, bib-cap-turned-backward type of guy. Nothing wrong with that casual fare, but it just wasn't Kevin. He knew who he was. Suddenly, Sarah caught herself involuntarily shaking her head. Kevin looked so good to her, not just in the way he dressed, but as the person she knew him to be. As the two waited for each other, they exchanged admiring smiles from moment to moment, beaming briefly and then sobering quickly, each searching for an opening line. This was a demanding moment for both of them. They glanced at the ground and into the air from time to time, between smiles. Finally, they nodded firmly to each other as if to say, *"Okay, this is it,"* and Kevin spoke the first words.

"Thank you for coming."

"A little bird sent me."

"Well, he is forever my friend."

"Mine, too."

"I like your hair."

She pushed a hand under her hair and turned her head ceremoniously as if modeling the style. "Thank you; this is my courtroom hair."

"I see, and by the way, congratulations!"

"I'll accept that. Mostly, I'm just glad it's over."

"My Sarah, you're still not free, are you?"

She didn't answer. In a moment, she bowed her head and held it there, staring at the ground, as if praying for Kevin to pick up on something else. In that time, he came on up to stand directly in front of her. She didn't flinch. Then, he took her shoulders and squeezed and rocked them gently until she looked up. When she did, he pulled her into his arms, and she yielded. They embraced and held on to each other, eventually snuggling their heads close together. When they eased apart, they continued to hold hands and smile, but their smiles were pleading.

"I'm sorry I didn't answer your question, Kevin. But, you see, the thing is ..." When her voice stalled, she cleared her throat, forcefully, and began again. "The point is I will not likely ever be free."

"Nonsense! Someday, you *will* be free, but, Sarah, dear beautiful Sarah, whatever your circumstances, I will love you, and I will do all that I can to help you get free. I would jump an ocean for you!"

Sarah chortled, "I actually think you would, and, my Kevin, I thank you for caring. She paused a moment. "But there's nothing anybody can do to help me."

"They can love you—and they do."

"Okay, let's drop that subject. Please understand, Kevin, I didn't come out to build your hopes but to give you the courtesy of a response to your precious note. Now, there are some things I need to go over with you. Shall we sit in the swing?"

They sat side by side, lightly swinging, looking out over the meadow as Sarah began to speak. "First of all, Kevin, I know you love me, and to have the love of a person of your character and bearing, I should be the happiest woman in the world. Indeed, I am grateful and honored to have your love, but it would be cruel of me to lead you on. How can I be happy for your love when I can't return it? It would be easier for me if you didn't love me."

"I don't mind waiting, Sarah."

"No. Waiting is not the thing here. Okay, I might as well get this out even though it's going to sound contradictory. The fact is, Kevin, I *do* love you. Now, hold it; don't go anywhere with that! I simply cannot have a relationship, ever again. So, you know, it would be better for both of us if you just go your own way, and I'll go mine, whatever that turns out to be."

Kevin just nodded and looked away from her. *How do I do this?* he wondered. *My sweetheart is captive of herself, sold out to her guilt feelings, choosing her own punishment. What can I do?*

"You going to say anything, Kevin?"

"I have an idea; let's start over. Let's play like all this other jazz didn't happen in your life."

"This is no play-like issue."

"It doesn't *have* to be. I mean, let's literally start over—boy meets girl under new conditions."

"Kevin, you're a dreamer."

"So come on; dream with me."

"You amaze me. How did this get started in the first place? I mean why did you come into the meadow that first time?"

"I just wanted to stand inside it, absorb its peace, indeed its glory. Then I saw you and my life changed. Why did *you* come out?"

"Same thing. I guess I have to admit that it was also a sort of catharsis for me."

"I felt that."

"From all that way?"

"Absolutely."

Sarah folded her arms and tilted her head as if questioning his claim. Kevin just looked straight at her, smiling confidently, as a way of backing up his assertion.

"Why did you keep coming, Kevin?"

"Hoping to find you. I fell for you the first time I saw you, and really, all I saw was this little dot way down the meadow. But I could see you weaving and swaying, lifting your arms to the heavens and holding them out to bless the meadow. I was hooked, and yes, I sensed that something was troubling in your life, and from that moment, I found myself caring about that and wanting to help."

Suddenly, Kevin paused, wrinkled his brow, and sighed. It had just hit him that he was sounding very formal in his attempt to woo this young maiden. It was as though he were making an argument before some high tribunal. Immediately, he shook it off and pressed on.

"Anyway, the air just seemed sweeter as I watched you from a distance. As I say, I couldn't tell anything about you physically, but I felt you, and I sensed that I was being drawn toward you, like there was some magnetic force pulling me in your direction."

Sarah was smiling broadly as he finished. Then she quipped, "So I'm a dot, huh?"

"Yeah, but you materialized so beautifully."

They both laughed and resumed swinging, but their chatter was missing until Sarah was taken with a sweet memory.

"Kevin, yesterday, while I was sitting in the backyard, this little bird—"

"Of course, we can always fast-forward the thing."

"Got a point there. Anyway, this little bird—"

"We could skip all those mornings when you didn't come out."

"For sure."

They halted the swing and sat in awkward silence for a few minutes until finally, Kevin broke the spell.

"What about the little bird?"

"What little bird?"

"Sorry."

"Forget it."

"Ooh, do I detect a bit of anger in that sweet voice? I do believe I do, and I'm glad. It's time you got angry."

"Well, you *were* rude, you know."

"Yes, I was, but that's not the point."

"And, Mr. Professor, the point is?"

"Like I said, it's high time you quit being scared and demoralized and get angry. You need a new emotion. Go ahead, get angry with *me*. This may be the breakthrough you need."

"Well, it would be nice if it were that easy. Anyway, enough of that stuff; let's get back to the subject. Do you understand the things I've explained to you about my situation, the impossibility of a romantic relationship in my life? And please know that I'm sorry it has to hurt a nice guy like you."

"I understand your words, but I don't buy your premise."

"Haven't you been listening?"

"Yes, I hear you loud and clear. But nothing you've said or nothing you *can* say will stop me from loving you."

"Please tell me, how can you love me, knowing I cannot crown that love and carry through in loving you? Really, Kevin, why do you punish yourself, seeing the way I am? How can you love me, knowing I can never return your love? How *can* you?"

"My dear Sarah, it's okay. My love for you is a gift I give myself."

～✽～

After her meeting with Kevin, Sarah went straight to her room and slammed the door. She decided to skip lunch and just brood for a while. She kept drumming the arm of her chair as she thought of the morning's escapade with Kevin. It seemed to her that he had been somewhat overbearing. Then it occurred to her that he had been insistent on only one thing. *Stubborn. Do I want a stubborn guy?* As she thought about that, she caught herself in a little smile. Presently, she got up and headed for the kitchen.

Around midafternoon, she set about to make a sweet-potato casserole to go with the leftover pork chops and butter beans they were having for dinner. In a while, her Aunt Gina came in, looking weary. "Hi, sweetheart." She sighed as she flopped into an easy chair in the den.

"I'm sorry, Aunt Gina. It must have been a trying day."

"Mostly just trying *people*, but what the heck? I'm blessed to have a job. How'd *your* day go?"

"Okay ... sort of."

"Uh-oh. I'm leery of *sort of*. Wanna talk about it?"

"Ummm. Well, Kevin and I spent a couple of hours together in the swing."

"Sounds pretty good so far, certainly better than *sort of*."

"Oh, we got along fine, but, you know, Kevin's tough. I gave him the word, and he acts like I can't make it work."

"The word?"

"Yeah, I was very candid. I pretty much told him he needed to go his own way." Gina's response was simply to lift her eyebrows, so Sarah continued, now through tears. "So, as I say, I told him to go his own way." She started crying outright as she wailed, "Problem is—I *am* his way."

Gina reached out, took Sarah's hand, and squeezed it. "Just let it happen, sweetheart. That man loves you. If the two of you are destined to be lovers someday, it'll happen. But, please, don't fault the guy for trying. I think he loves you so much that he hurts for you. He so wants to do something for you."

"You're right; he does. *He does.* He told me he'd jump an ocean for me." She leaned forward and let her head rest in warm hands while tears soaked into them. Finally, she pulled up straight and nodded. "But it's over."

Not quite, apparently, for an interrupting phone call might bring other news. Gina answered. "Yes, she is," she said and handed the phone to Sarah.

"Hello?"

"Sarah? Buford Crump. A little something has come up."

"Oh, no, please."

"Nothing we can't handle, but I do have to ask your permission for something. Here's the background: your former husband has sued for nonpayment of those alleged debts he billed you for."

Anger flashed immediately as Sarah blurted, "Oh that must be that silly bill he gave us. I thought the ball was back in his court, that we were waiting on documentation from him, substantiating those stupid charges."

"It *is* in his court. He did respond, but all he furnished was his own notarized statement, swearing his charges were accurate. That does not qualify as supporting documentation. When I so informed him, he said nothing. Then, today, the constable's office called, saying they needed to serve you with a subpoena to appear in court, and asking for your address. I knew the problem at once, and when I checked it out, I learned of Turbo's suit. Anyway, I declined to give the officer your address until I checked with you. So here's my question: Do you want them to serve you there or at your home in Dallas?"

"Here is fine. I am no longer in hiding, and I'm quite willing to be served right here, right in front of my aunt and uncle. Yes, right here, damn it."

"Very well, then. I don't blame you for being angry."

"Well, I really am, but I'm sorry I used that word."

"Hey, it was the absolute right one."

"Well, the thing is, I'm tired of shaking in my boots. I'm ready to put an end to this madness."

"Great. Give me your address there."

Sarah complied and ended the call amiably. However, she hung up the phone with a taunting kind of wave of her hand. Then, in a mocking tone of voice, she sneered, "Dear Aunt Gina, his majesty the Turbo, is suing me for nonpayment of debts. Wow! Isn't that just really cute?"

"It is, indeed. Poor baby, he's gonna lose another one."

"Yep. Kevin's right. So I'm gonna go sink that little turd, come home, get a job, and fall in love."

Sarah *did* go; the next morning, she sailed out to the meadow early. True to form, Kevin was already at his spot. In a totally unprecedented move, she waved and headed out in his direction. Now, they were rushing toward each other. As they came near, Sarah held out her hand, signaling she did not intend to embrace. However, she did take his hand and, essentially in stride, turned around beside him as they walked on toward her house. She was clearly in the leader role here, leading them into her agenda.

It was clear to Kevin that his unpredictable, reluctant young sweetheart was excited. Her disposition had changed radically. He was at a loss as to what might explain this sudden reversal in her mood. She was plainly on a mission, leading him along at the same nippy clip they'd already had going when they were rushing toward each other. They didn't talk much as they skipped along, partly because Kevin didn't know what was going on and Sarah chose to wait for a more suitable setting in which to explain her extraordinary initiative. Finally, she squeezed his hand, looked up at him, beaming, and spoke.

"Kevin, what say we go lounge on that poor old fallen log we found in the woods that time, you know, in that cozy little alcove?"

"Let's do it."

With this momentous decision, they slowed their pace and began to play, veering deliberately off course at times, stumbling without reason, one time wandering out into the tall grass, and in general, just whooping it up like a couple of clowns.

"Guess we better be careful over this terrain," Kevin said and laughed. "I remember one time I was severely scolded for getting fresh when I had to rescue you from a pothole."

"No, now, not *severely*."

Soon, they were at the narrow trail that cut through the timbers and led to the wooded cove. When they got there, they headed straight for the old log and without fanfare, robotically sat down on it.

When they finally caught their breath, Kevin joked, "Wanna run through that one more time?"

"Another day. For now, wanna check the mail?"

"Huh?"

"You know, that little pocket somebody carved into that tree over there."

"Oh yeah!" exclaimed Kevin as he sprang off the log. He was at the tree in three abnormally long strides. He lifted the little door and fished around ostentatiously inside the hole, all the while looking back at his escort for approval. "Nothing," he said. "So I guess that means there are no illicit lovers roaming around out here, exchanging mad, passionate love letters."

"*Illicit*, you say? Is that supposed to be a dig?"

"Not at all, but you know, by your own admission, we do sort of fall in the category of frustrated lovers. Really, sweetheart, I'm just funnin' around. Please, no dig intended. Really."

"I know, my Kevin. I'm just jostling along with you. Now, you're probably wondering why I called this meeting. Well, the fact is that I think you're entitled to the rest of the story, so to speak, and I'm fixing to lay it on you." Unlike previous exposé sessions, Sarah was speaking in a completely upbeat manner—and with a smile. "And, mind you," she continued, "I'm happy to finally be doing this, but really, well, it *is* serious."

"Believe me; I take it in that spirit."

"How sweet," she joked. "Thank you for your sterling attitude. Now, here we go. Until last Friday, I was married to a young boy my age named Mack Turbo. We had courted for about six months, and he seemed perfectly dedicated to me, agreeing with me on everything and faithfully doing all for me that he thought I wanted. To make a long story short, this guy is a colossal phony. All he ever wanted of me was to go to bed. However, on our wedding night, after sex, he slammed a fist into my face so hard it dislocated my jaw slightly. Then, I took his truck and some cash and ran. I sneaked back here and went into hiding, here with my aunt and uncle."

Kevin was off the log before she finished, pacing and fuming. "That son of a bitch is not only a phony; he's a despicable coward." He kept pacing, wringing his hands and cussing. He tried to calm himself and finally knelt before Sarah and pleaded, "I'm so sorry you had to go through that, Sarah. Nobody deserves that, but of all people in this world, you deserve a lifetime free of any such outrageous stunts. Oh, I'm so sorry ..." he stammered, wringing his hands and cussing.

Sarah took his face in her hands and said, "It's okay, Kevin; it's done. It's history. Well, almost. Come sit with me again, and I'll finish this sad tale."

"Okay, but first, how's your jaw?"

"It's actually doing pretty good. I can chew all right, but I can still feel a little tenderness when I yawn. So I've learned to yawn with my mouth barely open."

"You always make things work, don't you, sweetheart?"

Sarah nodded as he returned to his place on the log. With him at her side again, she continued her sad briefing, "As you know, I was granted a divorce last Friday. I'm free, right? Not exactly; my lawyer called yesterday and informed me that law enforcement people would be serving me a subpoena to appear in court." She laid a hand on Kevin's leg and said, "Now, keep your seat, Kevin; I know how this is going to hit you, but be assured, we're taking care of business, so don't get yourself all incensed over it. I just wanted you to know the whole score. Anyway, it happens that sweet old Mr. Mack has sued me for nonpayment of monetary debts owed him. He's claiming all kinds of foolish stuff."

By now, Kevin was sitting straight up, his body rigid, with a fist propped under his chin, staring straight ahead. Sarah gave him time, for it was obvious he was wrestling with something in his mind. Then, as he brought the hand away from his chin, he punched it into the other one as though reaching some profound resolution.

"It's pretty hard to just sit here and do nothing, but I realize my anger will solve nothing."

"Right." At that, Sarah filled him in on all the relevant details she could think of. When she finished, she asked him to stand with her. They faced each other for a few moments, respecting and waiting for impulses to guide them. When Kevin reached for her, she yielded wholly and came into his arms. They held their loving embrace for a while, and then Kevin pulled back just enough so they could kiss. They did, and when, eventually, it was given up, both agreed that this was a first for them. Soon, they strolled back to Sarah's house and parted blissfully.

Later that afternoon, someone from the constable's office in Dallas served Sarah as expected. She accepted the subpoena and dutifully signed the papers at the officer's request. Kyle and Gina stood a ways back, not interfering but clearly in a position to witness. The court date was set for Thursday, June 7.

As the officer departed, Sarah thanked him and wished him

well. He politely acknowledged and said, "I wish you ever good luck, miss."

When it was done, Sarah turned to her family and smirked. "Well, it ain't over till it's over, right?"

7

WHAT DO YOU DO till the judge appears? That was the question. Court was a week away. For Sarah Lock, the question was whether to do nothing and sweat or get busy and suppress. She chose the latter. It helped that she was already pursuing a new level of liaison with Kevin. She had started it when she invited him to the woods for a strictly nature-loving venture. It was *their* woods. That unusual initiative on her part was the result of a new attitude she had developed toward her situation and the much harsher regard she now had for her adversary, Mr. T. This new perspective arose in great part out of Kevin's insistence that she needed to get angry.

Even in her new framework of thinking, there were still compelling questions nagging Sarah about herself on this Friday evening. Most of them involved Kevin and their present and future.

What must Kevin think of me? One day, I tell him I can't love him, and the next day, I say I do, but I can't follow through on it. Surely that must sound like gibberish to him. One day, I send him packing, and the next day, I rush to him reaching for his hand and finally let him kiss me. How will he react when he has time to think about all those inconsistencies in me? And what's he going to think of me when he reflects on all that scandalous stuff I told him about me and my affair with Mack the Ass? How can he possibly still love me? I think I'm my own nemesis.

Sarah would soon learn the answers to all her questions. In fact, she would know by noon of the next day. As it happened, that day, Saturday, started in normal fashion at the Evans home. After breakfast dishes, Sarah had immersed herself in household chores and was faring quite well with that. Suddenly, there was a knock at the door. "I'll get it," she sang out as she shuffled through the front room, merrily rocking her head side to side. With a gleeful flair, she swung open the door. At once, she gasped and almost lost her balance as her hand flew up to cover her mouth.

There stood a bouquet of red roses, supported by an impishly smiling Kevin Eric Lane.

"Kevinnnn!" That was all she could get out for the moment. When, finally, she regained some measure of composure, she invited her surprise guest to come in. She directed him to set the flowers on the cocktail table, just as Kyle and Gina came marching in. There followed much commotion and babble over the beautiful bouquet, which contained one lone snapdragon in the very center, apparently stuck there in an act of mischief.

Sarah was simply beside herself. She couldn't talk. She stood at the vase and held her arms just to the outside of the flowers, symbolically hugging them. Eventually, when she regained her senses, she stepped back, cocked her head, and looked straight at Kevin.

"My dear Kevin, please tell me what that tall snapdragon is supposed to represent? That's not a standard floral touch, you know."

"Glad you asked."

At once, everyone turned to face Kevin and leaned in to listen as he began his answer. "Sarah, whether you accept it or not, my dear, you are a precious jewel—thus the roses. Now, those cute, clever-looking snap blossoms are the sparkles. Those are the cunning little gibes and quips, which you generously share with us to brighten our lives."

Kyle and Gina applauded, and Sarah rushed into the open

arms of her suitor. "Ahem," mumbled Gina, and she and Kyle crept out of the room.

Kevin and Sarah held their embrace, and it was warm and absorbing for both of them. They eased apart, smiling together when they heard activity in the dining room. Momentarily, Kyle stomped in, put a hand on Kevin's shoulder, and said, "Kevin, please have lunch with us; can you stay awhile, please?"

Kevin accepted, and the family of four enjoyed lunch and a genial time together. Afterward, Kevin graciously thanked them for their hospitality and the delicious lunch. Then, the men retired to the front porch to talk about hunting and fishing while the women set about to restore the kitchen.

In a while, the women came out to join the men. After an hour of happy banter and merriment, Sarah asked Kevin if he'd like to trek to the woods to check on their favorite spot there. He said he would, and they were off.

As they bounced along their way, Sarah was mumbling about the roses and how sweet it was of Kevin to present them. "I guess the roses are an answer to questions I had been asking myself about how you might react to all that I revealed to you yesterday. In fact, Kevin, I have to admit that you've been on my mind a lot the last twenty-four hours." She laughed and added, "Hope you don't mind being thought of."

"To have one minute in your blessed mind is an honor, sweetheart. Now that you bring up the subject, I had also been wondering if honoring you with roses would please you or anger you, whether they would make you think more or less of me. I finally decided it didn't matter, that after all, I love you, and roses are one way of expressing that love."

"Kevin, I love them, and I accept them as the loving gesture you say they are. Truly, they touch my heart."

In a moment, they came to the trail and started into the woods. When they reached the cove, they turned their backs to the log and stepped straight into the center of the little room. They turned to face each other, as if on common impulse. Their embrace was spontaneous and mutual. They held on to it as if it needed to last a lifetime. They cuddled tightly, affectionately, and inevitably, they lapsed into near frenzy. Soon, they felt the tides of passion sweep through their bodies and souls. Sarah started to push away, but Kevin only tightened his hold. When she again tried to pull back, he conceded and released his beloved soul mate. At that, they shared a wow-smile and turned toward the old log. Before they could sit, Sarah held out a hand to stop Kevin and said, "Hey, why don't we explore the trail further into the woods. Who knows? There might be bigger and better hideaways in there?"

"Sounds great. Let's be about the woods," said Kevin.

"You gonna lead?"

"Well, I'll be glad to be the front man, but I need to warn you: I flunked scouting."

"Well, you know, you have the trail to guide you."

"But what if it runs out?"

"Just follow your nose."

"Yeah, well, I also flunked instincts."

"Kevin, you lead and we'll pray."

"Was that a little sparkle?"

Sarah giggled bashfully and mocked, "My dear, it's whatever you deem it to be."

Kevin raised a hand high in the air and then pumped his arm and ordered, "Okay, everybody, line up; we're going in."

Bravely, the young pioneers mounted their dangerous excursion deep into the woods, with nothing to guide them but a well-cultivated, clearly discernible pathway. Wow, what courage!

Oops! Within minutes, the well-marked trail started to lose definition. It had thinned and no longer had the character of a bona fide pathway. Neither said a word. They just stumbled ahead. In a while, there was no trail at all. They were simply in the woods. Still, they surged ahead. Kevin continued to lead, twisting vines to the side, stomping down briar bushes ahead of Sarah, and stretching low-hanging limbs so she could duck under. As they ducked and dodged along, they grew weary and short of breath.

In a while, Sarah cleared her throat noisily and pleaded, "Where are we going?"

"To the creek, my love, to the creek—to what I believe to be Whistle Creek."

"Why?"

"To see what's on the other side. Where did you *want* to go?"

"Just into the woods a ways. But that's okay; that's okay. Lead on, my dear."

Kevin sensed that uncertainty was beginning to grow in Sarah, partly because he was uneasy himself and partly because he could hear a little frenzy in her panting. Moments later, he touched a hand to her shoulder and they stopped. Then, they sat on the ground at the foot of an ages-old tree, trying to catch their breath. Although they both knew the score, neither talked. Finally, Kevin broke the disturbing silence.

"Pardon me, ma'am; may I say something?"

"Sure; you talk, and I'll rest."

"A couple of things," began Kevin, wedging his words in between puffs of breath. "First of all, ma'am, I just want to say that I think this is a lovely wooded setting you have here."

"Why, thank you, my noble scout."

"The second thing is … I think we're lost."

"We *can't* be," said Sarah diffidently.

"Then, why are we just stomping headlong through these woods?"

"Well, we've just got to get to the creek, like you say—so we can turn around and try to find our way back."

"We're lost."

"We're not *lost,* Kevin; we're right here," she insisted, pointing to the spot where they sat.

"Funny."

"Kevin, we know *generally* where we are. And ... see, we can't be lost because we're ... we're .... We're lost!"

Kevin turned to face his sweetheart, and for a moment, he just gazed adoringly at her sweet, innocent face; her remarkable, accepting countenance; and those deep-blue, knowing eyes. She met his gaze and smiled. They were breathing more easily now as Kevin remarked, "At least we're not alone."

In that moment, a light breeze leaked through the trees, making it a little easier to relax.

Suddenly, Sarah jerked and held a finger in the air as if to make a point. "Kevin, do you smell that?"

"I smell the woods."

"No, not that; I smell something else."

"What does it smell like?"

"Mud."

"That oughta help us."

"No, I mean mud, like wetness, *water*. Can't you detect that dampness in the air, that seedy, algae-like smell?"

"By golly, you're right. Now, we really *can* follow our noses."

They sprang up and were off again, trusting that their backs were turned away from the direction from which they had just come. Sure enough, in just a couple of minutes, they emerged into a narrow clearing and beheld a quiet, gentle brook just trickling along downstream. They high-fived and celebrated for a while and then settled down to study their surroundings and calculate ways to ford the stream. Soon, they decided they didn't need to go any farther on this particular day, even though they were curious about an old barn they could see in the distance on the other side.

"This has been so fulfilling," said Kevin as he reached out for Sarah. "We've done something together, as one." In one flurry, he brought her into his arms and pulled her as close as he could, pressing her firmly against his body. By this time, they were both panting and their hearts were pounding against each other.

As their sexual frenzy began to pick up, Kevin let his hands slide down to Sarah's hips and pulled her pelvis hard against him.

Sarah yielded breathlessly, but even as she did, she was beginning to shake her head frantically, slinging it from side to side in front of Kevin's face. Watching his anguish build at her sudden resistance, she wrenched away and cried her way to the ground at the foot of a tree, still rocking her head.

Kevin waited, finally mumbling, "Another time, maybe."

Sarah pushed up and leaned back against the tree, now somewhat better composed. "Kevin, please understand that it wasn't that I didn't want to. I so wanted you. Believe me, I did ... I did!" She swiped a hand across her face and tried to smile, but it was a lame effort. "I know we would be perfect. But, Kevin, I'm still a prisoner of my—what? Something. Can you understand?"

Kevin nodded but said nothing, clearly showing his disappointment. Finally, he walked up to her and took her hand. "Shall we start back?"

"Yes, we should. It's getting late, but someday, I would like to explore the other side and check out that old barn."

"Me, too—among other things."

As they turned around to head back through the woods, Sarah frowned and muttered, "So where is that nontrail?"

"Really, I don't know anything to do but just barge into the woods and proceed. Now, we're on instincts for sure."

So they just marched boldly into the woods and shoved on, somehow building confidence as they met their challenge. Now, they were just slinking along, Kevin groping in the lead, Sarah at his heels with two fingers hooked into his belt. In a while, miraculously, they passed by the tree where they had rested, and later, clearly by the will of God, they came to the actual trail. They were not headed directly into it, but were close enough to see it off to the side. They also noticed, to their surprise and chagrin, that the trail actually made a right turn and headed laterally for a few yards and then turned frontward again, obviously toward the creek. Kevin was embarrassed, but Sarah hugged him and said it was a natural and reasonable choice to forge straight ahead as they had done coming in. She pointed out that she hadn't noticed the offshoot either. In any event, they cheered and high-fived again, extoling their first random sojourn together.

Back home, Sarah paused at the flowers on her way through the living room. She contemplated them for a while, taking them in, trying to absorb the enormity of what had just transpired with her and the bearer of those beautiful roses and their sparkles. The venture she and Kevin had engineered on the spot was big. She nodded to herself as she reflected on it. Except for one little detail, that undertaking now loomed as the most decisive event in their relationship so far. It told her exactly what she had hoped to find out when she proposed their woodland hike. It was the first significant thing they had done together, as one, and it worked.

In Sarah's mind, Kevin had passed the test, not as a skilled navigator of the woods, but as a potential mate. Their tandem effort on the hike, their unassuming interaction, the spirit in which they conquered challenges with mutual ease and understanding, indeed their passionate sexual play, all seemed so easy, so natural. Only the aborted sexual foray stood in the way of an absolutely exhilarating adventure together. It now loomed as the one thing that prevented her from completely relaxing at this moment. She could still feel the tension of their bodies as they hung together and oh, how she still wanted him. *Can it ever be?*

Attempting to squeeze her way out of these last deflating thoughts, she tried again to count up all the things that had gone right. Nothing had been forced by either of them; nothing was allowed at any point to strain their rapport. Moreover, their banter and good-humored teasing seemed to arise naturally as a means to unite their effort and keep them calm. It wasn't that they blindly agreed on everything; rather, it was the fact that they just seemed to fit. Clearly, they were building a bond.

Sarah and Kevin started meeting every day, doing *their* things: a leisurely stroll to the Meadowlark Café for pork ribs and fries, a picnic in the ballerina patch (as Kevin called it) to which they invited Sarah's aunt and uncle and Kevin's landlord, and another hike through the woods and across the creek to explore the dilapidated old barn, which appeared to have been abandoned years earlier.

All of it was exciting, mostly because they were doing it together. To Sarah, Kevin's love was undeniable, and though she no longer inhibited *her* love for *him*, she sensed that he was not completely certain of it. *Why can't I tell him how very deeply I love and adore him, how surely I want him in my life forever?*

Ultimately, it occurred to Sarah that her reticence lay in the fact that she still was not a free woman, that a dreaded appearance in court unconsciously haunted her, and that she was still skittish about having a romantic relationship. She fully accepted that these doubts kept her from completely giving in to her feelings for Kevin and giving herself wholly to him.

On the eve of her scheduled court date, she was simply low in spirits, flat down, and Kevin knew it. When he asked to attend court with her family, she begged him not to, explaining that Mack would undoubtedly be suspicious, and she didn't want him to have anything to react to. Kevin didn't go.

Then came the day. The procedure was different this time. Four people stood before the judge, Mack and Sarah and their attorneys. They answered questions presented by the judge and asserted their claims about the issue at hand, namely the alleged delinquent payment of debts claimed by Mack Turbo. The judge seemed to be irritated by the whole affair and soon cut off all debate and issued his decision.

The court held that Sarah was clearly liable for charges relating to retrieval of the truck. Otherwise, it found that the defendant's requirement for verifiable documentation on the other charges was reasonable and proper and that the plaintiff had not, in fact, furnished acceptable documentation. The judged ordered that Mr. Turbo's notarized statement did not reach the threshold of acceptable evidence. The entire procedure lasted about twenty minutes.

The instant the decision was announced, Buford Crump, Sarah's attorney, scampered out of the courtroom. Like the judge, he was obviously out of sorts himself. *Everybody seems ticked off,* thought Sarah. *Do they consider this little matter too trivial to take up their time? Come on, guys; it's your job!* On that impulse, her mind drifted back to the day she marveled at the little bird flying with a broken wing.

As Sarah lingered, she was aware that her adversary was holding his ground also. She continued to wait for him to leave, feigning preoccupation with something in her purse. At once, Mack started sauntering toward her. His lips were pooched out as though he'd just swallowed a wooly worm. Sarah turned to face him squarely, lifted her chin, and waited, keeping her expression cool and indifferent. She held it even as he stopped directly in front of her. Then, she cocked her head and rolled her eyes as if to say, matter-of-factly, "Yessss?" She said nothing.

Mr. Mack groused, "Do you have anything to say to me?"

"Only that I'm very tired; aren't you?"

"Well, better get some rest. Get ready for the big one." On that stinger, Mack wheeled around and strutted out of the room.

As stunning as those last words were, Sarah refused to be ruffled by them. Even so, while this man had now exposed himself as a colossal phony, she knew better than to underestimate what silly pranks he might yet try to pull. Still, she could not help but be troubled by all that was taking place in her world. This whole affair with Mack Turbo stood out as a huge failure in her life. She continued to stand in place, thinking, rehashing her mistakes.

To Sarah, it seemed that she had lived a lifetime since that dreadful night in April when a ghastly shot to her face hurled her into a terrifying runaway nightmare. She had pinned all her hopes on Mack Turbo, who had seemed to bend over backward to please her. Even now, as he threatened her and huffed away, she could not help but feel some sympathy for him. Really, it was sad to watch him groveling, slinking away, trying to be brazen, faking confidence. Poor man, he had nowhere to go with his own life. But, although she felt compassion for him because of his ineptness and deranged mind, she decided that if he continued to mess with her, she would go all out to defeat him.

In a while, Sarah shook herself out of her lethargy and strolled outside to join her mom and dad, who waited patiently by the car. Unlike her previous success in court, the ending on this day did not lead her to revel in victory. In fact, she was sorely depressed. This time, she elected to go on back to her home in the country rather than spend a few days with her mom and dad. At that hour, she so yearned to be with Kevin, to hear his gentle, loving voice, consoling her but not trying to tell her how to feel. As much as she ached to see him, she opted not to visit the meadow the next day. She was afraid she would break down, and she didn't want Kevin to see her in a moment of weakness. *What does he see in me, anyway? I'm a wreck. Oh, but I wish he was here with me now. I love him so very much. Dear Lord, what shall I do?*

18

SARAH SAT QUIETLY IN the shade of an old tree, lonely as a lost feather. She had a foreboding sense that she was giving up on herself. She felt that she was losing control and that she was on the brink of doubting that her life had any value to herself or anyone else. As she started to develop that thought further, her aunt Gina came to the back porch and announced that Kevin was there to see her.

"Shall I have him come out here, or would you rather come inside?"

"I'll come inside; thanks, Aunt Gina."

Sudden excitement raced through Sarah; the unexpected appearance of Kevin was the answer to a prayer. Even though she hadn't prayed to God specifically to bring them together, so many of her thoughts carried that hope. In fact, she was convinced that humble thinking had the same effect as praying. So she bounded away. By the time she reached the house, she was fully uninhibited. When she saw Kevin, smiling in his inimitable way, she rushed to him and threw her arms around him before he could get his ready.

Nerved by this sudden show of affection, Kevin pulled back and kissed her, and then they kissed again—and once more, this one, a passionate, lingering kiss. When finally they slacked off, they were panting, and for a few moments, they just looked admiringly at each other. In a moment, Sarah took his hand and led him to the front porch swing for their visit.

"What brings you to these parts, old man?" teased Sarah, her eyes sparkling.

"I'm chasing girls ... well, one girl."

"Better be *one*," chortled Sarah, and they both laughed.

"Right. Actually, my little prairie ballerina, I came here on a mission, a very specific mission."

"And that is?"

"My Sarah, I'm here to ask you for a date."

"Isn't *this* a date?"

"Okay, you score one sparkle on that. Seriously, you know, sweetheart, we've done a lot of wonderful things together, but they were all sort of, what shall I say, impromptu. I would like to date you formally and ... err, get serious."

"Wanna go steady?"

"You bet."

"Okay, my young hero of the woodland foray, I'm in."

Over the next few days, Kevin and Sarah spent hours with each other, exploring ways to be together in all kinds of situations and places: joining for worship services at her church, dining out in Dallas, taking in a Texas Ranger ball game in Arlington, attending a hip-hop concert at the American Airlines Center in Dallas, and getting around to malls and other enclaves. It was exciting and very refreshing. As rewarding as it was though, they invariably returned to the wilderness, walking the country lane and just hanging out in their meadow.

Of all the exciting things they did and places they went to, there was no place like their meadow. After all, it was where they met. It was home. So the time came when they would sit peacefully in the tall grass on a lazy, partly sunny day, exchanging soft, calm, innocuous mummers. For some of the time, they didn't talk at all. They didn't need to talk. They couldn't have been more in communion than they were, just sitting there in silence, absorbing the peace of each other and the tranquility of the countryside.

In that moment, they spontaneously glanced up, looking at

the clouds that seemed so very patient, just resting for a while and then floating in a leisurely manner—all in one direction. The small clouds seemed to mimic children, straying at times and then catching up. They watched one of the child clouds as it wandered away from its family, and then all by itself, drifted over the sun, casting a thin shadow over their place in the grass. In a while, it moved on in its effortless journey, drifting ever so slowly away from the sun.

Sarah and Kevin were again bathed in the warm light of sunshine. Sarah wondered if Kevin felt the sun's love the way she did. As they bowed their heads, still wordless, she felt she knew what he was thinking and that he was, like she, feeling a quiet, awe-inspiring sense of eternity and love. In a while, they simultaneously raised their heads and nodded, without a word. As for Sarah, she felt there was simply no way to characterize the awesome ambience of that moment.

Finally, she sighed and spoke in a voice a little louder than a whisper, "This is just one moment in time, but it will live in our hearts forever. Kevin, my dear, this is ours!"

"Yes. It's our song; it's our dance."

After that brief exchange, they just stared innocently at each other for a while—two philosophers, introverts, basking in total acceptance of each other, with no word for it. Finally, Kevin squirmed, caressing the grass with his butt, cleared his throat, and opened his mouth to speak. All the while, Sarah was leaning over her knees, propping her chin in her palms, looking wide-eyed as if waiting for breaking news, ultimately displaying a playful smile that seemed to say, "Yes, go on."

"I was just thinking that this wilderness seems to say so much about how to make life work."

Sarah nodded, and as she gazed vaguely out across the prairie, she said softly, "You know, Kevin, life's best can only be felt; it can't be talked about very well. I think love's like that."

"Sweetheart, I think you're right; the word *love* has no meaning until you feel it."

"Uh-huh. You know, I like hearing you call me sweetheart. However, most of my family calls me that, and they usually mean 'sweet little, subordinate child of ours'—which is great; I'm not complaining. But I just wonder what you mean when you say sweetheart to me."

"Well, I certainly don't mean anything subordinate. That would be the farthest thing from my intentions. *Sweetheart* has a different meaning when used outside a family. In my situation, I intend it to reflect a powerful romantic interest in you. For example, if we were married, I'd probably call you sweetheart. There's an old classic song entitled 'Let Me Call You Sweetheart,' and it's pleading for the privilege of loving someone so much that they can use that ultimate expression of affection. In my case, when I call you sweetheart, it means I love you."

"You know, Kevin, one time, I thought I had a sweetheart, but I didn't. Now, I think I have a sweetheart, and I'm afraid."

"I understand, my darling. I just hope that someday, I can win your heart to the point where you won't be afraid anymore. And, as I indicated once before, I'm willing to wait."

"Okay, I think the time has come for me to go where I haven't gone before. The fact is, Kevin, you've already won my heart, and although I've intimated it, I've never said outright to you that I love you."

She swallowed and looked away briefly, seeking nerve—in a way, praying. Now, she pushed up to crouch on her hands and knees so she could come closer to Kevin. Then she moved right up to him, rocked back on her heels, put her hands on each side of his face, and squeezed gently.

"Kevin, I love you. Do you hear me? I love you, and I love you more than I ever thought it was possible to love."

"Oh my darling, I love you, and I want you. I want to get on my knees right now and thank God for your love. It's so blessed and priceless." As he squirmed up to his knees, he reached for Sarah's hand, and she gave it freely. At this point, both were crying softly, giving up tears of sheer, humble gratitude. Holding hands, their heads bowed, Kevin submitted to God their eternal gratitude for their love for each other and their promise to honor God's blessing, namely their love.

They fell into each other's arms, though it was a little tricky, considering they were on their knees. However, love triumphs over everything, and so, they made it work. In a while, they fell away and sat again in the grass, closely snuggled side by side.

"My Kevin ... See, I can call you mine now. Anyway, I wish I could somehow tell you how deeply I feel for you, how I care, and how I want you in my life forever. But I've never gone this far with love—the other was essentially academic—and so please forgive me if I stammer. Someday, Kevin, you'll know just how profoundly I love and care for you."

Kevin was sniffling and trying to talk at the same time. "My little princess, you've just said it; you've said it all, and you've expressed exactly how I feel about you."

Sarah was also crying a little as she spoke. "Tell me, Kevin; I want to hear it. I could never get enough of hearing you talk about loving me."

"It just means I want you in every intimate way; I want everything of you. I want to love you, serve you, care for you, and let you teach me. I want to live for you."

"I want all that for you, too. Tell me more; I so need to hear it."

"Well, my darling, I want you to be the happiest girl alive, and I want you always to have good health and meet with goodwill every day. I want people to treat you with kindness and love, and I want to watch you smile because of it. I hope things happen around you every day that make you tingle with joy and that you always feel good about yourself. And I want to always be where I can see all this wonder in your life."

"Oh my, how blessed could I ever dare to be? You know, I have to be honest, I really think our love was just about instant, so much so that I could hardly believe it."

"My dear Sarah, this is the real thing. You know, there's

no pretext in feelings. You can never really hide them from yourself."

"I know, and it's hard to verbalize them. Still, we don't have to be in each other's arms to feel."

"Right you are," said Kevin. "I felt you in the meadow that first day, from all that distance. But even now, when I hear myself say I love you, it doesn't begin to convey all that I'm feeling."

Abruptly, Sarah clapped her hands, pointed down the meadow, and whooped, "Oh look!"

Kevin looked up and saw a young mother deer hop across the field into the woods. Then, they watched in awe as her fawn came wobbling along some distance behind her.

"Amazing," said Kevin. "We've seen so few animals in these fields and woodlands. In all our rumbling around, I think we've scared up maybe three rabbits and one old beady-eyed coon. I just wonder why we don't see more animals out here."

"Because they're not out here."

Kevin chuckled and declared, "Now, that *would* tend to explain why we don't see them, wouldn't it?"

When Sarah laid a hand gently on Kevin's arm, a little quiver rippled through him, and he gazed in wonder at the beautiful— now serious-looking—face of his woman.

"Know what I think, Kevin?"

"I'm all ears."

"Okay, this is not an authoritative explanation, but it's what I've reasoned out. It may be that the animals don't find suitable nesting places in these particular woods, and maybe it's the scent of man that scares them away. Huh?"

"As far as I'm concerned, that *is* authoritative."

"Thank you, sir."

"Don't see a lot of chickens in the woods either, do we?"

"Yeahhh," sighed Sarah, drawing out the word. "That's really baffling, isn't it? Seems we would at least spot a runaway chicken now and then."

After this little round of homemade humor, they stared at each other for a while. Sarah could tell by the look in Kevin's eyes and his shifting around in place that he was feeling passion. Surely he must sense that she was feeling the same thing. In a moment, he started to lean toward her with that beckoning look in his eyes but stopped short when she started to shy away. Sarah was on the brink of giving in, for she knew his passion was no stronger than her own. It took her back to that day in the woods when they almost went the full course. Now, she could virtually hear his ending words, "Another time maybe." *Unfortunately, not now,* she thought. Momentarily, she pointed upward, and they both stood up and strolled out of the meadow arm in arm.

When the two met again, they both sensed that something mysterious was hanging over them. As it happened, Kevin had to work all day and into the night the next day, for he had received an e-mail from *Lands Alive* requesting a status report on his project. Apparently, he had been neglecting his assignment, and the magazine staff was starting to get nervous about it. Then, Sarah was missing the next day, reportedly shopping in Dallas with her mother, who'd come to be with her on an unexpected day off.

Finally, the two lovebirds met again. As they came together, Sarah smiled awkwardly and chimed, "Hi, Smiley."

"And a hearty hi to you, Miss Sparkles," sang Kevin. With that, he stepped forward and nervously took her hand, and they strolled away. Kevin was ambling along as if there was absolutely nothing to worry about. But clearly, something was in the air. He felt there was something eerie about their newfound love—something foretelling disappointment—some ominous threat hanging on the edge of it, pulling it down. It was his sense that Sarah was feeling the same thing. It was like the wind picking up before a storm. Perhaps their love was so strong that it was just scary, he thought.

So it happened that their first meeting after their confessed mutual love was virtually formal. They were jovial enough as they ambled along the woodline, yet the atmosphere seemed strained.

After a while, Kevin stopped them and said, "Hold on; what's wrong here?"

"I *hear* you," said Sarah. "Now that we've confessed our absolute love for each other, something seems to be trying to take the luster out of it. I can tell you feel it, too. I still feel the same way about you; nothing has changed one iota. I love you with all my heart, and I know you love me as well. Maybe we're just being challenged by the enormity of it all?"

"I think you've hit on it. Love is a ... Well, really, love is a grave matter, probably the most critical element of life."

"That's gotta be it. So nothing really to worry about. Reality is just heckling us, as I guess it does all love affairs in the beginning, trying to see if we really mean it."

"And we do. I've never been more positive of anything in my life than I am of my love for you."

"Same here, my dear Kevin. You are—and always will be—the man of my dreams."

In that moment, they arrived at their trail into the woods and turned onto it with renewed enthusiasm. Soon, they were at their favorite room in the woods. It was just natural for them to pause in the middle of it for a while and savor the full essence of their consummate bond. By now, they had dismissed their earlier premonition that something was wrong.

The two devoted lovers stood quietly, beholding the wonder they saw in each other. They had no fear of being interrupted, because for one reason, the chance that someone else would be stomping around in the woods at that hour was remote. Also, they felt risk was an element of their adventure, part of the dare, making it more exciting. As Sarah so aptly put it one day when they were lolling around in the meadow, "True love is willing to take risks."

In Kevin's view, considering the present state of their emotions, *Who cares?*

Now, there was no force of any kind that had any chance to contain the sexual passion they were beginning to feel for each other in that extraordinary moment. Sarah could see that Kevin was becoming increasingly amorous, and he could read the passion in her eyes. She had never wanted a man sexually in her life so much as she did that man right then, and she could see the same frenzy boiling in him. So they held each other as if it would be their last time, allowing their spirits to fuse them together as if they were just one essence. Their kissing had always been thrilling, but this time, it was imbued with downright sexual craving.

They paused for a moment in their lovemaking, and then Kevin cuddled her to him again. At that point, they were panting and their chests were heaving. They could each feel the frenzied pounding of the other's heart. Soon, Kevin began unbuttoning her top. When he finished, he pulled the sleeves a ways off her shoulders. He placed a finger lightly underneath her lips and let it rest there for a few seconds and then began to draw it lightly around her chin and on down her neck to her chest. With two featherlight fingers, he traced around the perimeter of her bra.

"Kevin, sweetheart," wheezed Sarah, "I'm sorry, but you know we're not supposed to go where we're headed."

"We're both single," he puffed.

"That's not the thing ... just ... it's just that we're not supposed to do it out of wedlock."

"I thought that was just a cultural thing."

"It's also in the Bible."

Kevin slowly pulled her sleeves back onto her shoulders and began to rebutton her blouse. Sarah felt that he was probably remembering their last sexual outing that had ended so abruptly and that he was deliberately conceding defeat because of her expressed doubts. Ironically, she had never been so consumed with sexual passion in her life, and she now decried her earlier resistance. As she looked into Kevin's desperate eyes, she knew he was fighting the same battle, fiercely struggling to hold back his own craving. Soon, she murmured, "So maybe it *is* just a cultural taboo."

Now, they lay naked on their shed clothes in a bed of leaves. Kevin was over her, loving her from her neck to her knees, caressing and kissing her everywhere there was Sarah. In a while, he came to rest fully, but lightly, on her nude body. Moments later, they became fully intimate. So caught up had they been in their feverish lovemaking that Kevin's penetration came as a sudden, exhilarating surprise to Sarah. Now, they were fully united, and it felt to her as though it was the ultimate physical expression of love.

Once they were finished, they held on, cuddled together as one—inseparable. When Sarah sighed, Kevin rolled over to lie beside her. In a while, unintentionally, they fell asleep, side by side, their shoulders and hips touching. Sometime during their sleep, they turned toward each other and snuggled together, still snoozing—still dreaming and thanking God.

After they awakened, they again lay side by side. Kevin was groping for Sarah's hand, which he expected to be down beside her leg.

"Are you getting fresh with me?" she teased as she reached her hand down to join his.

"As much as you'll let me," he drawled.

"By the way, hope it's a boy," she crooned.

"I don't."

"Really? Why?"

"'Cause if it's not what you want, we'll have to try again."

At that, he felt the pulsating of her stomach and knew she was laughing. *What a breakthrough,* he thought. *She seldom laughs at my really funny stuff.*

After her laughter subsided, Sarah said, dryly, "Well, so much for planned parenthood."

They came out of the woods renewed, no longer tormented by the ominous dread they'd suffered earlier. At Sarah's house, they parted and headed home to rest and reminisce.

19

SARAH WAS BUBBLING WITH joy, reveling in her love for Kevin, when Gina handed her an envelope. She sobered at once. There was something ominous about receiving unexpected mail in the midst of pure bliss. She shuddered at the thought of it even though she hadn't yet looked to determine who the sender was. When she did, she screamed, "No!"

She ripped open the envelope, thoroughly disgusted. What could the police possibly want of her at this stage? She jerked out the one-page note and began to read. Instantly, she felt lightheaded and started to sway. On the edge of fainting, she began backing toward the nearest chair, still reading the letter. She fell into the chair and let the letter drop to her lap. She was still sitting there staring at the floor when Aunt Gina came in from the kitchen.

"What's wrong, Sarah? You look like a little girl who lost her puppy."

Sarah said nothing, choosing simply to hold out her letter for the taking.

Gina was shaking her head as she read the short note, ordering Sarah to report to the police station in Dallas. When she finished reading, she said, "I'm sorry, Sarah; you don't need any more of this. But we don't have choices sometimes—unfortunately. Anyway, I'll drive you in there Thursday, no problem. Wonder what they mean by you've been charged with theft of a motor vehicle."

"It's the truck. Mack's behind this. Anyway, thanks, Aunt Gina, for offering to drive me in, but the fact is ... I'm not going."

"Oh, sweetie, you have to go. You've been directed by law enforcement to appear, and you simply have to."

Sarah shook her head. "I'm not going."

"I understand your feelings. Tell you what: talk to your uncle Kyle tonight. He can help better than I can."

"I'm not going."

This was the only order of business the instant Uncle Kyle came on the scene. He asked Sarah to sit with him at the dining table while they talked.

"Sarah, this has to be the work of Mack Turbo, but be assured, he's gonna lose another one. All you have to do is comply with this directive. I'm sorry; it's unfair, and it's a terrible way to have to spend your time, but as you know, bad things happen to good people."

"Uncle Kyle, I don't mean to be impolite, but I have to tell you right up front, I'm not going."

"Yes, you are."

"You gonna make me?"

"That's not the question, darling. The fact is you *have* to go."

"No! I won't go in. I *can't* go in. I can't handle any more of this."

"Yes, you can. Come on now; you're a strong person. You can handle whatever you have to. It's that simple. Go, Sarah."

"No."

"Call your lawyer," grumbled Kyle as he jumped up and stalked out of the room, clearly annoyed.

When Sarah called Buford Crump the next morning, he indicated he'd check into the matter and get back with her. He called back in the late afternoon and confirmed that she had been charged with theft and that she had to respond to the summons.

"Mr. Crump, I thought this was all over with. What's going on here? You didn't warn me that this kind of thing might come up."

"Miss Lock, there was not the tiniest suspicion that this would take place. There were no signs to tip it off. But the point is that it doesn't matter what's right or wrong in cases like this. The only point is that we have to obey government authority."

"Well, I hear you, but it looks to me like they're just conceding to Mack Turbo. Where does he get all that leverage?"

"I'm sure that he and his attorney talked the state into filing the charges. The thing is that you're under suspicion. You'll get your fair trial later, but right now, the police consider that they have reasonable cause to regard you as a suspect."

"I understand all that, but I just simply can't go to the police as they say."

"Okay, listen carefully. As your attorney, I have to advise you to appear as directed. That's all I can say. Think about it."

That was it. They hung up. Like her uncle Kyle, her attorney also seemed perturbed that he had to spend his time with her, apparently because she refused to acquiesce. "Next?" she scoffed. "Get ready, Kevin; you're on."

If Sarah thought her uncle and attorney were irritated with her, she would soon find their response to pale in the light of Kevin Lane's.

When Kevin read the letter, his first words were, "Damn that pathetic little misfit. One of these days, I'm gonna have his ass."

"Strong words, coming from you, Kevin. Wow, I've never heard you talk like that."

"I'm sorry for the language, but this really pisses me off. Oops, sorry again. Anyway, what can I do to help? Will you let me go with you?"

"I'm not going."

"Oh, you *have* to. We don't have any choice there. If you fail to answer this summons, they'll get a judge to issue an arrest warrant for you. I'm so sorry, my beloved, dear sweetheart. I'm so sorry."

"I'm not going."

"You just don't have that choice, Sarah."

"Wanna bet?"

"Sarah, what happened to your strength? That's been a trademark of yours. It's one of the qualities I've admired in you from the beginning."

"Does that mean you don't love me anymore?"

"Oh, that's ridiculous. Come now; be reasonable. I will always love you. It's just that I won't stand idly by and let you give up."

"I'm so tired ... so weary ... and now, you're angry with me. So, Kevin, I hereby set you free. You can go your own way." With this uncharacteristic declaration, Sarah reflected back to those times in the divorce trial when she was woefully aware she was building horrific memories that would come back to haunt her.

"I'm not leaving you," said Kevin.

"You didn't hear me; you are free to go your way."

"My darling, my way *is* you."

It was downhill from that point, and their session ended just as the others had, with the exception that Kevin didn't leave her. However, he was clearly put out with her, and their impasse held. Ultimately, they parted for the evening, still brooding.

Sarah didn't go. Early on Friday morning, the day after she was to have appeared at the police department, her attorney called and advised that law enforcement officials were on their way to arrest her. He didn't expand on that point, nor did he offer any further advice. *So what choice do I have when they show up to arrest me? All I can do is hide.*

Ironically, Kevin had the uncanny sensation that he should hang around on Friday, so he gave himself the day off. Now, he was hurrying toward Sarah's house. The instant he got there, he heard Gina scream out his name.

"Hurry, Kevin! They're on their way to arrest Sarah." She was standing limply in the doorway, rubbing her arm. "Hurry, Kevin, she's running from them; she's going to hide. I just fell in the doorway trying to stop her. Please, Kevin!"

Kevin shot forward like a missile. He called up reserve he hadn't used in years and literally streaked toward his soul mate. He could already see her, trying to sprint along, headed in the direction they'd taken many times along the woodline. He was wearing down fast, but he was gaining on her.

Soon, Sarah heard his heavy feet pounding the earth behind her. She whirled around and screamed, "No, Kevin!" When he kept on coming at her, she let out an agonized squeal, like a dying animal, and dropped to the ground, folding her arms over her head.

Kevin was there in the next instant, crouched beside her, trying to calm her, to no avail. She continued to scream and rail at him. "Go, go, go!"

Kevin winced at the sight of her, the little heap of wailing fury, crying, pleading for help. Kneeling beside her, he reached his arms fully around her, but she twisted out and started beating on his chest two-fisted and berating him. "Go away! Go away! Kevin, I hate you! I hate you! Why, Kevin? Why? You don't love me." She continued to pound away on his chest and shout for him to go away.

"Knock it off, Sarah. Listen to me. Please, Sarah; you'll never be free if you run."

She raged on unabated. Kevin was beginning to tremble, and he was rapidly growing desperate. At once, he rammed an arm under her legs and pitched the other around her back. While she twisted and squirmed, trying to wrestle free, he grunted fiercely and started pushing up with his legs, giving it every last measure of strength he could possibly muster. As soon as he was standing, he started back to the house. Sarah raved the entire way.

As they arrived at the house, Gina hobbled out to meet them at the steps, then preceded them to the door and held it open. Kevin carried his stricken Sarah to the couch and gently lowered her onto it.

In a while, Sarah twisted around on the couch, sobbing, and curled into a fetal position. Kevin's heart was pounding so unmercifully that he thought it would explode through his chest. He knelt at the couch and laid a hand on her shoulders, but she fought it off and moaned, "Go away!"

Gina stood by weeping.

When there was a knock at the door, Sarah jumped and whirled upright. "No! I'm not going!"

"Please, Sarah," begged Kevin, "if you refuse to cooperate, they may add a charge of resisting arrest."

"I don't care. Do you understand me? I don't care."

Two officers stepped into the room, and one of them spoke directly to Sarah, asking, "Are you Sarah Grace Lock?"

Sarah nodded.

"Okay, I regret to inform you that we have a warrant for your arrest. Stand up, please, and step forward."

Sarah didn't budge.

"I'll ask you again, Miss Lock, please stand up and step forward."

Sarah didn't move; she just sat at the edge of the couch, mumbling, "I'm not going."

Thereupon the officers stepped up to the couch and handcuffed her with her hands in front. Strangely, she didn't resist; there was nothing left. When they asked her to stand up, she shook her head and refused. Now, the officers lifted her to her feet and began dragging her toward the door. Sarah was mortified but still resisted, forcing them to drag her on across the floor. As they did, she lost a shoe, and her bare foot started bumping painfully along the way. Kevin swooped down to retrieve it, banging his knee on the floor, and scooped it up. He handed it to an officer, who declined to take it. Uncharacteristically, Kevin shouted, "Take this shoe!" The officer snatched it out of his hand, and they dragged their victim on out of the house and into the police car.

Kevin and Gina walked out to stand a ways from the police car and watched it pull away. They continued to stare after it in disbelief, wordless, for several minutes.

"Aunt Gina, I'm going to follow that car on to the station. I mean, I won't be right behind it, but I'm going to show up there before they get her booked in. Do you want to go with me?"

"No, but thanks, Kevin. Kyle is on his way home. We'll see you there."

"Have you called her mom or dad?"

"Yes, but I need to call them again to let them know when they picked her up so they can be there also. Guess we'll have quite a squad of supporters there." She tried to laugh, but it came out as a silly little chuckle.

"Okay," said Kevin, "I'm out of here. I'll stop at the bank and pick up some cash because I believe bail money has to be in cash. I'm not sure, but I'll have some in case. You might mention this point to Kyle also, in case I don't bring enough. See you." With that, he sailed away, leaving Gina standing in place, waving.

At the county jail, the little crowd of murmuring supporters waited patiently while officials worked on the papers taking Sarah into custody. By this point, Buford Crump was on hand to help with the technicalities of bail and other details. Fortunately, the officials were able readily to find a judge who set bail and ordered that, upon payment, Sarah Grace Lock was to be released into the hands of her mother and father, with whom she was to reside until her trial. At Sarah's request, it was also established that she would have a jury trial. Family members got the bail together and paid it. Then, into their arms, they gathered a stunned, thoroughly beaten Sarah and took her home.

On invitation, Kevin visited for a while at the home of Ed and Denise Lock. At first, he and Sarah respectfully avoided contact, and then in a surprise move, Sarah came to him, and they embraced. When she stepped back, she rested a hand lightly against his cheek for a few moments. Smiling meekly, she said, "I'm sorry."

Kevin reached to hold her again and afterward spoke softly, "My sweet Sarah, you'll never have reason to be sorry. Thanks for letting me love you."

In the days that followed, Kevin visited with the Locks three times at Ed Lock's insistence. During those times, he and Sarah hit it off well, but it was not like old times in the meadow. She was unusually reserved, but Kevin attributed that to her anxiety and uncertainty about her future. He didn't raise a question about it or otherwise call attention to it. She deserved to be allowed to deal with the adversity in her life her own way.

On his last visit, Kevin learned that a date for Sarah's trial had been set, and it was now only eleven days away. When he asked Sarah if he could be present in court, she readily agreed. During the little time they spent together before the trial, there seemed to be some instinctive effort toward reconciliation. It was almost as if they wanted to pretend the alarming events on the day of Sarah's arrest never happened.

Kevin's last visit was on the eve of the trial. Surprisingly, Sarah seemed reasonably relaxed. She indicated that her attorney had briefed her on what to expect in the upcoming procedure, and she felt very confident about it. She explained that he said he couldn't believe the prosecution took on this case. He said there just wasn't anything there for them to build a case on.

As Kevin was leaving, Sarah rapped him on the shoulder and chuckled, "See you in court."

20

SARAH GLANCED AROUND THE courtroom. All seemed to be in order. The judge was on the bench, the jury was seated, and the bailiff had called the case. Sarah had already been sworn in and was sitting gracefully in the witness chair. Mack Turbo and his attorney were across the room, sitting stiff and tight-lipped as if they owned the place. At once, the judge spoke.

"Prosecution, present your case."

The prosecutor stepped up to Sarah, politely introduced himself, and began asking questions.

"Miss Lock, do you acknowledge that on the morning of April 13, 2012, you accessed a truck parked at the home of Mr. Mack Turbo and removed it from its location?"

"Yes."

"Who owned that truck?"

"My husband, Mr. Mack Turbo, held the title to it, but we had just been married a few hours earlier."

"Where was Mr. Turbo when you took the truck?"

"I presumed he was at work. I saw him leave the house about seven o'clock."

"So you waited until your husband was gone before you took his truck; is that right?"

"Yes."

"Where did you go with that truck?"

"Oklahoma City."

"Please tell the court what you did after you got to Oklahoma City."

"I parked the truck at an apartment building, got out of it, locked it, and left."

"Why?"

"I was running for my life."

"Why did you lock the truck?"

"To prevent someone from easily stealing it before Mr. Turbo could reclaim it."

"And just how would he know to find it where you left it?"

"I sort of left a trail. I mean, I phoned my mother and told her where I was. I knew Mr. Turbo would call her first thing."

"What did you do next?"

"I caught a bus back to Dallas."

At that, a little murmur ran through the jury, and the judge rapped his gavel.

"Okay, Miss Lock," continued the prosecutor, "so you testify that you were running for, as you put it, your life, yet you immediately return to the scene. What made sense about that to you?"

"I needed to hide, and I figured that nobody would think to look for me in the place I ran from."

"So what did you mean when you testified that you were running for your life?"

"I had just had my jaw dislocated, and I didn't know what the next hit might bring."

"And you really consider that life threatening?"

"I was just scared to death, sir. It was extraordinarily painful and frightening."

The prosecution continued to plod along, tramping mostly on irrelevant matters aimed at impeaching Sarah as a witness, attempting to find inconsistences in her testimony, and straining to discredit her motivation.

Sarah's attorney was next. His questioning was noticeably limited. He had advised Sarah that this would be his approach.

No use wearing out the jury when they could tell there was nothing there, he claimed.

"Miss Lock, did you steal a truck?"

"No."

"You testified that you took a truck from a driveway and drove off in it. Who's driveway, please?"

"Ours. It was at the house where my husband and I were living."

"Where were the keys to this vehicle?"

"In our house, in a kitchen drawer."

"What was your regard for this truck?"

"I considered it sort of like community property, that it was there for me to use—for shopping or anything else that I might need transportation for."

"Am I correct that you left the truck in an open parking lot at an apartment building in Oklahoma City?"

"Yes."

"Why?"

"I believed that the owner would easily find it there by tracing the license number and obtain help from the police."

"One more question and then I'm finished. Why did you wait until your husband wasn't home to take the truck?"

"Because it's hard to run away if someone's watching you."

A little titter ran through the courtroom, and the judge rapped his gavel again. He said nothing, but he was clearly struggling to stifle a smile of his own.

Thus ended the awesome exercise. The prosecution elected not to reexamine Sarah. It also opted not to call Mack Turbo. Also, Buford Crump confidently chose not to call Turbo as a hostile witness. Sarah's testimony had fully covered the details of the matter at issue, and there really were no facts in dispute. As Buford Crump had already intimated to Sarah, the case was academic; it all boiled down to the definition of theft. Hence, no other witnesses were called.

During closing arguments, the prosecution held that Sarah's

removal of the vehicle was unauthorized even if it was parked in her driveway. The attorney also argued that this access met the definition of theft. Further, he contended that Sarah abandoned the vehicle in another state and that this disclosed a motive for stealing. Finally, he asserted that her claim that she was running for her life didn't have credibility.

Buford Crump argued simply that the vehicle in question was clearly left at Sarah's disposal. Further, he argued that nothing in her actions indicated a motive to steal, but rather only to hide from further abuse at the hands of her husband. Finally, he pointed out that the owner had presented the defendant with a bill of charges related to reclaiming and returning the vehicle and those charges had been paid.

The jury was out for only about forty-five minutes and returned a verdict of *not guilty*. Otherwise, the court held that Sarah had good cause to take the vehicle, which had been left for her use. It concluded that the truck was already in her possession and the circumstances of her use of it did not rise to the level of a premeditated crime or a crime of opportunity.

Before leaving the courtroom, Buford Crump came up to Sarah, grinning broadly, and said, "Sarah, one thing was obvious throughout this exercise: the jury loved you."

"Thank you, Mr. Crump, and thank you for all you've done. And I want you to know this: I'm convinced I have the best lawyer in the world."

As on the previous occasion, the family, including the Locks, the Evanses, and Kevin (on invitation) all met back at the Locks' home. Sarah was in deep shock. She felt everyone could tell that. She really felt no sense of victory. She had been cleared but not restored. In that tragic moment, she knew positively that she would never be the same Sarah. She tried to be gracious and cordial with everyone, but she just couldn't escape the stupor she was in.

For one brief period, she actually showed some semblance of the old Sarah, but quickly that little flare was gone. It didn't stay, and it didn't return. However, while it lasted, there was a little teasing tone to her voice when she said, "Maybe I ought to get a job at the courthouse; that way, I'd already be there when ... you know."

When it seemed to be the appropriate time, Kevin indicated that he should mosey on and let the family have their time with each other. As he was leaving, Sarah stepped outside with him and they stood together for several moments. Then she hugged him perfunctorily and said, sort of plaintively, "Thank you for coming, Kevin."

"You're certainly welcome, but you see, it's where I needed to be—by your side. Dear Sarah, please, may I offer a humble suggestion? I think at this point, more than anything else, you need some quiet time, and I pray that you'll have it. Although my heart will ache to see you, I'll not bother you for a while. But if you could somehow get word to me when I can see you, I'll come running. In the meantime ... know that I love you."

Sarah nodded, and Kevin started away. When he was a couple of steps out, she managed to murmur, almost inaudibly, "I love you too."

Kevin immersed himself in his work. Actually, he was on the verge of needing work to do, for he had almost wrapped up his assignment for *Lands Alive*. He needed only a couple of pictures of prairies at night and a few shots on a rainy day. Fortunately, the editors had indicated they were considering a new project covering lakes, rivers, and the woodlands. Meanwhile, he had picked up a couple of local weddings and some part-time work, assisting a friend at his studio in Dallas. *Come on rain!*

In the middle of the week following Sarah's trial, he learned that she was back with her aunt and uncle. True to his word, he did not attempt to contact her. But she was seldom off his mind, and he so pined to see her. It ripped at his heart to see his Sarah so helpless, so addled and surrendered. Surely, somebody could do something—if not him, someone else. He was of a mind that she would benefit from seeing a doctor and was very nearly ready to suggest that to her family—just in case they weren't already considering it.

During the following week, Kevin grew so desperate that he felt he could wait no longer. He had received no word from Sarah that she was ready to see him. He simply had to find out how she was doing, even if it meant breaking his pledge not to bother her. So one evening after dinner, he walked to the little blue house and knocked at the door. Kyle warmly welcomed him in and led the way to the TV room where Gina was blissfully watching an old rerun of *Cheers*. When she saw Kevin, she smiled and reached for the remote to turn off the TV, but Kevin held up a hand to stop her.

"No, no," he said, "I'm not here to interrupt, and I hope you all are well." Then he laughed and continued, "Besides that, I'm sure you've already guessed the other reason I dropped in."

"Absolutely," Kyle assured him, "and your reason is perfectly honorable. God bless you. Wish we had better news."

By this time, Gina had turned off the TV, notwithstanding Kevin's concession. She nodded at Kyle's last comment and then tuned to Kevin and began to speak.

"Sarah is in a really bad way. I'm sure you have deduced that. She's still in what we'd call shock. She just stays in her room day and night and sleeps most of the time. We can hardly coax her out of the room to eat. Honestly, I think she would hunker down in there and starve to death if we didn't make her eat. Sometimes, we have to carry the food in to her, but she hardly eats three bites of it. Kevin, your Sarah is in a deep depression."

Kevin could not talk for a few moments. His patient hosts waited politely for him to collect himself. He clinched his fists and stretched his arms, trying to brace up. Finally, he said, "What can we do?"

"Mostly just stand by her," said Gina. "This has to end sometime."

"Do you all mind if I drop by from time to time to find out about her and see if there's anything I can do?"

"We don't mind at all; by all means, do check with us as often as you want."

They did not offer to let Kevin see his girl, so he soon left, graciously thanking them for their hospitality and for taking care of Sarah. When in three days, he did not hear from them, he called again. Sadly, Gina reported that there had been no essential change in Sarah's state of mind or overall condition. Suddenly, she snapped her fingers, obviously in readiness to add a vital point.

"One day—now listen up; this might mean a breakthrough—one day, still in her room, she asked me, 'Have you heard anything from Kevin?' I told her that you had been in touch and that you were deeply concerned about her."

"Thanks for that, and thanks to you all for all you do." He hesitated, clearly studying the situation, and then asked, "Do you think I might see her now?"

"Tell you what: I'll go in there and tell her you're here and that you're desperate to see her and ask if she will let you." With that, Gina hustled away and was gone for several minutes. Finally, she returned with the news.

"Kevin, she asks that you come and stand a ways back from the door to her room. She intimated that she would continue to think about it and that she may or may not come to the door."

"That's probably the best deal I'm gonna get," said Kevin stoically. "So here goes."

Kevin waited near Sarah's door—and he waited. When he could not hear any commotion behind the door, he cleared his throat and continued to wait. He'd been there at least ten minutes, when suddenly, the door began to ease open. Now, a limp, frail-looking Sarah stood in the doorway, motionless, expressionless. She just stood there, like a zombie, staring vaguely above Kevin's head. Finally, she lowered her chin a little. Then she sighed and spoke quietly but firmly.

"What are you doing here, Kevin?"

"I need you."

Silence. Neither felt obliged to attempt a follow-up on that terse declaration. Momentarily, tears washed over Sarah's face, streaming into the corners of her mouth. Still, she stood immobile in the doorway, just letting her tears take over. Finally, she raked over both sides of her face with fierce hands. Then, she spoke again, weakly.

"Well, I'm sorry about that, Kevin, but ... you might ... might as well forget it, for I am a hazard. So really, you don't *need* that."

"Come on now, Sarah! Not another label. Please."

"You sound angry."

"I *am* angry, but not at you, my darling. I'm angry at the forces of nature, the seeming indifference of the world. You should not be treated this way; it isn't fair."

"Well, I hear you, but really now, you *are* angry at me a little bit. I think everybody is."

"Okay ... well, maybe I'm, like, irritated. I guess I expect you to be pulling yourself up instead of pushing yourself down, giving in to all that isn't fair to you."

"I think maybe you need to go now," said Sarah as she backed into her room and closed the door.

It was clear to Kevin that her aunt and uncle could tell by his countenance that he didn't have good news. Before he could say a word, Kyle said, "I'm sorry."

Gina just looked at him sympathetically and said nothing.

Kevin said, "Well, she didn't invite me back. Anyway, it's time I leave and not be a bother to anyone. Do you mind if I continue to check with you from time to time?"

"Of course not," said Gina.

Kevin dived into his work again. Then, on the weekend following his brief meeting with Sarah, just out of the blue, came word from Kyle Evans that Sarah had asked to see him. Her instructions were that he should come to the meadow Saturday morning at nine o'clock.

When Kevin saw Sarah standing in the ballerina patch in the meadow, his heart began to race and he had to force-swallow a thick lump in his throat. He hustled on. When he was near Sarah, he hesitated to allow her a chance to speak first—his trademark show of respect.

Sarah stepped up to him, looking serious, placed her hands on his shoulders, and said, "I haven't treated you right, Kevin. You've loved me, you've stood by me, and you've tried to help me, and I haven't treated you right."

"Oh, my precious Sarah, not at all. I'm the one who should be apologizing for being so impatient. Please forgive me. I just love you so much that it makes me selfish. I want you."

"You don't need to apologize. I've really been out of it for longer than I should have been. Truly, I've been feeling sorry for myself and haven't known what I'm supposed to do with my life. Kevin, in the days since that dreadful trial, I've spent most of my time thinking about life, questioning its purpose and railing at its cruelty."

"I think, sometimes, we can do little more than agitate ourselves, thinking about this … whatever it is we call life. If you think about it too much, you learn nothing and just get depressed."

Sarah did not respond to Kevin's philosophical comment. Instead, she put a finger to her lips and said, "Kevin, do you have to work today?"

"Unh-uh. I give myself Saturdays off, most of the time. So you want to do something?"

"Let's go through the woods and check out that old barn again. Something about it fascinates me."

"That old barn across Whistle Creek? You want to go there again?"

"Yes. Do you mind?"

"Well, no, I guess not."

"Well, hey, don't strain yourself any," she huffed. "Never mind; I'll just go myself."

"No, now, don't get upset; I was just trying to understand. By all means, let's go."

At the barn, Sarah wanted to go inside, but vines had completely overtaken the door.

"Well, I guess that says nobody's been in this old shack for, I guess, years," said Kevin.

"Good point; it's clearly nobody's clubhouse. Maybe we could make it ours."

They laughed and started pulling and tugging on the stubborn old vines. Finally, they were able to wrestle the door open enough they could squeeze in sideways. Inside, Sarah just wandered around, thoroughly looking it over, paying particular attention to the ceiling. Kevin stood by, disappointed in himself for being hesitant when Sarah proposed this outing. *That was me at my worst, and she needs my best. It was such a simple request, yet I had to be such a moron.*

At one point, Sarah sat down on the bare dirt floor by the sturdiest looking wall and leaned back against it. As she sat there, apparently relaxing, she glanced at the ceiling and said, "As dilapidated as this old thing is, that tin roof appears to be in fair shape."

"Yeah, pretty fair; there are a few cracks in it, but it probably keeps out most of the rain … at least the light showers."

Soon, Sarah scrambled to her feet. "Okay, that's it. I'm satisfied. Let's head back."

No way was Kevin going to ask what it was she was satisfied about or question anything else about the venture. He'd already used up his one boo-boo. In any event, Sarah seemed to be regaining some of her characteristic optimism, and nothing in creation could make him happier than that.

When they got back to the meadow, Kevin suggested that, since they had done so much walking, they ride into nearby Gun

Barrel City and have lunch at Vetoni's Italian Restaurant. Sarah agreed, and they enjoyed a fairly friendly though somewhat passive lunchtime together.

Then things changed again. Kevin watched painfully as Sarah slipped back into her gloomy mood. He knew better than to attempt any comment on it because that would only make her defensive, a characteristic she had picked up only after the three court trials. So they rode back to her house in near silence. Their parting was a bit formal, and they failed to set another date.

21

SARAH WAS LOST, DRIFTING like a straw blowing in the wind—with no way to land. She seemed immune even to the touch of love. *When will it end? Can it end? Oh, saving grace, where are you?*

Sunday, after church and lunch, she fled to her room. Now, she stood beside her bed, cradling her violin, studying it sadly, pondering its place in her life from that moment on. She turned it around and cuddled it closer to her chest. She was beginning to tremble. In a while, she gingerly placed it back on its shelf in her closet, while a lone tear glistened in her eye. "Good-bye, dear friend."

After dinner that evening, she apologized to her family and went straight to bed. The next morning, she was up early but skipped breakfast, much to the consternation of her aunt Gina. "I just want to get in an early morning walk before it gets too hot," she explained as she headed for the front door.

Sarah kept close to the timberline, trusting Kevin would be unable to spot her if he was out. Though he was in her heart and would forever remain so, she needed some private time to meditate outside the bland confines of her room. In a while, she was far down the countryside, well out of sight of Kevin's house. At that point, she strayed into the meadow, expecting to find the bliss it had always held for her, hoping to pick up some healing from its wonder and the glory of the day itself.

The day had broken with the best that days ever have, early

summer's Sunday best—cool, quiet, and clear, with a gentle breeze blending it all. It was a day perfectly tuned for peace of mind. Sarah stood immobile and closed her eyes, hoping the splendor would wash through her. She forced herself to sway lazily, submitting to the glory and wonder of it all, offering it every opportunity to penetrate her gloomy, defeated mentality. It wasn't working. She felt as though she were standing somewhere high above, looking down on herself, worrying about how she fit into that unblemished picture, what her role was in the world. She had the consuming sense that she was standing on the edge of life itself. She shook her head and trudged on out of the meadow. It didn't work.

The next morning, Sarah conceded to having breakfast so as not to antagonize her aunt. When finished, she scooted briskly away from the table and hurried through the dish-washing routine, while her aunt was getting ready to head for work. Active as she was, she was still growing nervous and struggling a little for breath. Suddenly, she rushed outside with her violin and set it on the swing. She paused for a moment, pondering its meaning in her world, and then skipped into the meadow, hoping Kevin would be in his spot. He was.

Kevin came running. When he got to her, they embraced, but Sarah couldn't help but grimace. She hoped Kevin hadn't noticed. But she felt almost insulted, because it seemed to be just a procedural embrace for him. Nevertheless, she smiled at him and he smiled back pleasantly, again seemingly matter-of-fact.

They stood in place, glaring at each other. Sarah was shocked by this sudden turn in Kevin's behavior. It was so uncharacteristic of him not to show some initiative. In a few moments, she asked him to join her on the porch swing. She could tell by his countenance that he had decided her state of mind hadn't improved. So they just let the swing rock them for a while. Finally, Sarah stopped the swing, twisted around to look directly at Kevin, and began to speak.

"Kevin, if something should ever happen to me, I would

want you to have my violin. Will you take it?" She chuckled modestly and added, "Maybe you could learn to play it."

Kevin looked stunned; he just stared at the violin, frowning and shaking his head. He said nothing for a few moments. Finally, he spoke. "What do you mean, if something should ever happen to you?"

"Oh, you know, we all meet with unexpected developments in our lives, and since I'm not playing it anymore, someone should have it who might come to enjoy it."

"First of all, I'll gladly accept your violin if you feel absolutely compelled to give it away. But I must have you know, Sarah, I don't like seeing you give it up, and I'm still baffled that you spoke about something that might happen to you."

"I see." She said no more.

"Sweetheart, you never play your violin anymore, and I think I know why."

Without a word and trying to look a little winsome, Sarah tilted her head, indicating she was waiting for him to explain. She said nothing.

"My Sarah, you don't play anymore because you don't have a song in your heart."

"Well, you know what they say, 'All good things must come to an end.'"

He nodded.

"So whatever. Will you just take the violin—please, Kevin?"

"Of course, I already said I would, but let's get back to your comment about something maybe happening to you."

"There's really nothing else to say on that. It was just an offhand comment to introduce my request for you to take the violin. Do you understand, Kevin? There's no big deal about that. You're making too much of it."

"I am not making too much of it. It just worried me; that's all."

"Why?"

"Because I love you."

Sarah laid her violin aside and then leaned over and pressed herself against him affectionately. In a moment, she pulled back and wrapped her arms around him. When they released, she said, "I should be so lucky."

Kevin placed a hand behind her head, pulled it gently toward him, and kissed her. Sarah accepted it with unbridled love and passion. At once, she squirmed out of the swing and then knelt before him and meekly placed the violin in his lap. She patted it one last time.

"I'm the one who should be kneeling," said Kevin as he fondly caressed the sides of the instrument. Suddenly, he sucked in a deep, fluttering breath and, faltering somewhat, pressed on. "We both know what this means."

"Oh?"

"The dance is over. Gone."

Kevin decided to sound out his landlord on a critical matter simmering in his mind *and* his heart.

"Gro, what I'm gonna talk about now is top secret. Okay?"

"You got it. I'll not breathe a word of it," growled Grover Geesling in his low, raspy voice.

"Well, the thing is … I need your wisdom, and I mean yours particularly."

"How flattering."

"It's true. Anyway, my Sarah has become the love of my life, and I care about her … more than anything else in the world."

"Lucky for her."

"Thanks. But we have a problem. Gro, Sarah is in a bad way. I mean, a bad, bad way, and I have to find a way to do something about it. It's so heartbreaking to see her suffering like she is, this sweet, innocent little angel. You know that she's been through three traumatic court proceedings, and, of course, you know what started all that."

"Yeah, I know generally, based on what you and the Evanses have told me. I agree with you that no one should ever have to suffer all the agony she's been through. What are you thinking?"

"All right, she's sick; let's face it. That's it in a nutshell. She is so bewildered and demoralized that she has essentially quit living; that is, she isn't responding to life at all. She is no longer Sarah. Gro, the simple fact is that she is in a *deep* depression. I'm even worried that she might have bipolar. Now I haven't mentioned any of this to her, but I want her to see a doctor. She needs help, and no one in her life is qualified to help her with what she really needs."

"You're right, Kevin, my boy, but keep this in mind, not just any doctor will provide the right kind of help. Some, especially highly specialized physicians, won't have the foggiest idea what to do. So your major job is to locate the right one."

"Okay, I understand that; what kind do you think she needs?"

"No question about it; she has to see a psychiatrist."

"I don't know … I think they just talk to you and ask a lot of questions and say 'Hmm' while they take notes."

"No, no. Psychiatrists are medical doctors. They do everything."

"Great. Clearly, that's what we have to shoot for. Now, there is another problem, maybe more serious than the first one."

"And that is?"

"I'm not the one who has half a chance to motivate or direct Sarah to see a psychiatrist. If I approach that subject with her, she'll reject me out of hand. Somehow, I have to get someone in her family to take that initiative."

"On that point, Kevin—and, by the way, I agree with you—the Evanses are not the ones. Even though they are very close to her and love her as if she were their own, they would not carry the weight to convince the girl. There is only one person who qualifies for this role, and that's her father. Do you know him very well?"

"Somewhat. I've visited with him on a couple of occasions."

"Then he's your man. And, Kevin, soon! Do you hear? Soon!"

"I'm on it. I'm glad I came to you, my good buddy. Your counsel is indeed very wise."

"Probably because it makes sense to *you*," squawked Grover, laughing and slapping his knee.

"Just one thing," began Kevin, "what persuades you to have the father rather than the mother—or both of them—take on this task?"

"The father-daughter relationship has the most leverage in this situation. The mother-daughter connection may be too judgmental or even too aggressive. Most daughters see old dad as the parent who is more out in the world and the one who will steer them right in critical matters. This may not be true, but many of them see it that way. Keep in mind, now, you don't want to leave Mom out of it, but Dad is probably the focal point."

"I'll call her dad right away. Thank you so much, my good, good buddy."

With that, Kevin decided he would indeed call Ed Lock, but first, he would sound out Sarah in a disguised way.

A couple of days later, Kevin and Sarah were having lunch at the Meadowlark. There was very little interaction between them. They were just together, for whatever that might mean. From time to time, they would glance at each other and flick a perfunctory grin and go back to eating. In time, Sarah paused and raised her eyebrows as she stared at Kevin.

"Kevin, something's on your mind."

To him, it seemed indicative that she had made a statement instead of asking a question. He decided to patronize the statement rather than get defensive.

"Glad you noticed. Very astute of you, sweetheart. The fact is that I have indeed been pondering your situation, wondering what you might be planning in your ... let's say, *rehabilitation*."

"I don't know what you're talking about."

"Your outlook on life, regaining the old Sarah. I know you're unhappy, as well you should be, for you've been through so much."

"I'm okay with everything."

"But you're so down."

"Down?"

"Okay, how do you see yourself right now?"

"I know what you're driving at. Yes, Kevin, I'm depressed, and I know it. Just gotta give it some time. Okay already?"

"Okay, okay. Just wondering if you could ... ah ... could use some help. What do you think?"

"Do we have to talk about this at lunch? This is a very private subject. I think it's thoughtless of you to bring it up in here."

"Sarah, darling, there's nobody within earshot of us. If there were, I wouldn't bring up anything like this. I'm sorry. Besides, you know this started when you said I had something on my mind."

"You still don't get it; we *are* trying to enjoy lunch, you know. After all, that's the essential reason for coming here."

"It's also to be together, but I'm sorry, darling, I shouldn't be adding to your burden. Please forgive me?"

"Burden?"

"Excuse me—challenge."

On that note, it seemed that Sarah had decided to hold her peace and think for a few moments. After a while, she looked at Kevin and then dropped her eyes again. Kevin looked at her sympathetically without a word. The thin little smile she finally gave him had no spirit in it. Ultimately, she quit eating altogether, laid down her fork, and started to speak.

"Kevin, it just occurred to me that I'm being pretty hard on you, and I guess that proves your point. If I weren't burdened, little trivia like we're talking about wouldn't matter. I realize that your questions mean you care, and you're right; I *am* depressed. Another day, we'll talk about it, maybe in depth, because there are some realities about my life that I need to read you in on. For now, my Kevin, I want you to know I *do* love you." With that, they ended their date pleasantly and pledged to meet again.

The next day, Kevin called Sarah's dad and asked if he could visit for just a little while. That evening, he drove to the home of Denise and Ed Lock in Dallas. En route, he had decided it would be inappropriate to try to isolate Sarah's mom from the discussion and so met with both of them together. Even so, he directed most of his questions and concerns to Dad Lock.

"Thanks for having me, y'all. First of all, Mr. Lock—"

"Call me Ed."

"Thanks, Ed. First of all, by way of this visit, I'm actually doing something behind Sarah's back. If she finds out about this, she'll hate me. But I can't be worried about that. If it takes her hating me to help her, I'll gladly take the risk."

Denise Lock responded instantly. "She won't hate you, Kevin. She may take offense, but she loves you—that, Ed and I are convinced of—and she will never hate you. And, be assured, we will be discreet; you have our promise on that. Right, Ed?"

Ed nodded. "So what's up, Kevin?"

"Sarah is ill. Okay, so far?"

"You're right," said her mom. "We sense that very keenly, but I'm sure you know more about that than we do because you're around her pretty much every day, I think."

"Pretty much," said Kevin, turning to speak directly to her dad again. "Ed, she's in a deep depression—in my opinion, that is. She's beyond being demoralized; she's still in a trauma. She seems to be terrified by the process of living."

"Oh, oh, oh!" cried her mom. "Oh no. Kevin, we have to do something. Please, Ed, Kevin, we have to get going on this. Oh no."

She bowed her head and began to weep.

"Agree," chimed her dad, trying to appear calm.

To Kevin, it appeared that Mom Lock was coming forth as the stronger force in this grave matter, contrary to the advice of one Grover Geesling. So he looked from one to the other as he continued to talk. *After all, Grover, this is really a family matter.*

"Here's the really scary part, y'all; I have a very compelling sense that Sarah is giving up. She's beginning to say and do little things that signal strong cynicism about life itself. Y'all, listen to this: she has essentially kissed her violin good-bye. Please, I'm telling you some highly personal things about her ..." Now, Kevin was blotting tears. "Personal to her, I mean. But I have to reveal all this because I know you want to know."

Mom Lock jumped up and began pacing the floor. "We have to get a doctor, and she's going to resist with all the might she can muster."

Ed Lock pushed up and went to his wife. He put his arm around her and tried to comfort her. "Sweetheart," he began, "I will talk to Sarah early in the morning. I don't know how much we can do by phone, but as you say, we have to get going on this. I realize it's going to be her will against mine, but—you know our Sarah—she will ultimately concede if we just don't let up."

Denise was nodding as he talked, and then she turned to Kevin. "We will hold this in complete confidence, but Sarah is a smart girl; at some point, she'll figure it all out, and, Kevin, I'm honestly afraid you'll be exposed, strictly on her intuition."

"No problem; I'll gladly accept whatever she has if it'll help her."

"I wonder if Dr. Debosky can help her on this?" said Ed. "I can always get in with him right away."

"Is he a psychiatrist?" asked Kevin.

Before Ed could say anything, Denise stepped up to Kevin and laid a hand on his shoulder. "Kevin, was that a leading question? If so, it's a good one. Right, Ed? Let's face it; Sarah's problem is mental or should I say emotional? So she needs a psychiatrist."

"No question about that," said Ed. "I'll find a good one. At least, Dr. Debosky can give me some referrals. He won't be offended by that; he's very savvy. I'll start that process even before I talk to Sarah. Let's see ... I'll wait till tomorrow afternoon to get with her."

Sarah resolved to skip a day or two before returning to the meadow. The decision was easy to make, but she had failed to consider the consequences. She had not predicted the melancholy that would set in. Now, she sat on the side of her bed, picking at her fingers and wrestling with her feelings. Then the phone rang.

"Hello."

"Hey, punkin," came the voice of her dad. "We need to talk. Can Mom and I come out tonight?"

"Fine, Dad, anytime. What do you want to talk about?"

"Well, sweetheart, we're concerned that you haven't been in touch and we suspect that's because you're still down in spirits."

"Dad, you didn't answer the question."

"Well, don't you want to wait until we're all together and get the whole thing at that time, rather than having to worry about it for the time being?"

"I smell a rat."

"Okay, Sarah, the fact is that it's clear to us that you are not coming out of the depression that set in after ... well, you know."

"I don't want to talk about any of that."

"We *will* talk about it, period! Sarah, whether you want to admit it or not, you need some help. That's pretty blunt, but that's going to be the way it is until we get you some help, and let's face it, none of us is qualified to help you."

"Thanks a lot, Kevin."

"Say what?"

"Kevin's behind this; I know he is."

"Only that he cares about you and asked me to help him help you."

"So what do you have in mind?"

"Sarah, the way we're going, we might as well talk about this now. I didn't want to do this by phone, but it looks like we're doing it anyway."

"You want me to see a doctor, don't you? And yes, let's settle this right now; we don't need a meeting to do this."

"Right you are. The point is not what *we* want; the point is that you *need* a doctor's help."

"Daddy, seeing a doctor right now would do nothing but add to the trauma in my life. The answer is no."

"The right kind of doctor will not add any trauma or other adverse reactions. The right kind of doctor will know what you're facing and will be sensitive to that."

"Right kind of doctor. Uh-*huh*. So what are you thinking?"

"You need to see a psychiatrist."

"Oh, no you don't. I know what that kind of doctor will do. I know exactly what he'll do. He'll ask me lots of questions. Well, dear Dad, I'm tired of answering questions by so-called authoritative figures."

"No, sweetheart; a psychiatrist will examine you completely. And, my dear, it doesn't have to be a 'he.' How about we find a woman doctor?"

"You're assuming I agree with this, which I don't. Not only that, no matter what they figure out, what can they do about it?"

"They can give you new ways to look at your situation, get you out of your mental rut, so to speak, tell you how to rally your resources. Also, they can prescribe some medication for anxiety."

"Come, Dad; have a heart. You're sure putting it brusquely. How can you be so demanding like this?"

"I'm your dad, sweetheart ... and besides that, you know I *am* paying your bills, which as you can imagine, are pretty enormous at this point."

Ouch! Sarah was rapidly becoming infuriated with her dad even though she knew he was right. She held the phone down to her chest and tried to think of a way to counter his proposal. She couldn't understand why he and Kevin had to torture her so mercilessly. They had always said they loved her; why couldn't they see how cruel it would be to put her through another round of agony? *Is that love?* At once, something hit her like a slap from behind. It was a word—a word her dad had used. He had said something about *medication*. Initially, that word had just slipped past her; at this moment, it was taking on meaning. She was still thinking about that when her ever-patient father suddenly became impatient.

"Hello-hello?" he said. "Sarah, are you there?"

"I'm sorry, Dad. Yes, I'm here. I just took some time to try to think through all you were saying, and I decided that I was being too stubborn."

"Hey, that sounds promising. So may I get the doctor?"

"Okay, Dad, reluctantly, I guess I'll have to agree."

22

SARAH WAS THE ONLY one in the waiting room of Dr. Elouise Romain, psychiatrist. Her dad had dropped her off and gone to work. She was to call him when they finished. She wondered why there weren't more people in the room. Was the doctor not in demand? Wasn't she good enough to attract more patients? Then, it dawned on her that psychiatrists dealt extensively with one patient at a time, holding forth lengthy, dedicated interviews, unlike other doctors, who were able to schedule a lot of patients for the same general time frame and scatter them out to wait in tiny rooms, containing weight scales and exam tables and walls papered with copies of their credentials and brightly colored, explicit diagrams of entrails and clogged arteries.

She was actually quite satisfied with the situation, now that she had argued it out in her mind—except for one thing. On the wall directly in front of her was a big-screen television monitor featuring scenes from the animal world, a sort of running story of life in the wild. Presumably, this subject matter was supposed to help nervous patients relax. The fact was that the life depicted in these scenes of animals grousing in the woods and grasslands was mainly violent. She shuddered as she watched panic-stricken creatures running for their lives, driven by raging forest fires; a cougar and a jaguar fighting it out to the death; alligators biting off the heads of prairie dogs; and a bobcat chasing down a young deer, forcing it into a river and leaving it there to drown. *This is about as relaxing as a traffic jam.*

Mercifully, Sarah was saved from a complete nervous breakdown by the plastic voice of a nurse, inviting her to the back chamber. "The doctor will see you now, Miss Lock."

After the nurse weighed her, measured her, took her temperature, and checked her blood pressure, she directed Sarah to sit in one of two plush chairs located a little distance apart and angled so that they somewhat faced each other—but not directly. The room was very nearly as bland as her bedroom back home, essentially void of accouterments of any kind. Soon, the nurse spoke kindly and left the room.

In a few moments, the doctor walked in, smiling. She was a petite, very alert-looking woman, probably in her early sixties, with short, loosely combed, straight hair, which was completely gray. "Elouise Romain," said the woman politely as Sarah rose for the dutiful greeting.

"I'm Sarah Grace Lock, and thank you for taking me."

In the short span of the time it took them to sit down, Sarah mulled over how she should perform, whether to take a role that disguised her depression or perhaps minimized it or just avoid all pretense of any degree. Surely she didn't want to come across as so depressed that she needed to be hospitalized. At the same time, she wanted to be troubled enough to qualify for the medication. She finally decided that she would stay in the middle, with emphasis on just being herself. As they got situated, Dr. Romain responded to Sarah's comment.

"You're welcome; it's a pleasure to have you as a patient. Thank you for choosing me."

"You're sure welcome." Sarah chuckled and added, "So I guess we're off and running." *Oops, that didn't sound very depressed. I shouldn't have laughed.*

The doctor shifted her notepad over her lap and continued, "Right you are. We're going to spend a little while together, going over things very personal to you. As you might expect, I have a good number of questions; however, you don't have to wait for a question on a particular subject if there's something you want me to know. So just jump in anytime you want to mention something you think is relevant, and feel free to develop your answers as fully as you want to. This is all about you. Woohoo, right?" With that, she laughed, obviously trying to be a little animated. It was clear to Sarah that she was genuinely trying to help her relax. "Anyway," the doctor continued, "I want you to be fully at ease with the whole process. So please, stop me anytime you are not comfortable with a question or any trend in our conversation."

"I understand," said Sarah, "and thank you for explaining all of that. It helps a lot, because I don't know a thing about these procedures."

"Good. Okay, here we go. Tell me, are you here of your own free will?"

"Yes ... definitely, but honestly, my parents did urge me quiet sternly."

"What does that mean to you?"

"It means they think I'm depressed."

"What do *you* think?"

"I guess I *am* somewhat, simply because I've been through a series of traumatic events. Still, I accept all that's happened, and personally, I think I'm getting along with life quite well. Sure, I'm anxious, but it doesn't seem to restrict me." *You're talking too much, Sarah.*

"Do you want to talk about those traumatic events you mentioned?"

"Well, sure, I *can*." Thereupon, Sarah outlined the whole messy story, minus a few highly personal details, such as the specific form of physical abuse that was inflicted on her.

"Okay, okay. Is there anything else you want me to know about that matter?"

"No, not really."

"How do you feel about all that?"

"It sucks."

Dr. Romain laughed heartily. "Probably not a better way to

put it," she said. "Anything else you want to say on the traumatic times you've been through?"

"Not really. Honestly, I think that covers it."

"All right, tell me, what's a typical day like in your life right now?"

"I have been sleeping a lot lately; otherwise, I help with housework where I'm staying, with my aunt and uncle. I also spend a few hours a week with my boyfriend." She paused to smile. "Oh, and I indulge in nature some, you know, walk in the woods and play in the meadow, that sort of thing, and ... I guess that's about it." She had already decided that she deliberately would not rehash the retarded-label issue. Her mother had asked to be forgiven, and Sarah and forgiven her. That jazz was history.

"Tell me, Sarah, what's important to you in your life?"

"Right now, it's getting through this interview." They both laughed, and then Sarah held up a finger and explained, "Seriously, the most important thing to me is to lead a full life and in the course of it, give something back to life."

"Thank you, Sarah. What else is going on in your life?"

"Nothing, really; I just take one day at a time."

"Hmm." The psychiatrist continued to look at Sarah; finally, she pushed up her glasses, crossed her legs, and then cleared her throat. It seemed to Sarah that all this body language was a signal that the woman was not especially satisfied with her last answers. Picking up on that possible clue, she decided to try a short clarification to see if that worked.

"I'm generally satisfied with my situation," said Sarah, this time with some enthusiasm.

That seemed to motivate her interviewer. She scratched her forehead and continued with a little more vigor. "Do you get angry?"

"Not much."

"Not much?"

"Only if someone goes against my wishes."

"Want to expand on that?"

"No."

"Sarah, have you ever considered suicide?"

"I can't picture me doing that."

"But have you ever considered it?"

"I just can't picture me doing that."

Now, the two just sat quietly, sweating each other out. After a noticeably long period of silence, the interview slogged on in the same manner, with the two reaching the point at which they were very nearly like competitors. Sarah was getting weary of the endless chain of nondirective questions, with no indication from the therapist concerning what anything meant. Finally, it ended.

"Sarah, you were great. Don't give up; you're going to get it done," said Dr. Romain.

"Get *what* done?"

"Living. You've got the tickets, as they say."

"Is that all?"

"Yes; we pretty well covered everything about your situation—how you see it and how you feel about it. As I said, you were great. I'll call your dad and tell him essentially that."

"Aren't you going to tell me what I ought to do?"

"You don't have a lot of changes to make. Clearly, it will take time for you to be fully restored, but you've already made progress. That's the really promising point. Be yourself. Otherwise, here's a little trick that often helps: change up your daily routine—sleep later or get up earlier, find new projects, interact with people, spend either more or less time with your boyfriend, order something different in the restaurant at times ... You know, just change it up; get a new pattern to your life. By the way, the healthiest, most genuine smile I saw on your face during our entire meeting was when you mentioned your boyfriend."

"Maybe I ought to tell that to Kevin. He could use a boost, considering all that he's had to put up with from my antics."

"Sure; let him know how you feel about him. Romance is

not a tactical game. Be honest. If you love him, say so." Now, they were standing, and the doctor was leading her toward the door.

"Dr. Romain, I *do* get pretty anxious during the course of a day. Can you prescribe me something for that?"

"Sure. Glad you brought it up."

The ride back to the Evans home with Dad Lock was very low-key. Actually, based on her less-than-scintillating interview with the doctor, Sarah had very little to report. However, they did pick up her prescription en route, and this caused a brief exchange of viewpoints concerning the dangers of medication. In that context, her dad warned, "Be sure to take it exactly as it's written on the bottle; don't double up on any doses no matter how you feel!"

Later, Sarah sat in her bedroom, an open magazine resting in her lap, squeezing the little bottle of pills, pumping it up and down as though hoping it held some special promise. Momentarily, she got up and stashed it in a coat pocket in her closet. She went back to her magazine and attempted to get interested in it, to no avail. Then, she fell to thinking about Kevin and wanting to be with him.

Kevin and Sarah were not to meet until the next day when they hailed each other from their places in the meadow and then came to rest in the porch swing. They hugged, kissed, bantered a little, and then sat back, smiling and pretending to be relaxed.

"How'd it go with the doctor?" asked Kevin.

"Okay; it was actually kind of fun, matching wits with the doctor."

"Did she help you?"

"What do you mean?"

"Never mind."

"Well, you know, they can't help you on the spot. They just kind of try to redirect you and let you help yourself."

"So what's your overall impression?"

Sarah chuckled and chimed, "You sound like the doctor."

Kevin grinned and shrugged as if to say, "No more questions."

"Okay, Kevin, this is it: sure, the interview was interesting and thought provoking, maybe even a little fun, as I said, but as uplifting as it might have been for the moment, it changed nothing. I'm still whatever I was—*depressed*, as you all want to put it—and it's true; I'm still disillusioned with life. So that's where we are, okay? Now, could we get on to something else?"

Kevin's expression seemed to hint that he knew it was pointless to proceed any further with the matter of Sarah's condition. Possibly, he figured that to persist would only irritate her and produce nothing worthwhile. If, indeed, he was thinking along these lines, he was entirely right.

"Okay," he said. "Can we talk about the violin?"

"Let's."

"The thing is, I'm not sure lessons are gonna help me. See, I can't even get a tone on it. I tried to just stroke it with the bow—" At that instant, he was distracted by Sarah's sudden change in demeanor. He had hardly gotten started and already, she was holding her sides and shaking with amusement. She knew at once the experience he was about to relate. But when Kevin suddenly stopped, she cleared her throat, straightened up, and said, "Do go on, my dear."

"So it just screeched. I tried it several times, and each time, it did it again, just gave out a shrill, scratchy kind of squeak. It was awful. No matter how I tried, I couldn't get an actual musical tone out of it."

"You will, sweetheart, you will. What you went through happens with all of us when we first pick up a violin. Don't be discouraged. Here's the thing: it's all in the bow, how it picks up the essence of the one holding it. That's what determines the tone. The sense of the player descends to the bow."

"So you're saying it's in my touch."

"Yes, but you'll learn. It's something that you have to feel out—and keep trying. Your teacher will help you with that."

"My teacher? Aren't you going to be my teacher?"

"Kevin, my dear, sweet Kevin, I'm afraid that is possibly an unfortunate segue. It forces an issue I've been afraid to broach with you—or anybody else, for that matter. But for now, can we go for a walk and try to drink from this beautiful countryside for a precious little while? Who knows? We may not get many more chances."

They set away, two confused lovers, uncertain of the future, unsure of each other and doubtful as to what life held for them, either as individuals or as a longed-for unit. It wasn't like old times. The bliss was gone. As they piddled along, Sarah was thinking that the good Dr. Romain would have her walk a different pathway other than this well-worn, familiar one.

"Would you like to go to our log, Kevin?"

"Sure."

When they arrived at the cove, they just stood in place for a while, as usual. Momentarily, they took up their regular positions on the old log, but they had difficulty getting any conversation going. Finally, Kevin groaned; pushed against the log, stiff-armed; and said, "I'm getting log butt; how about we sit on the ground in front of the log and lean back against it?"

Without answering, Sarah rose from the log and plopped down in front of it. Kevin sat down beside her, and they both started to lean back against the log. It worked.

"You know, this place has fond memories," said Kevin, grinning like a mischievous kid.

Sarah looked at him with dreamy eyes and nodded. "If I didn't know better, I'd think you were trying to seduce me, young man."

Soon, the laws of nature took over, and they left the log for a more private section of the cove. There, they just gave in to the mutual passion they were feeling for each other in spite of the ominous curse that seemed to envelop them. The power of sex trumped their misery. They became intimate as they had before, but this time, they didn't fall asleep in the leaves. Neither seemed hurried, and eventually, they dressed and returned to sit on the ground in front of their log.

Still, they didn't talk. After a while, Sarah turned her back to Kevin and then leaned into him, ultimately curling up there in his lap, resting her head against his chest. Kevin could feel her slow, deep breathing, and it worried him. In time, with her head still snuggled against his chest, Sarah murmured, "Kevin, why do you love me?"

"I wish I could tell you, darling." He paused, trying to measure her question and his answer. "My dear, beloved Sarah, my love for you just can't be translated into words. I guess the best I can say is that I love you because I *feel* you—in my heart. And that feeling, that unspeakable sensation, makes me glad to be alive in this world we share. I feel complete with you in my life. I just want you near—beside me."

Sarah let the matter lie there. Neither said a word for a while. Then she began to labor out of his lap. It appeared to be such a struggle for her. She seemed so heavy, so helpless. Kevin tried to help, but he was afraid he'd cause her to fall. Moreover, she seemed willfully determined to do it herself. When finally she managed to wriggle her way up, she dropped to the ground and leaned back against the log.

Kevin was startled as he looked into her face, stunned to the point that he was unable to restrain an instant, reflexive gasp. She looked terrible. He'd never seen her look so haggard at any time in their relationship. She looked so desperate, as though she'd been pulled from a lake seconds before she would have drowned. It startled him that her somber conversion had taken place in the short time she'd hidden her face against his body.

What could she have been thinking in that time? She'd only asked why he loved her.

They stared impassively at each other, wordless. Sarah was glad that Kevin didn't try to make her talk, and she didn't offer any comments. Now, she just looked around the cove, glassy-eyed, as if she were surveying it for the first time. Then, very suddenly, she stood up, wandered out to the trail, and turned toward its entrance in the meadow. Still, she spoke not a word.

As Kevin caught up, she noticed he slowed somewhat, possibly so as not to frighten her. They had just reached the meadow, and at that point, she stopped, still staring straight ahead. Then he eased on around her until they stood face-to-face. He held her bleary-eyed gaze, his lips drawn tight, and watched as her frown spread, wrinkling her brow. He stood erect, arms down at his sides, his gaze drifting back and forth from her face to somewhere out in space. They just hung in their tracks for a seeming eternity. Finally, it appeared that Kevin wanted to talk and get her to talk. But he had no chance to get that started. She couldn't talk at that moment because she was suffering too much emotionally to try to think how to say the things that were bothering her, namely that her life was in spoils.

Sarah didn't respond to Kevin's efforts to generate a conversation. At that moment, she felt useless and totally incapable of pulling herself out of her doldrums. She just stared past him, clearly dazed. His talking didn't seem to get through at all; it didn't penetrate. When he tried to hold her, she didn't resist. In fact, that seemed to be the only thing that registered with her at all. Time marched on, and nothing changed. It looked like Kevin was getting desperate, for now he was praying silently. Then something changed her mood, inexplicably, possibly with the right question.

"Sweetheart, would you like to go home and lie down for a while?" pleaded Kevin.

"Unh-uh. Sleeping is about all I've done lately." Her voice was so weak.

"May I do something for you or get you anything?"

She laid a hand on his shoulder and managed a tiny smile. "My dear Kevin, this is so unfair to you. Is it any wonder that I love you so much?" Now, her voice was picking up. "By the way—you'll like this—the doctor said my brightest smile during our entire interview was when you came up."

"That makes my day. You know, our love is mutual and complete."

"There's so much I wanted to tell you today, and the more I tried to begin, the more impossible it seemed that I ever could. Anyway, Kevin, what I have for you is … well, I guess a little brutal. The fact is that I am not giving anything to your life or anybody else's."

"I'm sorry, but I beg to differ with that. By just being yourself, you give something every day to all of us who are privileged to know you."

"No. Now, please, just listen. Really, I'm not adding anything to this world, and, my Kevin, I've come to realize that there is no such thing as life; there is only living. Here's the rub: I am not living. So just take a few moments and think about that."

Kevin was devastated and feeling totally inadequate. There were things that he could say that might have some positive effect, and there were other things that would only reinforce her fatalistic obsession. Unfortunately, he had no idea what would work. *What can I say? What will help, and what will hurt? I gotta face it; I have no idea.* Finally, he shuffled in place and again curled her into his arms. When he released her, she showed no emotion of any kind.

"Sarah, I'm not understanding any of this."

"I'm telling you, I'm useless! Pray tell, what would you have me do?"

"Run the race."

She seemed stumped with that shot and appeared to be pondering it. Finally, she lifted her head and said, "I'm afraid I've fallen too far behind."

"Run the race! You don't have to beat anybody—just run."

23

By this time, Kevin was scared witless. He was frantically trying to wrap up his meadows project with *Lands Alive* and completely free himself to concentrate on ways to help his troubled sweetheart. He felt that she was literally hysterical at this point. He could not just let it go. Sarah had to be the top priority in his life. He really cared about nothing else. By day's end, he had submitted the requisite last section of range photos to the magazine. *Okay, it's done,* he thought, sighing deeply.

Now, he decided it was high time for Sarah's entire support group to rally around her. With that, he resolved that, *somehow,* he absolutely had to talk to her aunt and uncle as well as her mom and dad. How? Getting a private audience with Mom and Dad was no problem, but how could he corner Kyle and Gina alone, away from Sarah? That was the big challenge. Until he could figure out how to tackle that one, he elected to call the Locks.

The next evening, Kevin was in the Lock living room, pleading his concern. "Sarah is getting worse. I'm sorry, y'all; she just is. She has drifted way out. For one thing, she doesn't believe she's needed. We've all told her that we love her and need to be loved by her. What can we do?"

Ed Lock jumped in immediately. "Kevin, wonderful friend, you've focused on exactly the right issue. I say this based on what the psychiatrist told me after their interview. She said that Sarah knew she was needed emotionally by those in her life, you know, such as giving all of us her love. But, said the doctor, that's not enough, because it's so subtle. She said Sarah needs to feel she's meeting some concrete needs in her world. On that point, the doctor said it would help if she had some kind of activity—some responsibilities—where she can feel she's making a tangible contribution."

"Like a job," blurted her mom.

"Right," said her dad, "She also indicated that some social interaction would help her conquer depression. She said Sarah is mostly a loner right now, which feeds depression. Also, a job would do other things for her psyche. That may well be the best medicine for her."

"So what's our best role in this thing?" asked her mom.

"Good question," began Kevin. "I just wonder, what are some things we can do on this issue? I guess it's clear to everyone that our Sarah has been in such a deep depression that she's not looking for a job, nor is she even interested in having one. Her depression is feeding on itself. It's like a baby crying; it hears itself crying and figures there must be a reason for crying, so it keeps on crying."

"Maybe I can help on this job issue," said Ed Lock. "Let me call Buford Crump to start with. He recently asked me if I knew of someone who might replace his pregnant receptionist. If that doesn't pan out, I'll make some other contacts. Thanks, Kevin, for that observation. I figure you know her situation better than any of us, because you're on the scene with her more than we are. Fortunately for all of us, you care about our little jewel, and please know that we are forever grateful."

Wiping away tears, Kevin said, "Thanks; caring for her is so easy. One thing I *can* do is give her transportation to look for a job. Our biggest obstacle is in trying to get her motivated. As I indicated, she's not even interested in living right now. This is really serious, y'all; I can't stress that enough."

"You've convinced us that it is," said her mom. "For one thing, I think Dad and I have to indulge her more. The only thing is we can't afford to overdo it, because she'll suspect it's all contrived and not genuine. You think of anything else, Kevin?"

"I'd like to speak to the Evanses about this, but Sarah is always there, so it'll be hard to find some private time with them."

"We'll talk to them," said her mom, "and we can begin with a phone call before Sarah gets up in the morning. Gina says she sleeps very late. Anyway, that's a good idea, Kevin. Anything else?"

"Just a couple of concerns. For one, it worries me that she may be bipolar, but I'm not an authority on that. As to the other point, this is something I touched on once before. Remember, I mentioned that she was saying things that sounded dangerously like she was not really interested in living? Well, that tendency has become stronger and more direct since her meeting with the doctor. Let me just be blunt about it: I'm frightened that she's entertaining the notion of suicide. I don't mean to be an alarmist about this, but we can't casually dismiss that possibility."

"So we have to mobilize immediately," declared Ed.

The next evening, Kevin walked down to the blue house.

"She's sleeping," said Kyle.

"Already?"

"Still. Not already—all day. She dragged in here for about three bites of dinner and then moped on back to her bed. I don't know if she ate any lunch."

Gina said, "Kevin, Denise called and told us of your visit. I'm so glad you confronted them with the reality of Sarah's state of mind. They really needed to hear that."

"What are we gonna do?" asked Kevin.

"For one thing, we have to keep her awake long enough to talk to her."

Kevin's worry had taken him to the point where he wasn't functioning normally. He couldn't remember lifelong routines, stumbled over things he didn't notice because he was rambling around in a daze, and in general, was simply not tuned in. He was also a little miffed that Sarah's family hadn't already taken some really positive steps to help her. With that thought, he chastised himself for being critical, for he really hadn't accomplished anything either. One thing he *could* do was shake himself out of his own maudlin stupor and get creative. He needed to quit concentrating on *his* anguish and put himself inside Sarah—try to feel what she must feel. He decided he would get an appointment with Sarah's psychiatrist to discuss her lack of progress or persuade her dad to do so. Meanwhile, he would visit the Evanses every day to check on Sarah.

On his next visit, he found her again swaddled in daytime sleep. This time, she didn't wake up, and he didn't try to rouse her. He just stood quietly and looked at her for a few moments, praying silently. She had thrown her covers off and drawn her knees up to her chest. Kevin shook his head as sadness welled inside. She looked as though she had just crumbled into a little bundle of pain. In that gripping moment, he yearned to take her into his arms and dream them both into eternity.

Later, Gina told him there had been no change of any kind, except for one "tiny little relief scene," as she called it. "Kevin, last night—it must have been a little after midnight—I heard some racket in the house and got up to check it out." She laughed and continued, "Well, when I walked in the dining room, there sat Sarah chewing on a sandwich, with her elbows resting on the table. I mean, there she was, just propped on the table, nonchalantly mauling a sandwich."

"I'm inclined to say that's good—I mean at least it's different; it's not *sleeping*. But most promising of all, Aunt Gina, it's a positive sign of her trying to live."

"Touché. Now, I don't want to sound negative, but there is

just one thing on the downside. When she glanced up at me, she put on a big, big smile. Okay so far, but, Kevin, it was not a normal smile; it looked downright silly, goofy looking."

"Hmm. You're right; that's a little disturbing, but it's kind of in character for her, considering her new self. Perhaps she was just embarrassed at getting caught."

"Maybe. Anyway, I'm going to be with her every day. I'm taking a week's vacation beginning today."

"Bless you, Aunt Gina. That's probably the most positive thing any of us have done toward helping her objectively. If it's okay, I'll see you tomorrow. Do you need me to get any groceries or anything for you since you're kind of homebound at this point?"

"No, thanks; we're pretty well stocked up. Do come back tomorrow though."

The next day produced nothing new. Although Sarah did come forth a little more, she essentially slept the day away. Fortunately, she was up when a call came in from Buford Crump. Reportedly, she almost fainted when Gina held the phone out toward her and announced the caller. Then she recovered quickly and said something like, "What the heck? Nothing matters now," and she took the call. Gina said she didn't hang around, so she didn't know what they talked about.

On the third day, Kevin's landlord got a frantic call from Gina Evans. She was yelling, "Sarah's missing!"

Kevin shot out of the house like a rocket and ran toward the Evans place at a dead run. As he passed a hysterical Gina, he shouted over his shoulder, "Check out the country lane, and call the Meadowlark; I've got the woods covered."

He rushed on. When he reached the woodland trail, he spun into it and charged ahead. His target destination was the old barn, but he glanced at the cove as he lurched ahead. Suddenly, he skidded to a dead stop, almost falling on his face, instinctively flailing his arms to restore his balance. Then, he backtracked a few steps to the cove. There, on the old fungus-covered log, sat Sarah, calmly musing at the situation. Kevin was reeling and panting so hard he could utter not a word.

"Hi, Kevin."

"My goodness, Sarah, what's going on?" wheezed Kevin as he pounded his chest.

"Oh, Kevin, you're so exhausted. Please sit down, darling. Here, sit beside me," she pleaded, patting a spot on the log close to her. When he was seated, still trying to catch his breath, she asked, "So what's all the commotion about anyway?"

"Just got a frantic call from your aunt Gina that you were missing."

"Well, dear me, what's so alarming about somebody going out for a walk?"

"Because it was five o'clock in the morning, and this is way unlikely for somebody who's been sleeping till noon every day."

"I'm so sorry. I just ... I wanted to see what the air was like at that time of day."

"It's okay, sweetheart; it's that we're all on edge right now because of what you're going through."

"Oh." She turned away, and as she moved her hand across her legs, she noticed Kevin staring dumbfounded at the bottle of pills lying in her lap. She dropped her chin and stared at him wide-eyed, as if to say, 'You got a problem with that?"

"What are you doing with those?"

"These are my depression pills. I never know when I might need them ... ah, but hold it at that for right now! I'll have more on that issue later."

"If you say so," grumbled Kevin. "Meanwhile, we need to get word to Gina that you're okay before she has a heart attack."

"Okay, Kevin, let's go to the porch."

As they walked back toward the house, Kevin had trouble

setting a brisk pace because Sarah lagged. When they were near the house, they spotted Gina rushing toward them. As she drew near, she opened her arms wide and, in a few more steps, embraced Sarah and held on for several moments. Then, the three tarried in place for a while as Sarah explained her behavior to an obviously skeptical aunt. Then they all proceeded on toward the house.

At the porch, Sarah suggested, "Let's all sit out here and relax for a while. Huh?"

"You two go ahead and get started," said a breathless Gina. "I'll join you in a few minutes after I get some laundry going."

Kevin and Sarah swung for a bit, holding their legs out straight, looking at their feet as if they expected some divine inspiration from them. Then Sarah stopped the swing and started to speak.

"Okay, Kevin, it's time for some serious talk—round two!" She giggled. "Seriously, you know we talked about life and living one time and what the purpose is and all that philosophical stuff. Well, Kevin, my love," she said and began to sob, "my problem is real; it's not philosophical. The fact is that I am not giving anything to this world; it doesn't need me. All I'm doing is complicating the lives of others. Look at *us*; I'm just making your life miserable ..."

"That's just simply not true, Sarah. Sorry if that sounds brutally blunt. The point is that I'm alive when I'm with you. I'm not miserable. Love doesn't work the way you say. I *need* you. If I didn't have you, I wouldn't care about anything. I wouldn't have anything to care about. And as far as the world is concerned, we can't really ever know what we're giving, because there's no one out there, applauding and waving a flag ... and ... and saying, 'Thanks.'"

"I don't agree. But, Kevin, please know this: I care about you, more than anything, but sometimes, you can't have what you care about. Now listen to me, I'm sorry to have to say this, but I'm not really living. Maybe I don't have the will—I don't know. Look at me now—most of my living is sleeping."

"I think you're right about your will. I think you can will yourself to live just as you've willed yourself to sleep. Please, Sarah, please. Give us something to do! Don't be so pessimistic. There is always help. Are you telling me you don't want help?"

"I don't agree that it reduces itself to that question. Think of my history: first, I let a mindless label cripple my life, then a mad beating plunged me into total panic, then three stupid legal battles just threw me down. I'm just not up to the cause."

"It's not the events, Sarah; it's your reaction to them."

"What the heck are you talking about?"

"The beating you referred to, is that the vicious hit you took from that lunatic on your wedding night?"

"Right."

"Your therapist says it wasn't the hit that got you but rather the run."

"What are you doing talking to my doctor?"

"She talked to your dad. We just wanted to find out what our role is."

"So is she saying that running away caused my depression?"

"She's saying that was a large part of it, because that was your reaction to the trauma. She also said the pills might help you with your mood, but since they're systemic, it takes a while for them to work. So I hope you're taking them regularly."

Sarah was stunned by that revelation for two reasons, for one, because Kevin was nosing around getting into private matters and for another, because she was counting on the pills to put an abrupt end to it all. She wondered if Kevin was trying to set a trap for her, sneaking around the way he did. She would just have to be cautious and keep her eye on him. *As to the pills, I know how I can make them work.* She smiled and lifted her head to Kevin.

"Don't worry; they're in my system." *He doesn't have to*

know that I haven't taken a one of them, because it's just none of his business. "What else did you find out from the good doctor? I mean, let me have it all, so we can be on even footing here."

"That's about it. Oh, she did say that a jolt sometimes shakes a person out of depression."

"A jolt. Woohoo, a jolt. How promising," she sneered. "So, Professor, what's a jolt? I mean, will just any old jolt work?"

"You know, a shock, unexpected event, a blow to the head. I guess anything that jars your senses. You know, jolt!"

Sarah sat quietly at this point, contemplating this turn of events. *A jolt. If I could come up with a good jolt and practice acting normal, maybe this crew would all leave me alone. Hmmm, a jolt, indeed.*

After a while, Kevin cleared his throat and said, "But anyway, sweetie, at least we're talking. Praise God for that. Let's not ever quit talking."

"I don't think that's the saving grace here. Anyway, Kevin, all I know is that I can't live like this. I'm ready to give it up." At that, she broke down crying. When Kevin reached for her, she wiggled away.

By this point, Kevin was woefully aware that words wouldn't help his sweetheart in her highly emotional condition. She was not open to reason, which begged the question, how could he impact her emotionally? Could he pitch a fit? Could he break down crying with her? Kevin was shaking his head as he thought, *She'd probably figure out a way to intellectualize anything I do.* "Please, dear God," he begged aloud.

In time, Sarah straightened up, rubbing her eyes and looking halfway composed. Then, Gina came to the porch and pulled up a chair. "What are you guys talking about?"

Kevin lifted his eyes toward Sarah. "Life," she said finally.

"Awesome subject," said Gina.

Not much of any consequence followed Sarah's evasive

comment. However, the three tried to make it a social situation. Still, nothing seemed to have any power to lift Sarah from her pessimism. In a while, she yawned and said, "Think I'll go get some rest."

That same day, Kevin called Ed Lock and briefed him on the events of the morning. Dad Lock said Gina hadn't called him until after the crisis was over. When Kevin insisted that Sarah simply had to be hospitalized, he totally agreed and said he would personally get it done. He also said that he and her mom were already planning to come out and talk to their daughter and her aunt and uncle the next evening after dinner.

On the day in question, Kevin decided to start it out by checking on Sarah, as he had done regularly for at least a week. It was ten o'clock in the morning when he arrived at the house. Gina told him she was sleeping. She herself had lunch underway on the stove and was resting in the living room, reading a magazine.

"Do you think she'd object if I peeped in on her?" asked Kevin.

"Kevin, I really don't think it matters if she *does* object. It's time we all got a little more forceful with her. She's failing rapidly."

"Okay, I'll reverse my approach and start to push her a little. She's gonna resent it, but as you say, at this point, we simply have to take that chance. So, ah, okay, I'll ease into her room and take it from there."

"Good idea," said Gina. "I'll check on her just to make sure she's presentable." She was back in seconds, nodding. "You're good to go, Kevin. She's sleeping on her side, facing the far wall. Good luck!"

Kevin slowly opened the door and tiptoed toward Sarah's bed.

24

KEVIN STARED DOWN AT his little fallen ballerina, pitched in darkness, oblivious to life, so broken—just a little bundle of heartache. He wondered what treasures it would take to buy her freedom. Where was the enemy that he might beat on him? The way it was, there was nothing to grasp, to get a grip on. Sarah's submission was in charge. *We can't let that be; we have to take over!*

It was crushing to look on the one he loved with all his heart and mind—one so innocent, so capable, so accepting—and to realize her dream was empty—the song was ended. And there was little hope for getting it back, because she had clearly surrendered to the menacing forces that had hovered around her from the beginning. At first, she had danced in the delightful meadow and played her music, and it all worked, but the powers of evil had swelled to the point where nothing helped anymore.

Even though her spirit had given in, Kevin could still see, deep inside his little jewel, that captivating wonder, that fascinating glow, that he saw on the first day he watched her twirling in the meadow. Even then, though from a considerable distance, he could see in her what he would one day come to cherish and hold so dear. She was winning then, but her adversaries came at her with new weapons. Suddenly, the dance no longer worked; even the ingenious little gibes and teasing retreated and finally died.

Once, he had watched her twirling and winning; now, he watched her surrendering—again from a distance, this time a mental distance, then in the light, now in darkness. The sparkles were dead, but there had to be a light, though dim, deep in her somewhere. Only God could bring it back to shine through her as before. With God's help, those who loved her would have to step it up.

Sarah was so still now, her breathing shallow, almost undetectable. Surely she felt that sleep was the only ally she had, the only saving grace she'd been able to find, the only peace with herself. But one day, it would fail her, and that would certainly spell disaster, for she might well be unable to find relief anywhere else.

Suddenly, Sarah flinched and then shifted slightly. In a few moments, she turned to rest on her back—signs of waking up. Indeed, in time, she drew in a deep breath and opened her eyes, staring for a while at the ceiling. Then, she blinked a few times and let her head roll to the side on the pillow to behold her visitor.

"What time is it?" she asked.

"Ten o'clock. Want some breakfast?"

'No."

"Sweetheart, would you like to get dressed and go for a walk in the meadow?"

She looked at him for a long time, possibly waiting for him to say more. Finally, she started shaking her head very lightly, and then, softly, politely, she said, "No."

Following that little round of non-conversation, Kevin just shifted in place for a few minutes, leaned in, kissed her brow, and drew back smiling. Sarah showed no change of expression. She just stared at him. In a moment, he pulled a chair up to her bed and sat down.

Before he could start a conversation, Sarah rolled over, facing the other way, pulled the covers up a little tighter, and said, "Good night, Kevin; I love you."

He stood up, struggling to keep any semblance of hope. Whatever their spoken relationship, whatever her regard for their love, she was his soul mate, pure and simple. He continued to stand at her bedside. His thoughts were almost aimless now. He couldn't think of anything hopeful at all except that his love for Sarah Grace was forever.

Now, Sarah was sound asleep again. Kevin shook his head vigorously once and sighed deeply. "Okay, Sarah," he whispered, "I'm not going to stand idly by and watch you surrender. Hate me if you will, but I'm not going to let this happen. I'll be your enemy; I'll be whatever I have to be, but damn it, Sarah, you're staying in this world."

Kevin sat down to plot a new strategy. When Sarah's breathing turned to near snoring, he bounded to her beside. "Wake up, Sarah." Nothing changed, so he took her shoulders in both hands and shook them—gently at first. "Come on, baby; wake up." She shrugged and forced a deeper breath as if she could blow him away.

"Sit up, Sarah!" She flinched, and Kevin raised his voice, he hoped not loud enough to catch the attention of others in the house. "Come on! Sit up!" He took her shoulders and rolled her over as she fought feebly.

"Quit!" she cried.

"No. I want you up; I need you."

Sarah slowly began to prop half up on her elbows, straining her neck toward him. "What do you need?" she groused.

"This is it! I've made a decision. I know I don't have any say in your life, but with whatever influence I may have ..." Now, he was gaining grit from the sound of his own voice and shoved on, even more determined. "With whatever will I can wield, I'm not going to let this go on. I'm not going to let you go down!"

Sarah dropped back down and flung her arms out across the bed. She heaved a deep, aggravated sigh and stared straight up at Kevin. "Please, Kevin, go away!"

"No way. You-are-going-to-get-help, period. I'm not going to watch you sleep yourself into a coma and die."

"I hate you!" she screamed. At once, she grimaced at the

startled look on Kevin's face. She punched her chin and cried, "Oh, Kevin, please. Okay, I'll give in to your wishes, but for just a few more minutes, let me rest and regain my energy. Then I'll get up and find you."

"Okay, but I'll be back."

When he came out, Gina was at the door, looking frightened, apparently ready to come in. "I heard commotion in here. Is everything all right?"

"Not really, but we're okay, physically. To make a long story short, I think we need to get her to a hospital right away. I've already talked to her dad, and he says they will move out on that."

"You're entirely right," said Gina. "We can't help her here. Ed and Denise are coming over tonight to discuss that issue and Sarah's overall condition. We'll get together—Sarah included—and hash it out. The way her dad sounded, she will not have a choice."

Kevin was overcome with emotion and having trouble talking, but he pushed on. "The way she's going, she'll sleep her life away—eventually die from lack of enough oxygen getting to her lungs."

"Yeah, we have to move out on this. She has to be hospitalized."

Thereupon, they both fell quiet. There seemed nothing more to say. Kevin was patiently waiting for Gina's initiative. He was a little miffed that he hadn't been invited to the big meeting. However, it seemed evident at this point that he wasn't going to get that invitation. He decided it was time for him to leave.

"Oh, by the way," he said, "have you found out any more about Buford Crump's call the other day?"

"Only that he offered her a job at his front desk."

"What was her response, or do you know?"

"When I asked her that, she just shrugged and started walking away, mumbling something about having three weeks to make up her mind."

Sarah finally roused in the late afternoon. Getting out of bed was a curious struggle, but she finally wiggled and shoved her way to the side of it and sat up, yawning heartily. She decided just to sit there and think about her situation. Clearly, her family—fired by Kevin's insurgence—was on the brink of committing her to a hospital or asylum or some other stupid ordeal, and she simply couldn't let that happen.

As she looked at her fingers curled inwardly toward her palms, apparently in readiness to make a fist, she began to hit on some ideas for a change in her behavior. She could stop sleeping so much; that was a piece of cake, but that would not be enough to make her look and act like her old self. Now, she began talking quietly to her curled fingers.

"I think my sparkles have disappeared, so I'll have to dream up some more and get back to my old teasing self even though I don't really feel like it." She paused for a moment, dropped her hands to her lap, and gazed up at the ceiling. "Come to think of it, I better not improve too fast or they'll get suspicious. Oh, and what about this *jolt* thing? Maybe I can get creative with something in that area. Seems like the prospect of going to the hospital would be jolt enough, but I'm fixing to defuse that one, so it'll be history."

By now, her mom and dad had arrived for what was touted as an all-hands meeting, at which her attendance was mandatory. Initially, she had planned to decline, but now thought better of it in light of her newborn ploy to appear well and normal. Soon, she was called to dinner and went tripping along beside her uncle, smiling cheerfully. *Oops, don't overdo it, Sarah Grace. We have to take our time with this synthetic reformation.*

Chatter was light and innocuous during dinner. Afterward, her dad rose and announced jovially, "Okay, everybody, let's gather in the living room for our sure-to-be scintillating all-hands meeting."

That sounds so parliamentary, thought Sarah, *like a company staff meeting at headquarters.* "Hope I will be able to contribute something scintillating," she teased. *Nice try,* she thought, *but that really doesn't qualify as a sparkle. Maybe later.*

"Sweetheart, it's all about you, so it's bound to be," assured her dad.

Sarah took the initiative to be the first to speak at the meeting. As she entered the living room, before taking her seat, she glanced around, making eye contact with each one, and started to speak.

"I don't really know what my role is supposed to be here, but whatever it is, I want all of you to know that I am so very grateful for all your support. And I want to apologize for the trouble I've inflicted on this, my beloved family, and I'm sorry that you had to get involved in such a mess." Pushing a tear from one eye, she added, "Again, thank you for bearing with me through everything and for supporting me the way you have." She sniffled and started for her chair. "I guess that's all."

There ensued a conspicuously frank but good-humored exchange of observations among all the participants about Sarah's troubles, including an admission by Sarah that she had been clearly depressed.

"My main concern," barked Ed Lock, "is you're sleeping so much—way too much, and—"

Sarah interrupted before he could finish. "I know, I know, but I'm coming out of that, even as we speak." She giggled to make it sound convincing.

"Good girl. Meanwhile, we're going to get you some help. It would be unmerciful of us to let you suffer this alone. So, my precious Sarah, we're going to get you into the hospital for some dedicated help—"

"No! Didn't you hear me?" shouted Sarah as she bounded out of her chair and began ringing her hands. As she paced the floor, throwing her arms out toward everybody in the room, she continued to shout, "No, no, no!" She was simply out of control, clearly in a total breakdown because her efforts to avoid confinement obviously hadn't worked.

Gina was the first to react and jump to Sarah's aid. She rushed to her, took her in her arms, and spoke softly, very softly, so much so that only Sarah could hear. She continued consoling until Sarah began to settle down, at least to some degree. In a moment, Gina drew back.

Now Sarah was shaking her head, bawling, and trying to talk all at the same time. It was as if she were flinging her words to the floor, which she likely held as symbolic of her family members.

"You can't do that to me! Please! I'm already starting to get better. Please, y'all. Won't you please just help me this way? I'm just plain begging you … just begging … *please*!" She slumped to the floor and buried her face in hot, tear-stained hands. "Where's Kevin?"

Her dad knelt beside her and put his arm around her shoulders. "We were afraid you wouldn't want him in on this."

"I want him in on everything; he's my buddy," she sobbed. She started pushing up, still sniffling somewhat, and her dad helped her pull on up to stand. Intense fear struck deep into her as she realized that her fit denied her claim that she was becoming normal. As she surveyed the room, looking into the astonished faces of her family, she started to speak, this time fully composed.

"I guess that gives you all some idea of how frightening it is to me that I might be confined in a hospital or somewhere else. It wouldn't have upset me so much if I weren't already coming out of my depressive state. But that hit me at a time when I was making real progress. If you really love me, you all can help me with this, and that's my plea. Just give me your support, and you'll see the old Sarah rushing back." She lifted her arms over her head, like … well, like the ballerina she was.

It was uneasily quiet in the Evans house for a few minutes. In time, a little subdued mumbling set in, and Dad Lock turned to Sarah. "Okay, sweetheart, we'll hold off for a few days to see how it goes with you. If you show strong signs of improving, we'll drop the idea, at least for now."

A little light applause followed, which Sarah acknowledged with a surprising full-blown smile. The party broke up shortly thereafter as her mom and dad started shuffling around in readiness to leave. As they were bidding sweet good night to Sarah, she grinned and smirked. "Think I'll sit up tonight and watch a late-night movie." *Is that a sparkle, or what?*

Then it was quiet again. For the rest of the evening, Kyle and Gina Evans were unusually indulgent toward their niece. Sarah did indeed sit up late. She also got up early the next morning.

She tried to smile a lot at breakfast and vowed she would stay awake throughout the day. She felt guilty that she was playing a role simply to protect against drastic measures threatened by an honestly concerned family. Then, her mind turned to Kevin. *Where is he, anyway?*

A knock at the door answered her question. "I got it!" she shouted as she headed to the front door. When she opened the door, Kevin smiled, lifted a hand, and jiggled it playfully.

"Do come in, Smiley." Sarah smirked.

Inside, they embraced and, at Sara's invitation, took seats in the den. At once, Gina came in to greet Kevin and welcome him aboard. Then she wheeled around and headed out, babbling something about having stuff on the stove.

"Want to hear a good one?" chortled Sarah.

"Right on, especially if it'll keep you smiling like that."

"I pitched a walleyed hissy yesterday."

"Wow, that's really out of character for you."

"Well, my dad was threatening to install me in the hospital, and I just went delirious over the whole thing. Anyway, he has backed off for now, contingent on my staying awake and coming out of depression."

"Oh, I see."

"Uh-oh, I detect some misgiving in that. Don't tell me your allegiance is with the other side."

"Sweetie, there are no *sides*. We all care deeply about you; we love you, and we want to get off our butts and do something that may help you."

"I understand. Okay, let's talk about something else."

"Good idea. Want to take a little walk in the meadow? It's cool this morning."

"Sure. I know what; let's go sit in the grass in the ballerina patch, as you call it, and bask in the sweet meadow ambiance."

"Great idea."

Once seated, they took a few moments to gaze at the sky and suck in the morning air. Then, Kevin held up a finger as if asking for the floor—to speak, that is.

"Okay, it's my turn to talk."

Sarah beamed, slapped his leg, and scoffed, "Fire away, Chief."

"This may not be a subject you want to talk about, but it's one that is in the center of our lives, and we have to face it, so please bear with me."

"I know exactly where you're going."

"Mainly, I'm facing reality. See, sweetheart, I know what you're planning to do. I just don't know when."

"Like I'm going to end it, right?"

"Right."

"Well, relax, that's the furthest thing from my mind."

"I'm concerned about that bottle of pills that always seems to be around; you seem to have them around at the most unsuitable times as if just waiting for the right time to overdose."

"Oh, Kevin, don't be ridiculous. I keep them around because I feel guilty about not taking them as the doctor directed."

"Whatever."

"You know, Kevin, let's get out of this rut. Let's do something different for a change."

"Okay, like what?"

"Maybe a little weekend excursion. Maybe we could drive to the hill country, do some sightseeing and, you know, just loaf."

"Great idea ... just us and the hills." He chuckled as if trying to sound enthusiastic. "Let's see; let's make it weekend after next because I have a briefing to attend at *Lands Alive* headquarters next Friday."

"Kevin, my dear, that's great. We'll make plans," she whooped, smiling joyfully.

Kevin winked and jabbed the air with a confirming fist. Then he seemed to drop into deep thought—about what, Sarah had no idea. So she used the time to do some thinking of her own. *Wonder how long he'll be gone? How can I find out without raising doubt in his mind?* Suddenly, he jerked back as if springing out of a deep trance. As they turned again to face each other, beaming, Sarah gathered in the most unassuming countenance she could muster and began to speak.

"So, Kevin, you'll be back on Saturday. Right?"

"Probably not."

"Well, if you *are* back, maybe we can do something on Saturday and attend church together Sunday."

"Well, I don't know so much about that because they could hold us over another day—at least me; you know how these things go."

"Sure, I understand." She thought for a moment and then asked, "So what's the probability they would hold you over?"

"Actually, there's a very good chance they would. There are some other projects they want me to do, and they're planning to use part of the time to map these out with me."

"I see. So it seems unlikely that you'll be back before Sunday."

"Correct. In fact, I'm thinking very strongly about staying over in any event. I've made reservations for both days at the hotel."

"Sure, I understand. I'll just miss you; that's all."

"Me too. Look at it this way: that'll make our reunion ever the sweeter."

Thereupon, they arose resolutely and strolled out of the meadow, holding hands.

After dinner that evening, Sarah headed for the front-porch swing, hoping to demonstrate she no longer needed to lie in bed and sleep the hours away. As she began to rock gently, her thoughts turned to Kevin and his odd demeanor during their last outing, especially when she brought up the idea of taking a little weekend excursion. Though he had been patronizing about the trip, it didn't seem that he was all that enthusiastic about it. He really didn't spark at the idea. Missing was that old trademark Kevin glow in his expression as he just sort of concurred with her plans.

Even more unsettling was Kevin's seeming indifference to the changes she'd made in her behavior in contrast to what it was during her admitted depression. It was as though he suspected it was contrived. Somehow, he just didn't seem convinced that she was truly making progress in resuming her old persona. If he had been convinced, why did he bring up the bottle-of-pills issue?

She needed to do something to seal the matter in Kevin's mind, convince him that his *old Sarah* was really back. Suddenly, the idea of a *jolt* ploy entered her mind. Maybe an unexpected shock to her status quo, followed by a showing of overwhelming enthusiasm for life, would convince him that she was no longer a threat to herself.

Sarah called Kevin at once and just bubbled into the phone. She was teeming with excitement, like a little child going to a party. "Please, forgive me, Kevin, something extraordinary has come up, and we need to talk about it right away. I think it's good, Kevin; I want to know what you think. Can you come at once? I'll be in the swing." She giggled eagerly.

"I'm on my way," chimed Kevin.

While she waited, Sarah practiced smiling, hoping to come up with a smile that was both innocent—kind of little-girlish—and enticing, piquing his curiosity. *I could use a mirror for this.*

Kevin was there in ten minutes. "What's up, my love?"

Sarah, following her plan, didn't answer. She just motioned him to the swing beside her. As they turned to face each other, she bowed her head and, looking sideways at him, began to grow a smile, now believing that it probably fell somewhere between devilish and devious.

"My dear Sarah, that's the most seductive-looking smile I've ever seen on your pretty face. What's going on in that mischievous little head?" He chuckled and twisted further around in the swing. "Wow! I'm so glad you called."

Sarah continued to look up at him playfully, and let the suspenseful silence bear on. Kevin waited. After several moments, she rested her chin on clasped hands, still holding her disarming smile, and spoke to her mate. "Err ... Kevin, you know about women's periods, right?"

"Sure. I mean, I know there are menstrual cycles; that's about it."

"Well, okay, get ready for this, Kevin." She began rubbing her stomach as she talked. "The thing is, I've missed a period. I'm overdue; know what I mean?"

Kevin's face grew solemn, and he just stared alternately between Sarah and the back of the swing. In a moment, he raised his hand and began pointing a hesitant finger in the air, finally puckering his lips as if ready to say something profound. Before he could say anything, he smiled.

Sarah took the clue and laughed full throttle. "You've got it, Kevin." Then she tossed her head back and hooted, "Kevin, you're gonna be a daddy!"

Without further ado, Kevin eased out of the swing and

dropped to his knees in front of Sarah. He smiled up at her and then grew very serious as he began to speak humbly.

"My dearest Sarah Grace Lock, love of my life, will you let me be your husband and you be my wife?"

She softened her expression and in a steady, quiet voice, said only one word: "Yes."

Kevin arose, and, stretching himself as tall as he could, he reached for Sarah's already yielding hand. "This begs a trip to the meadow."

They embraced and headed out. All they could do was hold hands and savor this awesome moment at their favorite spot in the world. It was where they had met, and it was where they had courted implicitly. To Sarah, there were no words big enough to express what she was feeling. She had good reason to believe Kevin was caught in the same ecstasy. So they strolled the meadow, glancing at each other from time to time, smiling proudly. In a while, they paused and embraced again—they held it and held it.

"This is all ours," said Sarah, finally pushing back. "And from this moment on, I will consider us engaged to be husband and wife."

"I'll call a preacher," said Kevin.

Sarah quickly suppressed the temptation to frown.

They parted sweetly after about an hour and headed to their homes. Inside her bedroom, Sarah murmured to herself, "I deserve an Academy Award for acting." Suddenly, she slapped her head, disgusted with her mockery of such a gripping hour in their lives. *Please forgive me, Kevin; the fact is, my period isn't even due for another week.*

25

KEVIN MET BRIEFLY WITH his bride-to-be the next morning and then sailed away on an unprecedented mission—for him, that is. Now, he was drumming on the steering wheel and singing "Everything Is Beautiful" as he cruised toward the North Park shopping mall in Dallas. He had only one task to complete, a simple purchase from Tiffany's.

North Park was inviting enough, as malls went; it was actually one of the premier shopping centers of the world. It was a dazzling city in itself and—perhaps more popularly—it was a social center. Shoppers ambled along its galleries, sometimes six abreast, with iPhones glued to their ears, hardly aware of the remarkable landscaping along their routes. Indeed, flower beds, fountains and pools, lush tropical gardens, and spacious courts—all immaculately maintained—were scattered along the clean, wide promenades.

Still riding a cloud of unabated joy, Kevin skipped along, dodging pregnant women, disoriented old men, carefree teenagers, and baby buggies, until he reached the door of his jewelry store. He hustled on in without breaking stride; he knew what he wanted.

"Let me help," invited a pretty, polite young Spanish lady, smiling graciously. *Whatever happened to "May I help you?"* wondered Kevin.

"Thank you. Yes, I need a genuine ruby engagement ring."

"This way, sir. Sounds like you've already got it narrowed down," she hummed, looking back over her shoulder.

"True."

"So you've ruled out diamonds?"

"For my little jewel, absolutely. Diamonds are stunning, but rubies are beautiful, absorbing, breathtaking. Not much personality in diamonds really. They glisten; rubies glow. Diamonds shine and look expensive, but rubies are radiant and they actually sparkle more. How long can you look at a diamond without getting bored? But gaze into a ruby, especially if it's caressing the finger of a lovely lady—" Abruptly, Kevin shut up. It suddenly occurred to him that he was preaching a sermon and his sales associate didn't need that.

When they stopped, she raised her eyebrows, smiled toward a showcase of jewels, and said, "Let's look here."

Kevin picked several rings from each of three trays and held them aside until he was satisfied he had all the best choices. Then he studied every candidate intently as his diplomatic saleslady modeled each one on her finger. It took him only about ten minutes to find the winner, the one he felt best reflected his Sarah's incomparable personality without overshadowing it.

"Now, sir, would you like to look at some wedding rings?"

"Yes, indeed. Once again, I'm looking for a simple gold band, not too flashy."

"Good decision. You're right; you'll want something pretty conservative to place next to this precious ruby. I really admire your taste."

"For a man, right?" drawled Kevin, modestly shifting around in place.

"Well, no; you just know what you want, and that's admirable. And before we finish, I want to wish you and your bride good fortune and much love."

Kevin nodded, and they set about the task of choosing a gold band. Again, Kevin knew immediately when the right one surfaced—a solid gold band engraved all around with a chain of interlocking wedding rings. The engraving was somewhat faint, so it didn't detract from the simplicity of the band. The job was done.

On the road again, Kevin was smiling and nodding, pleased with what he had accomplished. Although he still felt upbeat and encouraged, for some reason, he didn't feel like singing about it. After a while, he actually turned a bit somber. Something had crept into the back of his mind and was just sitting there, gnawing away at his euphoria.

Suddenly, a little scene out of his celebration with Sarah the day before caught his full, conscious attention. Somehow, their exchange about his upcoming trip to *Lands Alive* had crept back into his brain. It was a little conversation that seemed perfectly innocent at the time but now loomed as a big question mark. Upon reflection, it struck him that her indulgence in the subject of his trip was more of an inquisition than a matter of idle curiosity. What was behind her questions? What did it matter as to precisely when he was going to get back? He recalled one particular question that he now thought was altogether too pushy: *"So it seems unlikely that you'll be back before Sunday?"* She seemed bent on pinning that down. He couldn't help but wonder whether she might be planning to do something with her bottle of pills while he was gone.

He cruised on, trying to draw his attention back to the happy turn of events in their lives, especially their pending marriage. Unfortunately, that had the opposite effect of what he wanted. It made him recall another curious statement Sarah had made just before they parted: *"From this moment on, I will consider us engaged ..."* *That sounds as though she never expects us to get married. Something's going on here, and I don't like it.*

Back home again, Kevin continued to wrestle with the pesky little questions that had invaded the happiest moments in his life. Maybe he was just delirious from it all, picturing things in his mind that really didn't have the meaning he'd been worrying about. Perhaps it was all very innocent. Surely, Sarah seemed to be on a fabulous high since the shock of her pregnancy. Indeed, he should just drop his suspicious curiosity and enjoy the news with her. Actually, it was the prospect of marriage to his little prairie ballerina, rather than the thought of being a father, that excited him. He wanted to be a husband first and a daddy later—thus, his ruby ring.

Suddenly, his bemusement was invaded by the grating base voice of his landlord. "What's up, Kevin? You look lost," he chortled.

"Just lost in bliss."

"The frown on your face didn't look blissful." When Kevin instantly bobbed his head and grimaced, Grover raised his hand like a crossing guard and quickly blurted, "Just joking! Really, I know you've got a lot of serious thinking to do, considering the big event coming up in your life. Did you get the ring?"

"I did, indeed; I got *two* rings, even though Sarah seems to be satisfied with just being engaged. Anyway, I'm trying to figure out the right setting for presenting her with our, err, *engagement* ring. I can't just waltz in and say, 'Here's your ring,' and pell-mell hand her the box."

"Right on! She'd never forgive you. It may seem like just a procedural thing for a man, but to a woman, it's sacred. You gotta make something of it. Be sure to bow; take your time. Linger with it a while. Know what I mean? After you slip it on her finger, continue to hold your fingers around it and smile. Make it a little-boy bashful smile."

"Gro, you're a scream. But I must admit there's a lot of practical merit in what you say."

"Go, boy!" croaked Grover, piercing the air with a finger as he shuffled away.

Early the next morning, the eve of his departure for St. Louis, Kevin dressed himself neatly and headed for the Evans house.

Sarah was a bouncing bundle of chuckles and smiles when she met him at the door.

"Wow!" whooped Kevin. "I've never seen that prissy little

butt wiggle so enticingly before. Shall we just head straight for the cove without further ado?"

"Oh, did you lose something there?"

"No, but you did."

"Cute."

"Seriously, I have something for you, and I'd like to present it in a place we've come to think of as ours alone. Really, could we?"

"Let me get on some slacks, and we'll be away." After a few steps, she stopped and looked back at Kevin. "Aren't you a little overdressed for the cove?"

"Guess so, but what the heck?"

At the cove, they stood quietly for a little while, looking all around it, taking it in, as they often had. Kevin was feeling very sentimental, and it appeared to him that Sarah was as well. In a while, she reached out for him, and they embraced with the same fervor as they had that special time when passion took them all the way. They continued to smooch and pet until finally, and spontaneously, they eased to the ground and made love. At one point, their lovemaking was ended, but the affection lingered. Kevin could see it in Sarah's loving eyes and feel it in her repeated squeezing of his hand. It was clear to him that they both felt the profound caring that followed sex where there was love.

In a while, they both started to shift around in readiness to get up. With that, Kevin chided, "If we're going to keep this up, we need to stock this place with a couple of blankets."

Sarah laughed and whopped his shoulder. "Keep what up?"

"Yeah, right. So okay, now, we need to have our clothes on for this next feature. I have some protocol to honor."

"Yes, my beloved fiancé."

Kevin gently turned her around and positioned her on their steadfast old log. Then, he dropped to his knees before his soul mate, took the ruby ring from his pocket, and started easing it onto her finger, speaking softly.

"With this ring, I commit my life to this, the sweetest, kindest, brightest, most beautiful and deserving woman in the world. And it is my solemn vow that I will come to be her husband and serve her."

Smiling through tears, Sarah placed her hand over Kevin's and spoke tenderly, "I accept this ring with enduring love for this, the finest man who ever lived and with eternal devotion to him and all that he is and that he stands for."

They sat again, side by side, on their trusty old fallen tree trunk. "Know what?" said Sarah, with a friendly chuckle. "I think this wasn't fair because you knew what you were going to do and had time to compose what you were going to say and I didn't."

"Sweetheart, from what you *did* say, it's obvious that you didn't need time to prepare. I'm humbled by your response just exactly the way you stated it."

They stayed in the cove for another half hour, doing mostly nothing, murmuring to each other from time to time, and just letting the quiet ambiance hold them. Kevin was thinking about his heretofore reluctance to propose to his soul mate for fear it would insert another quandary into her confused life. He also wanted to assure himself that she loved him. When the betrothed finally came out of their cove, their exuberance had returned, and, with arms swinging merrily, they literally pranced along their way back through the meadow to Sarah's next-favorite spot, the porch swing.

They both sat forward in the swing as if to signal that it was time for business. Sarah was the first to speak. "You're leaving out tomorrow morning, huh, Kevin?"

"Yep." Considering the reservations he had developed in his mind since their last outing, Kevin had decided he would be essentially noncommittal on any question that came up about the trip.

"Darn, that means we probably won't see each other again

until Sunday night." The little pouting look on her face seemed contrived.

"Not necessarily."

Sarah waited, apparently giving him time to offer something more specific. After an awkward silence, she continued, "Oh, not on your part. 'Cause, you see, Kevin, an old high school friend called me yesterday, and, to make a long story short, we're planning to hang out together until probably sometime Sunday night."

"An old high school friend?"

"Yeah. She still had my cell phone number. We were chums all through high school. Anyway, she wants to pick me up here and prowl around in Dallas for a day and then drive on into the hill country, mostly sightseeing, and then on down to San Antonio for the river walk and other fun stuff."

"You've never mentioned her before."

"'Course not; we hadn't talked since graduation. But she sounded so enthused about her plan, I didn't have the heart to turn her down. And, you know, since I can't be with *you*, I could use a little diversion myself."

"I understand." He felt his brow wrinkling as he continued, "Tell me, Sarah, what's your friend's name?"

"Ah ... Eloise Moore."

"She lives in Dallas?"

When Sarah nodded, he asked, "With her parents?"

"No, no, she lives alone."

"I see. Anyway, sweetheart, I wish you all a safe journey and a happy, carefree time."

"Thanks, Kevin. You too."

In a while, they parted, namely when Kevin noted that he'd better get back to the ranch and do some packing. The minute he stepped in the door of his quarters, he went straight to the Dallas phone book Grover had acquired somehow. He thumbed right to the M's. There was no Eloise Moore. He realized this was not a conclusive disclosure, but it was some indication, enough to at least raise a question. *Oh well, if there is such a person, she likely doesn't even have a landline phone.*

Kevin decided he'd consult the wise old man, his sage house mate. After briefing him on his earlier conversation with Sarah about her professed absence for the weekend, he asked, "Gro, what does all this mean to you?"

"It doesn't mean a damn thing. Young girls often have close friends, and they get together at times for girl talk and girl walk."

"Isn't it odd that this so-called Eloise Moore invites Sarah for an out-of-town vacation at the exact time I'll be away? It sounds a little contrived to me."

"Well, yeah; it's certainly coincidental, but that by itself is not enough to raise a doubt—at least in my mind. But, Kevin, listen up! You're talking to the wrong person. I don't know this girl. I don't know the things that typify her. I wouldn't be able to sense when she's contradicting herself. I didn't see her face when she was speaking all this. Do you see? An untutored third party is not a good source of advice."

"I get you. But, look at this, Gro. This is all too sudden to be credible. She's never even mentioned *having* a close high school girl friend. Don't close friends talk about each other sometimes?"

"Don't get hung up on that, Kevin. It likely means nothing. Really now, how many times have you mentioned past friends to her?"

"Touché," chimed Kevin. Then with a somewhat yielding smile, he kidded, "I'm glad I talked to you, Gro, but really, good buddy, it sounds like you're on her side."

"Quite the contrary, Kevin; I'm on *your* side, trying to help. If I weren't, I'd be telling you what I suspect you've already concluded—what you want to hear."

"Actually, Gro, I haven't made a definite conclusion, but I've certainly raised a lot of doubts in my mind. See, I *do* know this girl. After all, I love her—so deeply. And I have watched her face and looked into her eyes as she talked. Really, I'm not trying to make a mountain out of a molehill."

"Good thinking. Trust your instincts; they're not infallible, but they're usually pretty reliable. They're a strategic part of our God-given survival mechanism. So I don't blame you for being doubtful."

Kevin shuddered at the word *survival*. He wondered if that was an instinctive reaction or a biased one based on misgivings he had about Sarah's intentions. Finally, he slapped his knees and started to push up. Looking doggedly at his friend, he declared, "I'm just afraid Sarah's preparing to do something dreadful—to herself."

Kevin was spellbound as he cruised down boring highways through unattractive scenery toward St. Louis for his pivotal briefing. He was well aware that *everything* was boring and unattractive to him in his frightened mood. He could not shake the premonition that the love of his life was about to commit suicide. There were altogether too many indications to dismiss this possibility. *The feeling of guilt has such endless power,* he thought. Now, he wanted to go find her, hug her, and pour all his love into her. *Oh my sweet Sarah, please—for you, darling, not for me.*

He continued to think about Sarah as he cruised along. He felt this was the second time he would have to go against her wishes, the first being when he chased her down and made her give over to the police. He pounded the steering wheel and swore that he would do all in his power to keep her from destroying herself. He would stay in constant touch with her family as to her status and would bolt his meeting if necessary.

As it turned out, officials of *Lands Alive* seemed to have things pretty well organized. Friday afternoon began with a general meeting of staff from various departments. To Kevin, it was a worthless waste of time. He really couldn't fault company officials because, at that moment, anything would have been an intrusion on his time. He was getting restless to the point he was sorely afraid it showed. If they didn't wrap it up soon, there wouldn't be time left for the private meeting they had arranged with his main point of contact. That meant they would likely hold him over to the next day.

On their break, Kevin called the Evans house. Kyle answered and when questioned, indicated that, to his knowledge, Sarah had left with a girl. He pointed out that he had left for work before she got out of bed.

"What about Gina?" asked Kevin.

"Actually, Gina called in sick this morning. Hold on; let me get her."

Gina seemed a bit vague in speaking to Kevin's interest, indicating simply that Sarah had left on an intended weekend trip with this girl from her high school. She confessed that she hadn't actually watched her leave, but she had every reason to believe she did so.

The company general meeting adjourned soon after they reconvened. Kevin hurried to his contact man, Shaun Simmons, and said, "I'm yours."

"Good, Kevin. How about … say, how about a cup of coffee before we get down to business?"

"Oh, I don't do much with coffee." Realizing that this was not a politically correct response, he quickly added, "But I'll be glad to sit with you while you have a cup."

"Tell you what," said Shaun, "it's getting late. Let's just get together in the morning. We'll put you up at the hotel for the night."

"Oh, that's all right; I don't mind working late if you don't."

"No, no. We'll do it in the morning!"

The man sounded a little irritated, so Kevin didn't press the matter. The next morning got underway on the same note.

Shaun Simmons began with a few challenging observations about Kevin's behavior. He indicated Kevin seemed nervous and didn't appear very focused. When Kevin apologized and admitted there were some compelling distractions in his life, the man dropped the subject and moved ahead. In a short while, they finished on a pleasant note and parted amiably. *Crap! We could have done this last night, and I'd be home by now.*

As he raced down the highway, Kevin's first thoughts were of Sarah. That set him to brooding about some plans his employer had in mind for him. Namely, they wanted him to explore the Midwest in the same manner he had covered East Texas. That would essentially contrast desert landscapes with the terrain of mountainous regions. *Bully of an idea,* thought Kevin, *but there's no way I'm going to leave my Sarah behind and I will not subject her to a move away from her home in her present state. Maybe I ought to start looking for a new job.*

Kevin screeched to a stop at his Mabank quarters, barked a quick hello to Grover, and set out at once for the Evans house. It being Saturday, he expected they would be home unless, heaven forbid, they had opted for some shopping. Thankfully, they were home. Gina met him at the door, hugged him, and escorted him on in, mumbling blandly on inoffensive subjects, as they trailed along.

As they started to take up chairs in the den, Gina tapped her forehead. "Oh, before I forget, I have something for you!" she exclaimed as she hurried out of the room. She was back in seconds, holding her hand out toward Kevin. "Here's a note in a sealed envelope that Sarah left with me asking that I give it to you when you get back."

Kevin couldn't wait. He snatched the envelope and shoved it into his pocket and then blurted, "What *about* Sarah?"

"Guess she's having a good time. Certainly hope so. The last thing she said before she left was something like, 'I got my cell phone, Auntie, but be patient and keep trying. You know me; I usually forget to turn it on.'"

"Oh, you were still here when she left?"

"Yeah, I got up sick yesterday and didn't go in. I'm okay today."

"Great. So you actually saw the girl pick her up."

"Not exactly. They had arranged to meet at the Meadowlark for breakfast because Sarah wanted to get in her morning walk."

"Did you see her as she started her walk?"

"Unh-uh. My stomach was hurting unmercifully, and after we hugged good-bye, I just fell back into my chair."

By this time, Kyle had joined their conversation. "Kevin, old boy, you'd be proud of your girl. You should see the way she left her room—immaculate."

"I can imagine; I wouldn't expect any less of that little jewel."

"Here," said Kyle, motioning toward Sarah's bedroom, "let me show you." He rattled on as they stepped well into the room. "Notice how everything is so neat and picked up? And check this; she actually placed the decorative pillows up at the headboard. She never does that."

Kevin just nodded, thinking, *It's as if she left it for eternity, like she didn't expect to be back and wanted to be remembered for something positive.* He said nothing.

As they turned to leave the room, Kevin suddenly stopped, jolted by what he saw on Sarah's dresser. He stared dumbfounded at the beautiful crystal bowl where she'd placed her dried red roses, so proudly. They were gone. Quickly, Kevin made an excuse that he had to get back, thanked his hosts warmly, and left.

Now, he was sprinting down a familiar trail, headed for the wooded pathway to their cove. By that time, he was overwrought with sadness and fear. And it was so lonely down that cherished lane without Sarah. Then he shouted into the woods, "Sarah, my darling, where are the roses?"

He glanced for an instant at the cove as he zipped by and

then stopped suddenly, remembering the envelope in his pocket. He retreated a few steps to the cove, plopped down on the log, and ripped open the envelope Sarah had left with Gina:

My dear Kevin, there is no baby. I'm sorry I deceived you this way. I didn't mean to hurt you, but I was holding out hope against hope. It meant so much to see how happy it made you. Do take care, my darling, and know this: I will always love you.
Your Sarah.

Kevin was devastated by the note, not because his fiancée wasn't pregnant, but because the tone of the note sealed his hunch that she was on a mission of death. He sprang from the log and raced away again. He could not dwell on the note; something far more compelling had priority. Soon, he reached the creek and swung around in stride heading upstream for the crossing log. He literally scampered across it to the other side of the creek and shot up the grassy knoll and into the meadow. He didn't even look out into the meadow as he cut across it, speeding toward the old abandoned barn. Soon, he was at the barn swishing through the tall grass toward the front door.

26

SARAH WAS UP EARLY Friday morning and calmly idled her way through the business of getting the day started. She straightened up her room meticulously and then took her shower as a matter of course. She was skipping breakfast, for it was totally unnecessary at this point. She donned a fancy, long-sleeved blouse and her favorite dress slacks. She paused for a moment, measuring her image in the mirror and then carefully applied her makeup. When finished, she glanced at her hands and smiled at how steady they were.

She took her bottle of pills and headed for the kitchen for a bottle of water. All at once, she stopped dead in her tracks, instinctively rising up on her toes to keep from falling on her head. Gina was sitting at the dining room table limply leaning into her hands, as though studying an insurmountable problem.

"Aunt Gina!"

"Good morning, darling." Gina let her head drift a little toward Sarah, hands and all, never looking up.

"Are you okay?"

"I'll be all right; just got a queasy stomach, bad enough I had to call in sick. Don't worry; it'll go away by day's end."

"Can I do anything for you?" pleaded Sarah.

Gina shook her head, which was still in her hands. "When's your ride supposed to get here?" she muttered.

Sarah gulped and glanced at her now fidgeting hands. "Oh,

ah … we've changed our plans. My friend is meeting me at the Meadowlark … by mutual agreement."

"Sounds foolish to me," began Gina, now a little more animated. "Seems it would be so simple and accommodating if she just dropped by here and picked you up."

"That's not it at all. She *is* accommodating me; I asked for this because I needed my morning walk—which, as you know, I have neglected for quite a while. I thought this would be an ideal time to get back in the swing of it. Actually, my friend is going to walk down and meet me halfway and then walk on back to the Meadowlark with me." Sarah's punctuating giggle sounded a little fake, even to her.

At that, Gina lifted her head and said, "You're goin' walking in that classy outfit?"

"Special occasion."

"So you're going to wag a suitcase and walk half a mile on this warm morning. Right?"

"No suitcase. I have very little to carry, just a couple changes of underwear and my pajamas, and it'll all fit in my small backpack."

"Whatever. You having some breakfast before you head out?"

"We're having it there," said Sarah, drifting away toward the refrigerator.

In a short while, Sarah came to her aunt to bid her good-bye. They embraced and exchanged sweet wishes for each other, and Sarah was away. At the porch, she looked back. Gina was not visible. As she started in the direction of the Meadowlark, she looked back again to assure herself she wasn't being watched. Gina was nowhere in sight. Now, she changed courses and angled across the meadow to the familiar woodline trail, which would take her to the connecting pathway to their cove and on to the old barn across the creek.

The trail was so lonely without Kevin. There could have been a dozen people there, and it would have still been lonely. *Please don't grieve, Kevin. This is best for you—especially you.*

Sarah lingered inside the cove, reminiscing. She would not desecrate this, their special chamber in the woods, by the dreadful act she would soon commit. In a while, she strolled wearily out of the cove and trudged on through the woods to the creek. She stopped to get her bearings and then turned upstream to the old crossing log Kevin had taught her how to navigate. She shinnied over it to the other side and labored up the grassy knoll and on to the deserted old barn that sat at the edge of a meadow near a small patch of woods.

Inside, she just wandered around aimlessly as if mystified by being there. She looked at her hands again. They were still steady, yet she felt so bewildered. Where was the magic that had been in this old relic when they first explored it? Where was that instant sensation that she was doing the right thing? Something had suddenly intruded into her confusion. Had she inexplicably fallen into the grips of nature's instinctive will to live? Was she having doubts?

With that last question, Sarah pulled the little bottle of pills out from her backpack and started to study them—*for the hundredth time,* she thought. She bowed her head and continued to roll the bottle around in her hand, finally shaking her head slowly. She sighed and dipped her head resolutely; nothing could take the conviction that she was earmarked for downfall out of her. Otherwise, why was that cruel stigma slammed on her when she was just a child? Why the inexplicable exploitation by a perverted phony? Why the mocking temptation to love again by one so genuine as her dear, priceless Kevin?

Immediately, she shook herself out of her thoughts about this unsolicited dilemma and started to drag around over the dirt floor from one corner of the barn to the other. She hadn't noticed the smell when there on her one previous visit with Kevin. Now that her mind was clearing, she was picking up on things that didn't meet the threshold of interest before. Actually, the smell was not unpleasant. Basically, it was the smell of *old*, the pervading scent of deep, cold dirt—not bad, really.

In a while, Sarah wandered to the back of her final resting place and set her backpack against the wall. She sat down beside it and leaned back to rest—emotionally, that is. *Wonder what Kevin's doing right now? Wonder if he's thinking of me or if he's too tied up in meetings to think about—us? Dear God, please forever bless my man.*

The day was still young, and Sarah hadn't planned to start her process until that evening. Then, with another heavy round Saturday morning, she should be at peace by the next day. That settled in her mind; she decided to amble out to the meadow for one last survey of God's world. Before leaving, she lifted from her backpack a small, orchid-colored bag about the size of a coat pocket, with two scarlet ribbons for handles.

Fully resigned and unafraid, she rambled along through the tall grass, letting the soft morning sun caress the back of her neck and the gentle breeze gather in her hair. As pleasant as she pretended it to be, everything looked different and felt different here in this new meadow. It was not as captivating as her and Kevin's. In a while, she decided the meadows were the same; it was *she* who had changed.

Now clouds began to cover the sun and the wind picked up a little. *This is the right time,* she thought. She fingered the simple ruby ring on her left hand and stared hypnotically into it for a long time. Then, she took up her pretty little sack and brought up some of its contents in one hand. She bowed her head and stared into the handful of dried rose petals she had pinched out of each stem. They still had their reborn color, a refreshing purple tint, and they still had the sweet smell of spring flowers. She continued to gaze into them, taking them in, thinking of the dear man who had given them to her. She could very nearly make out the image of Kevin—almost see him in the petals, smiling that bashful boyish smile with which he was so generous.

She stirred the sacrificial petals with her finger, thinking of the caring man who had given her the roses. She knew he intended them to be both a token of his love and a symbol of the peace he longed for her to have with herself. There were so many things she admired in him and that she loved about him. He had tried so hard with her, and his love was tough—the only true love there was. He was just simply her man. *Oh, my Kevin.* Suddenly, she clutched the little handful of roses to her chest, dropped her head, and wept.

Sarah continued to grieve with no urge to curb her feelings or hurry through them. After a while, she slowly raised her head, still sobbing, and lifted her hand high, palm side up. She held it there as if beckoning a bird to come and light on it. Then she tossed the cherished petals into the breeze and watched them swirl around and around. *Kevin, my dear, our love is blowing in the wind.*

After a while, the wind let up a little, and the roses settled slowly to the ground and sifted into the tall grass to become one with it. She repeated this solemn, poignant ritual until all the purple petals were gone. When she finished, she looked up toward the heavens and felt under her eyes. There were no tears. She was numb.

Sarah stood in place for a while, letting her arms dangle down beside her legs, essentially immobilized. Then, she started to make her way further down the meadow. The sun had squeezed out again and cast a faint glow over the field. Slowly, she raised her head and with her arms lifted upward toward the heavens, she pleaded, "Oh Lord, why does life have to be such an argument?"

Sarah remained in the meadow until clouds started to form and the wind got really serious. Soon, she came to a lone tree near the end of the field. It was a sweet gum tree, its prickly, shiny green balls glimmering with life. She tarried there for a while, looking far up through its limbs at the darkening clouds and then turning away to scan the meadow and neighboring woods. As booming thunder blasted away, a vigorous breeze swept through and swirled around her body, making her shiver as she held to the tree.

At this sudden shift in weather, Sarah decided she'd better head back to her special quarters. Before she could take her first step, the wind rose even more fiercely, tossing the grass around in the meadow and rattling limbs on the tree. When she glanced up into the tree, trash slammed into her face. She pushed it away and hurried through the meadow.

Back in her shelter, Sarah huddled beside her backpack, listening to the wind whipping around the barn, scraping over the old tin roof, shaking the walls and rocking the door, making its hinges cry. A vicious storm surely was upon her.

All at once, the rampage stopped and it became dead still and quiet. After a while, she came to accept that it had all passed by. Not a drop of rain came from it, a fortunate turn of events since the roof did have some cracks in it.

As darkness settled in, Sarah decided it was time to begin. From her bottle, she poured out six pills. She pondered whether to take them one at a time or dump in all six at once. She planned to take the rest of the bottle the next morning. She thought a while, and then opted for the one-at-a-time approach.

Thus, Sarah got underway with her daring journey into death. She was gagging horribly after three pills but kept trying. Now, the cramping was unbearable, and at once, she coughed out what looked like two of the pills. She couldn't tell for sure. She grabbed them up immediately, stuck them far into the back of her throat, and gulped a big swallow of water. They stayed down, but now the pain was piercing her throat even down into her chest. *What am I doing wrong?* She summoned up all the will she could muster and downed the remaining three pills. She was so weakened from the ordeal that she just toppled over onto the bare dirt floor and let her head flop down against it. Soon, she felt no sense of anything.

Sarah awakened ever so slowly. All she could feel were the tremors all over her body and the twitching of her neck and hands. But something was going on because she was rousing. *Where am I? What happened?* She gradually became aware that she didn't have her senses, or she concluded that she didn't, as lifeless as she felt. She touched a finger to her lips. *I felt that.* She tried to open her eyes, but they seemed not to budge. She squeezed them tighter together and tried again. Now, she saw faint shadows and finally a murky glaze. All at once, her head jerked at the smell of urine.

Sarah slowly came to accept that she could understand and that her basic senses were still intact, though blunted. After all, her thought processes were still working. *Is this virtual death?* she thought. She had no energy, and she still had many more pills to get down. *I should have done some research on this,* she thought, *but really I just didn't want to know.* She squirmed and pushed with the heels of her feet, all to no avail. Finally, she managed to turn over to her stomach. Then she drew her knees up under her and began the pushing and shoving again. It took several minutes to finally rise up enough she could lean back against the wall. However, the effort had taken its toll, and she was painfully exhausted.

Catching her breath somewhat, she started to focus on her surroundings. Clearly, the day was dawning. She could smell the grass warming up in the sun and hear a timid breeze sweeping across the tin roof. She struggled to clear her mind even more. She was now conscious enough to know that in this one moment in time, she so wanted to see Kevin, to tell him she loved him. As though in a fantasy, she reached for his hand and had the sense that she was holding it.

Sarah's mind started to drift. Now, something was beginning to come into focus. She was watching an actual scene from her recent past. It was growing brighter and coming closer. Soon, it loomed clearly in her mind's eye. She saw herself sitting in a swing in the backyard. She couldn't imagine what was so significant about this that she would flash back to it. In that instant, she saw something that made her gasp.

There it was, a little lone bird, perched on a tree limb, yes, a little bird with a broken wing. She recalled her words: "Hi, little friend, I'm sorry about your wing. How can you fly with it broken like that? Oh, I know; it's because you *want* to fly. For you, little spirit, flying is living ..." She studied this poignant event for a while and tried to make sense of it at this particular point in her fading life. Ultimately, she denounced the idea that, deep down, she really wanted to fly—not to give up. As she continued to think, the sway of this little memory waned, and she dropped it from her consciousness.

It was time. Sarah dumped all of the remaining pills into the palm of her hand. She had to figure out how to get this done. Especially critical was the fact that she had very little water left. At some point, she felt her senses again. Now, she realized that she really didn't have time to try to calculate anything; she had to assault the problem. She heaved half the pills into her mouth and sipped some water. Some went down; some didn't. She swallowed as hard as she could, and it worked, but the pain was severe. She gagged and pitched in the remaining pills. Choking and retching, she put all her meager force against them. She tried for leverage by pinching her throat and slinging her head up and down.

She carried on. In this early moment, it seemed as though her stomach would explode and her throat felt as though it had been seared with a hot poker. She was so very, very tired. She feebly became aware that her mouth had fallen open and was just drooling whatever was there onto her chin. Now, she started to weave and she had the feeling that she was fainting. She couldn't remember ever fainting in her life but suspected this must be what it felt like.

Now Sarah had the sense that her body was collapsing to the

ground, and she was so drowsy. She couldn't feel where her head was or anything else. Soon, she heard her breathing morph into what must have been a snore, and …

It seemed only minutes after she had passed out that she roused again. She could feel herself breathing, but her body felt like a diffused glob, a lifeless mass. Somehow, her ears were still working, for she could hear the air hissing in her room. Now, her confused mind started to drift again. In that moment, she was stirred by something outside. She could hear the swish-swish of legs moving through the tall grass.

27

Kevin continued to hustle as he thrashed through the meadow to the front of the barn. At the door, he turned sideways to squeeze in. Still trying to hurry, he whirled around to begin his search. In that instant, he gasped and shouted, "*Sarah*!"

He was at her side in three giant steps and immediately dropped to his knees beside her. He was panting heavily, so he took a moment to regain some energy lost during his desperate race through the woods and meadows.

Sarah was alive but motionless, and her breathing was alarmingly shallow. She just stared hollow-eyed at the ceiling. Her body was limp and lifeless, and her clothes were soaked with perspiration and body fluids. So as not to frighten her further, Kevin decided not to talk to her for a few moments. Soon, she let her head roll a little toward him, still looking hysterical. There was enough left in her that she was trying to focus, but Kevin had never, in all his life, seen anyone as sick as she was. Clearly, she was at the edge of death.

Kevin leaned into her, and as he started to touch her hair, he noticed the empty pill bottle resting in her hand, her fingers curled loosely around it. Then he saw two pills lying on the ground beside her. Apparently, she had passed out before she got them down or they came back up again. When he touched her, she groaned and whimpered something unintelligible. As Kevin held an ear close to her, she murmured, "No, Kevin." She waited. Again, she tried to speak, but nothing was coming

out. Then she dipped her head limply and sighed, "Is too late …
and … and I'm not worth … worth it."

Kevin gently nestled her face in his hands, kissed her brow,
and spoke softly and very slowly, "My Sarah, if you weren't
worth it, you wouldn't be here now." He paused and continued,
"And if you weren't worth it, *I* wouldn't be here—now. Don't
try to move, and don't talk. Just rest; we're getting help."

Kevin hopped up, his breath somewhat restored. He jerked
out his cell phone and walked toward the barn door as he
talked. Fortunately, in two rings, he reached a responsive,
savvy operator, who listened and asked a few questions. She
seemed to grasp everything, as if she were actually on the scene
looking down at Sarah. She indicated that a helicopter would
be airborne in just minutes. Kevin then explained that he would
be in the meadow with Sarah in his arms, because it would be
nearly impossible to conduct a rescue through the narrow, vine-
entangled barn door.

He went back to Sarah, described everything, and explained
what her role would be. Much to his relief, she no longer seemed
interested in resisting. "Okay," said Kevin, "here's the thing: I
will lift you up into my arms. Please be as still as you can. Don't
try to help me; it'll be easier if you leave the lifting up to me.
I'll be doing it mostly with my knees. Sweetheart, when we get
to the door, I'm going to ease you down to the floor and walk
around you and on through the door. If you can raise up a little
at that point, it will help, but don't sweat it. I'm going to pull you
through the door. Then I'll pick you up again, and we'll head on
out to the center of the meadow."

As he was finishing up his briefing, he noticed that Sarah's
eyes had softened a little and he thought he detected a thin smile
on her face. Then he heard her breathe out a couple of words.
"What, darling?" he asked.

"My … man," she uttered, holding up her left hand and
turning it so he could see her ring. Her smile seemed a little
stronger.

Sarah was getting some of her senses back as the paramedics lowered her to the helicopter pad at Parkland Hospital in Dallas. She was at least alive enough to feel the torturous pain of nausea and internal trauma. It was horrifying, and she wanted to scream out and just cry herself back to sleep. Suddenly, there was commotion, and she was at once aware that Kevin was coming out of the helicopter. She rolled her head toward him and immediately gasped.

Kevin had fallen, banging his head on the steel rail as he hurtled to the ground. He jumped up immediately to his hands and knees, but when he tried to stand, he fell back to the ground where he now lay—still and lifeless. While hospital attendants hurried inside to get a stretcher for Kevin, the paramedics started moving a heavily protesting Sarah toward the building. She tried to shake the gurney, to squeal and flail her feeble arms, but there just wasn't enough life left for all that. All she was able to get out was a feeble whimper, "My man."

Sarah and Kevin were placed in separate rooms in intensive care at the Parkland Hospital. Both had been pronounced as near death. That didn't mean that they would die at any minute, but it did mean that, without extraordinary intervention and the will of God, they well could soon pass from this world.

Sarah was lucid enough to beg that she and Kevin be placed in the same room. She won. Perhaps that concession by hospital officials was part of the intervention. Now, they occupied beds across the room from each other. *Nothing's perfect*, thought Sarah, who seemed to be regaining some of the life she had lost. But, oh how she shuddered at the sheer misery, the sickness … the horrific pain.

Then, there was sleep. While IVs percolated hopefully lifesaving nourishment into their bodies, Sarah and Kevin slept the hours away. Though Sarah clearly was regaining her conscious life, Kevin hadn't awakened since his fall. Now Sarah was alert enough to feel deeply for her mate and yearn to be near him.

After rounds of stomach pumping, food was brought to Sarah for, as nurses explained, a test of her capacity to hold it and metabolize it. The fare was limited to pureed food, such as mashed carrots and spinach. She was only able to eat three bites of it before she started to gag and writhe. "Three bites is three bites," said the nurse optimistically, "and that's the good news. We'll try again tomorrow, sweetie. Meanwhile, you're doing well. I'm proud of you."

Kevin was a different story. They were unable to get him awake. Try as they would, he refused to rouse even to a semiconscious state. Other doctors were called in, and Kevin was pronounced technically comatose. Later, they indicated that it was likely he would come out of it with a concussion.

Sarah begged to be allowed to get up, so that she might go to his side and comfort him. The nurses refused, saying she would be unable to stand, and it would unnecessarily use up some of the energy that had been restored in her. Ultimately, Sarah prevailed, notably when nurses walked in on her trying to get out of bed. With one at each elbow, they guided Sarah to Kevin's bed and held her while she stood beside it.

She just looked at her man, wordless for a while, praying. Fortunately, her nurses stood with her patiently. After a while, she reached for Kevin. She touched his hair and caressed his brow. Then, she leaned in further, her head swaying, and spoke softly to him.

"My love, I need you. I know you're tired, but, sweetheart, we've been to hell and back together. Now, it's time to live. Please know that I want to live. I want to live now more than ever. Come with me, and I'll dance for you. Isn't it a miracle that I can talk now? God has one for you, too, my dearly beloved. Kevin, my Kevin, faith darling, faith." She raised herself up ever so slowly, her head steady now. She touched under her eyes—tears.

The nurses helped Sarah back into her bed. One of them left at once to answer a call. When Sarah looked directly into the face of the remaining nurse, she saw moisture in her eyes. "It's okay," she said to the nurse. "He's going to be fine."

"I agree," chimed the nurse.

"You know something?" began Sarah. "Well, I don't want to hold you up, but there's something I don't understand. As soon as he fell, he got straight up on his knees, then slumped back to the ground and passed out ... like he is now. I don't understand. What explains that? Does it have to do with the will to live?"

"No, not at all, else he wouldn't have bounced up so quickly. But that bounce took it all. Actually, his getting up immediately was instinctive. Then those instincts were overridden by the physical trauma and possibly the concussion that was forming after the fall. Even though he's in a coma at the moment, he'll be fine; I'm sure. But, my dear one, don't stop praying."

In the days that followed, Sarah's family came to visit the two of them—her mom and dad, Aunt Gina and Uncle Kyle. There were times when all four of them were there, but only one at a time was permitted to come to their room. While Sarah was comforted by her mom's visits, it was Gina who seemed the most indulging. She and Sarah would talk quietly and peacefully, with Gina standing at her bedside for as long as the nurses would let her stay. She also spent time with Kevin, who had his own dedicated visitor in the person of Grover Geesling. To top it all, Sarah's loyal attorney, Buford Crump, came by several times.

During these periods, staff doctors counseled Sarah on the subject of suicide. Ultimately, they called in her psychiatrist, Dr. Elouise Romain, who visited with her at some length. Her questions were candid and terse.

"Do you think you'll ever consider suicide again?"

"Not on a bet," Sarah assured her sincerely. "Never, never, never! But, Doctor Romain, I must say, the attempt certainly showed me what life means, how dear it is, and how ridiculous and useless guilt feelings are."

"Tell me about that."

"Well, during that morbid time after I decided to end my life, I came to realize that guilt feelings are the height of conceit. There's nothing admirable about them at all."

"Hmm."

"Yeah, it's just the notion that by feeling guilty, you excuse yourself—you know, of your perceived misdeeds, or whatever."

"What are you saying?"

"I just simply think suicide is a form of self-punishment."

"You've just hit the nail on the head. What else?"

"In my case, I literally got hooked on suicide. I became addicted to the idea."

"Not so anymore?"

"Not anymore! Doctor, I'm free!" As she shouted out that declaration, Sarah lifted her head and threw her hands high in the air above it.

After a while, it was clear to both parties that the interview had accomplished all that it could. As she rose to leave, Dr. Romain touched Sarah's shoulder and confirmed, "I agree, Sarah; you *are* free. You have liberated yourself."

"Thanks for your assurance, Doctor, but in all humility, I must tell this: my Kevin's trust in me was the greatest part of that liberation."

"And it was the person you are that generated that trust. So take some credit, Sarah! You've earned it."

Sarah flinched as she felt the instant stretch of an all-out smile and the little quiver of thankful feelings that ran through her body.

The doctor nodded and left.

On the sixth day after Sarah's rescue, while she was lying wide awake, staring at the ceiling, she had the impression that Kevin had stirred in his sleep. There was an overwhelming sense of his essence even from that distance. It was as if he were at her side at that very moment. She pushed up to her elbows and looked toward his bed. Nothing different was apparent. She decided that, just in case he was cognizant enough to understand things, she'd speak softly to him so he'd know he wasn't alone.

"My Kevin, just in case you can hear me, dearest, there's one thing above all else that I want you to know: I love you. And I'm right here with you, just a few feet away. Let me know if you need anything." She giggled because she knew he had always found comfort in her laughter.

Later that day, she thought she heard him rustle just ever so slightly in his bed. When she raised herself up to check, she detected that possibly his head had shifted a little. Then, while she was still propped on her elbows, she heard a sound, sort of like a weak groan. She waited. Nothing else happened, so she settled back and fell asleep.

That night, after her mushy dinner, she lay awake, vaguely aware of the TV noise. Suddenly, she heard a distinct sigh emanating from Kevin's side of the room. Moments later, she heard her mate clear his throat.

"Sarah?" he mumbled.

"I'm here, sweetheart. I'll be right over."

She labored out of bed; took some time to get her balance before she circled around her bed, using it for a crutch until she felt steady; and then stepped gingerly to Kevin's bed. When she looked down at him, his expression was blank, as though he were sleeping with his eyes open. Clearly, he was wanting to say more. She said nothing, electing to give him time to line up his thoughts. Trying to prompt him might delay rather than aid his waking. A couple of minutes went by as they studied each other. Then, to Sarah's delight, Kevin raised a feeble finger to his chin and opened his mouth to speak.

"Did you call the preacher?" he asked, grinning full tilt.

With that, Sarah fell over the bed; she wedged her way up onto it and came to rest prone on top of him, laughing and shaking with joy. "No, darling, I didn't call yet, because I didn't know how much longer you were going to sleep. I can't have you dozing off during our wedding."

Kevin's quick chuckle was barely audible, but it was real.

Sarah rolled off to lie beside him, and they visited low-key for a few minutes. After a while, she started to dismount the bed, explaining, "I better get back to my roost before the authorities catch me."

"Yeah, they might expel both of us."

"Oh, that being the case, I'll stay." On that note, she laughed her way back to her own bed.

Later, as the nurse bounced into their room, she noticed Sarah's wide grin and immediately glanced toward Kevin. "Hooray!" she shouted, clapping her hands. "Look who's back."

After the nurse left, Sarah advised Kevin that he was in for the treat of a lifetime. "Kevin, now that you're back, you're gonna have the privilege of feeding on mashed potatoes and carrots. Woohoo, huh?"

"Can't wait." Soon after that brief round of teasing, both fell asleep.

The next morning, they awoke to a new world, and their lives would never be the same again. They had won, thought Sarah. Praise God! They were back to their old lighthearted, fun-loving selves. Their love was for real, and it was eternal. As they met in the middle of the room, both yawning and stretching, Sarah was thinking of a subject she realized had heretofore been the sole province of Kevin.

"Good morning, my little prairie ballerina," whooped Kevin.

"Good morning, Smiley. Now before you get started on other profound subjects, tell me something."

"You're on."

"So what about this preacher business?" she quipped.

"Funny you should ask. Anyway, since you did, I'll take care of it."

"Why don't we just call the church and talk to the preacher together. Hopefully, he'll be in."

"Tell you what, the day we get out of here, let's just drive over there and do it face-to-face. That way, he can do his counseling and we'll get the information we need."

"Fine with me."

The next day, Sarah was aware that Kevin and his landlord were spending a good deal of time together. At one point, they were mumbling as if sharing secrets. Even so, she could tell Kevin was telling Grover how to find some object in his bedroom.

The day after this covert conference, Sarah and Kevin began sitting up in their chairs, and the day after that brought solid food. Soon thereafter, they were walking separately in the halls with the aid of a physical therapist. Then, they were allowed to walk together, shoulder to shoulder, sometimes holding hands.

They dreamed, and they shared their love. Visitors continued to come by every day. Now, they were rapidly gaining back their weight. One day, they were discharged into the caring arms of friends and loved ones, who literally applauded as they were wheeled out of the hospital at a side exit.

The greeters promptly left Sarah alone and met in a little cluster at the bottom of the steps as if checking signals on some pivotal point concerned with getting Kevin and Sarah to their homes. *What about me?* thought Sarah. *Hey, I'm over here. Remember me?*

The flock soon broke up and headed away to find their cars. Simultaneously, a smiling Kevin came to Sarah and said, "Come with me; we're riding with dear old Grover Geesling. He begged to be our chauffeur."

Soon after they got underway, Sarah looked all around and said, "Where are we going? This is not the way home."

Kevin grinned full tilt and felt for the little ring box in his pocket. "We're going to church," he hooted.

"Oh, I get it." Thereupon, she twisted around and looked out the rear window to behold a little convoy of three cars trailing behind them. Her mom and dad were in the first car, and she was sure her aunt and uncle were in the second one. She turned to Kevin, smiling like a bubbly young bride, and asked, "Who's in the third car back there?"

"Your very loyal patron, one Buford Crump. He specifically asked that he be the anchorman."

The two lovers nestled their heads together as the modest little convoy of bonded family and friends poked along toward Mabank and on to the Harbor Baptist Church in Payne Springs.